RELEASING THE CATCH

"Oh, for chrissake!" Faith said, disgusted, and all three men jerked their attention toward her, as if slapped. "My father," she gestured at Mack. "Is an asshole. It's not his fault, he was just born that way. He didn't tell me about any of this."

She waved a hand at them and the table. "Until I got here, a little over an hour ago." She flicked an accusatory glare at Mack, who had the excellent sense to stay quiet, and went on. "Look, I don't have time for any of your good-ole-boy superstitious bullshit. I've lived on a crab boat since I was eight-years-old. I became a full share deckhand at sixteen, and I've worked as deck boss and as an engineer."

Her glare now fell on Jake, who stared back in fascination. "I just left my last job because it was time for a change, not because I couldn't hack it. I work well on the hydraulics, stack, rail, bait, wherever the hell you want to put me. I'm a fast learner and I don't expect to find your boat to be the space shuttle. Either you want me or not. I'll be on the pier tomorrow at seven a.m., so you have the night to decide. Right now, I'm tired and I want to go to bed."

She grabbed Jake's drink, the closest and fullest, with three fingers of some strange, yet horrific alcohol, she discovered. She drained it in one large gulp, turned on her heel and left the bar.

BOOKS BY JENY

The Heaven & Earth Series:
The Sea Archer
The Warrior's Progeny
Dee's Cornucopia (2021)

Other Works:
"Dancing Through Tears"
(Australia Burns Anthology, Vol. 2)
The Catch

RELEASING
THE
CATCH

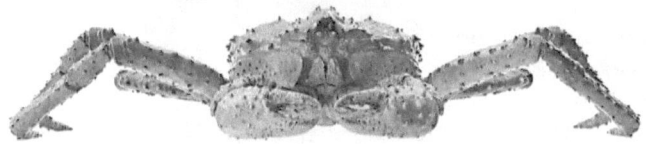

CELTIC BUTTERFLY PUBLISHING

Releasing the Catch

Celtic Butterfly Publishing
PO Box 2661
Stanwood, WA 98292-2661
Visit us at: www.celticbutterflypublishing.com

Cover Art by: Elizabeth Berie
To the extent that the image or images on the cover of this book depict a person or persons, such person or persons are merely models, and are not intended to portray any character or characters in this book.

Publishing History
Women's Fiction Romance Edition, 2020
Print ISBN: 978-0-9965096-9-5
Digital ISBN: 978-0-9965096-7-1

Published and printed in the United States of America

PREFACE

When I first wrote, *the Catch,* back in 2008, I'd never written anything before in my life. My father-in-law, Chuck, was in the final stages of non-Hodgkin's lymphoma, and I was a nursing student. Rather than go back to school, I chose to stay home and help take care of him. It was one of the best decisions I've ever made in my life. I got to know him on a level I hadn't in the fifteen years I'd been married to his son. Not that we weren't close, we were, it was just different.

I knew he was dying, but my family wasn't accepting it very well. He'd battled the same disease for nineteen years and beat it every time. I'd come home in the early evening, a little stressed because I didn't know how to get through to them, that his time was limited. So, I walked... a lot.

My favorite show at the time was, *Deadliest Catch,* the reality show about Alaska crab fishermen on the Bering Sea, and their incredibly dangerous job. I watched everything they produced on it, including the little vignettes on their website. Things like how does a crab pot work? The anatomy of a rogue wave, and my personal favorite... superstitions. I found out one of the biggest omens involved women onboard a fishing vessel and how they aren't very welcome. Taboo, I think they said, during one season. Being someone that has always beat to my own drum, naturally I thought, *what a crock of shit!* One evening after staying with Chuck, I watched that little side show on superstitions, and started coming up with a story.

I've done this all my life, having ideas for stories and making them up in my head, or reading stories and thinking how I would have written them differently. As I walked, I started wondering what would happen if I wrote my imagination down. So, I did. Four hours later, I had my plot and a fleshed-out outline. I wrote the story, in a few months, but painfully we lost my father-in-law, and were all devastated.

Both of my children were in middle school and heavy into sports and their friends, whom always congregated at our house, and we had a business we needed to run. So, *the Catch*, stayed shelved. However, after a time, my son, Charlie, asked me about it and even read some. Not being a huge reader, I was tremendously happy he deemed me worthy, and when he asked me to publish it, I decided to do it.

I decided to self-publish it, and as time moved on, I started writing down more stories and going to conferences to learn more about my craft. My second book, *The Sea Archer,* was picked up by New York publisher, the Wild Rose Press, and thus began the award-winning, *Heaven & Earth* series. However, I always thought about *the Catch*, because I'd learned a lot and believed so much of the story was still rough. My grammar, and other mechanics weren't as polished as I wanted, but I loved the story about survival, fathers and daughters and a woman in a man's world. I decided to improve it, make it cleaner and republish it. However, certain story arcs changed a lot in the re-telling, thereby changing the tenor of the story somewhat. So, I decided to create a new book and entitle it, *Releasing the Catch,* which is actually a better name for the story, in many different ways. The result of which now lies in your hands and is published five years after the first. I'm very proud of it.

There's a million memories for me in this book. You'll probably wonder how or why by the end of it or what I have in common with rough talking salty sea dogs. More than you might think, down in my core. I love Faith and Mack's strength and growth in this story and sincerely hope you do to!

Thank you for taking this journey with me.

DEDICATION

For Charles Anthony Heckman Jr.

Because this all started and ended with you.
I miss you every day.

FOR THOSE IN PERIL ON THE SEA

Eternal Father, strong to save,
Whose arm hath bound the restless wave,
Who bidd'st the mighty ocean deep
Its own appointed limits keep;
Oh, hear us when we cry to Thee,
For those in peril on the sea!

O Christ! Whose voice the waters heard
And hushed their raging at Thy word,
Who walkedst on the foaming deep,
And calm amidst its rage didst sleep;
Oh, hear us when we cry to Thee,
For those in peril on the sea!

Most Holy Spirit! Who didst brood
Upon the chaos dark and rude,
And bid its angry tumult cease,
And give, for wild confusion, peace;
Oh, hear us when we cry to Thee,
For those in peril on the sea!

O Trinity of love and power!
Our brethren's shield in danger's hour;
From rock and tempest, fire and foe,
Protect them wheresoe'er they go;
Thus evermore shall rise to Thee,
Glad hymns of praise from land and sea.

By Reverend William Whiting, 1860

PART ONE

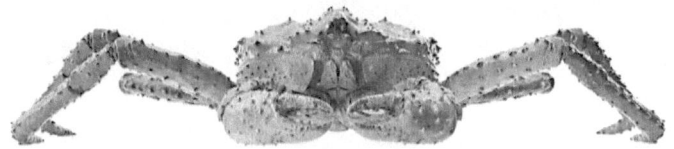

CHAPTER 1

The odor of rotten sludge wafted from the dilapidated dumpster. Mack Carter, a tall, muscular, sixteen-year-old with inky black hair, walked by and tried not to breathe in the acrid stench. He loped down a back alley, off Rainier Avenue, toward his apartment building, in Seattle's seedier part of town. Optimistic people would call the day beautiful. A perfect first day of Spring. Mack called it Thursday.

The events of the morning also wafted over him, and he didn't look forward to the continued and inevitable diatribe with his mother when he arrived home. Michelle Carter, once disclosed to her son aspirations of becoming a classical dancer, despite growing up in the projects. However, escaping the shit hole that held her ankle deep in stripping, prostitution and an ever-increasing drug habit, seemed to extinguish that flame a long time ago. Mack stopped to light a cigarette and remembered the scene.

"Ma!" he bellowed for the hundredth time that morning. "Get up, you gotta go to work." When he received no reply, he swore under his breath, walked down the shabby hallway and kicked open her door. "Ma!"

The door bowed and quivered but remained whole. He narrowed his eyes as Michelle made a huge production of waking up, rubbing her red swollen eyes and giving a loud yawn. Dried drool etched the side of her mouth in a white cakey crust. The stench of unwashed female, stale breath, and alcohol mixed with sweat evaporated from every pore and the distinct smell of pot followed her movements. Mack turned his head, wrinkled his nose, and drew his eyebrows together, all at the same time.

"Christ Ma, you reek!" He leaned back against the door jamb. "Fuck, that's nasty. Come on, get up, I have to go to school, and you gotta go to work or Butch'll fire your ass." She continued her movements and passed gas in response. "Come on, just one foot on the floor, so I know you're getting up," he tried to encourage her, yet when she didn't make any further attempts to rise, he lost all patience and kicked her sweat-stained mattress. "Goddamnit, come on!"

"Okay, fine. I'm up," she growled and raised herself into a sitting position. The grimy gray sheet fell to reveal one bare limp breast, wrinkled from too many tanning beds and occupational hazards. Mack quickly looked away, as she clutched both sides of her head, like they cleaved apart, and she wanted to hold them together. Irritation radiated off her.

"Fuck, Mack! Would a little peace and quiet be too much to ask? I worked my ass off all night?" From the smell of her, Mack decided she'd spent any pitiful amount she earned on her various addictions. "Ungrateful piece of shit."

"Fine, whatever, get fired," he muttered, and frustrated, gave a wave of his hand, and walked down the hall to the living room. He folded his bed back into the couch and grabbed his smokes out of the corner cabinet, placing one unlit one in his mouth. He flung open the rusted screen door and let it close with a loud reverberating bang. The barrage of curses in its wake caused him to smile, and he raised his lighter to light the smoke.

Now, after school, Mack walked past the weathered and chipped Claremont sign of his apartment building, and turned to go up the back steps, taking them two at a time.

"Hey dude."

Kevin, his dealer, struggled to a sitting position on the top step of his floor. The rusted iron handrail squeaked as it shifted under his grasp. More focused on inhaling whatever he just rolled than becoming vertical, Kevin extended the joint to his friend. The sweet, pungent smoke drifted toward Mack and he accepted his turn. Somewhere in the distance, a police siren passed through the massive slum complex, and he raised the joint to his lips for the first delicious hit. By the time he made it the last few steps to his apartment, the space loomed in quiet darkness and, to Mack's surprise, laid empty.

"Ma?" he tested the silence, then listened. Taking in the small postage-stamp size of their living room, he turned a circle. Most of her stuff, and a lot of his, vanished. Running through her bedroom and into the small moldy bathroom, Mack called his mother's name. He returned to the living room and stared in disbelief at the moth-eaten curtains.

Dappled sunlight peeked through them, displacing millions of dust motes.

"Are you fucking kidding me?" he hissed. "You bitch."

A panicked laugh escaped him, fracturing the silence. Mack glanced at the end table, where his five-hundred-dollar stereo used to sit. Panicked, he ran to the broken fixture and looked inside the secret compartment he created within it. She'd taken his large stash of weed and the wad of cash containing three-hundred dollars from his sales of the drug. Money he owed Kevin outside, but the stereo enraged him more because he'd worked an honest job at a local golf course the summer before, to pay for it.

Disgusted, he walked back into the kitchen and almost put his fist through the wall when yellow notepad caught his attention. The corner edges curled up as his mother's scrawl taunted him. She'd left in a hurry, and he wondered if she knew what she wanted to do that morning when they fought. Two greasy twenty-dollar bills sat limp on the counter next to it.

Mack- Nothing's working out here. Butch just said Jason stole some money, which is horse shit. He told him to fuck off and quit. Now he wants to go to California, but he didn't want to wait until you got home. He said I gotta figure out if I want to go too. This is my shot, to get the hell out of this shit hole. You're sixteen, Mack, and it's not about you anymore. Besides, we hate each other, and I'm done with all of it. I left you some money for the radio and rent, so make it last and you'll be fine. -Michelle

"Forty dollars?" He snatched up the money and crushed it in his fist. Some dirty dishes sat on the counter, and he snatched up a plate and overhanded it at the wall. "And when were things ever about me, you bitch?" He breathed heavy and closed his eyes for a moment before opening them again and looking at the forty dollars sitting on the counter.

Screaming, he picked up a dirty glass and threw it against the wall. A musical tinkle filled the room with an ironic melody, as he felt something inside him shatter as well. "That goddamn stereo cost me five hundred dollars!" he screamed and punched a fist through the sheetrock. Retrieving it, he punched another next to the first. Without a doubt, he stood alone in the world now.

Hours later, Mack sat huddled on the filthy, matted carpet, in a corner of his mother's empty bedroom, staring at the walls. Light spots remained where a few photos once hung, and the space collapsed in on him. Soon, he'd suffocate under the weight of it. Standing, he ran for the door and jettisoned into the night. He needed to think about his survival and made his way to the abandoned lot he frequented for such things, to wait out the dawn. *How would he pay for the apartment? How would he pay back Kevin or go to school? Or even just... live with forty bucks.* He thought about Mason, his absent father, who visited only a handful of times as he grew up. The trips often cut short because of Michelle's constant bitching. He tried to remember if his mother ever said anything about his whereabouts but came up with nothing.

Mack's steel-gray eyes made icier from current events, scanned the abandoned lot. Once a small playground, it now played host to drug dealers and prostitutes in the neighborhood.

A couch, launched from the back end of someone's truck sat in the dirt, beckoning to him, as the sun inched its way up to greet the day. He reached into the pocket of his dirty flannel and retrieved a pack of Camel's. Shaking a cigarette out, he lit it and drew in a deep lungful of smoke, before scanning the forgotten wasteland. *Is this the best it's gonna get?* A few stolen minutes before school... work... life?

Out of the corner of his eye, a toddler in a red plastic superhero cape, swung through the legs of his mother, dressed in a server's uniform, as they waddled down the street. Mack's eyes shifted up from the pair to the storefront window, and the painted words, *McKenna's, A Gentleman's Club.* The oblivious duo continued to play their game, and he closed his eyes to drift off into sleep.

****

A car backfired, causing Mack to jerk awake and blink a few times before the extreme heat between his fingers registered in his brain. Confused, he looked down. The cigarette burned down to within an eighth of an inch from his skin.

"Ow, shit!" he muttered, and threw the butt on the ground, before shaking his hand to cool it.

The sun, notified him the first period of his school day was already over, and he still hadn't figured out anything. Having nothing better to do, Mack stood and walked the two blocks to his high school, then maneuvered from class to class without staying present in any of them. He couldn't shake his earlier thoughts, as they once more drifted to his father.

Mason Carter breezed in and out of Mack's existence, telling him stories of an exciting, adventurous, and profitable life. Though he hated Michelle, Mason enjoyed his time with his son, yet not enough to stay long or take the boy with him. The two often fished for the day, leaving Mack yearning for more. During one such visit in early 1970, Mason informed his son, he was leaving for Alaska, to fish in a gold mine, describing it as a paradise, and the one place a man could still accomplish something magnificent. Mack never spoke nor saw the man again.

"Mr. Carter?" Someone nudged him under the table, and he turned to consider the emerald green eyes of Murron Middleton, his crush since the summer before. Concerned about something, her gaze skittered toward the front of the class and their teacher, Mr. Sanders.

"Mr. Carter, would you care to stop daydreaming and join the rest of the class in this discussion?" The biology teacher gestured toward the chalkboard where an arc and a stick figure marred the mossy green surface. Sanders stared down his nose at Mack with a patronizing expression on his face.

"I'm... what?" Mack asked, confused.

"I asked you what helped shape Darwin's concept of descent with modification?"

The teacher spoke each word with distinction, then sneered, like a large animal playing with its prey. Mack glanced back at Murron, who raised eyebrows in sympathy and pressed her lips together, as if willing him to read her mind. A jar on the work-station countertop captivated Mack's attention. The tiny pickled pig from inside taunted him, and the class tittered at Mack's discomfiture. To his mind, the students and teacher morphed into dreamlike, obsequious creatures. Trapped and vulnerable as the specimen, something inside him cracked and emotion bloomed across his face.

"Well, how the fuck should I know," he retorted with indignation.

The stunned class went from titters of repressed glee to outright guffaws at the turn of events, and all eyes turned with expectation to the teacher for his response.

"I-I beg your pardon?" Mr. Sanders face reddened like someone slapped him and his nose pinched as if he smelled something horrendous. "Office... Now, Mr. Carter."

"Oh, absolutely. Right away," Mack muttered and stood up in mocked defiance.

Reaching for his books, he paused a long moment, then took a fresh course of action and left them on the table. He turned and leaned down close to Murron. In a smooth gesture, he did what he'd always wanted and brought his lips down on hers, leaving the redhead surprised and speechless. Mack wasn't coming back and for the first time in almost twenty-four hours, a huge grin crossed his face, becoming excited for the future.

With three weeks' left on their rent, Mack made the most of the time before becoming homeless.

Stealing a rucksack from a local thrift shop, he filled it with more stolen items. Heavy denim overalls, work gloves, jeans, tee-shirts, socks, underwear and toiletries, all found their way into the travel bag. Careful never to hit the same store twice for needed items, Mack worked with a single-minded determination in preparing his kit. He relieved people of their wallets and hocked anything he could lift that fetched a decent price. When he got hungry, he dined and dashed, and squirrelled away any edible transportable items he could. By the time he planned his route and thrust a thumb out for a ride to Alaska, his well-worn wallet possessed two-thousand, eight hundred and seven dollars, with the sum of his belongings on his back.

****

It took him a week to hitchhike from Seattle up to the Canadian border and along the Al-Can Highway before arriving on International Road in Anchorage, Alaska, at eleven-thirty at night. Mack spent every second planning and dreaming. His mother provided his formative years, such as they were, but maybe his dad provided the helpful information to begin his future.

Exhausted and hungry, Mack called up to the trucker, "Thanks, man. Hey, Arnie, you know where I might find a cheap bed around here?"

"Yep," the man rumbled out in a low crunchy voice. "Six-zero-three, just down the road."

As the teenager closed the door, he thought he heard the old guy cackle. The dank, oily road, and something like curdled milk, just under it, assaulted his nasal passages. Music with a deep bass vibrated somewhere in the night, as murky puddles rippled with the impact. Streetlights lined out in front of him, bulbs burned out and silent. The ones that remained gave a valiant effort to flicker an ominous, dingy yellow. He shook back his sweaty hair, grabbed his bag with all his worldly possessions, and heaved it onto his shoulder before making his way down the street.

When he reached the destination, Mack stood open-mouthed and tilted his head back as he stared into the lights of The Alaskan Bush Co. He tried to reason that major responsibilities loomed around the corner, as a tall and built blonde rushed into the employee entrance. Fuck that. Stepping forward, he handed the bouncer his fake ID, while shifting the weight of the bag from his left shoulder to his right.

The beefy man gave a brief glance at the photo, chuckled and grunted, "Have fun, kid," before letting Mack enter the establishment and transition into sensory overload.

Topless waitresses worked the crowd, mingling and serving drinks, their nipples jutting out from cherry red areolas in free invitation. On the center stage, dressed like scientists, with lab coats open, two well-endowed women painted geometric shapes onto each other's body, then tried to mix the colors by rubbing themselves together. The goggles stretched around their foreheads, fogged with humidity and perspiration. Mack stared in open-mouthed wonder.

He sauntered toward the back of the room and glimpsed two men getting lap dances. The girls, gyrating on their laps, leaned over and made out with each other. *Each other!*

"Holy shit," Mack grinned.

"You want a drink, honey?" A squeaky blonde, all lean lines and small perky breasts, approached him, holding a platter of drinks that almost defied her tiny frame.

He gave the room another sweep of his eyes, suddenly energized and grinned.

By the time Mack left that night, he'd gotten his own dance in a private room, a belly full of food and drink, and most important, though not necessarily to him, a new job in the kitchen. Now, oblivion awaited, in the form of a lumpy mattress in a recommended cheap motel room, nearby.

****

Mack quickly discovered washing dishes would not provide enough money to sustain him, and as the weeks pressed on, his funds dwindled. He scanned and answered the Help Wanted ads for construction jobs, and when a local excavating company took one look at the strong powerhouse, they hired him. Long days of working hard manual labor and longer nights of cleaning up after the club's patrons, left the young man exhausted and yearning for something more.

"Smoke break, Tony," he called to the bar's cook, and shuffled outside to sit atop an old picnic table behind the club. Blowing out a smoke ring and then another to interlock with it, the sound of two men talking pierced the quiet evening. The fishermen in filthy overalls and flannels walked toward the front of the building. They stopped to finish their own cigarettes, oblivious to Mack in the staircase's shadow.

"That's bullshit, Shawn." The speaker, a short and stocky man, had deep auburn hair that winged out from under a stocking cap. It connected to a patchy beard and swirled around a wide mouth. "There's no way a greenhorn made thirty-five k in three weeks."

"I shit you not." Shawn, a scrawny man in his late twenties, shifted from foot to foot to stay warm. "I'm telling you, Mark, you could make a fortune on those boats."

Before his friend could answer, Mack's deep voice growled out from the darkness, "What kind of boat?" Shawn jumped before he realized a kid his own age spoke, and relaxed again.

"Crab boats. Ya know, crab fishin'?" Shawn rolled his eyes at his companion, as if to say, *you believe this guy?*

"Crab fishin'? Have you done it?" Mack asked, his interest now piqued.

"No, man. It's hard to get on those boats." Shawn stubbed out his cigarette. "You've gotta know someone or have some serious fishing experience. It's super hard, and fucking scary, man."

"Scary?"

"Turn your short hairs white."

Mack drew his brows together in doubt and studied the kid. "Whatever."

"No, dude, for real. It's dangerous on the chain." When Mack just looked at him blankly, he said, "You know, the Bering Sea?" Mack shrugged, and the man continued. "The weather, the boats... they break down all the time or something else goes wrong. Been over thirty people died just this year."

"But you make bank?" Mack asked, not put off in the slightest.

"Yeah," Shawn admitted. "It's like winning the fucking lottery, man. Ya work for a few weeks, then make a shit ton of money."

"Where do you go to do that? How do you get there?"

Shawn shook his head and shrugged. "The guy I was talking to was from Dutch."

"Dutch?"

"Dutch Harbor, you know, on the chain?" Mack gave him a blank stare again, so Shawn continued. "You can leave out of Homer, it's about three hundred miles south of here."

"Come on, Shawn," Mark complained and heaved out an irritated sigh. "I came here to see some pussy."

"Okay, thanks man." Mack sniffed and gave a nod of his head as the two men disappeared around the building. Mack chewed on a hangnail, then took a final drag off his Camel, and flicked it away. Shrugging his shoulders several times, he jerked his neck from side to side to loosen it up and go back to work.

For the rest of his shift, Mack rewound and dissected the conversations with his father. *Was this the fishing he talked about?* In the short time since his move to Anchorage, Mack tried to locate his father, only to discover the elder Carter died in a bar fight earlier that year. However, the revelation triggered no emotion from his son. After work, Mack traversed the five blocks back to his rented room, and counted his meager savings. One thousand-two hundred-ninety-seven-dollars.

"It's got to be enough," he muttered, and shoved his belongings into the duffel bag, then jerked out a thumb for Homer, Alaska.

CHAPTER 2

"**N**els!" Captain Montgomery bellowed over the intercom. "Get up here, I need to talk to you."

Nels Pearson took in a frigid lungful of fall air, then exhaled it hard through his long nose, and swore under his breath. *What did the damn fool want now?* He threw down some coiled line and stepped over it. *I swear to Christ, if Campbell doesn't replace this moron soon...* By the time he reached the bridge, his face reflected a mask of reverent composure.

"Hey Capt'n, what's up?"

Docked and ready to offload for a quick two-day turnaround, Nels and his crew needed to get a substantial amount of work completed in a miniscule amount of time. Shooting the shit with the captain would take manageable effort and cut it down to nothing. *Christ, the man liked the sound of his own voice.*

The captain of the F/V *Nordic,* Harold Montgomery, looked up from his nautical charts to take in his first mate. Nels relaxed his six-foot-three frame against the wall, and ran a hand through his thick, coal black hair. It floated on the straps of his waterproof overalls, reminding him he desperately needed a haircut.

"Yeah, Pearson, I've been looking at some of these names to replace Anderson, but I just don't know," Montgomery drawled. He removed his captain's hat and scratched at his balding head with vigor. Dry skin floated down like feathers onto the papers. Nels reached into his shirt pocket and withdrew a pack of Marlboro Red's, and tried not to sigh as he lit the cigarette one handed.

"You know," the captain droned on. "You're the one in charge down there and I think it's important *you* make this decision because *you* gotta work with whoever comes aboard." Montgomery stopped scratching his scalp and placed his cap back on his head. He looked both overwhelmed and confused at the same time. "Besides, I've got enough shit to think about up here. Why don't you go pluck out a new greenhorn from wherever you find them?"

"Sure, no problem, Capt'n." Nels smiled at the aging seafarer. "Happy to do it." He turned and left without another word, clenching the cigarette tight between his teeth.

Pluck out, Nels thought. *Jesus, where did this guy come from?* He stopped and gazed down at the deck and her crew and decided not to get angry after all, maybe it was a blessing in disguise. If left to Montgomery, he'd hire someone even worse than the college puke that quit after one turnaround, and left them high and dry.

It took a special man to work aboard a crab boat. Lean, yet built like a brick shit house from years of grueling physical labor, Nels' long body stood out as an anomaly amongst many of his shorter and stockier counterparts. Like most Scandinavians, his skin illuminated light by nature, but after working in the harshest of weather systems for so long, it tanned and hardened, like weather-beaten leather. Physical presence notwithstanding, having the mental capacity to endure the pain of the intense physical labor and days of no sleep during some of the bleakest weather conditions, without falling into the water proved the greatest feat.

After instructing his subordinates on their tasks, Nels made his way towards Mildred's Cafe with a stack of résumés. All he desired in the world was one keeper crew member and a great cup of coffee. After a few words with the café's namesake, he sat down and turned over the first paper. *Mack Carter.* Nels stared at the wall, trying to recall the name and kid's face. He glanced up at a movement by the kitchen. The live specimen backed his way through the swinging doors, a gray plastic tub in his hands.

Mack heaved the container up on a table and cleared dishes, before he wiped down the surfaces with meticulous precision. *A fast, efficient job, even just cleaning tables.* Nels narrowed his eyes and grinned. *Young, strong, and he would only get bigger, once the remaining edges of youth wore away. The perfect greenhorn.* He liked the kid and looked down at the paper for his age. *Twenty-five.* The deck boss darted a look back to the worker. *My ass, you're twenty-five.* His size and deep baritone voice made him sound older for sure, but the older fisherman placed the boy's age somewhere around seventeen or eighteen. Nels tried to determine how it could affect the dynamic onboard and once more studied the paper. drawing deep on his cigarette.

****

Mack learned how to fish in Homer, but over the past year worked odd jobs to earn enough money for gear and a plane ride down the Aleutian chain. He found himself in Dutch Harbor at *Mildred's*, the only restaurant across from the docks, bussing tables and washing dishes. The café's namesake understood fishing came first with most of the young men that worked for her and possessed a revolving door mentality. The teen ended the summer salmon fishing and tried to make himself known to the crab captains.

"Hey," an older man called, startling Mack out of his thoughts. He turned, and recognizing Nels' studious face, gave him a friendly grin. "You got time for a quick break, kid?"

"Ah," Mack glanced over at Millie, who gave him a quick nod of her head. "Sure."

He slid into the booth, and the old woman shuffled over to fill another cup with coffee.

"Thanks Mil," Mack said and sipped. She laid a papery hand on his shoulder and winked at Nels, before attending to her other patrons.

"So, how you doing?" Nels asked.

"Good."

"How long have you worked for Mil?"

"Little over a year." Mack sipped his coffee again, a little perplexed at the line of questioning.

"How is it you came to Dutch from... where the hell was it?" Nels flipped some pages as Mack set down his cup. "Oh, right, Seattle? Rainier Valley?"

"Ah, yeah. My dad left a while back but always talked about fishing up here and my ma just... ah...

she left too. So, I figured it's time to earn my place in the world."

"Uh-huh," Nels frowned. "And how did you wind up here?"

"Worked and hitchhiked mostly."

"How old are you? No," Nels asked, then held up a hand. "Never mind, I don't want to know."

"Old enough," Mack stated anyway. He reached into his pocket, withdrew a cigarette from the pack, lit it and took a pull off it. He considered Nels and realized the impromptu job interview for what it was, straightened in his seat and cleared his throat. "Um, I'm a fast learner, once you show me what to do. I think I'd be good at it, crabbing I mean." He paused and the older man continued to survey him. "I'll play you straight, man, and bust my ass trying. You'll get two hundred percent from me every day, I swear to God."

"Yawp, well, that'll do."

Nels leaned back in his chair and scratched at the black stubble on his chin. Mack smelled the salty sea in the movement. After several seconds, the deck boss leaned forward again and sipped his coffee before shifting his gaze back to Mack, and the corner of his mouth quirked into a curve.

"Okay, we're gonna try you out, Carter. You'll be a greenhorn. Bottom of the food chain, and you'll get every shit job we have. It'll be fucking miserable, but you'll do exactly what I tell you. You won't complain and you'll have no opinions. You understand me, boy?"

"Yes, sir. No opinions, you got it. I won't let you down. Thank you." They shook hands, and both leaned back in their respective seats, relieved.

****

"No, damn it, not like that," Nels frowned at his young protégé, disgusted. "You'll rip your head off or get caught in the line."

"Fuck me," Mack muttered.

"Okay, hold up," Nels said as the last pot flew off the deck. "Remember what I said? Long-lining is different from just dropping a pot by loader." He kicked the buoy off and turned toward Mack.

"Yeah."

"Okay, what did I say?"

"In long-lining, the anchor pot floats at sea level and hooks onto a set of buoys." Mack rose his hand in the air to indicate a plane of water.

"And?"

"And the ground line goes from the anchor pot to the string of pots." He moved his other hand underneath the first.

"And how many pots are there?"

"Thirty to sixty." He took a glove off to bite a fingernail, and Nels slapped his hand away. Mack re-gloved it and put his hands on his hips.

"All connected to each other, right?"

"Yeah."

"So that means what?"

"A lot of fuckin' pots are flying around."

"Hundreds of them over the course of the week. Not to mention the lines you can step in." Nels faced his greenhorn. "You've come close to steppin' in two."

Mack clenched his jaw, ashamed of disappointing his mentor. "Sorry, Nels," he mumbled. "I'll get there. Sooner or later, I'll get there." He took in a deep breath of frozen air, shredding his lungs into painful icicles.

"Well, let's hope it isn't later, after you're lying in the muck with a fucking pot sitting on your ass."

They cleaned up the deck, and Mack, curious about the older man, asked, "You come from a fishing family, Nels?"

Pearson grabbed some line and began coiling it. "I'm a third-generation commercial fisherman."

"Where are you from originally?"

"Helsingborg, Sweden. My dad fished Bluefin tuna in the Øresund."

"Where's that?"

"Between Sweden and Denmark. Grab those tubs." He indicated four containers they used to haul bait. "He followed the tuna to the Kattegat, then into the North Sea. I learned everything I know from my old man. He was one tough sonofabitch. A calloused Scandinavian fisherman through and through."

"A true, blue blood."

"Yawp."

"When did you come here?"

"Nineteen-sixty-one, two years after Alaska became a state." Nels grunted as he stooped to pick up the deck squeegee and scraped the deck. Fish guts, slime and other bycatch squished its way across the deck and through a hole back out to sea. "My dad died, mom remarried, and I was stupid enough to want some adventure." He paused, a

21

little breathless, and leaned on the handle of his charge. "Heard about crab fishing over here. Fell in love with the challenge, sense of adventure and accomplishment from all the hard work, and... well, damn, look at this place."

Mack stopped wiping down the sorting table he worked on and looked out to sea. The sun, close to setting, turned the sky into a color byplay of reds, oranges, yellows and purples. As the boat rocked with the waves, far off in the distance two large animals, maybe seals or walrus, played without reservation.

"The wild frontier?"

"Exactly. Found out I had a knack for crab fishing. Been doing it ten years now, wouldn't dream of doing anything else."

Mack grinned at him. In ten years, his boss also solidified himself as a no-nonsense, hardworking, but fair-minded crew member and deck boss of few words. He didn't lose his temper because he didn't need to. The men followed his orders without complaint, because they all accepted they weren't arbitrary orders. Though uneducated, Nels also innately understood all the breakthrough technologies almost before they happened. Things like the new live tank systems, or hydraulics and power blocks, that became common place onboard the vessels, in his tenure. Not to mention, everyone understood who helped the aging Captain Montgomery find the crab, thereby giving them their livelihood.

The putrid smell of rotting fish hung all around them, as they slid on their slime, and cleaned up the cold, iron deck. Catching his breath for a moment, Mack straightened and smiled. He stretched his aching back for a moment and looked across the deck, past the peeling paint on the rails, and out to roiling sea again. He made it and knew he could do the job.

****

As the season closed, they asked him back for the next season, and elated, the greenhorn accepted. "After this run, what're you doing for the summer?" Mack's voice floated up to Nels from the bottom bunk of their crew quarters.

"I rent out a piece of shit cabin on Kodiak." Nels said, as he thumbed through a fish and game magazine.

Mack fluffed the pillow under his head and tried to figure out how to say what he wanted to say. Coming up with nothing, he blurted, "Want some company?" The pages of the magazine stopped rustling and his face flushed crimson. "If not, it's cool... I just..."

"No, it's not that. I was thinking about going to Seattle this summer. I've never been there before and was gonna ask if you knew a good place to go."

It never even occurred to Mack to go back to Seattle. The boat and the Bering Sea felt more like home than his birthplace ever did, and he wasn't sure if he wanted to go back.

"You could teach me a thing or two," Nels continued with a smile in his voice.

Mack thought about it, then grinned too. "Okay, Pearson, we can try you out. You'll be a greenhorn, though. Bottom of the food chain, and you'll get every shit job I can think of. You gotta do exactly what I tell you. No complaining and no opinions. You understand me, boy?"

The older man chuckled. "You got it, kid."

CHAPTER 3

The fishermen found a two-bedroom apartment to sublet above a convenience store, on the corner of University Way and Fiftieth Street, in Seattle's University district. One unseasonably warm evening in early June, they wanted to catch a movie at the Old Varsity Theater, five blocks away. After standing in line for twenty minutes, sipping on warm, concealed whiskey in flasks, they reached the box office ticket counter.

Behind the glass, a woman, in her late teens to early twenties, with ginger-red hair curling in a haphazard queue down her back, raised heavy-lidded emerald green eyes, to address the men. Her skin, like porcelain, yet washed with thousands of tiny freckles, glowed.

"How many?" she queried.

"Murron?" Mack asked with incredulity.

Murron Middleton blinked as if to clear her mind and gazed back at Mack, brows drawn together. She blinked again before realizing who he was, and the corners of her wide mouth, with a full upper lip, quirked into a genuine smile.

"Mack," she asked, a little hesitant. "Mack Carter?" The lilt of Scotland in her melodic voice, she skittered a look to Nels, but not recognizing him, refocused her efforts back on Mack. He stared back, with his mouth half open.

"Oh man, you're gorgeous! Been a long time, huh? You graduate?"

"Aye." Her gaze returned to Nels again and locked.

"Ah," Mack turned to his deck boss. "Nels Pearson... Murron Middleton. Murron, this is Nels, we work together up in Alaska."

"Ah, so that's where you'd be keepin' yourself?"

The group behind the men complained about their reunion chatter, so the men stepped out of line to wait for the young woman. As they waited, Mack explained to Nels how the couple met when he worked at the golf resort her parents belonged to. He'd been saving money to buy a stereo, and Murron's family just moved from Paisley, Scotland, several months prior. Wealthy and blue-blooded, her father wanted her to learn the game of golf. Having no interest in the game at all, she spent most of the summer sitting next to the pool, reading books and drinking root beer.

Mack worked in the cabana and noticed the beautiful girl in his first hour of work. She recognized a kindred spirit underneath Mack's guarded exterior, and the two became friends. Mack omitted to his boss he'd developed a crush on the girl the second he met her. Though secure in his abilities with girls of his own socio-economical class, he never worked up the courage to ask her out and settled for friendship.

When Murron's shift ended, she crossed the street to them, hair flying behind her. Both men ran their gazes down the tall and slender length of her five-foot ten-inch frame in appreciation. The green micro mini dress molded to her curves and black patent leather go-go boots stopped just below her knees.

"So, ya could've knocked me over with a feather when I saw ya! You're looking weel, Mack," she gushed with eyes shining and threw arms around her friend in a proper hug. The rich lavender scent that always surrounded her like an aura filled his nostrils, and they settled into the night to catch up on the events of each other's lives, as Nels listened.

"There was a huge shindy when ye left that day. Someone said at graduation you'd moved to California, but dinna ken where."

"Naw, I went up to Alaska," Mack's rich whiskey and gravel voice filled the small restaurant booth they sat in. "I worked a while doing all kinds of shit, but now I work on a crab boat with Nels here."

He clapped a hand on his boss's shoulder and Murron's gaze shifted to the older man. She gave him a bashful, yet radiant smile that he returned.

"And where are ya from then, Nels?"

"Helsingborg, Sweden."

"Oh," she gushed. "It's so beautiful there."

"You've been there?"

"Of course, the *Karnan*, and *Sankta Maria Kyrka*... that beautiful *Norra hamnen*."

"You know the harbor?"

"My Gran brought me on holiday one year, when I was just a wee thing."

Mack grinned as he listened to the two speak of foreign locations and the magic of the Baltic and Celtic lands.

****

The attraction Mack experienced in high school for Murron softened but remained. However, the young woman slipped into romance with Nels, rather than his protégé, as the weeks progressed.

Mack shuffled into the kitchen one morning and grabbed a box of *Cheerios* off the counter. He shook some cereal into a bowl and reached for the milk in the refrigerator, when Murron bounced into the kitchen wearing a pair of Nels' boxer shorts and aquamarine tank top with no bra. The kitchen shrunk by half as she reached around him and grabbed the eggs.

"Morning Mack. Oh, don't eat that, I'm going to make some pancakes."

"Ah..."

"Ya want some?"

"Sure." She bent over a retrieved a pan to use as a griddle as Nels padded into the kitchen and wrapped his arms around her waist. He nuzzled her neck, and surprised, she squeaked and giggled. Mack shifted uncomfortably in his seat.

"Your hands are freezing!"

The older man snickered and flicked his eyes up to Mack's.

"What are you up to today?" he asked his roommate as Murron expertly flipped over a cake.

"I'm gonna row boats on Lake Union with Lizzy," he replied, referring to one of Murron's friend he'd met the night before.

"Oh, brilliant," Murron exclaimed. "I'm so glad you like each other. She's a keeper, that one is."

Mack brightened, turned to his plate and poured some syrup on the fluffy flapjacks delivered fresh off the griddle. He spoke around a large bite of food, "She said she likes me?"

"Aye, that she did."

"Well, we'll see. Two hours in a boat is a long time when you aren't fishing or doing something."

"If she blethers, just give her a wee kiss, and see what comes of it."

"And," Nels added with a laugh, "we're thinking about getting out of here for a few days and letting you have some privacy."

"Where're you going?" Mack asked, interested.

"We're thinking Vegas, but maybe Canada. It's just for a few days," Nels replied.

"Cool." Mack went back to his food but observed the couple from his periphery.

An urgent need developed between the couple over the course of their two-month courtship, the loving warmth so foreign to Mack, he didn't trust it. In his world, relationships between men and women were comprised of fighting, tears, and satisfying physical needs in a dark room. *Could something that special exist?* Mack didn't have a clue.

****

The couple's vacation of a few days turned into two weeks. Mack returned from a rather more interesting date with Lizzy to music playing in the apartment. Excited about his friend's return, he rushed in just as Murron launched herself into his arms, hugging him hard. She stepped back and handed him a cold beer.

"We have a surprise," she giggled with excitement. "We're pregnant!"

"And," Nels added, walking around the corner, grinning like a fool, "married."

Mack, taking a sip of his beer, gagged and spewed the contents all over the counter. He coughed and sputtered as beer dripped out of his nose. Giggling, Murron rushed over to help clean him up.

"Um," he coughed. "Congratulations?" he asked, a little unsure of what he should say, and glanced at each friend. Murron's bright green eyes flashed, and her cheeks flushed.

Christ, pregnant women do that... glowed with pregnancy. He felt the familiar drop in his stomach at her beauty, then eyed Nels, also transcendent with happiness.

"Holy shit, you guys aren't kidding?"

"Nope." Murron threw out her left hand with a small diamond set in the middle of a gold band and beamed down at it. Mack clasped her fingers and squinted at the diamond.

"Pretty pitiful there, Nels." He grinned and looked over at his best friend.

"Fuck you." The two men embraced, clapping each other on the back, and when they parted, Nels said, "I promised her after this next run I'd do it one better."

"Why the hell didn't you tell me any of this shit?" Mack scolded. "I would've stood up for you."

Murron went to the fridge and pulled out two more beers, and an apple juice for herself.

"Oh darlin', there wasna time." She handed the men their drinks, then stooped at the kitchen sink cupboard for some cleanser and a rag. The potent scent of Pine-Sol permeated the room as she rid the counter and cupboards of the foamy amber splashed onto their surface.

"She's not kidding." Nels watched his new wife's progress. "I wish you could've been there, man, but everything happened so fast. We were having a great time in Vegas, even won twenty-five hundred bucks, but then she started getting really sick every morning." Murron threw the rag in the sink and placed the cleanser back in the cupboard. "She did the math and thought she might be pregnant. So, we went to see this doctor and begged him to check her out."

"He gave me this test, right there in the office, just like that." She snapped her fingers. "And said it was very accurate."

"How far gone are you?"

"He thinks about six weeks."

Mack did the math and discovered they got pregnant with one of their first sexual encounters. He looked at the older man with new admiration at his virility.

"So, here's a toast to my wife, Mrs. Murron Pearson, and my son," Nels said, raising his bottle.

"Darlin', I told ya, it'll be a lassie. You may as well start gettin' used to the notion." She smirked but still drank deep. "Okay." She turned Mack. "So, before you say anything else, my parents aren't knowing nothing about it yet. And... we," -she gestured between herself and her new husband- "wondered if, as a weddin' present, would you like to be the one to tell 'em?" She gave Mack her most luminescent smile.

"Oh, hell, no," Mack retorted. He'd met her father, Angus, on the golf course the summer he worked there. They also crossed paths on Murron's birthday, three weeks after the couple started dating. A first-rate asshole, her old man made no pretense of liking the two fishermen, even a little. "But you better be damn sure I'll be there to watch... you know, for moral support."

"Oh aye." Murron's smile faltered just a little. "Moral support. We'll be needing that for sure."

****

Angus Middleton, a proud patriot of his homeland, lived by a strict and righteous compass. At fifty, he still exuded power and propriety, with unfriendly hazel eyes, and thin lips which never deemed to bend themselves into a smile. Angus inherited his substantial fortune through the property dynasty of his family. As a man of status and position, Murron said he expected his daughter to align herself with the same.

Defiant and headstrong, Murron, an only child, believed her father respected her personality, but also expressed concern about her naiveté about two "hapless, gold-digging parasites". Attributes he attached to the fishermen she befriended during the summer and voiced his displeasure with frequently and with loud ruminations. Every night, the young woman listened to her mother, Fenella, coo and counsel him through the thin walls. She chided to give it time and the relationship would cool on its own. At this, the patriarch always declared he looked forward to the day they'd go back to Alaska and "splash" about in the sea.

When Angus learned his beautiful young daughter not only married a man ten years her senior but also carried his child, he could barely be restrained. The old man warned Nels he'd never amount to a damn thing and would only take his innocent daughter with him to the devil.

"Then I'll wear a halter top," she retorted and stomped out of the house, with the two men glancing anywhere but at the melee.

"Thank you for supper, Mrs. Middleton," Nels said, but didn't spare a glance at his new father-in-law.

As the pregnant woman seethed in the front seat, Mack asked, "What the hell is a *gomeral?*"

"What?" She turned back to him, holding back a giggle. "A *gomeral?* What is it?"

"Oh, Mack, I'm sorry. I'm their only daughter and Da was nothing but a horse's arse tonight."

"Yeah, okay, but what the fuck does it mean?"

"Oh, it's Scots for an idiot."

"Damn, if the man has to insult us, the least he could do is say it in our language. He is in America, you know, Murron."

"Sorry, I think the only help for it is time."

"That and a grandson," Nels chimed in, grinning. When she gave him a shaky smile back, he reached over, clasped her hand and brushed a kiss across her knuckles. She grinned again with determination.

"Aye," she replied. "Except for the fact he'll be getting a granddaughter, *mo cridhe*." She reached out a hand and stroked his cheek. *Mo cridhe*, Mack thought, my heart.

****

As the twilight of summer faded and fall solidified, the men prepared to leave. Standing on the pier at Fisherman's Wharf, Mack opened his arms to the expectant mother.

"Be careful, Mack," she said and moved into his outstretched arms. "Will ya take care of him for me and keep him safe?" she whispered.

"You know I will, Murron." He breathed in her scent before releasing her. "I promise, and next time I see you, you'll have a snot-nosed brat running around."

"Aye." She giggled and hugged him again. "Take care of yourself too. I hope it isn't too bad out there."

Mack gave her a wink and walked to the Nordic, grabbed the remaining gear and fed his superstitious soul by stepping aboard with his right foot. Throwing his gear in their bunk room, he returned on-deck to help with the lines and run through the final checklist before leaving.

The day was crisp, yet the sun shone as Nels and Murron clung to each other in an embrace, heads bowed together. Dotted along the dock, families on the pier said goodbye to one another. Some jovial, and some in tears. Mack breathed in through his nose to smell the foamy brine of the harbor and left to grab a cup of coffee. In the galley, the skipper's wife washed several dishes and mugs, turning everything upside down to dry. Mack darted a look around the room and quickly flipped each mug upright. Lore prophesied glasses or mugs turned upside down on a boat foretold of an evil wind. If Montgomery observed the ominous sign, he would've postponed the trip by several days.

Thank God, he corrected the blunder in time.

CHAPTER 4

The F/V *Nordic* started its slow motor toward Alaska, leaving loved ones' mere specks on the dock of the misty harbor. As Mack and the other deckhands unpacked their belongings, Nels climbed the stairs to confirm the intended fishing route, checklists and weather reports for the first run of the season with the captain.

"Hey, Capt'n, the guys are settling in. We still on point for..." Nels trailed away, as his eyes fell upon new charts unrolled on the man's desk. "What's this?"

"We're going to my honey pot at St. Lawrence Island."

"St. Lawrence Island?" Nels asked with concern. "What are you talking about, Skip? There's nothing there. Haven't you been reading the reports?"

"Of course I've read the reports," snapped Montgomery. "Campbell suggested to me over the summer, maybe I should step down. That there were several complaints. Is that where we're at now, Nels?"

"What?" *The man finally lost it.* "I don't understand... you think I said something?"

"Save it. Why don't we go back to me being the captain of this vessel and you go back to being the deck boss? What's for dinner?"

"Montgomery..." Nels began but didn't have a clue what to say to the accusation.

"I'll take it up here. That's all, Pearson."

At a loss, Nels returned to the galley and explained to the crew the alternate course they now found themselves on. If he had to pick a day, the plague of cataclysmic events began for their season, he'd declare the first day as the point of no return.

In the first week, a rogue wave capsized their sister ship, the F/V *Triton*, and all six of her men - friends- were swallowed by the Bering Sea. Their new greenhorn sliced open his hand with a knife used to cut open bait, causing them to return to Dutch and acquire a new beginner. Training the unknown man set them back weeks, and the season as well as all their efforts resulted in empty pot after empty pot. Not only could they not land on crab, but the boat fell into disrepair from several years of basic neglect. At every turn, the boat required another major overhaul or expensive part, dipping into the crew's profits.

"Fuck!" Nels screamed uncharacteristically off the aft end of the boat.

Some crew glanced back as they scurried inside to warm up. Mack, halfway through the door himself turned to observe his best friend. Nels paced over the deck next to the stacked pots. The ship began its slow turn to make yet another trip back to Dutch Harbor for repairs. The brief red crab season closed its doors on barely any profit for anyone.

"When we get into port, I'm calling Campbell and getting that asshole thrown off this fucking boat or I swear to Christ Almighty, I'm walking," the deck boss announced. He glared up at the cockpit and screamed, punching a fist in the air and raising his middle finger at the captain. "Dickhead!" Montgomery peered down at them but didn't switch on the intercom.

"It's gonna be okay."

"Like hell it is. How the am I supposed to support Murron and the kid when I work my ass off and still owe the goddamn boat?" Mack handed Nels a smoke, as the smell of diesel oil and exhaust rolled over them. A flock of seagulls rained shit across the deck, illustrating the men's attitude perfectly.

"Campbell will listen," Mack encouraged. "And every one of those guys would walk with you in a minute, too." Mack paused. "I can help with some money..."

"Don't be an asshole," Nels interrupted. "You don't have a fucking pot to piss in either."

Nels wasn't just blowing off steam. Over the dozen years he'd been a deckhand, he received his own captain's license and learned not only the deck and engine room but the bridge. He believed himself more than capable of running a boat from the wheelhouse. However, fishing vessels weren't in infinite supply and regulated as to number.

When they pulled into the harbor, and the captain ordered Nels to see to the offload, he retorted, "What offload?" He flung open the door and stomped onto the outer deck, as the captain followed. The crew turned their heads to the spectacle. "You're done."

"I'm done," the captain shouted. "I'm done? We'll just see who's off this boat in an hour."

As Nels used his hands on the ladder to catapult himself from the boat to the dock, and retorted, "You bet your ass we will."

A day later, the repairs and provisions complete, the *Nordic* disembarked for the long Opilio season, with a new captain. Though Nels knew it erased any chance of coming home for the birth of his first-born child, he plotted his course and fell on the crab with his first soak, and the crew sighed with relief that some of their efforts were salvaged.

****

In the late days of April 1973, Murron's water broke. She waddled with excitement into her parent's bedroom in the early hours of morning and announced, "It's time, Mam."

Excited about the impending birth, Fenella grabbed her belongings and Angus drove them both to the hospital. However, after forty-eight hours, and still laboring hard, the young woman's strength waned. With each contraction, the baby's heart rate plummeted to dangerous levels, as did Murron's, causing black spots to creep into her vision.

Fenella held her daughter's clammy, shaking hand, trying to provide a small measure of comfort, while encouraging the weakened woman to push. In a mighty effort, Murron bent her head to her chest, face turning the color of a ripe eggplant, and pushed with everything she had left, until a tiny, pink-faced, furious baby slid from her womb. The obstetrician suctioned the neonate's mouth and nose before placing it onto a warming bed for inspection and APGAR score. After the brief examination, the RN placed the baby in the new mother's waiting arms. Exhausted but exultant, Murron gazed at her newborn daughter and beamed at Fenella with tears streaming down her face.

"Ah, *mo nighean*... I was telling Nels she'd be a girl." Breathless, Murron looked down at her the baby again with decision. "Faith, Mam. I want her named, Faith." Weeping, she grasped her mother's hand and gazed into the warm green eyes, so much like her own. "Isn't she bonnie?"

"Aye, *mo cridhe*..." Fenella cried too, "... *bòidheach*. She's the spit of you, love." She stroked her daughter's damp hair, as Murron's body went limp.

Fenella reached out just in time to grab the baby before she rolled out of her daughter's arms, then turned with confusion to look first at Murron, then at the doctor. Tension rose to a palpable level and buzzed all around the room. The obstetrician, not a part of the emotional exchange between mother and daughter, struggled to deliver the placenta. Murron's bleeding increased as a nurse scanned the monitors.

"Heart rate's one-fifty, BP ninety over forty and dropping!" the woman pronounced to the room.

The older woman's cognition, as fractured as the doctor's orders, only picked up scattered words. "Fresh frozen plasma... manual massage... get me some sterile... STAT!"

Things happened with such speed Fenella couldn't decipher the words. Terrified and unable to move, a nurse nudged her away from her daughter and tried to distract the new grandmother by saying she needed to check the newborn. However, Fenella wrapped her arms tightly around the newly bundled being and huddled in the room's corner, crying and praying at the same time.

****

Murron regained consciousness, but the dark void all around mocked and enticed her just out of reach. A calm and soothing voice filtered into her consciousness, almost musical, if not lyrical.

"Murron? Honey, hang on," another voice encouraged, then faded. Words blinked in and out. "Uterine atony... DIC... Deliver placenta... Now." Pressure came down on her sternum.

"Hold on, Murron," someone ordered. "Now push!"

Arms wrapped around the young woman and bent her in half, as hands pressed down on her uterus. Her body hardened with a contraction, as pain exploded into her and Murron unleashed a bloodcurdling scream of agony. Without warning, over seven hundred cc's of blood gushed from the mother's womb, along with the placenta. The fragrant earthy odor of iron enveloped the room, which stopped time for a moment, as if flash-frozen in an ice storm. Murron glimpsed herself in a mirror placed at the foot of her bed for the birth. Her face, ghostly white, almost transparent, and covered in a fine sheen of sweat. Her eyes rolled back into her head and her body went limp again.

"She's bottoming out..."

The words spoken, now detached from her world. *Should she be fearful of something?* As if in answer, an intense peace permeated through the membranes of her being. No pain resided from that shell now, where moments before tiny explosions of agony set off inside her. Floating upwards, she was a whisper. Her fluid body turned to look down on the scene unfolding. Nurses and doctors applied paddles to her bare chest and her body spasmed, arching upward. However, in her state of being, a featherlike tickle crossed her chest. Bright crimson pooled all around the bed, draining her life essence from arteries and veins within her womb.

A movement to the left captured her attention. A woman huddled in the room's corner. Her soft white hair glistened in the bright brilliant light radiating down. Sobbing, she cradled a compact bundle in an arm, close to her body. The woman genuflected repeatedly with the other, and something about the bundle troubled Murron. The woman folded down the blanket as if to answer an unspoken question, and the new mother saw the baby... her baby... her baby with Nels. Realization the precious child would not know her, suffused through her. And her husband... her Nels. *What will happen to them both?* She received the answer almost before the question and peace glided into her, through her, once more.

A desire stronger than anything she'd ever experienced, beckoned to her, and Murron raised her head serenely to its purpose, before she blended her energy with the light.

****

A thin voice crackled over the radio as Mack climbed the stairs to the wheelhouse.

"Campbell to *Nordic*, over…"

"This is *Nordic*. How do, boss?" Nels inquired, but before the man responded, he continued. "Man, are we on 'em now. You'll be happy to know the boat's almost full."

He glanced up as Mack set a cup of coffee and an enormous tuna-fish sandwich beside him. They finished setting their gear for twenty-four-hour soak, and the sun shone high overhead, promising an unbelievable day.

"Pearson, you alone up there?" Campbell asked.

"No," Nels cocked his head at the odd question and responded with a brief hesitation. Mack also paused mid-bite of his own sandwich at something in the owner's voice. "Mack just took his break and came up. Everything okay?"

"Pearson, your wife had the baby this morning," Campbell responded without preamble.

"No, shit!" Relief spread through the cabin, and Mack clapped Nels on the back, with a laugh. "Well, all right. What did she wind up having?" the junior asked.

Relieved, Nels laughed and hunched over, rubbing the palms of his hands over his thighs. "Oh, man," the new father said. "You scared the absolute shit out of me. I thought…"

"Pearson!" Campbell's tone snapped both men to attention. "Something went wrong. Something about bleeding too much. Nels, I'm sorry to have to tell ya this, but sh-she died. Your wife. She's gone, man."

Silence crept over the wheelhouse for several moments.

"What?" Mack asked as the information processed. "What do you mean? Where is she?" He looked over at Nels, who sat like a stone in his chair.

"What about the baby?" Nels murmured. Campbell didn't hear him and answered Mack's question instead.

"She's at one of the funeral homes by now. We had a hard time reaching you. Her mother… Fenella, is it?" Nels shook his head in affirmation, but the caller couldn't see him. "She said to call her at home when you can. The kid… you have a girl, Pearson, she's with the grandmother and from what I understand, doing very well. I'm sorry, son."

"A daughter," Nels said, a full five minutes later. He bobbled confused eyes to Mack, who could no longer move his body. At the statement, the younger man snapped out of it and paced the bridge, like a large, caged cat.

Nels whispered, "Well, I'll be damned. She was right, Mack. She *was* carrying a girl."

Mack clenched his teeth at what the new widower managed to say, then gazed out the window. His friend followed suit. The ocean, serene and calm, floated in obvious reverence to the situation, but the beautiful sunny sky appeared to mock the two men with cruel intention. Unable to accept the information, Mack closed his eyes to it. The sandwich he'd eaten roiled in his gut, and fled the room to throw up.

****

"Mrs. Middleton... I..."

"I think from this point on ye should start callin' me Fenella, Nels."

"I... I..."

"Where are ye callin' from?"

"In port. I'm trying to arrange a flight, but some weather just moved in and it's hard to get a flight out and..." Nels trailed off, then said, "But I *am* trying. I'll be there just as soon as..." He trailed off again.

"Nels, there's naught so urgent right now. Murron wanted cremation and to have her ashes spread over Scotland." Nels doubted it but didn't argue, and her mother continued, "She wanted to name the babe, Faith. It... ah... it was the last thing she said." The fisherman closed his eyes, trying to make the words stop. "Is that okay with ye, too?"

"Of course." He paused and thought for a moment. "Faith *Murron* Pearson."

"Aye, that's lovely. And the cremation? We can wait until ye get here if ye wish to see her."

"No, I can't see her that way."

"Well, then, we'll see to it. The lassie is bonny... she's thrivin'." Fenella paused as if searching for words. "Look, I ken the season's been hard. There's a lot to do here, so why don't you see it through? It's just two or three weeks more, then when you come home, we'll have a wake so fine, my Murron can't help but sleep easy."

"Okay," his breath exploded out from him. "Fenella, I'm so, so sorry."

A long pause ensued until the mother said, "Darlin' this wasna your fault. You loved my

Murron, and she loved you. She and I spoke of it many times since you left, so I ken it very weel. This was God's plan to take her now, and though I dinna ken why at all, I must trust there's a purpose for it. You must trust it, too."

Nels trusted nothing.

****

The new widower kept to himself during that time, only allowing Mack into his grief. They spent the evenings smoking cigarettes, talking of Murron and their summer together while going through bottles of Johnnie Walker Red. Mack raged over the injustice of a God that would separate a wonderful mother from her child. Nels often raised the flask to his lips unseeing, and allowed the liquid fire to dull the pain. More than once, he'd look down to discover the long tip of ash lengthened to the filter on his cigarette. When the men worked, the skipper focused on the job at hand, wanting it over. However, when the men slept, and he'd motor across the quiet night, numb as the immense waves rocked the boat in a cathartic rhythm.

Three weeks later, the morose *Nordic* motored back into Puget Sound and Fisherman's Terminal in Seattle, and the crew closed the ship down for the season. By the time Nels and Mack rang the bell at the Middleton's door, Nels barely recognized himself. Fenella held him hard against her for several moments before she escorted him to Murron's old room, now the nursery.

She opened the door for him and stepped back, placing a hand on his arm. "I'll be in the living room, should ye need anything at all."

She tiptoed down the hall and Nels stood alone with his daughter. He occupied the doorway for a long time, just listening to the infant breathing. Moving to her crib, he peered into it and took his first reluctant look at the monster that killed his wife. *Tiny.* Something inside him thawed. *So, small. So, vulnerable.* A revolving nightlight moved underwater lights and sea creatures around the room in an eerie golden glow. He reached out a clumsy hand, roughened with work, and stroked her soft, perfect cheek. As if sensing his presence, the tiny being woke, searching for him in the dim light. He stroked her cheek again and watched in fascination as her mouth opened, searching for her mother's breast. When it didn't come, she whimpered.

"Yes, darlin'," he whispered. "I want her too."

In that moment, he found the connection. An intense love for his daughter and their mutual loss. Without another thought, he picked the newborn up and brought her to his chest, breathing in her fragrant baby breath, and the scent of baby lotion and powder. He smoothed her silky-soft auburn curls and counted her tiny fingers and toes. Her fast heartbeat tattooed underneath his palm, solidifying her presence, and the living part of his late wife. Nels sat down on the floor, leaned against the dresser, and laid her head against his chest. As if sensing the man her protector and father, Faith resumed her slumber, and Nels kept her there until morning.

****

The older couple traveled to their native land and released Murron's ashes into the River Clyde. By mid-summer the Middleton's returned and Fenella recognized the intense despair and sorrow bubbling just under the surface of her son-in-law. He'd found no release and cried no tears. Angus, vehement in his blame, accused Nels for the death of his daughter, even as his wife expressed hope they would share their grief and bridge the gap, for the sake of wee Faith.

The new baby thrived, unaware of the surrounding loss. Fenella insisted she get baptized into the Catholic faith and scheduled the ceremony to coincide with her daughter's wake. After the service and small reception in the Middleton's home, Fenella went to the baby's room to change her. Through an open window, she watched Mack approached Nels, sitting on some brick steps in the backyard. A glass of whiskey tilted in one hand as he held a cigarette in the other.

"So, you getting wasted by yourself?" Mack asked, closing the French doors behind him. Fresh cut grass and the summer sunshine permeated the air. "You know, some might say you have a problem." Deep grief etched in grooves around the skipper's eyes.

Nels snorted, "Yawp, well, way I see it is, I got a few too many problems. So, why face them sober?" A slight hiccup escaped from his diaphragm, and he gave another loud snort of laughter.

"Well, fuck it," Mack responded with solidarity, laughing, too. "Give me the bottle then."

"You aren't supposed to say fuck when you're the godfather, you idiot."

"Yeah, well, I thought you knew what you were getting into when you asked, dipshit."

Angus walked into the room and placed his hands on his wife's shoulders. He cooed at the baby before he lifted his eyes and noticed the two friends obliterating themselves. One whooped and said something rude, and the other followed. Tears of laughter streamed down their faces as they held their sides. Watching the path of destruction, fury at the perceived desecration of his daughter's memory erupted within him and the older man started for the door. Fenella put the baby on her shoulder and reached out a suppressing hand.

"Ye canna interfere, *mo luaidh*. He weeps for her."

"The bloody hell he does," Angus spat. "Look at him! The man's nae fashed at all. He's a clot-heid, and so is the other one! I canna allow that, Nell, I canna!"

"He does, Angus," she spoke softly but with defiance. "And I dinna think *do nighean* would want ye to kill him, making her wee Faith an orphan."

Angus looked at his wife. Her eyes brimmed with tears, so he brought her close to him. They looked out the window. Mack's arms now locked tightly around Nels massive shoulders, who clung back and sobbed.

****

As the summer progressed, and Faith grew stronger, the adults held many conversations regarding her future. Nels was fractured in his need to provide for his daughter, and his desire to experience her life in the present. *How did he move forward?* He only knew one way of life... fishing. The Middleton's, desperate to care for the living piece of their daughter, made the decision easier, and eventually, the trio determined Faith would remain with her grandparents during the fishing season, so the men could return to their livelihood. However, when the season ended, Nels would spend the summer, and any other time off, with his little girl in a small cabin he purchased on Camano Island, about thirty nautical miles north of Fisherman's Terminal in Seattle.

As the new father kissed his daughter goodbye before motoring back to Alaska, a piece of his heart irreversibly ripped from his chest.

"I promise, we'll take good care of her," Fenella said, gazing at the bundle in her arms.

"I know you will, Nell." Nels looked down at his daughter too and placed a hand on her ruddy, fuzzy head. He leaned down to kiss her temple, then kissed his mother-in-law's wet cheek. "Let me know if you need anything."

"I will." She patted his cheek. "Now, off wi' ye, and safe travels on ye all."

Nels extended a hand to Angus, who scowled at it, but decorum soon overruled, and the old man shook it. Progress, Nels thought and hid a smile, as he gazed down at his daughter one final time before turning to walk back to his truck. Mack gave Fenella a friendly wave from the driver's seat, which she returned, and they drove back to work.

CHAPTER 5

Six hard and determined years later, Nels thrived as captain of the *Nordic* and reveled in his knack for finding crab. While Mack, now deck boss, found an aptitude for leading men. The two became a strong and efficient team and cemented within each other and Faith a family. They spoke a kind of shorthand, knowing what each other needed. Nels changed after becoming a father. The guilt of leaving Faith each year clung to him like an unwelcome burr. Mack tried to soften the pain, while stuffing down his own feelings of anger and loss.

They filled their quota for the season much earlier than expected, and Nels made it home in time for his daughter's kindergarten graduation. Mack stayed behind to clean up the boat, and get some minor repairs done, before motoring the boat back to Seattle with a skeleton crew.

He sat in Pearson's chair, sipping whiskey and staring out into the night. Twilight, and all its mystical hues, reflected off the calm surface of the harbor, only breaking when another crab boat puttered in to offend it. His gaze fell on Faith's school picture. Her bright red, curly hair was tied back in pigtails, as freckles already dusted their way over her face, creating a striking resemblance to her mother. His gaze shifted to the immediate right and the picture of Murron and Nels on their wedding day in Vegas. Both beamed at him through the cameraman's lens, and he lifted his glass to it.

"You should be there too, doll."

He took a deep breath and exhaled hard through his nose as he stared down into his drink and smelled the strong whiskey in a cloud around his head. Setting it on the counter, he decided he didn't want to get wasted alone in the wheelhouse. He wanted company... female company. Mack looked at Murron's face again before he grabbed his jacket and his pack of Camels off the table and walked out into the night.

The notorious Elbow Room in Dutch Harbor appeared as if someone built a cabin in the middle of town, threw down some old remnants of linoleum and hung a shingle out to announce its opening. Customers of every nationality crammed inside the tiny dwelling and sucked the air from the space in a matter of minutes. Once called the second most dangerous bar on the planet, the establishment lived well up to its name. The various odors of many nefarious activities permeated the surfaces and crevices of every corner. Because of its size, when fights broke out, patrons shoved the two brawlers outside until the heat of it cooled off or someone either went to jail or the hospital.

Mack loved the atmosphere and felt at home among the ruffians. He ordered a drink and eyed the huge brass bell, affixed to a beam on the bar, with the rough inscription, Elbow Room, etched in its dull metal surface. When fishermen came in from months out at sea with money burning holes in their pockets and wanted to buy drinks for all the patrons, they'd ring the bell, announcing their intentions. State law prohibited over two drinks on the table per customer, so the bartender handed out special coins until its recipient collected the spoils. Another limited commodity in the small town... women. Single and married women alike could pick any partner on any night, if they chose to. However, Mack Carter never longed for companionship. His cool detachment, rugged good looks and steely eyes drew women to him like fly-paper.

Tonight, she came in the voluptuous form of Roslyn Hoover. Daughter of a Russian fisherman and Aleut Native, Rosie stood nine inches shorter than Mack's six-two. Her shiny, jet black hair matched her lively, dark liquid eyes with thick full lashes. The young woman believed the only way off the chain was to use what nature gave her, so she allowed her ample breasts to all but pour out of a top two sizes too small. Her worn jeans shrink-wrapped around a tiny waist and well-rounded ass. She zeroed in on Mack and sat down on the barstool next to him. Giving a discreet lift of her bosom, she laid it out for display on the bar, and ran two red-lacquered fingernails down her chest.

"I'm Rosie. Who are you?" Her voice, deep and throaty, only hinted her native accent.

"Mack," he answered, running his gaze down the length of her body and up again.

A feline smile stretched across her face, unabashed. "You wanna buy me a drink, Mack?"

"Sure doll," he replied. "What're you drinking?"

"Whiskey, three fingers," she said, enunciating each word while holding up and wiggling her middle three fingers. Mack gave a wicked smile and through glazed, unfocused eyes raised his hand to attract the bartender.

****

He woke the next morning to blinding light, and a splitting headache. The stench of stale vomit lurked nearby, and beer bottles laid everywhere. A naked woman sprawled out halfway on top of him, her hand still gripping what he'd used in every workable way the night before. *Christ, is there anything worse than the morning after?* He needed to take a piss and maybe -he eyed the congealed mess beside him- vomit, again.

Reaching down, he disengaged himself from the unknown woman's hand and swung his legs to the side of the bed. He started at his own reflection in a mirror above her dresser, then glanced up and did a double take, as his reflection bounced back on her ceiling too. Hair standing on end, and a small cluster of hickeys dotting down the length of his neck, he looked closer at his face. *Fuck, is that a black eye?* He drew his brows together. The small woman rolled onto her back when Mack sat up. Perplexed, he tilted his head, squinted, then smiled at the Elbow Room coin stuck to her cheek. He tried to make a study of her, but pain cleaved his head in two. *God, who is that?* His eyes darted down and noted her beautiful body, then grinned despite himself.

On the floor beside his feet, his underwear laid guilty, so he snatched them up and slid them halfway up his legs before standing. With a careless snap into place, he left half of one butt cheek exposed, and yawned. He scratched the neglected cheek with one hand and slid the other down the front of his jockeys, just in case anything fell off. The pain drummed a tattoo in his head, so he raised both hands to it, and tried to soften the internal blows.

A door sat ajar, and he crossed over to it, to discover a small bathroom with a tiny rust lined shower, and almost wept with joy. Thirty minutes later, after he pissed, puked and took a long, hot shower, he felt more human, and discovered his clothes, folded in a neat pile on the toilet seat. A bottle of aspirin sat on top of them. *Shit, she was an angel from God.* Shaking out four tablets into the palm of his hand, then popping them into his mouth, he cupped his hands under the tap, and drew in the cool liquid to wash them down. Discovering her toothbrush, he brushed his teeth, and pulled on his jeans, not bothering to button them, then padded out to the kitchen barefoot.

The blissful aroma of strong, fresh coffee brewing and bacon and eggs frying filled the air in heady invitation. At least he knew he could threaten his breakfast and peered around the corner into the kitchen. The woman from the bed stood at the stove. Her long, black hair piled on top of her head in a messy knot and she wore a short red silk robe belted so loose he wondered why she put anything on at all. Not having a clue as to her name, he slid both hands into his pockets.

"Um, morning?" Mack smiled and took a hand out of his pocket to wave, feeling like an asshole.

"Good morning back." She turned to look at him and leaned a hip into the cupboard. She crossed her arms, one hand holding a spatula, as she asked in her deep, throaty voice, "Feeling better?"

"Ah, yeah." He ran a hand through his damp hair. "Guess I have you to thank for that, ah..." He gestured at her, helplessly.

"Rosie." She giggled and sauntered over to him with a smile. Reaching out, she ran a hand down the length of his chest, before she kissed him hard on the mouth, tasting of cigarettes and orange juice. Her hand moved down further to stroke the bulge in his pants. "And you are?" she purred.

"Mack," he said, a little strangled, as her hand moved with more aggression. "Mack Carter." He groaned when her hand reached down into his pants to cup his testicles.

The flimsy robe fell off one shoulder, revealing a large, perfect breast. He grabbed it, rolled the nipple between his thumb and forefinger, watching her, before he stooped and took it in his teeth, then suckled. She gasped and Mack moved his hands around her hips to cup her bottom and lift her legs. Rosie locked them tight around his torso, and he carried her to the table, knocking over glasses. He reached into his pants and freed himself before entering with a violent thrust.

Crying out, Rosie dropped the spatula onto the dirty mosaic tiles of her floor. Mack arched back, their lovemaking and her body fascinating him as pounded into her. He came violently and pumped a few more times until she cried out too. Breathless, he rested his forehead on hers until he could pull back a little and consider her glazed eyes. He scraped his upper teeth over his bottom lip, causing her to smile.

"Well, all right, Mack," she panted, and disentangled herself from him. Bending over, she picked up the spatula and tossed it into the sink, before straightening her robe and re-belting it. "Whew, okay, let's eat."

They spent the morning talking about fishing and Rosie's work as a hair dresser. He explained he needed to leave the next day to motor back to Seattle for the summer, and Rosie asked to see the boat. After giving her a tour of the *Nordic*, she surprised him by helping him get her ready for the journey back to Washington state, and even further when she proved herself a hard-worker.

"You wanna go back with me?"

Rosie looked up from cleaning out the refrigerator. "Go back?"

"To Seattle?"

She wiped the back of her rubber gloved hand under her chin, while biting her lower lip. "What would I do when I got there?"

"I don't know, get a job, hang out." He slid his thumbs into his belt loops. "I'm going back for the entire summer to hang out with my friend and his kid. We have a lot of fun."

"Hell, if it'll get me out of here, I'm in."

"Yeah?" He grinned at her as she approached and stood on tip toes to kiss him. He wrapped his arms around her waist. "You got to tell your boss or something?"

"No, he'll figure it out."

A day later, Mack left Dutch Harbor to go home with two deckhands and one twenty-two-year-old nymphomaniac. He recognized with relish those two things never went hand in hand.

****

Nels and Faith waited on the dock at the Port of Seattle's Fisherman's Terminal. The little girl sat on her father's shoulders, holding up a sign that read, *Welcome Home Mack,* in a child's handwriting.

The interim captain all but leapt over the railing and sprinted down the dock before the little girl spotted him and scrambled to get down. She launched herself into his outstretched arms and kissed him all over his face. His heart lifted, and he hugged her back hard, pressing his scratchy face into her soft fragrant curls, breathing her in.

"Gueth what, Mack?" She grinned and jutted out her chin, pointing a finger to her mouth. She stuck her little pink tongue through a vast gap where her two front teeth once resided. "And the thecond one fell out thith morning and you know what?"

"What's that, baby?" Mack grinned, trying not to laugh as he reached out to shake hands with Nels.

"Daddy thaid that the twoof fairy will come again tonight." She put both of her small hands up to her mouth and giggled, then bounced up and down in his arms, like an energized bunny.

Mack gave her a huge squeeze again before setting her down and said, "I bet she will, too." He gave Nels an evil grin. "You know what else? I hear the Tooth Fairy is loaded. I bet you'll get at least a hundred bucks from that chick."

"Weally?" Her eyes grew as large as saucers and she turned to her father to ask with awe, "Do you think tho too, Daddy?" Without waiting for a reply, she giggled and twirled around on the dock before hugging Mack's legs. Mack grinned at Nels, who shook his head and flipped his best friend the bird.

"Whoth that?" Faith asked, one arm curled around Mack's thigh, and the other pointed at a woman making her way over the rail of the boat and down a ladder in six-inch stilettos.

The trio watched her progress open-mouthed, as if an interesting attraction performed just for them. Rosie removed her work attire in Mack's bunkroom and said she'd be damned if she'd arrive in a new city looking like a street rat. Except for the heels, she dressed down in dark skin-tight jeans and one of Mack's extra-large football jerseys.

Mack snapped out of his stupor first and pulled away from Faith to help Rosie off the vessel. Nels and Faith followed.

"Okay, so, Nels, Faith... this is Rosie," he said as they approached. "Rosie, these are my good friends, Nels and his kid Faith, who just graduated from kindergarten." He gave the little girl a wink and a quick tug on one of her pigtails.

The young woman sprang forward in animation, with at least ten metal bracelets clanging together on her wrist, as she extended a hand to the father.

"Pleasure to meet you. Mack has told me everything about both of you."

Nels stood with his mouth still half opened, then looked at Mack and closed it, taking the proffered hand. "Nice to meet you too, um, Rosie, was it?"

"Yep, that's me," she said and winked.

"Your hair ith weally pwetty and thiny," Faith observed.

"Oh, yes. Well, thank you, sweetheart." She flung her dark mane over a shoulder. "What a nice thing to say. I always wanted curly hair like yours." She curled a ringlet around her finger, and beamed at Mack, as the little girl giggled again.

Rosie stayed with Mack and the Pearson's at their island cabin. She liked anything and everything her new inamorato liked. Fishing, boating, camping, car racing and motorcycling, she wanted to experience it all. Although Mack suspected she did it more for his benefit than hers, he took it all in stride and patiently taught her the finer points of each activity. More importantly, she worked hard to get along with Nels and Faith, which endeared her to Mack even more.

Her biggest drawback? Rosie liked to party... a lot. After she partied, she wanted sex, but not just any sex, some of the craziest shit Mack ever experienced. He couldn't figure out the woman or her moods. Adoring, relationship-driven and maternal one moment, angry, jealous and judgmental the next. Each intensified with her level of inebriation.

One day, halfway through summer Rosie took Faith shopping and to get their nails done. The men spent the day on an impromptu crabbing trip. They just set their small pots, and Mack carried a full cooler of beer up to the cockpit of his well-worn twenty-five foot Bayliner. He popped the top off one beer with the cap of another before handing it to Nels, who just finished lighting two cigarettes. They traded beers for smokes, and leaned back in a companionable silence, as they sipped their beverages.

"We've got to think about when to head back up," Nels said after a while, and took a drag off his cigarette. The song of several chickadees pierced the quiet.

"Yawp," Mack replied, and blew out a smoke ring. "You got a time frame in mind?"

"No, I just need to get a few things done on it. The engine's still a little too sluggish for my taste. Don't you think? I want to get Harry down to take another look at it. Maybe get a look under the prop too, before we run out of time."

"Okay, let's get down there next week and see what's what."

"Aren't you and that gal going to Copalis next week sometime?"

"Yeah, but we can go the week after." Mack blew another smoke ring, then glimpsed Nels' raised eyebrows and said, "What? The ocean ain't going nowhere."

Nels sipped his beer. "What's going on there, Mack?"

"What? You don't like her?"

"I don't know, she's... she's..."

"She seems kind of perfect for me." He glanced at his friend, looking for confirmation. "I'm twenty-five, maybe I want a brat of my own. I sure like hanging around with yours well enough."

Nels smiled at him. "You'd be a great father, but it's all moving quick, isn't it? I mean, you don't even know the woman."

"You didn't know Murron very long."

Nels' head snapped up to Mack, and his eyes held some anger in them, but even more pain.

"So, you're telling me you think you're at that level with this woman."

Mack stubbed out his smoke and took a deep breath. "Shit, I don't know. My ma was a piece of shit. My dad was a piece of shit. I don't even know if I'm built for marriage. I don't know if she's a hundred percent real, but I like her." Both men tilted their beers back and sipped, listening to the water and seagulls fight. "I expect we'll just see how things run."

Nels opened his mouth to say something, then closed it again, before tilting his head back for another swallow of beer.

****

"We painted our fingernails *and* toes, see?" Faith stuck out her hands and wiggled her neon green toes. Nels winced as his daughter sat on his lap facing him. She maneuvered his face around this way and that, contorting his flesh to create funny faces.

"Wow, that's bright..." Her face fell a little, and he added, "... and pretty, it's pretty too. Is that like glitter or sparkles or something?"

"Yawp." She brightened. "And Rosie said that if you said it was okay, we could go to get my ears pierced tomorrow." She showed all her teeth in a smile. "So, can I, Daddy? Get my ears pierced, I mean. Just like Rosie's." She tried her best manipulative grin again, and Nels shook his head. *How did girls learn that so quickly?*

His gaze swept over the alternative role model, who straddled Mack backward in their living room recliner. Legs swinging over the arms of the chair, her hands ran suggestively down his chest. Rosie wore a yellow and black polka dot micro mini skirt that Mack ran his hands up. Both chortled like loons, as huge metallic red mesh earrings swished on her ears.

Nels shifted a little so Faith's back faced them and sighed. *My six-year-old daughter idolizes a slut.* He refocused his attention back on his offspring, who looked back with large, pleading green eyes. He was a goner.

"Maybe just some small ones, okay?" he responded and kissed her forehead. Exultant, Faith laid her head on his chest to listen to his heartbeat, and he recognized the moment for what is was... special.

****

A few weeks later, Mack's nymph wasn't as agile, seductive or attentive, except to her own needs, which now included her head at the bottom of a toilet. The fifth day in a row, and Nels feared they'd all been exposed to illness two weeks before the men needed to leave for Alaska. He expressed some concern to Fenella when they stopped by for dinner after work one evening.

"When was the last time the lass had her courses?" Fenella asked Mack.

"Aw shit!" Mack muttered. "Are you kidding me?"

"Aye, shit is right ye *amaideach asal!* That's what happens when ye take up with a *siùrsach!*" Angus said in a superior tone.

Mack learned over the years what "ridiculous ass" sounded like in Gaelic, but had no idea what a *siùrsach* was. He did know from the sound of it, that it wasn't flattering Rosie overmuch, and stepped forward to snap the Scot's neck.

"Angus Middleton!" Fenella snapped. "How dare you! *Bu chòir nàire a bhith ort! iarr maitheanas!*

Fenella proved herself no dormouse, and Mack enjoyed watching her tear her husband a new asshole. *Christ, he hated the man.* The fact he couldn't even insult him in his own language made Mack believe him a coward.

The older woman's anger only occurred in rare moments, and Angus appeared appropriately abashed, mumbling, "Weel, please be accepting my apology, *Mister* Carter." Mack just grunted back at him and turned to Fenella.

"Thanks Nell, I better go. I gotta talk to Rosie about all of this." He looked at Nels for confirmation, who gave his father-in-law the stink eye as well, then nodded in agreement.

As the men collected their coats and turned to leave, Fenella patted Mack on the back, and smiled at Nels, before embracing him. United in raising Faith, the two became very close. She'd come to enjoy regaling both men with anecdotes of Faith and of Murron in her youth. Fenella even taught the two fishermen some Gaelic. Mostly endearments to say to Faith. Mack knew Nels' favorite endearment was, *mo bréagha ròs,* 'my beautiful rose' and favorite sentiment of all time became, *Je suis prest,* or 'I am ready'.

The skipper smiled at his mother-in-law now and said, "Thanks Nell, we'll see ya next week then."

"And this is where we'll be," she said. As she closed the door, her scowl deepened and everyone knew the old woman wasn't finished with her husband yet.

CHAPTER 6

When the men left Fisherman's Terminal and embarked for Alaska and the Bering Sea that fall, Mack's responsibilities increased, as he left a pregnant wife waving in the misty distance. Nels glanced over at Mack's perplexed face and chuckled. The younger man, seated on a wheelhouse stool, appeared as if someone brained him with a two-by-four, but couldn't remember what happened.

When Mack did become a father at the end of May, he missed his son's delivery by sixteen days. Rosie named him, Charles, but wanted to call him Charlie. They arrived home and Faith decided it was her duty to show Mack how to take proper care of his infant son.

"Okay, now you have to hold his head very carefully," Faith instructed Mack in serious tones, as she hovered in front of him with her hands up, challenging his competence for such matters.

"Oh, I will," Mack assured her and smirked. "Christ kid, but you got bossy."

"Well, you have to do it the right way or Gran said you can drop him and hurt his brain, but Grandpa said he might already be dangered because of you. When did you fall, and hurt your head, Mack?" She peered at him, great concern flooding her vivid green eyes. She wrinkled her forehead, studying for traces of impairment.

Mack drew his brows together as realization sunk in. "Angus told you that my kid might have brain damage because of me?"

"Damaged! Oh, yeah, I forgot." Faith bounced her palm off her head. "That was right, damaged. I didn't know your brain was..."

"It isn't," Mack snarled. "That little fucker."

"What?"

"I said, look at this little bugger, isn't he cute?" Mack would deal with Angus later. "Are you gonna be the babysitter?"

"Yes, and soon he'll get to play with me too, and then I can teach him some stuff about the boat."

"You'd be an outstanding teacher, too. Wanna hold him again?"

"Yes, yes," she cried, bouncing in her seat.

"No," Rosie snapped, glowering at the trio. She snatched up the baby and set him on her shoulder. Noticing their faces, she gentled a touch and added, "He needs to be fed soon."

At first, Rosie said she enjoyed the girl's presence. Mack suspected it gave Rosie the opportunity to demonstrate her maternal instincts, yet as time passed, those emotions changed. Rosie changed. Suddenly, she didn't want Faith around, got combative with Mack over it all the time.

"Does she have to be over here every fucking day, Mack?" Rosie spat after Faith and Nels left for their cabin. "I mean Christ, she's got her own goddamn family, doesn't she?"

Patting Charlie on the back, she strode from the living room to the kitchen, with a drink in her hand.

"What? She loves being with Charlie," Mack replied, following her. "And she's great with him. It's been a long time and I wanna see her when I can."

"I wanna see her," Rosie mimicked in a high falsetto.

"Christ." He let out an exasperated growl and walked over to the bar, threw his pack of Camels on the counter and searched for a glass. Pouring himself a glass of Crown Royal whiskey, he sipped it, sighed and sipped again, as she charged him.

"What about missing your goddamn wife or, I don't know, maybe make it home to see your first kid be born! Isn't he supposed to be your first choice now, Mack?" Rosie glared at him and bounced the baby as they argued, rocking back and forth on her feet. Mack stared back at her, face red and hysterical as a banshee.

"I thought Nels was supposed to be your best friend!" she continued her diatribe. "But, *no*, he couldn't be bothered to leave off just a little early, so you could make it to your son's birth. Selfish prick!"

"Roslyn," Mack growled again through gritted teeth, his face flushing crimson. "I told you I might not get home in time. Nels was going to stop early, and I was the one that told him to finish it out. It was an extra five grand." His temper transitioned from simmer to boil. "Don't worry, it'll buy all the stupid shit you've been loading this overpriced house with!" Her eyes shot daggers back at him.

"You can't bitch at me for working if you keep spending every fucking cent I make, then think more's just gonna blow out of my ass somehow!" He snatched up his tumbler, drained it, and moved around the bar to discharge another.

"So money's more important than me and Charlie, is that it, you prick?" She seized a vase she'd purchased and smuggled in just that day and hurled it at him. Startled, Charlie snuffled and a pitiful whimper promising something more vibrated in his chest.

"Jesus Christ!" Mack shifted to deflect it, but the vase glanced painfully off his left shoulder. "Are you crazy? Look, you scared the shit out of the kid. Go fix it, settle him down or give him a bottle or something."

"How about I leave him here for you to take care of?" She sang with patronizing vehemence, then set Charlie on the carpet and collected the keys to Mack's truck. "I've been dealing with this shit for two weeks now, non-stop... with no help from anyone. So, let's just see how you like it, Mack!"

She slammed the front door behind her, and Mack gave the closed door a weary sigh, before kneeling to pick up his wailing son. Holding him under his arm like a football, the father returned to the bar and finished pouring himself another healthy dose of whiskey. With the baby in one hand and the tumbler in the other, he sat down in his favorite recliner.

Leaning back, he held the baby out in front of him. Charlie's neck seemed to disappear into his body, and his enormous head sat in his clavicle area for a moment, before swinging back violently, almost as if decapitated by an invisible force.

"Whoa." Mack chuckled, and shot a hand out to help keep it on his shoulders, as Faith's words about supporting it rang through his mind. He did, and in a deep soothing voice intoned, "Your mom's a fucking fruit loop, isn't she?"

Charlie stopped screaming and stared at his father. Mack smiled back at him, and the two made their first genuine connection. The new father loved the idea of marriage and fatherhood but was quickly recognizing that dream might not be for everyone. Not all couples had what Nels and Murron achieved in such a few short months. And Rosie, well, she was no Murron.

By the time the young mother returned home, three hours later, the infant laid sprawled out across Mack's chest. The TV remote remained untouched on her husband's thigh, and both of her men slept with the sandman.

As the summer passed and fall regained its footing, the same scenario replayed itself in the Carter household. Abusive screaming matches, followed by moments of tender bliss, resulted in another pregnancy by the time the men returned to the sea, much to the couple's shock and chagrin.

****

Angus's strict upbringing softened, as the years passed, and Murron's parents lavished all the love for their daughter onto their granddaughter. Faith thrived in their care. The elderly couple spent hours showing her pictures and telling stories of the beautiful woman, frozen in perpetual youth, they called her mother. The little girl fell asleep every night staring at the wallpaper covered in roses, wondering about the stranger that picked it out.

Though Faith adored her mother's family, she lived for the summers, and the freedom, happiness and time she spent with her dad. A superhero in her eyes, Nels didn't treat her like a fragile eight-year-old girl, but more like a peer to have conversations with and teach things to. During the summer, she learned to tie boat knots, work the deck and handle the few "lines" of Mack's boat. From mid-June to the beginning of September, the Middleton's traveled back to Scotland while Faith learned to fish and crab in the San Juan Islands and in the waters off the Pearson's Camano Island cabin.

Every year, Nels' brought his daughter to her first days of school, and listened to her narrative about her new teachers and classmates at the day's end. Invariably she'd ask to return to Alaska with the fishermen, and every year Nels navigated the fine line of explaining the harsh conditions aboard a crab boat, without scaring her about their safety. To his chagrin, it always created more excitement than fear, and every time they headed north, it turned into a battle of wills between parent and child. After the men left, the battle continued to rage with her grandparents.

****

"Why can't it snow here like it does in Alaska?" Faith whined to her grandmother.

Winter descended upon their comfortable Beacon Hill home, but only enough to lay a thick blanket of frost and a light dusting of snow. The little girl let her curtain fall over the sparkling crystals on the window.

"Because lass, then we'd live in Alaska and nae in Seattle, ye ken?" Fenella replied.

"I just wanna go sledding. Can't I skip school just today, please?" She blinked prettily at the older woman. "Torrey Hill gets to stay home when it gets icy, even her mom says so."

"Weel, that's just fine and good for Torrey Hill." Fenella finished buckling Faith's Mary Janes. "But wee Faith Pearson goes to school when it's open for learning, ye ken? Now let me have look at ye. Ah, *mo cridhe*, ye'd just look bonny if ye'd give a wee smile."

"Yeah, okay," Faith said, distracted, but frowned down at her shoes. Inspired, she bobbed her head up and asked, "Do you think we could visit Daddy? I could get boots just like his for when I'm in the snow."

Her grandmother sighed. "Faith Murron Pearson, I havena been talking to hear to myself talk. Exhausting to the bones, ye are. We'll go when we can, nae a minute before. Now I'm nae too pleased wi' all this stalling." She glanced at the clock. "And look there, now we're late," she said and jabbed a finger into Faith's belly, who giggled. "So, reconcile yourself to the notion of school and go kiss Grand-da goodbye."

Angus sat in his Stickley-styled chair, sipping tea and reading the paper with his glasses perched across the bridge of his broad nose. He set the mug down on the coaster beside him when Faith crawled onto his lap and rubbed her soft cheek to his. His favorite moment of the day, or so he told his wife.

"Aye, now there's a good lassie." He kissed the top of her head. "Time for school, is it?"

"Yeah," Faith pouted. "But I want to stay home with you." She encouraged the co-conspirator. "We could think of something fun, Grand-da, like checkers."

"Aye, that we could, *mo cridhe*." He glanced up and saw his wife's irritated face, "But I canna risk a *collieshangie* with your granny just now, so off ye go." Resigned, Faith pressed her face into his chest and breathed in. Fenella could smell his familiar scent of Old Spice, chamomile tea and old tobacco pipe, from across the room.

"Granny, what's a collshingy thingy?" The girl asked when she hopped off her grandfather's lap and put her arm through the sleeve of her jacket with infuriating slowness. She shuffled over to Fenella who held open the door for her.

"A *collieshangie* means that your grand-da doesna want a fight with me, because he rightfully kens he'll lose the battle." The older woman glanced back at her husband, who chuckled, and raised a hand to tap his heart.

"Oh Angus, what a wee bugger is that lassie of ours." Fenella returned an hour later after running errands, still giggling at her granddaughter's tenacity, Fenella rounded the corner to the living room. "You willna believe what she..."

Slumped over in his chair, Angus laid motionless with his teacup broken on the floor beside him.

"Angus!" she yelled and ran to him. "Oh, Angus, what is it?" When he didn't respond, she ran for the phone and cried out to him. "It'll be okay, *mo cridhe,* wait only a moment."

Two hours later Fenella, grief stricken and in disbelief, watched as they covered her husband with a white sheet in the hospital ER. The physician worked on the elderly man for twenty minutes with no response, no pulse, no life. Angus Middleton died of a massive coronary event shortly after the girls left the house that morning. *Why didn't she let Faith stay home?* He died alone. The knowledge haunted Fenella.

****

Faith hopped off her school bus with a picture she colored special for her grandparents. Cars cluttered the street and driveway around the Middleton house. Confused, she ran to the front door, and walked inside to twenty people hovering in the living room and kitchen, crying and hugging each other, with strange expressions on their faces. Frightened, she called out to her grandmother, who sat almost unrecognizable in her grandfather's chair, sipping a whiskey, and ignoring her for the first time in her life.

"Gran?" Their eyes met after Faith knelt before her. "What's wrong? Why are all these people here?" She looked around worried. "Where's Grandpa?"

"Gone," Fenella hissed. "I wasna here." She collapsed into sobs and Faith backed away.

Unfamiliar hands patted her back, shoulders and the top of her head as she moved through the hot and crowded living room toward her grandparents' bedroom. Closing the door, she leaned her back against it and slid down to the thick carpet. Fenella beamed out of a picture on her grandfather's nightstand. She scanned the rest of the familiar room. How many times did she run in here from a bad dream or during a thunderstorm? She understood death was absolute and the despair that followed. Hadn't she seen the effects of it often enough from her mother's passing? The phone next to Fenella's picture beckoned to her. Faith sprinted to it and dialed the number of the boat owner, hypnotized by the slow rotation of the rotary dial. She wanted her father.

****

The memorial for Angus Middleton occurred two weeks later. Mack stayed on the *Nordic* as captain, while Nels returned home to care for his mother-in-law and daughter. Fenella, overcome with exhaustion and grief, slept constantly. Worried, Nels removed his daughter from the dark despair for the evening, to walk along their favorite pier around the Elliott Bay Marina.

"How you doing, *mo bréagha ròs*?"

Faith shrugged and looked down at her feet. "Daddy, is Grandpa alone?"

"Alone?" His forehead furrowed. "What do you mean, Sprout?"

"Granny said that he was alone and..." Her chin and bottom lip trembled. "What if he's really lonely?"

Nels rubbed his hands on his jeans and sat down, dangling his legs over the side of the pier.

"Come here, Faith." She jumped onto his lap backwards, threw her arms around his neck and cried. He rocked her back and forth, running one hand up and down her back while holding her head with the other. He leaned his face into her curls and breathed in. She smelled like sun-warmed lavender, exactly like Murron on the day he'd left her on the pier, and his stomach clenched. He closed his eyes and murmured endearments to her until she hiccupped.

"Your grandfather... well, he's with your ma now, honey." He pulled her away from him and considered the crystal green depths of her watery eyes. "Just like my mom and dad. He's safe and happy just watching over you, now... protecting you."

"Yawp?" She gave a loud sniff and took a deep breath. "Daddy, can I go with you on the boat now? Please, Granny's so sad and... and..."

"Now, Faith, you aren't old enough to go on the boat yet. It's too dangerous for a little gal. I've told you that so many times." He took a deep breath. "Besides, Grandma needs you a lot right now, do you know why?"

"Why?" Her lip trembled, and it nearly undid him, so he hurried on.

"Because with Grandpa gone, she's gonna need lots of help, and because you make her smile, and she needs that so much right now. She'd be so sad if you weren't here with her. You understand that, Faith?"

"Yawp." She sniffed again. "But one day I can come to live on the boat with you, right?"

"Yes, one day, when you're older, you can. Okay?" She nodded. "Now, what do you say to some dinner?"

"Can we go to Ivar's?" she asked, wiping her nose on her sleeve.

"You bet, anything in particular you want?"

"Can we have dessert too?"

"Don't push it, kid." However, the smile he gave assured her of a hot fudge sundae laid in her future.

****

Nels returned to the normality of his boat and crew, but life for Faith changed. Week after week, Fenella grew more despondent and too incapacitated to care for her granddaughter. Most of the time, the elderly woman stared off into space and forgot even the most basic things, often leaving Faith to fend for herself. The old woman slept later, went to bed earlier and her once meticulous house fell into disrepair. Faith learned to make sandwiches for herself and her grandma out of necessity and even learned to work the washer and dryer. Rosie took a renewed interest in the little girl and invited her to play with Charlie and their younger son, Brady, most weekends.

Faith woke one morning in a panic. She'd overslept and missed her school bus again. Running down her small mental list of people to call for a ride, she padded out into the kitchen. *Maybe I should try Granny first?* She called out to her but received no response. When Faith walked to the woman's bedroom door, knocked and still heard nothing, she stepped inside.

"Grandma, I'm sorry, but I forgot to wake up again." The room, dark, dismal, and foreboding, made her heart race just like it did every day since her grandpa died. Dead flowers in vases laid across every hard surface, and the room smelled sweet and rotten. Fenella's tiny form laid outlined in the bed clothes and didn't so much as twitch at Faith's appearance. She reached out a hand to her bare arm.

"Gran, I'm sorry but can you..." She trailed off as her finger brushed cold, hard skin. Terrified, Faith reached up to her shoulder and tried to shake her again, but the woman remained frozen.

"Granny, wake up, I have to go to school," she pleaded, even more panic settling into her voice. When that still elicited no response, she pulled down the covers and peered into the filmy, unseeing eyes of her grandmother. Yelping, Faith jolted and stumbled back into the corner, sitting down hard on her bottom. Images pocked her brain of Fenella's eyes, mouth, feet, hands, and hair, all imprinting in her memory. She tucked her bottom lip into her mouth and rocked back and forth, folding both hands over her head.

CHAPTER 7

Nels sat laughing in the galley with the crew to grab a quick bite to eat. They just offloaded their catch and wanted to take the evening off before returning to work. Mack's voice boomed over the intercom.

"Nels, get up here! Now!"

He launched from his seat, at Mack's voice and sprinted up the stairs, two at a time. His deck boss spoke to a hysterical caller in a soothing voice. Mack mouthed, *Faith.* "It's gonna be okay, baby, I promise. Okay? Hold on, here's your dad."

"What's going on?" Nels asked as Mack put a hand over the receiver without taking the phone away from his ear.

"Christ, Nels, I think the kid just found Fenella dead. She's freaking out, man." Nels ran to the phone and yanked it out of Mack's hands.

"Faith? Faith?" An animalistic wail screamed across the line. "Listen to me. Shh, listen, okay... Faith! Listen to me! Good, baby... good girl." He reached up and held his forehead, glancing at Mack, who wore a grim expression. Nels whipped the CB off the hook and threw it at Mack, mouthing, *Rosie.* The CB wouldn't accomplish what Nels wanted, so Mack ran for the phone booth just off the dock.

"Mack's calling Rosie okay? She's gonna be there real soon."

"Daddy, she's really hard and cold," Faith whimpered. "And she's looking at me."

He paled. "Are you still with her in her room, Sprout?"

"Yeah."

"Faith, I want you to go out to the kitchen, now... Okay? You hear me?"

"Yeah, but what about Gran?" She sniffed.

"It's okay if you leave Gran for a little while. We're gonna take care of her in a minute. Okay?"

"Okay."

"That's my girl, all right..."

"Don't hang up!"

"No, I'm not gonna hang up. I'm coming home, okay? It might take me a minute to get everything organized and get a flight out, but I'm coming home." Helpless, he listened to her sobs. "I'll be here honey, I'm not gonna hang up. Rosie'll be there soon."

****

Rosie dropped the boys off at daycare and sat in her chair at the hair salon organizing a grocery list. The phone rang and Mack's emotional voice came through.

"Rosie!" he yelled. "Rosie, oh God, I need you to do something for me, babe." His voice shook down the line, and she stood straighter.

"What happened... Mack? Are you guys all right?"

"Listen, honey. I need for you to go over to the Middleton's." He took a deep breath. "Faith just called here hysterical. Rose, I think Fenella died or something. Faith just found her. She was screaming, saying something like she was looking at her but not moving. I think she's still in the room with her when she called. I-I don't…"

"Mack," she cut him off. "I'll go right over. It'll be okay, just give me a second and I'll call you back as soon as I can."

She ran out to the car and her tires screeched as she backed out of the parking stall and down the street. *Christ, she's only eight-years-old, and now both of them.* By the time Rosie reached the door and pounded on it, panic set in about the emotional state of the little girl.

"Faith! Honey, it's Rosie!" She pounded harder, slapping her palms against the wood, causing them to sting. "Faith, come open the door now, baby!" After several more shouts and beatings, Faith's small, willowy form cracked open the door and launched herself into Rosie's outstretched arms.

"It's okay, baby girl. It's gonna be okay now." She walked her away from the house stroking and soothing, then sat down with her in the sunshine. Faith let out a torrent of sobs, arms folded in as she rocked with Rosie back and forth. "Shh."

Mack's wife asked a neighbor coming out to investigate the noise, to call an ambulance and continued to rock the little girl. It took Rosie fifteen minutes to calm her down and reassure her, before checking on Fenella, as Faith sat on the grass. Mack's wife walked into the old woman's bedroom and knew the cause of her death in an instant. Empty pill bottles tipped over on the nightstand with a bottle of wine, also empty, next to it, told the tale.

"Oh, Nell, what did you do?" She sighed and closed the door on death.

****

The EMTs suggested Faith go to the hospital for observation, but Rosie insisted they check the girl out there, and didn't wait for them to bring out the body. She picked up her boys, and they all played together, until dinner, bath and bedtime.

Roslyn cradled, sang and read Faith a story about beautiful princess's and happy endings. When the little girl finally went limp in her lap, Roslyn laid her down and dimmed the lights, without putting her in solid darkness. She grabbed a pad of paper, walked into the kitchen and sat down at the table, to try and start a list about what arrangements needed to be made. She poured herself a deep glass of wine before calling the *Nordic* and Mack again.

"She's sleeping," Rosie whispered in the dark, drinking from her wine glass. "It was a genuine shock and the ambulance people said she might need to see a doctor or like a shrink or something, but I thought she'd be even more scared, sitting in the hospital right now."

"She'll be okay once Nels gets there, which," -he paused- "should be in about half an hour or so."

"He could get out that quick?"

"Yeah, the stars aligned and one of the other skips was going home, and let him have his ticket."

"That was nice."

"Yeah, he was lucky to get out of here when he did. We got a big weather system moving in." He paused for several seconds before saying. "Was it a heart attack?"

"No. She killed herself."

"What?"

"Yeah, it'll probably be for sure in the next day or two, when they get the reports back, but there were a lot of empty pill containers next to her." Rosie gulped her wine again. "It's going to be hard for *me* to get her out of my mind, I don't know how Faith's going to do it."

"Rosie, you did so great today. I mean... Christ, darlin', you must be completely wasted. All the kids and shit. Thanks for being there, for all of it."

"When are you coming home, Mack? Can you get here soon?"

"Shit, I'm sorry honey, but it's gonna be some time yet." His lighter clicked on, then off. "Campbell's giving Nels shit for missing all this time, the little prick. He even asked me to take over."

"Jesus, what did you say?"

"I told him to fuck himself. As if losing your wife and your in-laws wasn't enough reason to take time off. Dickhead. Nels doesn't know anything about of it. So, can you keep it that way? He doesn't need this shit right now."

"I won't say anything." A light knock tapped on the door. "I think that's him, Mack. I have to go. See you in, what, about a month for Christmas?"

"Yeah, I'll try to get there as soon as I can." He gave a heavy sigh. "I love you, Rosie."

"Me too."

When she opened the door, Nels swept her into a long hug.

"You look exhausted," he said, squeezing her hand. "Honey, thank you. I won't ever forget this."

"Don't worry about that at all."

"Where's she at?"

"I put her in Charlie's room, the boys are sharing."

He gave her hand another squeeze, and walked into Charlie's messy room. He dropped his bag on the floor and laid down next to her, wrapping strong arms around her tiny frame. Deep in sleep, she curled into him. Rosie smiled and closed the door.

****

For the next two months, Nels tidied up the affairs of not one life, but two. Fenella, unable to cope with the magnitude of the estate dealings, along with her all-encompassing grief, did nothing but change her will. It left everything to Faith, except for a three-hundred and fifty-thousand-dollar stipend to Nels. After everything, the Middleton Trust gave a small allowance to Faith until her eighteenth birthday when she'd inherit the bulk of their fortune.

The generosity on the behalf of his in-laws gave Nels wiggle room, should Campbell be less than patient with his circumstances. He didn't finish the king crab season, and in fact, wouldn't make the beginning of Opilio's either. Knowing Campbell as he did, it wouldn't surprise him if the asshole hadn't already spoken with Mack about taking over.

Mack would tell him to fuck off, as would the rest of the men, but he couldn't say he blamed Campbell. Well, not much anyway. If he flew on the straight and narrow for a while he'd be okay, but his daughter's living arrangements were now the challenge.

Mack suggested she should come to live with Rosie and the boys while the men went back to sea. However, one look at Rosie's face told Nels that wouldn't happen. He needed to find another way., and find it fast.

****

"You ready for some breakfast?" Rosie asked Mack early one morning. "There's coffee over there, too." She gestured toward the counter.

"Sure." He grabbed two cups and poured, but before she cracked the two eggs she held, he said, "Let's go outside a minute."

Resolved, she nodded and grabbed a sweater. Once outside, they sat at a table with an overflowing ashtray on it. The neighbor had set their used Christmas tree on the fence and the scent of pine filled the backyard. Mack shook two cigarettes out of the pack, lit them and handed one to Rosie, but she shook her head.

"I quit. You should too." He drew his brows together in the universal sign of, *you're crazy*. "I know what you're gonna say, Mack, but it's never going to happen. You know, and I know that I have to take care of our boys first. What happened here is horrible... it's terrible. And I'm as heartbroken for Nels and Faith as I can be, but I *have* to think of Charlie and Brady first." Her eyes pleaded with him. "You don't pay enough attention to them. Not like you do her." She raised a hand when he started to speak. "I'm not trying to be mean here, I'm really not. They're my boys, though, and I don't have the time or energy to give to a little girl who is gonna need extra right now. A lot of extra. It's just not fair to them, Mack."

"I know."

"Do you?" She leaned forward, snatched his cigarette from him and stubbed it out. "Do you understand? This isn't about Faith *or* you or me. It's about our boys."

He nodded and contemplated the ashtray. His face pinched, holding back a potent emotion, the pain evident behind his eyes.

"Making things all fucked up is what I'm good at." He glanced up at her with a grin and she mirrored the gesture. "But I love those boys, Rosie. I do. And I love you. I'm gonna take care of all of you. Maybe not the way you want me to but... all I can do is give it my best." He stopped for a long moment. "If you need for us to call it a day... I will, if that's what *you* want. I'll still take care of you guys, but seriously babe, I really want you to be happy."

"I want you," she said simply. "You're all I've ever wanted. I've learned to take you as you are, Mack." He leaned back in his chair after she gave a final nod of her head, and they both looked across the lawn in silence.

****

Mack sat at the Pearson kitchen table with his head propped on a hand and a cigarette dangling from his mouth as Faith colored a picture.

"Do you like it, Mack?" Faith bit her bottom lip as big green eyes peered up at him. "I made the grass the same color as the water, so you would like it 'specially."

"I do like that." Mack yawned and pointed at something in the page's corner. "What's this here?"

"Oh, that... that is..." She itched the side of her head. "That is the fish. I meant the cod to catch the crab."

He sniffed. "The purple cod is jumping out of the blue grass to catch the green crab?" Mack asked, just to make sure.

"Yawp."

"Well, that's great kid, but where's the other crab?"

"Well, I haven't... I haven't drawed that yet," she said, a little miffed. "The crab has to go by the garbage, so you can throw away the shells. That's what Grandpa said, because it smells terrible."

"Yeah, well, how would he know?" Mack muttered. "Little fucker."

"What?" Faith asked and looked up.

"I said those crabs are sure cool little buggers. Why don't you draw me two pictures, so we can put one of them on the galley fridge, okay?"

"Okay, and I'm gonna draw them magenta." Faith's entire face lit up at the possibility of everyone onboard getting to look at her picture. She stuck the tip of her tongue out of her mouth as she drew. "Mack, do I get to live on the boat now, too?" Faith looked up again.

He shifted his gaze down to her and stubbed out his smoke. Her bright red hair, grown to shoulder length, hung in a tangled ball, after not brushing it for a week. Her freckles tripled in number and deepened in color and her catlike deep green eyes had a new depth to them, like an old soul.

"I don't know, Faith. I guess we'll just have to wait and see what happens."

He knew Nels had engaged in several conversations with an all-girls boarding school in Oregon. Neither of the men wanted the little girl to go there, but the choices evaporated. Nels could give it all up and do some kind of engineering or mechanical job, but what kind of money could he make? His practical experience, aside from the boat, equaled squat. The father would never survive crawling along in a car to and from a job he hated and didn't make money at, so broken, he'd be no good to Faith at all. Nels belonged on the water. It ran deep in his blood, something city people could never understand.

****

"Yeah, I'm here. Okay, thank you, Mrs. Follette," Nels said. "We'll be there in a few weeks, then. Yawp, okay. No ma'am that shouldn't be a problem, bye."

Walking into the kitchen, he leaned a shoulder against the door jamb with the phone in one hand, before he laid it across his thigh. Mack locked eyes with him in question, and Nels gave a quick nod of his head to acknowledge what he did. His best friend's face fell, and eyes dropped back to the table before scrubbing a hand over his face. He rested his chin in his hand, and both men watched Faith, her head bent to her work, mop of red curls bobbing up and down. Her lips clamped hard on her little pink tongue.

"That looks great, kid," Mack said. "You keep working on it and show me tomorrow, okay? I have to find out what the boys are doing."

"Okay." Her face relaxed, knowing she'd have more time to finish the drawing and set down the color crayons. She climbed into Mack's lap, wrapped her arms around his neck, and kissed his cheek before climbing back down.

Mack grabbed the phone from Nels and walked outside with the long line trailing behind him. As the deck boss closed the front door with an aggressive clang, Nels turned to his daughter.

"What do you think about going down to the pier?"

"Are we gonna fish?"

"No, not today, just a walk on the pier. What do you say, you want to go hang out with your old man?"

"Yeah!"

An hour later Faith sat atop her daddy's shoulders. The pungent smell of the salty seawater filled the air and seagulls called out for food. An ice cream truck idled nearby, as scores of children begged and pleaded for their favorite treats. When they reached the end, Nels set her down and held her hand.

"Faith, I have to talk to you about some stuff."

"About Grandma and Grandpa? I miss them."

"Yeah, honey, I know. It's not fair you've had to find this out so young, but death is part of life, and some of us get more than their fair share of it." She nodded in agreement. "But darlin', it's far better to be with someone you love for a little time than not at all."

"Okay, thanks for telling me Daddy." *So, smart,* he could tell she wanted to get off the topic, afraid of what he'd say.

"Well, yes, you're welcome. Remember that, but I also wanted to talk about you." They sat down on the dock with their legs dangling over the side into the water. "See, with your grandparents gone and me always out fishing, I'm not sure where the best place is for you to live right now."

"Oh, I'm gonna live with you on the water now. I decided that right away," she announced.

"Yeah... Well, that's just it, honey, you're not gonna be able to live with me on the water. It's only been a few months, and it's just too dangerous for a little girl. So, I just got done talking to a real nice lady who runs a cool school and..."

Faith followed her father's words with increasing horror. Upon hearing this last sentence, she shook her head and cried. "No! I want to be with you. Please... please, Daddy. I promise I will be so careful."

"Faith, it's *not* for little girls and you've got your schoolwork..."

"But.. but... I'll do all of my work, and I'll stay out of all the people's way. I can help. I'll work hard." He was about to take a more authoritative approach when her next words sliced through his heart. "Daddy, I c-can't do this anymore. I c-can't be without you, too." She bawled and stuttered, "P-please d-don't send me to live with p-people I don't know. Please let me live with you, I p-promise I'll be good and t-try to make you happy."

Undone, he opened his arms to her, and she crawled into his lap, wailing into his shirt. He patted her back and stroked her head, letting her have her cry. As she slowed down to hiccups, he pulled her away from him and considered her face. Swollen and red, with tears and snot running down the whole of it. He took in a lungful of air and puffed out his cheeks to let it out slow.

"Well, shit... how can I say no to a face as sweet as this?" He snorted and kissed her forehead, then stood and picked her up. She wrapped her arms and legs around him and laid her head on his shoulder as he carried her back to their truck.

Faith fell asleep to the quiet hum of the motor. He glanced over at her from time to time, determined he'd find a way to make it work. After they arrived back home, Nels laid his daughter down to sleep, only taking off her jacket, shoes and socks, before drawing the blankets up around her.

"I love you, Daddy," she whispered and curled her arm around her white fluffy teddy bear.

"I love you too, *mo bréagha ròs*," he whispered back and walked out to the kitchen to call Mack.

"Well, fucking A!" Mack exclaimed and slapped his hands together, before pouring them both three fingers of Crown Royal.

"It's gonna be okay, Nels. We'll all look out for her, keep her away from the rail and off deck with foul weather. It'll be fine. An adventure."

Nels took a huge gulp from his whiskey glass and felt the liquid gold burn down his throat. *Why in the hell did he think this could work?* Taking an eight-year-old girl onboard a death trap in the middle of winter, on the Bering Sea? No sane person did that.

"Well, look at it this way," Mack said after Nels voiced his concern. "If the ship goes down, we're all in it together."

"Comforting," Nels grunted and drained the rest of his drink, then nodded for another belt. "Not to mention that some of the worst excuses of humanity will be rubbing elbows with her."

"Now that's something we can control," Mack said. "Most guys are solid, and we're a relatively clean boat." Indicating, they didn't allow drugs onboard. "Tony, Alex, and Jesse are all solid. The only ones we might need to axe are Hardy and Johnson, then get a top of the line greenhorn." He paused. "The biggest problem I see is she's gonna want to help." Mack pointed at him, then laid his fingers across his lips in thought again. "Maybe on calm days, we could have her setting up some bait bags. Everyone hates it and she'd love it, maybe make her feel like she was helping a little, wear a life jacket the whole time."

Nels sighed again, and scrubbed a hand over his face as Mack poured out two more healthy doses of whiskey, and set one in front of him. He grabbed a bag of chips from the counter, ate a couple and set the bag out for both to reach.

"Christ, Mack, we want her to be safe, so let's have her grind up frozen herring and take a long, sharp knife the size of her entire arm and slash through some fucking cod."

Mack rolled his eyes. "Yeah, well, when did you start working bait and using knives and shit?" he countered. "I'm guessing it wasn't when you got onboard at sixteen."

"I'm a guy, she's a girl *and* my kid," Nels said, as if this should be something important Mack understood. "She's only eight-years-old."

"Well, if she's gonna be onboard a crab boat, we're gonna have to make the rest of the men forget that fact. No one likes women onboard, let alone a little girl, you know that. And Campbell -shit- I never even thought about him. How we gonna pull that one off? You'll be in the wheelhouse all day, you won't be able to watch her twenty-four-seven, and I won't be able to watch her all day on deck."

"Hopefully, she'll get onboard and realize she won't get to run and play or be with her friends and we'll do the school after all."

"If not?"

"She'll have to spend most of the day doing school work at the bridge cabin, regardless."

"Oh yeah, okay then." Mack paused then asked, "Wait, how are you gonna do that?"

"Well, I *did* have a long talk with her school teacher about it earlier, when I was trying to decide what to do. The lady said she's been worried about Faith for a while now." Nels and Mack both took a companionable sip of their whiskey, and the skipper went on. "I told her about her wanting to come onboard, and I'll be damned if she didn't say she thought it might be a good idea. But I don't think she understands how dangerous it is. She just said it would be best if Faith was with me and if I wasn't staying home, she shouldn't either. Said she's got a brother who actually lives and teaches in Dutch. You believe that shit?"

Mack smiled at things working out for once. "Maybe it's all meant to be."

"So, there's some new shit called home-schooling, but it hasn't taken off yet," Nels said, ignoring his comment. "She thinks it'll catch on, eventually. I guess the brother knows all the teachers there at the school and thought they might be willing to help too. So, between all of us, we might make something work." He poured Mack and himself a fourth whiskey and started feeling damn happy about the whole thing.

"What grade's she in now?" Mack asked, looking a little bleary-eyed.

"She'll be going in third."

"Well, it'll all work out. Neither of us finished school and I expect we turned out all right," Mack said.

Nels looked over at his best friend. Only twenty-seven-years-old, but the wind, cold, stress, whiskey and cigarettes all took their toll on him.

"Yeah, you're a walking poster child for success there, Mack, either that or birth control." He snickered at Mack's pretense of offense.

CHAPTER 8

"No! Goddamnit Frank, this is nothing but shit." Mack twisted the brick of bait delivered to the *Nordic* that morning. "Look, it's all burnt," he said, and held it up under the man's nose. "Look at the yellowing, and it's dry as the fucking Sahara Desert. I'm not paying for this shit. Get us some decent bait here tomorrow!"

Back on the *Nordic* and in Dutch Harbor, Mack reveled in his element. Now that Faith also lived with them, he took on the role of her guardian while on deck. The trio motored back to Alaska a month early, to not only check out the ship from bow to stern but also begin teaching Faith about life onboard, without the judging eyes of the rest of the crew on her. Not an easy process, the hours of coordinating and planning the new reality came slow, but piece by piece they found ways to make it all work.

Nels and his daughter first met with the principal and several teachers at the local elementary school. They'd donated books, workbooks, worksheets and several other learning modules. As Faith came into port, she'd turn in assignments and tests to one teacher, and pick up new ones. She would keep a notebook of anything that needed clarifying, or problems too difficult to solve and as the men offloaded she would work them through with a tutor in port.

Mack believed if Nels could entrust Faith to him on the deck, everyone's lives would be better, not to mention safer. Thus, the deck boss began her training, in the same manner her father taught him. While outside, he drilled safety first, taught her mindfulness of the waves, and how to walk on a rocking deck without falling. He instructed awareness of the men, crane, hooks, lines, buoys and pots, in a meticulous step-by-step approach until she understood.

Faith learned if he ever instructed her to go indoors, she obeyed with no questions asked. A unanimous sigh of relief came when everyone involved realized the girl was a quick study. Not even the ship's owner, presented as a factor, to everyone's surprise. When Nels informed Jamie Campbell that Faith now lived with him on the boat, Mack expected a quick and emphatic "Hell, no."

However, Campbell listened as Nels explained there wouldn't be any more emergencies back home with his daughter onboard, and that he could concentrate on going where they needed to go to land crab and make money. The owner didn't give any real resistance and simply told Nels not to let her interfere with work, and they departed the marina to the shaking heads of many a captain.

"*Je suis prest,*" was all Nels said.

****

"That's it," Nels said over the intercom to the deckhands. "We'll give her a long soak, so finish those two, eat and hit the rack."

One month into her first tour at sea, Faith sat next to her father on the bridge, working on some spelling words when she asked, "Why do the pots soak? What happens when they soak that makes the crab go in?"

Nels slid the throttle forward a touch while he talked. "Well, you know how we have the bait area?" She nodded. "Okay, so we take one of those bags down there and fill it with little bits of herring and like octopus or whatever, then take a nice big cod fish and slice it up the middle. One guy hangs both those in the pot and we dump it over the side."

"With the launcher thingy?"

"Yawp." He throttled back. "So, the pot goes way down to the ocean floor and all those crabs come running cause they're hungry, right?" She nodded again. "But not all of them come at once. So, if we picked up the pot right away, there might only be a few in it, and Mack and all the guys would have had to do a lot of work for nothing. So, we let them sit and soak awhile, that way all the crab in the area can go into the pot."

"How long do they soak for?"

"Well, it all depends." His head on a swivel, the captain scanned the waves for any rogues or danger barreling toward the men at the rail. "It could be a day, could be a week, depending on the captain, the weather, the tides, everything. These are gonna soak for about thirty-six hours, I think." He glanced over at her and smiled, and she smiled back. "How's the homework going?"

"Good, but I need help with two words."

"Okay, shoot."

"Okay." She scratched her head. "The first word is d-o-u-b-t-f-u-l."

"Okay, well, that's da-ow-t-ful," Nels sounded out. "It's like when you…"

"No, I know what it means, I just didn't know they spelled it that way. Why's there a b?"

"The b is silent."

"I know, but that's dumb."

Nels laughed. "I know, but that's the way it is. Hold on." He clicked on the intercom. "Mitchell, make sure you clean up that bycatch, that's sliding around. One of you guys are going to fall on your asses on the slime." He received a thumbs up. "Okay, what's the next one?"

"G-o-v-e-r-n-m-e-n-t?" Nels snorted. "Talk about dumb… Okay, that's guv-earn-ment. Like politics."

"Oh, it thought it was go-ver-ment. It just didn't make sense."

"Well, government doesn't make a lot of sense." He chuckled. "Wait, I thought you were in third grade? Aren't these spelling words a little big for you?"

"No. I did the third and fourth grade ones already. So, I skipped ahead to fifth grade."

"You're doing fifth grade words right now?" He asked to make sure.

"Yeah some of them. Is that okay?"

"Yeah, it's okay." Nels beamed with pride. "That's pretty awesome, kid." A weather warning flashed across his screen. "Hey, Faith?"

"Yeah," she said, still concentrating on her words.

"Darlin' we got some weather coming in and..." He broke off as she immediately collected all her things and placed them in her tote, then secured the tote with a bungee cord.

Stunned, he watched her go to her cubby and withdraw her life jacket and flotation suit. "Can I kiss you goodnight?"

"Ah... ye-ah." She ran over and kissed him quick on the cheek, but he grabbed her wrist. "Did Mack teach you that?"

"Yeah. He said if you say there's weather coming in, I have to put everything away quickly, if there's time, and get my life jacket and Gumby suit." Nels burst out laughing, but when she tilted her head confused he said, "That's fantastic! Then what?"

"Then I go to our room, unless you tell me to do something else and stay there until you tell me to come out. And don't walk around or go to the bathroom, even if it takes hours."

"Well, shit." He grinned. "Okay, well good for you, baby. You did that really well, I'm so proud of you." She beamed in his praise. "You have time to use the bathroom. So, brush your teeth, and use the toilet. It's late, so you shouldn't need to get up for the rest of the night. It might get kind of rough, so if you need me for any reason, use the master berth phone, okay? If I don't answer right away, it's because..."

"You're steering or doing something very important and can't be interrupted. And you or Mack will call me as soon as you can. I know."

"Right... well... come give me another kiss, then scoot to bed."

"Can I read?"

He looked at the clock. "For thirty minutes only."

"Okay, love you, Daddy."

"I love you, too, *mo bréagha ròs.*" She scampered off to bed and Nels peered down at his best friend, working his ass off, grinned and murmured, "Good for you Mack."

****

Some of the happiest years transpired next for Nels, Mack, and Faith. She found her lessons easy and often skipped ahead. Fascinated by waves and weather, she learned to understand the weather warnings and often helped in relaying them to her father and the crew. After her school work, she learned to cook simple things and enjoyed making lunch for the men, then cleaned up after they returned to work. On calm days, she brought bait components for the greenhorns, and loved helping her dad steer the boat into port, as well as load and offload supplies.

As the years progressed, he slowly expanded her duties, and let her experiment with the grinder, and help cut and prep the bait area under heavy supervision. As Nels taught her about the wheelhouse, Mack instructed her about the deck and internal workings of the ship. Faith absorbed everything like a sponge. Even the crew accepted her and answered her endless questions about the deck with the enthusiasm. By the time she'd reached her fourteenth birthday, she entered the equivalent of tenth grade in most topics. She handled more weather on deck, learned about repairs, and even learned some about the hydraulic system and gears for maneuvering pots. She learned quick, never wanting to give anyone any reason to doubt the decision to have her onboard. Beyond this, Faith blossomed and developed. Comments about her appearance, spoken under deck hands' breath caused one or two physical retaliations by Mack, ending the talk abruptly or in some cases, an immediate firing.

Faith rounded the corner to the wheelhouse with her father's lunch one day and heard him speaking gibberish. *"Kom igen, Nels du måste komma. När får du denna möjlighet igen? Allt är klart, vi behöver dig bara som kapten."*

"Who's that?"

"My friend from Sweden."

"What's he saying?" Faith inquired.

"Just a sec, darling," Nels said and pushed the radio button to speak. *"Det låter fantastiskt Andersson, men jag har min dotter med mig. Hon vill inte spendera sommaren på ett annat fartyg, även om det är i Sverige."*

Nels grinned at his daughter's stunned expression and smiled. "Didn't know your old man was so intelligent, did you?" She grinned back. "So, this guy's telling me a lot of guys from Sweden are going back to fish for Bluefin tuna and he wants me to captain a boat this summer." Her face fell a little, as the stranger's voice crackled over the radio again.

"*Låt henne stanna hemma. När gjorde du senast något för dig själv?*"

Nels frowned, he didn't want to leave his daughter at home, like the man asked. Glancing at Faith, who tried valiantly to make out what they said to one another.

"*Det här gjorde våra fäder... Du kan inte säga att du inte vill göra det. Om hon stannar hemma kan du också hitta en kvinna och ha sex. Hur länge har det varit?*"

"Now what did he say, Daddy?"

"Ah, just what he said before and that he wants me to go." He didn't tell her the man said it was time to do something for himself and get laid. He depressed the button again and answered, "*Sluta! Okej, jag tänker på det Johan. När behöver du veta det?*" He looked back at Faith. "I said, I'd think about it and when did he have to know by. Don't you have some math to do?"

"I already did it." She smiled at him, then listened to the caller's reply.

"*Två veckor. Vi måste gå den sista veckan i juni.*"

"*Okej, jag ska meddela dig.*" Nels said, then hung up the receiver and smiled to himself. Fishing bluefin tuna. He looked back at his daughter, who waited for the translation. "Oh, he just said we'd need to leave by the end of June. So, no fireworks. I need to let him know within two weeks."

His mind went back to the tuna. A gamble because fish weren't as plentiful in that area anymore, but even so. At forty-two, just a year older than his dad when he died, Nels hadn't stepped foot in the land of his birth over two decades. *When did his mother die? 1966?*

He caught Faith studying his face, so relaxed his features. "You sounded excited, Daddy. Do you want to go?"

"Oh, I don't know." He dismissed the notion, then changed his mind. "What do you think? You want to see where your ole man grew up, not to mention where my ole man used to fish?"

Faith paused and sat down in one of the wheelhouse chairs. "It's just that Charlie and Brady, well, we sort of have a plan for this summer. Remember, we're all going to the cabin, and Rosie's gonna make that cool watermelon basket thingy. We were all gonna go swimming and stuff."

"And you'd rather spend your summer on land." He stretched, trying to cover his disappointment. "Don't you, kiddo?"

"Yeah, we're even going to do some M80s." She eyed the floor, then met his gaze. "But you want to go, don't you?"

"Well, it's just something I was thinking about. No big deal."

"You're lying. If you want to go, it's okay, I know you think it's cool and stuff, but can I stay with Mack, if he says it's okay?"

"If he says it's okay?" Nels laughed. "Honey, sometimes I think the man loves you more than me and that's a lot. Come here."

She giggled and came up from behind and hugged him while he sat in his chair. He laid his hands on her forearms, wrapped around his neck.

"Just when did you grow up?" He pulled her around to face him. "Man, you're pretty."

"Oh my God, Dad," Faith said, rolling her eyes. "You always say that."

"Well, it's true. You look exactly like your mama." He pulled her onto his lap and hugged her. "Thanks, darlin'."

****

"Hi Daddy, we're all having a water fight and I'm winning!" Faith said, a little breathless on the Fourth of July. The rapt disapproval of this statement, from Charlie and Brady, came through loud and clear down the line. "Where are you now? Did you catch anything?"

"Yeah. I'm about to go out again and won't be able to talk to you for a while." He grinned at the receiver as his thoughts drifted to the day's coming events. "I just wanted to call and wish you guys a happy fourth, and to light an M80 off for me, okay? Are you all ready?"

"Oh yeah! You should see all the crap we got! Mack took us to a reservation. It was so cool there. Next year, we'll go back so you can see everything! There's so much stuff. I got these paratroopers that have real parachutes and we're gonna light off some smoke bombs when they land so we can run through it."

He chuckled. "Sounds like fun. I love you, darling. And thanks, this is just what I needed."

"You're welcome! It's been fun for me too. Okay, bye Daddy, I love you," she said, and he smiled at the dial tone.

Thirty–six hours later, Nels stretched out his full frame, on his bunk in the captain's quarters, for some much needed shut-eye. He yawned and scratched at his short, graying beard, smiling at the gratifying week. Once he'd committed to come, the operational wheels moved quick, and Nels had a trifecta of native pride coursing through his veins, with Sweden to the east, Norway to the west and Denmark due south. He hated to admit it, but the solitude in his homecoming transcended his wildest expectations. To return to his native country after a very long time, and captain a boat full of Swedish and Norwegian men, created a sense of accomplishment. Confident in his research and ability to land the tunnies, he believed he might earn the final amount needed to purchase his own crab boat with Mack.

The sea rocked the vessel as it creaked under him, lulling him into sleep. It felt as though his eyes just closed, when a high pitch screech, like fingernails raking down a chalkboard, vibrated across the hull. A jolt slammed into them as the piercing sirens of the master alarm punctuated throughout the boat. From sheer peace to full alert, Nels rose to his feet. Men spoke in frenetic overtones in their native tongues.

"What the hell was that?" Someone yelled in Swedish.

"How the hell should I know, we were both playing the same card game, you idiot!" Another retorted in Norwegian.

Just then, heavy footsteps raced past the door and faded down the hall.

"Turn on the pumps!" A voice bellowed in Norwegian. The two must have remained still, for the man screamed, "Now, you idiot, get moving! We are taking on water!"

"Where's the captain?"

"I don't know, move your ass! The engine room's flooding... now!"

The crewmen bellowed over each other in the hallway, yet no one listened. All the young men, in absence of leadership, would never follow orders of a peer, regardless of their experience. Something Nels worried might be an issue if a problem arose. He opened the door as the phone next to his bunk rang. He crossed the cabin in two long strides and answered with his usual, "Capt'n!"

"Aye sir," said a nervous but careful voice. "Aye... we, we've hit something, sir, and Karlsson's in the engine room and he said... well... we're taking on a lot of water, sir."

"How much water?" he asked. Nels, a captain of fifteen years, endured some harsh blunt impacts, yet never took on water from a tap before. *What the hell did they hit?*

"Already over eighty-five liters, sir." The voice quavered on the other end. *Three feet, holy shit, that wasn't a mere tap, they were fucking bleeding out and fast.*

"Start the pumps, now! I'll see where we're at and be in the wheelhouse directly. Everyone needs to get in their gear. Do you understand? Everyone."

"Aye, sir."

Nels made it to the engine room, and despite the frantic efforts of the two men to stop it, green water poured in by the gallons from a huge gaping wound in the hull's side. *That isn't just from an impact.* He scanned the walls, and eyes narrowed on a large open area with leaks next to most rivets around it. It's flooding way too fast. He couldn't fix this. Nels exhaled through his nose and pleaded, *God help me get these men off the boat.* He took another deep breath and began yelling orders over the melee before him, which stopped.

"Listen up! I want both of you on deck!" He commanded. "Get on your gear, tell everyone to get into their gear, get the rafts ready and launch at will. Do it now!"

"Aye, sir," Both men said in unison. Relieved their duty concluded, they scrambled over each other to get to the upper decks.

The strain on the archaic hull apparent now, Nels' forehead furrowed as he peered at the hole, then down into the ascending water. *Damn,* how had he missed this in his initial inspection of the vessel two weeks earlier, and every damn time he'd been down there in between? So eager to get started, did he neglect the most elementary procedure of inspecting for strong craft durability? The vessel sank before and was patched back up poorly. Those goddamn sonaofb... *Oh my God.* He blanched as the first real wave of fear coursed through his body like an electric current.

"Oh God... Faith... I have to get the fuck out of here."

He made for the door just as a violent shift rocked the boat, making it moan like a wounded animal. Now desperate, he tried to reach the opening to freedom and his daughter. Two large drums fell with the shift of the boat. One rammed against the door and the other wedged it into position, closing the door with a deathly thud. He moved one of the offending barrels and reached to move the other from the door, when another seam burst and more water swamped the area. Raised to hip level, the pressure of the frigid water against the door denied him the right to life. Even as he struggled against it, he knew the effort was futile.

Nels shivered violently and thought of the young men on deck in utter chaos. His men. His responsibility. *How many would live? How many would die?* The water rose up the length of his body. The smell of salt water, oil and fish filled his nostrils. If the young men of the crew didn't stand around waiting for him, they all had a chance, a good chance, of surviving. *Karlsson, what's his goddamn name, Jakob, Joshua?* For some reason, it seemed important right then to know. Could he hold it together long enough to keep them moving toward a positive outcome?

The water at chest level now caused him to shiver even more, and not just from the temperature of the water. The icy fingers of death slid in and out and down his spine as it approached, and life ebbed from his body into the abyss. He closed his eyes. Only his girl entered his mind now, laughing and playing, lighting off her fireworks and sparklers back home. Eating cubes of watermelon from the fruit's gutted hull. The one with the handle carved out of the top that Rosie made each year. *Rosie.*

The water lapped at his neck now numb from the cold, and his vision became filmy. A vision of red, curly hair, back lit in the sun, flashed to his mind. So much like her mother, so much. The vision shifted and smiled at him. In a few brief hours, they'd tell his beautiful little girl of her father's death. A tragic death at sea. Another death. *How would she survive this?* How would she survive him? His heart shattered for her and his eyes filled with tears. Nels could no longer see her. *She's no longer mine. She's Mack's now... Mack.* His best friend's face filled his mind. *His brother. His son.* He closed his eyes and when he opened them again, Murron floated before him, radiating warmth and love, and holding her arms out wide in welcome.

"I have missed you, *mo cridhe*," she whispered.

"But what will happen to our girl?" He received the answer and smiled.

"*Je suis prest?*" she asked.

"Yes, my love," he answered. "I am ready." As the water swallowed him, Nels closed his eyes for the last time and let the breath empty from his lungs.

CHAPTER 9

Mack scrubbed one large hand over his face as he held the receiver in his other. Both shook violently as his eyes brimmed with tears.

"Yeah... Okay." He choked back emotion. "I appreciate you letting me know." He listened without hearing and tried to swallow as the man on the other end expressed his condolences towards Nels' young daughter. He threw the phone onto the linoleum, then stared at it, breathing hard.

"Jesus, Nels." He let his hand drop, defeated at his side and sucked in a trembling breath. "Oh, God."

He turned and braced his hands on the oak table in the kitchen, and shook his head, struggling to free the news from it. His senses heightened. A vivid blue bowl on the table contained plastic fruit in it. *Plastic fruit? Why didn't she have regular fruit?* The charcoal smoke from the barbeque wafted through an open window. Everything slowed its motion, and his best friend... they would never go fishing again. Never talk about the kids or buy their own fishing boat together. He wouldn't be there when Mack needed him or captain the *Nordic* again. Just gone. Dead. Outside, the birds warbled and Faith laughed with Charlie.

"Charlie, that's not fair, you always win, I never get to."

For Mack, that declaration unleashed the overwhelming pain inside him. Both Faith and Mack just lost their father.

"Fuck!" he screamed, grabbed the closest chair and slammed it against the wall until it splintered. "You goddamn bastard!" he cried out as he rammed his fists through the kitchen wall. Pain radiated through his arms and down his spine.

Rosie sprinted into the house at Mack's agonized cry. "Mack? Where are you?" She ran around the corner and into the kitchen. He sat back on his haunches, the palms of his hands pushing hard into the sockets of his eyes. Blood dripped from his knuckles, and his ring finger bent in at an odd angle. Rosie fell onto her knees and wept.

"Oh God, Mack, how?"

He cried too and tried to wave her away from touching him.

"Mack!" she admonished as tears streamed down her face. "Let me, damnit!" She drew his head to her bosom and rocked him like a child. He clung onto her with deep wracking sobs. Several moments passed before either could speak.

"The men on the boat said they hit something... but something's off, it happened way too quick, and he was down low... they all made it to the life rafts, except Nels. Oh, Christ, Rose, I need a drink."

"I'll get it." She pulled him into a chair and brought down the bottle of *Crown* from the cabinet, pouring them each four fingers. He drained it, and she discharged another. Standing close, she ran her fingers through his hair, and he encircled his arms around her waist, burying his head in her breasts.

"Shh, it'll be okay," she murmured and continued to stroke his damp hair.

Both spent and half of the bottle gone, she sighed and stood. Walking over to a cupboard she opened it and withdrew a small kit, pulling out what looked like a small popsicle stick and some medical tape. She walked back to Mack and reached out for his hand. He laid it in her lap as she straightened his fingers, then taped the broken one and the two on either side of it, together.

"When do we tell Faith, Mack?" she asked as she worked. "Maybe we should give her today and try to settle down before... before..."

"I have no fucking clue." He shook his head, defeated, and gave an uncomfortable, almost hysterical laugh. "Not when, not where... I don't know how to do this, Rose. I have no clue what she'll do."

"She's gonna know something's wrong, Mack," she murmured. "Neither of us has been outside in over an hour now and she may have heard you."

The stove clock proclaimed it ten PM, and he scrubbed his hands over his puffy face once more before he stood. "I'll tell the boys to wrap it up."

"No," she said. "I'll tell them. You go find her." She left the medical kit on the table and walked outside to find their sons. Mack grabbed the bottle on the counter and poured himself one more drink before following her out into the warm summer night air.

He found her alone on the swing set in the backyard, staring out across the city skyline. Mack gazed out on it too. So many lights, you couldn't tell where earth ended and the stars in the heavens began. He approached her from behind, trying to put his thoughts and words together, but her soft statement jolted him to his core.

"Daddy's gone now, too, isn't he?" she asked, matter-of-fact, yet didn't look at him, just kept staring out at the city.

"Yes," he choked out in immediate response, then took a deep breath. "Yes, baby, he is."

"I'm fourteen. I'm not a baby anymore, Mack." Instead of taking this as a measure of defiance, he accepted it as a simple appraisal of her current situation.

"I know, but lump it, because you'll always be that way to me, kid." He sat down on the swing next to her and peered up into the night sky. "So, how did you know?"

"I heard you in the kitchen." She glanced over at him and he cursed his selfishness. "No, I'm glad I heard you first, before now, I mean. I've just been sitting here." She turned her eyes back to the city. "I know I have to go away now. I know you can't stop it but I don't want to, Mack." Her voice wobbled and her eyes filled with tears. She blinked furiously, in a valiant effort to stop their progress.

"We'll talk about all that later. Nothing needs to get decided right now. I do promise you, it'll be okay and you won't be alone." Two fat tears betrayed her, and rolled down cheeks, rounded with youth, and something stabbed into Mack's heart. "Come here, Faith."

She climbed onto his lap backward and keened, so deep, wounded and primal, it didn't sound human. No one from the party approached them. *Thank God for Rosie.* When every drop of energy was spent from Faith, she collapsed and fell asleep, her arms locked around his neck. He carried her long gangly body inside and laid her down in bed, but when he rose to leave, she cried out and begged him to stay. Mack laid down with her and they both cried themselves to sleep.

****

Admired, respected and loved, hundreds of people showed up to Nels Pearson's memorial. Faith heard Jamie Campbell, owner of the *Nordic*, ask Mack, to take on his vessel as captain and he agreed without even thinking about it.

"Nels was a hell of a skipper and good man." A man with a thick beard and no moustache shook Mack's hand.

"He was, thank you Mr. Rasmussen."

In a daze, Faith looked up into the kind warm eyes of the man's stylish wife. She bent to Faith's eye level and touched her hair. Their eyes connected and stayed connected. The woman didn't say a word her eyes just brimmed with tears for Faith.

For the little girl, it was the first and only exchange that made her want to sob, so she grabbed Mack's hand and he picked her up and excused themselves.

After the presentation of life and the congregants left to resume their lives, Faith and Mack walked along the promenade at the Elliott Bay Marina where she and her father always went to fish and talk. *This was when he'd tell her sorry, but she'd have to go to that all-girls school after all.*

"How would you feel about staying on the boat with me?"

"All right," she answered resigned, not understanding him at first. "Wait... what?"

"I want you to stay on the boat with me, Faith. I can understand if you want to go, there's a lot of memories there, but I can't imagine you not being there."

She blinked at him. "You *want* me to stay with you?" she asked, not daring to trust her own ears. His face reflected the truth of it, and her face lit like the sun. "Oh my God, Mack," she shrieked. "I don't have to go to that school?" She whooped and launched herself on him.

"Well, wait a minute now, I got some conditions." He grabbed her by the shoulders to face him, earnestly. "You always have to hear the whole thing before jumping into something, Faith, that's always, okay?"

She stopped hopping and took several breaths to calm down. *If he treated her like an adult, she'd behave like an adult.* "Okay."

"Now I haven't been the best dad to Charlie and Brady, and I sure as hell haven't been good for Rosie. I'm gonna make mistakes... a lot of them." He glanced at her. "I'm gonna try hard not to, but I'm gonna do it sometimes. I don't talk to kids like I should, Faith. I don't give a shit about your school work and I'm not gonna watch you twenty-four-seven. So, before you agree to this, you gotta figure out what's important to you. If you want to learn and graduate, you've got to be adult enough to remember to do it yourself. School's something your dad wanted you to finish up." He lifted an eyebrow, and she nodded, taking it all in.

"If I tell you to do something, you damn well better do it with no opinions. Some of it you might not think is important but just like before, you're gonna do it anyway, because I say so, understand?"

She nodded her head again. "If any of those fucking assholes on deck act weird towards you... you have to tell me about it right away. I can't always see everything that's going on down there, and you're getting older. You know what I mean, right? Some of these guys are real jerks and you're not to be alone with any of them, ever, okay?" She nodded her head again. The "looks" and "weirdness," already started. "So that's it. You're older, and each year you'll get more responsibilities onboard. If you can hack it and live by all the other shit I just told you, well then, I guess we're golden."

"How is this possible? I mean, how do I get to live with you?"

"Nels, left me everything. I didn't understand it at all at first, but then I found out about your grandparents' thing."

"What thing?"

"Didn't your dad tell you?"

"Tell me what?"

"They left everything to you."

"What?"

"There's a little money coming in for all your expenses, it's why Campbell let you on the boat so easy. Your dad paid him, and he contributes to the school too, to work with you... the tutor... everything, to help get you educated." Faith stared out at the water. "Campbell worked with me to get some money from the company that..."

"From Sweden?"

"Yeah, someone did a bad patch job and they want to settle. I told Campbell I'd continue the original arrangement Nels set up, but he wasn't getting any extra money, and if he didn't agree I'd but my own boat. He finally said okay. Between all of it, when you turn eighteen, you'll come into a lot of money. And I'm talking a lot. When that time comes, we'll make sure you talk to someone, so you can be smart about it all."

"So, when you say Dad left everything to you, what does that mean?"

"He wanted me to be your guardian. Like a dad, but obviously not your real dad." He shifted with nerves. "He left me his life savings to raise you up, but also combine with mine and eventually buy the boat we wanted to buy together."

"Why don't you do that now?"

"Because I'm not ready yet. Campbell doesn't know it but I actually can't afford to do it by myself yet. So, don't tell him." He grinned at her and she grinned back. "Right now, I just want to be on the Nordic and keep things as close to normal as we can make them. Your dad said, more than anything he hopes you'll finish school."

After a long moment, Faith said, "All right. I have some conditions, too."

"What?"

She smiled at his dumbfounded expression. "Conditions for if I stay on the boat with you. Okay?"

"All right," he said as his lip twitched. "Let's hear them."

"When I gotta get my school books and stuff, you have to take me in to get them, not just say we'll do it later because it's not important to you. And when we need to set up the school stuff, you know, like sign me up and meet my teachers and everything, you gotta take me when I say or they'll know you're not doing shit."

"Hey!"

She continued as if he hadn't spoken. "And if I need to talk to you about girl stuff, you gotta try and listen. Even if you don't know what to say, you just have to give me your opinion, okay?"

"Like what kind of girl stuff?" Mack asked with trepidation.

Her cheeks flamed red as she mumbled quickly, "Like, I-started-my-period-two-days-ago-and-I-need-to-get-some-maxi-thingys-and-I-really need-to-get-some-bras."

Mack jolted, horrified. "Are you kidding me?" When she said nothing, he stammered, "I-I'm not getting you that shit. I'll give you money or something and..." He started waving his hand as if trying to make it go away. "You're gonna have to get that crap on your own. Matter of fact, I'll just give you, like, an allowance. So, really, you don't have to talk to me about it at all."

"I can't do it! I'll be too embarrassed," she whined. "Mack, you have to help me do it."

"No fucking way in hell I'm ever gonna to buy you any of that shit... Ever... Ever, Faith! I'll do all the school stuff, but anything that covers or goes near your... um... areas..." he emphasized with flailing hands. "You gotta go buy that shit yourself or figure out a way to get it, because I'm not doing it."

"Fine, I'll just ask Rosie to do it," she said, her face the same shade as her hair.

"Yeah, there you go, she'd be the one. And she can get all that shit on the boat before we even go up to Dutch, because I don't want to even see it, Faith. I'm sure the other guys don't neither." As if arriving at something he'd not yet thought about, Mack said, "Hey, also, you've always slept in the captain's quarters with your dad before. Obviously, it's not a good idea with me, so why don't you just take that room, because I think I'm gonna throw a cot up in the wheelhouse or take a crew bunk."

"That's your cabin now, Mack. I'm part of the crew."

"I don't want it," he blurted. "I'm used to sleeping in bunks, and you sure as hell aren't sleeping with those damn animals. No more talking about it, okay? It's your bed, you'll have a bathroom right there and everything. Besides, it sounds like you could... you know... use some privacy, sometimes." Relenting, she nodded and he turned his attention to a colorful sailboat tacking her way across the water.

"Mack, there's one more thing." She took a deep breath, and he looked at her, nervous about what other revelations threatened. "This is what I'm going to do with my life. I'm gonna fish. I decided that a long time ago, and I want to learn everything the right way. Dad always said it was harder for girls because guys are stronger and the superstition crap, but..." She paused, and smiled at a couple that walked by with their toddlers. "So, I want you to teach me. I'm going to finish school and get college classes in, but when I turn twenty, I'm not gonna work on your boat anymore." His eyes snapped to hers, confused. "I want to do it myself, on my own, without family."

****

A million thoughts ran through his mind at her declaration, but his own journey came back to him in color. *Just two years older than her when Nels taught me.* Mack shook his head in disbelief at how fast time moved. There weren't many women crab fisherman in Alaska, period. Her education needed to include not only procedure and safety but also the realities of the world and people she'd work with more closely, not just the ones he and Nels handpicked. *My God, what the fuck am I doing?* As much as he regretted the reason, she *wasn't* a baby anymore.

"Okay," he replied and the air settled heavy for several seconds.

"What about birth control?" she asked, suppressing a smile.

"What? Why?"

"Won't I need it someday?"

"No... you aren't... never gonna need it, and if you ever say those two words to me again or even think about asking me about sex, this entire deal is off, got it?" He jabbed a finger at her as she snorted with laughter.

"That was fun, watching your veins pop out of your neck like that."

"Yeah, well, keep it up and you'll give me a heart attack." A heavy silence fell over them again.

"He'd have been proud of you today, Faith, you held up." Draping an arm over her shoulders, he let her turn into him, and wrap arms around his middle. He laid a cheek on her soft hair. "You know, he always told me how brave he thought you were, and how pissed that you had to be so young to prove it."

"I miss him already," she murmured. "Sometimes so much it's hard to breathe right."

"Me too, kid." He kissed the top of her head. "I'm sure it won't be pretty, but we're going to make it through this."

****

Several weeks later, in the early morning hours, with the *Nordic* packed and ready for the voyage up to Dutch, Mack and Faith said their goodbyes to Rosie and the boys.

"When can I come work for you, Dad?" Charlie asked.

"I tell you what kid, when you turn fifteen we'll see if we can't start with some summer runs, what do you think?"

"Okay! So, like…" He scrunched up his face and counted out the calculations on his fingers. "Seven years, about?" Mack nodded as the boy wrapped his arms around his neck and then hugged Faith.

"Me too, me too!" Brady pleaded. Mack picked him up and threw him in the air as he giggled and screamed. "More Daddy, more!" Mack obliged him while Faith and Rosie said goodbye.

"Okay, sweetie, well, good luck." Rosie gave her a hard squeeze. "It's gonna feel real weird at first, but you're gonna be just fine. If you need anything else in the girlie department, just let me know and I'll send it up, okay? Or if you need to talk about something, just call."

"Okay, thanks Rose, for everything. I'm gonna miss you." Faith squeezed her back, then turned for the truck. "Bye guys, I love you. I'll miss you." Mack kissed Rosie, and they held each other for a long moment.

"Crazy summer," he said.

"Life altering for sure." He kissed her again.

"Thank you, baby."

"When it gets quiet out there or you don't know what to do with a teenage daughter, call me, okay?"

"First person." He squeezed her hand and walked back down the path towards the truck. The summer took its toll and changed everyone, even Rosie. The five of them grew into a family of their own. As Mack's truck drove out of sight, with the boys chasing after it, Rosie raised a hand to her lips in the rearview mirror and walked back to the house.

A week later, the boat prepared, the mood quiet and somber, F/V *Nordic* left the harbor with a new captain and crew. The men all moved indoors to stow their gear and settle in. Faith stayed on deck and thought about starting her seventh year at sea. The water rippled from a slow-moving wind, and magenta streaks reflected in the sky, waggled in its surface. She sighed deep, knowing Mack watched her from the wheelhouse, sharing this moment with Nels close by.

Just six months ago, *he* steered the ship's helm and spoke with a man in Swedish about going back to his homeland. Neither realizing their last moments together on the water were upon them. Sunrise or sunset. Those would be her moments with her father whenever she could muster it. Faith took a deep breath and stepped inside to unpack.

CHAPTER TEN

Faith graduated from high school the year she turned sixteen, and Mack celebrated by making her a full-share deckhand, as the crew allowed her to throw the first hook of the season. No longer required to do only the mundane tasks, she ran the hydraulics fifty percent of the time, helped with boat repairs, drove the boat when Mack didn't, and during offloads, took control of the counts. Beyond that, she worked the rail more often, even in some inclement weather, and blended into the rigorous work with alacrity.

However, turning sixteen brought forth additional problems. Her ever-expanding breasts and curves brought unwanted comments and gestures by new or transient deckhands and greenhorns, no matter how well Mack screened them. Though the old timers on deck had her back, without Mack on deck, she needed to learn how to fend off the remarks, innuendos, and actions for herself. A problem she tried to hide from her surrogate father until she couldn't anymore.

Lance Delveckio, came to the *Nordic* as a new greenhorn. A nice-looking, athletic kid, with deep golden-brown hair and matching eyes. He finished his first season with pride. Attending college at the University of Oregon, he'd taken the job aboard the

Nordic for notoriety and to earn money for his third year of college. At twenty, Lance acted even younger than his counted years, drinking a little more than anyone else, and bragging about accomplishments he'd yet to achieve. One topic he enjoyed talking about more than anything else... Faith Pearson, and what he wanted to do to her.

Like the other crew, she removed her all-weather garments, and stood in the entryway in her long underwear while stowing her gear. She ran to her room, threw on sweats, a crisp white tee shirt and a worn sweatshirt for warmth. Most of the men enjoyed watching her strip down, and though it made her uncomfortable, she also accepted it came with the territory and tried to do it quick.

After the meal, all the men staggered to their bunks for a well-deserved sleep. However, Faith's shift for KP fell on that night. She'd just finished wiping down the sink and wanted to say a quick hi to Mack before hitting her own stateroom, when Lance walked up behind her. He strapped his arms around her waist, and she jerked in surprise. Laughing, she thought he only wanted to scare her, when the heady scent of whiskey clung to them like a cloud.

"Ah..."

"Hey, that was a great run, wasn't it?" He ran his hands over her stomach, then rounded over her ass.

"Um, yeah. Listen, Lance..."

"Shh, I know I'm a little drunk, so I'm a little more honest, but I think you know what I'm talking about?"

"No." She panicked, and tried to back up, but he held her in place. "Lance, I need to go see Mack. He expects to see me after dinner." She tried to step away again, irritating him.

"You don't need to see Mack," he said, pressing his hips into hers, pinning her to the cabinet sink.

Something hard pushed into her bottom. Having seen her fair share of morning boners, Faith did not wish to see this boner up close and personal.

"Stop."

His hands moved to her breasts, snaking up and under her tee shirt. She struggled, and tried to escape, which prompted him to pinch her nipple hard through her bra. Yelping, she pushed as hard as she could off the sink and tried to kick him. However, since she faced away from him, her feet, trapped under kick plate, could only shuffled at the base of the sink.

He grabbed her chin hard. "Shut up. I swear to God you make one peep, after being a prick tease this whole time..."

"Lance, please stop." She closed her eyes, and inspiration struck. "Look, if Mack comes down here he'd kill you if he saw you doing this. Just stop and go to bed. We don't have to talk about it or anything okay."

Ignoring her, he replied, "You sure enjoyed putting on a show earlier, wearing all that tight shit. You looked at me..."

"No... I didn't."

"You did, were you just being a fuckin' prick tease?" He kept a hand on her breast, and plunged the other into her sweats, under her panties. They almost penetrated her, when suddenly he was flying through flew through the air.

Breathless, she turned. Lance laid on the floor with Mack hitting him in the head. Lance gurgled out a scream, as the men stumbled out of their bunks. Eyes wide, face pale and shaking, Faith took in the scene.

"Mack!" She grabbed his arm, but he slammed the man's body into the floor, and each time, Lance's head pinged off the linoleum.

The crew observed first Faith, then Lance. Every man had told him to stay away, knowing the consequences of that refusal laid before them now. They pulled Mack off him and the greenhorn remained on the floor, bloody, with his face already beginning to swell. His eyes rolled back in his head.

"Mack, stop!" Faith screamed. "Stop it."

Wild eyed, Mack glanced at Faith. Her eyes shimmered but didn't cry. "Are you hurt?" he barked. She jumped at the volume of his question. "I said, are you fucking hurt, God damn it?" He climbed off the bloody mess on the floor and shook her a little.

"N-n-no," she stammered, "I just wanted him to s-stop."

"And that," Mack roared as he turned back to Lance, "is the only reason you aren't dead." Lance groaned on the floor, and Mack kicked him in the stomach, then crouched down, so only the boy and Faith could hear. "Get in your fucking bunk. Take a step out other than to piss and you're swimming. No one will ever know. Am I being unclear?"

"No," Lance wheezed and then coughed up a glob of blood.

"Now stand up, you look like an idiot," Mack said a little louder for the room to hear. "Piece of dog shit."

Two guys moved to help him, but Lance growled to leave off. He struggled to his knees and used the galley seats and table to stand. He hunched over, holding his stomach, as blood dripped down his face.

"Now apologize to Faith."

"Fuck you, Mack." Mack grinned and punched him in the balls. Lance fell over screaming and Mack hovered close.

"I'm sorry, what?"

Before the boat docked, Lance apologized, and courtesy of the crew, spent the rest of the trip back to the harbor in his bunk. The boy threatened to sue Mack, but one by one each member of the crew who served with Mack and Nels for years told Lance they didn't see or hear anything.

****

The event impacted Faith significantly. She shifted into a different person, and during the next summer break, she attended classes with Rosie to learn how to defend herself. Mack showed her more, using her enthusiastic brothers as attackers. Challenging strength training workouts and running gained Faith muscles and power, and ate all her calories while fishing, so she didn't lose too much weight, and kept her lean muscle.

Though no man wanted to cross Mack, jokes and innuendos still occurred. She never told Mack about inappropriate behaviors, but rather studied them, and learned the way men thought about their children, girlfriends, parents and wives. They didn't talk about such things as if sitting on a counselor's sofa, pouring out their hearts. Their conversations leaned more toward the rude, disrespectful, blatant and sometimes cruel.

She wore jeans and heavier clothes under her all-weather gear, often changing in the hot engine room, rather than in the line of sight of men, and found she blended in and was more accepted for her effort. In the off season, she tried to make friends with women but found them emotional, judgmental, and game players. So, found her way in a more solitary life.

Faith spent evenings in the wheelhouse with Mack when not working or sleeping. Over the years, they compiled ways to help her when she embarked down her own path. Most captains believed the superstition, that females onboard a fishing vessel doomed the season, the boat and the crew. Finding a position among her peers presented an enormous challenge.

"You won't be able to dominate anyone with physical strength," Mack said, as they motored back to Dutch at the end of the season. "Guys are just stronger, Faith. You're going to need to do it with your smarts and endurance. That means mind over matter. That means not complaining about work, even when it's unfair. It means getting on deck first, working until the job's done and being last off deck."

"Taking on the shit jobs," she suggested. "And doing them better than anyone else."

"Yeah, exactly, and you've got to be careful at the bars. Don't leave your drinks vulnerable, or get too wasted, even when you think you can trust everyone. If you're out there and me or the boys aren't with you, you can't trust anyone."

"Okay." She scanned the waves. In the back of her mind she resented that the onus of the path she embarked on was entirely on her. Why couldn't men recognize their behavior and their place in decency. *Why did she have to change everything?* One day she wouldn't and the rules would be hers and not theirs. "I'm signing up for the online engineering program. I need to see what I have to do for the practical work. See if they'll work with me."

"This summer?"

"Yeah, unless you want to fish."

"We might. Duncan says he's got one more season in him as deck boss. So, I asked him to train you up in it."

Her head swiveled over to him, thrilled. "Really?"

"Yep. It'll give you a bump in pay and get you some experience. I want you to get great on the hydraulics, too."

"I don't think I'll have a snowball's chance in hell for getting to run them on other boats. Everyone wants to do that."

"Yeah, but if an opportunity arises you need to be able to prove yourself. Ya gotta be smart, watch and understand the weather and conditions and not brain someone with an eight-hundred-pound weapon. You gotta be able to park them on a dime quickly."

"Then I won't only have to depend strength and endurance as assets."

"Yeah, then with all of that, you'll be seasoned."

CHAPTER 11

As her last season with Mack ended, just after Faith turned twenty, she applied for a deckhand position to many different fishing vessels, but no one so much as granted her an interview. One day, as her brothers wrestled in front of her, Charlie informed Brady, he fought like a girl. Something in Faith triggered, and she tried a different application technique, then waited without telling Mack, for it to pan out.

"So when are you gonna resign as captain of the *Nordic* and buy your own boat?"

"I don't know. Not now."

"It's what he always wanted for both of you and you know it." She argued and sipped a beer with him companionably in the wheelhouse, as the other crew members staggered their way into town.

"Just think Mack, you could get a bigger and frankly, much better boat than this piece of shit. Just do it. Charlie's coming to work with you, so you could buy it and have some test runs this summer to get used to it. That way all the profit would be yours and not Campbell's. It chaps my ass knowing what he takes."

"Maybe," Mack said noncommittally, and blew a smoke ring. He sighed at her frown. "Christ, Faith, you'll be leaving soon. I don't think now's the right time to be starting something new."

"You always say that. It's not the right time," she mimicked. "Right now is the *perfect* time, Mack. Things are gonna be weird for both of us next season. You can start fresh on a new boat, make some fresh memories with the boys."

"I like the old ones," he retorted.

"But they won't take you anywhere but backwards."

"What are you, Oprah now?"

"No. Did you turn into a pussy when I wasn't looking?"

"Watch it."

"Just come look at that one I told you about. The mechanics on it are solid. There's just a few repairs. Maybe some spit and polish issues, but we can fix all of that easy enough." The radio squawked.

"*Nordic, Sarah Anne...* over?"

"Whew, saved by the bell." Mack gave Faith a cheesy smile with his cigarette clenched in his teeth, and before she could say anything else, and barked into the CB, "Carter."

"Yeah, is this Mack Carter?" drawled a deep, Southern baritone.

"The one and only."

"Hey, Capt'n, this is Ray Cavanaugh over on the *Sarah Anne.*" Faith, who had propped her feet up on the instrument panel, removed them immediately and straightened in her chair. Perplexed, Mack narrowed his eyes at her, as the captain of the *Sarah Anne* continued. "We're out of Kodiak but had some business to take care of here in town. I have a sheet here on an F. Pearson, says he works for you, that right?" Mack raised his eyebrows at her and grinned. She rolled her eyes back at him.

"Ah, yeah, you could say that."

"Well, Carter, I know you by reputation, and I knew the last skip, Pearson, by name only. Is this his kid? I guess I always thought he had a girl, but as they say, the memory's the first to go."

"Mmm, yep, that's what they say."

"It says here he's twenty, that right?"

"Yawp, twenty-years-old now, ready to spread some wings."

"How's his work? Does he have any problems I should know about, recreational, personal or otherwise?"

"Nope, this kid's solid." Her eyes warmed on his. "Has everything to prove and is one damn fine member of my crew. Been my deck boss for the last year and took to it like bread to butter."

"Okay, well, I'm down a few from you, could you have him come over and we'll get some paperwork signed for next season?"

"Oh, no problem at all, man." Mack hung up the phone and howled with laughter. He hunched over and grabbed at his sides. Faith rolled her eyes again, stood up and looped her thumbs into the front pockets of her jeans, then waited for him to finish. "So, now you're a crab fishing *Tootsie?*"

"Dustin Hoffman was a guy becoming a girl."

"So, you're a Tooter." He howled again at his own joke.

"Okay, well, what else was I supposed to do?" He wiped tears from his eyes and hers merely narrowed more. "He wouldn't have even looked at my paperwork if I had put my name on it." Mack tried to inhale but had a hard time, so she continued, slumping back into her chair. "At least this way, if I don't get the job after he sees me, then I'll know that I had it to start with."

"I guess."

"I'm also thinking of padding up a little."

"Padding up?" Out of breath, Mack stopped laughing and wrinkled his nose in confusion. "What the hell does that mean?"

"Not look so skinny. You know, throw on some sweats or something. What should I do when I get there? Do you think he'll just say, *fuck off*, or will he humor me first?"

"I'll go over with you."

"No, I have to do this on my own."

"Faith." He stopped all pretense of laughter and held an exasperated look in his eye. "There's nothing wrong with me helping you on the first one. No one's gonna give you a chance until you have a job reference from someone other than me. So, kick ass on this job and then you'll get as fair a shake as you can after that. Deal?" He stuck out a hand.

"Okay, deal," she said and grabbed his hand, but before letting go she said, "But you have to at least look at this boat."

"Why can't we ever just shake on something and have that be the end of it?" he countered. "Fine, I'll look."

The meeting with the *Sally Anne* went as expected. The captain and crew appreciated the beauty and wares of the young woman, padded or not, but weren't having a woman on board for any reason when good men needed a job.

"Look, Cavanaugh, you're new up here, but you aren't gonna be sorry if you take a risk on the girl," Mack said evenly. "She's been living on a crab boat for twelve years now. She's been doing deckhand work for ten of them. Full share for four and my deck boss this whole past year. I'm looking around your crew here and with exception of you and your own deck boss, Willie there," -he gestured at the man with a nod– "she has more experience than the other three put together, and she's hungry to prove herself."

Frustrated, the captain eyed Faith. In her present condition, she finessed the illusion of stoutness. He couldn't deny her experience, superstitions notwithstanding.

"What happens when you can't lift something, or you break a fingernail, or get your feelings hurt? Worse yet, what if you start causing discord among my men because they all want to fuck the new deckhand?"

Faith ran a hand over the back of her head, losing her patience, and fisted it in her hair, before she vee'd it down the sides of her jaw, looking semi-disgusted at the insult. She concluded she just didn't give a shit anymore and at least she'd get her say.

"My mother, father, and close kin were all dead by the time I turned fourteen, so I don't expect they could hurt my feelings worse than that." She raised a hand, showing the captain her dirty, calloused middle finger. "Obviously, I don't give a shit about my fingernails." Some of the crew tittered. "I have some rules I follow that sets the tone for the crew regarding any kind of personal relationships while out at sea. I don't have them." Her gaze swept the men present. "Certainly not with any of these sorry pieces of shit." Her eyes locked with the skipper's again. "And... I've never had a problem with the weight of anything onboard a boat that a man wouldn't have the same problem with. But if you'd like to arm wrestle, let's throw down and go for it right now."

She raised an arm and waited in the stunned silence, never taking her eyes off the captain. His gaze darted from her arm, to her face, to Mack, to her breasts and back to her face. When he said nothing, she lowered her arm.

"Look, all I want is the work, sir, and a chance to prove myself. I'm gonna make you a fantastic deckhand, and if you don't like the way things go, you can let me off after the first turnaround, with no pay and no questions asked."

Mack beamed with pride at her, crossed his arms and looked over at the captain, wondering if he'd give her the chance. The captain narrowed his eyes at Faith, then frowned at his amused deck boss in the corner who gave an almost imperceptible nod.

"Okay... we'll give you a shot, but if I don't like what I see out of you or my men, you're gone. You got that?"

"Yes, sir," she said on an exhale, and returned a slow smile. *She fucking did it.* Looking over at Mack, she grinned broader.

"Okay, well thank you for the chance, I won't let you down, sir." She stuck out her hand and gave him a handshake that made him wince, before turning to Mack. "Okay, now, let's go see about a boat."

****

"It's gonna be fine." Faith exhaled yet another exasperated sigh, two days later. "You did the right thing, Mack, and come October, after you've learned her quirks, you'll be on cloud nine."

They both stood, thumbs in the loops of their jeans, staring at Mack's new, one hundred twenty-eight-foot house aft crab boat. It held two hundred crab pots and had the capacity for two-hundred twenty-five thousand pounds of King crab in her hull. It boasted three-year-old twin engines and over one thousand two hundred eighty horsepower, capable of motoring at twelve knots or fourteen miles per hour. The outside paint needed work, the interior cabins smelled of urine, the carpet threadbare, but the heating and cooling tanks purchased the year before still gleamed. She needed an updated radar, but the hydraulics system and gears also were in their infancy. Her name...

"That's the first thing I'm gonna change," Mack growled. "What a stupid fucking name, the *Mariner*. She'd sink just to spite me, with a name like that..."

"What are you gonna name her then?"

"I don't know, but not some stupid, predictable crap, that's for sure." He paused and glanced out of the corner of his eye at her, a little sheepishly. "It was a good idea, Faith, I didn't even know how good until right now."

Faith widened her stance and folded her arms across her chest. "Well, it looks as though we need to celebrate, steak dinner on me."

"On you! Shit, let's go!"

The season closed, and the *Nordic* became a bittersweet memory for both Mack and Faith. After flying both of his boys to Dutch, the new boat owner motored *his* new project back to Seattle and Fisherman's Terminal, each person noting any problems and issues as they arose.

He unveiled the new boat's name to Faith on the sixth anniversary of her father's death. They all sat at the picnic table, as the boys and neighborhood kids ran around giggling with sparklers. Mack approached and nervously threw down the battered manila envelope on the table.

Faith blinked at the envelope before picking it up. She turned it over, ripped the glued paper flap open, and pulled out the sheaves of paper, then knitted her eyebrows together, and rested her head in her chin, as she read. Her eyes shimmered, and lips moved as she scanned the text and read the new name of Mack's boat.

Tears collected in the corners of Rosie's eyes as she and Mack exchanged glances, then watched Faith. When she finished reading, Faith turned the papers over on the picnic table and placed her hands on top of them, as if gaining power. Only then did she lock eyes with Mack.

"For this alone I'll always love you, Mack." Her voice shook, just a little. "He'd have loved this."

"No," Mack mumbled. "He would have said it's about fucking time.'" She laughed, and the heavy moment evaporated.

"Yeah, that's exactly what he would've said."

Mack exhausted most of his money on boat licensing, registrations, mooring, fuel, and to replace the important things that needed replacing. He needed a successful season, just to break even. With no money left for cosmetic changes, he satisfied himself, knowing that everything would work out and in two years he'd make the extra money needed to make those repairs too and start profiting.

****

Toward the end of summer, Mack, Rosie and the kids took a month-long fishing and camping trip all over Washington and Oregon. At first, Faith said she'd come with them, just to make sure Mack would go, but at the last second opted out, making an excuse her new captain needed her for repairs. Disappointed, Mack let her go, but Faith planned a surprise of her own.

Mack would never allow her to help him financially fix up the new boat, so she opted to do it in secret. By the time her surrogate father arrived at the dock a little over four weeks later, wearing Ray-bans, jeans, a white tee shirt and a deep tan, he didn't recognize his own craft, just a gleaming, freshly painted fishing vessel.

The bottom sparkled a deep sapphire blue, which extended two feet above the water line. Above it, a foot-wide band of gold, followed by a three-foot band of jet black, and another foot-wide band of gold, glistened, before connecting to the boat's remaining color, of bright white.

Dumbfounded, Mack walked to the aft end where his gift to Faith shone back at him. F/V *Je Suis Prest,* with a hometown port of Camano Island, Washington in black and gold script, swirled across the stern. *I am ready.* Mack's Adam's apple bobbed up and down in his throat, and he turned to her, mouth open, but speechless.

"Wait, there's a lot more," she blurted before he could say anything and pulled him on board. "Come on, Pop."

Every deck surface, refinished and painted, radiated like the sun. Every wall in the hull, wheelhouse, engine room, galley and bathrooms, were resealed and the distinct smell of paint hovered thick in the air. Though the main area was bright white, the bunkrooms and master berth were all painted a softer tan. She re-carpeted all the living spaces, and each bunk contained a new full-size mattress, bedding, pillows, and a small built-in dresser. The new kitchen appliances sparkled, as did the mugs, dishes, glassware and silverware, each emblazoned with the new vessel's logo. She converted one berth into a storage area for food and supplies, and the galley boasted a new television, VHS player, game and CD stereo system.

When they reached the wheelhouse, a brand-new leather captain's chair, with F/V *Je Suis Prest* on one side and *Captain Mack Carter* on the other, each in gleaming gold thread, stood at attention for the new skipper. Behind the chair, hung a row of pegs containing brand new all-weather gear. On the last peg was a new leather jacket with the boat's logo on the back.

"I… How did you do all of this, Faith?" Mack asked, overwhelmed until her smug smile mocked him. "You do realize everything'll look like shit at the end of the first season, right?"

"Oh crabbers, fuck up everything." She smiled and said, "And the how… well, it wasn't easy, let me tell you. I had everyone in on it before you left, and I made Rosie promise not to let you come home early. We had an entire crew come in and they worked day and night after they got her to dry dock and gutted her. The chair, appliances and all the other stuff were in a few storage areas. We just finished up the spit shine a couple days ago. Do you like it, Mack?"

He put a hand to his forehead and let it slide down the side of his face, leaving the palm just under his chin as he reached for his pack of Camels with the other and lit one. "This is so cool, kid. You shouldn't have done this. All the money…" He trailed off and blanched as he calculated the sums in his head. "Jesus, this was hundreds of thousands of dollars, Faith! What the…"

"Oh, shut up," Faith said, a little snottier than she had intended. "Don't you dare throw my gift in my face, you shit! Just say, thanks!" She tried to glare at him, but couldn't quite keep the smile from the corners of her mouth. "I wanted to do it. I had some money…"

"For your future!"

"I wouldn't have had a future if it wasn't for you and Dad." She walked over to him and he raised an arm to embrace her. "If he were here, you guys would've done this so much sooner. When he died, he left you behind too, and then you took care of me. So, even alone, you would've done it sooner, and had the money to do it right. You know Dad would've loved this! Besides, now the thing lives up to its name. I wanted to do it, so I can be with you fishing next year, too." She gestured all around. "Now I can."

She leaned in, and he sighed. "I'm not sure what I'm gonna do without you kid, I really don't."

****

When they left for Dutch that season, Faith motored back with the Carters. She stayed in crew quarters and the three of them tested out everything. Charlie practically vibrated with excitement for the chance to fish with his dad, for a few weeks, before returning to school, but also nervous about his first run. He voiced his concerns to his sister during one of their morning jogs together.

"You'll be great, Char," Faith said, placing her arms on top of her head to cool down and walked back to the dock. "Just keep your head up and pay attention. You're gonna be messed-up at first. It's going to hurt bad, and you're gonna want to quit every single day. Just push through that shit, and you'll start to figure it out." "I wish I could quit school and do it full time like you did."

"I didn't quit school. I did high school and college on the boat, and it was fucking hard. It's going to be good to do it in intervals like this. A few weeks here and there between school breaks, you'll get used to it and not just burn out like so many greenhorns do. Just work your ass off every time, and when you come on full time, you'll be ready. You'll figure out what works for you and things will get easier."

"The guys are gonna treat me like shit," Charlie complained.

"Yawp," she confirmed. "They will. You're the captain's kid, they're gonna fry your ass, and Pop's gonna be hardest on you of all. But if you work hard, harder than the rest of them, you'll prove yourself to them and to him. Life's gonna suck every time for a while, Char, but seriously, don't complain and don't go running to Mack if things get a little hard. You only use him as a very last resort and he'll respect you for it. Each time and each season will get better."

"Why don't you stay and help me? Come on, it'll be better if you stayed. You know he wants you to."

"I have to do this on my own, just like you. Plus, you need time with your old man, I've had him a long time. It's you and Brady's turns now."

"You know, I never cared about that, Faith." The seagulls chased each other over the water, and he glanced at her when she gave a disbelieving grunt. "Okay, maybe when I was little, because I wanted to come too. But I never thought you were like taking him from us or anything. You've always been my sister."

"Thanks Char. I love you, too." She leaned her head on his shoulder. "But it's your time now and I'm thrilled for you."

They both eyed the marina, closing one part of their lives to embark upon the next.

PART TWO

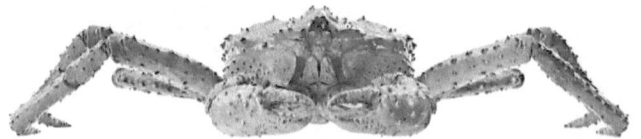

CHAPTER 12

Seventeen years later, Faith Pearson woke and struggled to hold onto the dream she'd had. A woman with her face beamed down at her, as they held hands and relaxed on the sun-warmed rim of the International Fountain, near Seattle's Science Center. They tilted their heads up in unison to the water spray in synchronization to *Mozart's Serenade No. 13* in G Major. That was it, the entire dream she experienced many times over the course of her life. Faith's mother, Murron, died giving birth to her in the spring of 1973, and the only memories available to her about the woman, comprised of a dusty scrapbook, embellished stories, two shoe boxes of personal items her grandparents and father saved for her, and this one dream. Now all of them, just dust in the wind. However, in her dreams, Faith recognized the woman as though she shared an intimacy only a true mother and daughter enjoyed.

A fist pounded on her door, erasing the misty, serene moment, and brought back the damp, molding stink and chill of her stateroom.

"Pearson, we gotta clear the decks," the deep baritone bellowed, paused, then said, "Come on, let's go bang some ice."

The voice and the fist moved to the next door and continued its assault, but met with suggestions of where the pounder should put his fist. A chuckle, and the scenario faded to the next door on its quest. The ship rolled over a wave, causing the hull to groan with frustrated indignation.

Resigned, Faith took a deep breath and swung her long legs over the side of the bunk. Aside from the few hardships of the past five weeks, the woman enjoyed this gig, as one of the few fishing vessels that gifted her a solo cabin. In fact, not since the *Nordic* did she have the luxury of her own cabin in the bowels of the boat. It didn't even matter, the engine and machinery roared at all times of the day or night. She loved it because of the extra level of freedom it allowed her. Sleeping naked for one, if she wished. Which she didn't on the Bering Sea in the middle of winter, but a girl loved to have options.

Who cared if she needed to lock the door to do it in peace? Better than overheating in the extra layers of clothes and the binding she wore around her breasts, or stuffing herself into a nasty bunk bed, where the odors of all previous tenants and their activities of the night lingered. Worse yet, cohabitating with some asshole snoring, jerking off to God only knew what, or flatulating overhead, the stench permeating into every corner of the room.

She sorted through some clothes in a pile on the floor and smelled them. *Another day's wear? Yes!* She pulled them on quickly in the frigid room.

At thirty-seven, Faith's lean frame lengthened to six feet in height. Built and strong, from years of daily physical use, she fleshed out into a crab fisherman her deceased father, as well as her pop, Mack, could be proud of. However, in those years she discovered most men didn't want to remember her gender at work. If they did, they tended to treat her differently. Either she was an object of desire or an object of envy for her work ethic. She preferred the latter. Even now, she bound her breasts tight to her body in two sports bras', and layered a complete set of fraying thermal underwear to keep out the cold. Next, she thrust her arms into an XL long-sleeve sweatshirt, a pair of sweatpants two sizes too big for her, and two pairs of thick socks. Her fellow crew members never saw her otherwise. Most men wouldn't care what she wore, as long as she did her job, but something in her irrational mind scarred that night with Lance in the kitchen, so many years ago.

She reached for two ponytail holders and wove her vibrant, shoulder-length, fire mane into a French braid, then a knot, twisting the bands tight around it before securing a faded, checked green and black stocking cap on top. She pinned it in place and glanced into a small stainless-steel wall mirror just to the left of the door to ensure nothing escaped for a while.

The reflection revealed an oval face, awash with thousands of freckles, high distinct cheekbones, and a shallow dent in her chin. All gifts from her mother's Scottish heritage, and the UV rays from the sun. As an afterthought, Faith grabbed her sunscreen and lip balm. She worked them in fast and smirked at her long nose, bent a fraction to the left, a memento from a picking hook that glanced off it three years earlier, fracturing it.

Reaching for the door, the delicious aroma of strong coffee, combined with the charred scent of burnt toast, overwhelmed the hallway. After eating breakfast and filling her thermos with scalding hot coffee, she maneuvered herself into her all-weather gear, slipped into her size eleven wellies, and stepped out onto the sub-zero deck of the F/V *Rosemary Sue.*

A frigid blast of wind slapped her face, and for a moment, took her breath away. The malodorous aroma of fish and the pungent sea filled her nostrils and tickled her eyes as she blinked back tears to clear them. Frowning at the ice-laden deck that accumulated to several inches in spots in the few hours they'd all slept waiting for the pots to soak, she psyched herself up for the hours to come.

The vessel, now a winter wonderland to the casual observer, appeared dangerous and deadly to the crew.

"Shit," Logan exclaimed. "It's fucking freezing out here! Christ, my sack's in my throat!" He glanced around. "Tell me again why do we got to do this."

Logan, the nephew of a skipper calling in a favor, never knew what he needed to do, without direction and questioned everything ad nauseam. Still, even stupid had a right to survive.

"A crab boat, as far north as we are, has temps that drop into negative double digits, right?" The kid nodded. "Since the seas are rougher, all that wind and spray turns into ice on anything." She gestured to the crab pots, gear, equipment, ropes and hoses and every other available surface, both horizontal and vertical, that fell victim to the blight. "So, all that ice creates weight."

"It can't be that much."

"A foot of ice build-up can weigh as much as the boat, and all that weight is above the deck line, so what happens then?"

"The boat gets heavy." *Jesus, the kid's brilliant.*

"The boat gets *top* heavy, which makes it vulnerable should a wave come that's big enough to make it list to one side. We can be swamped in minutes, killing all of us and sinking the ship."

Faith glanced over, as three deckhands and the deck boss stepped out onto the deck, to begin the tedious process of ridding the boat of its heavy burden.

"It's fucking freezing out here! My sack's in my throat!" Logan repeated, now that the *men* arrived.

"Ah, nothing to worry about then," Mikhail joked, tugging on his hoodie strings. "No one will notice anyway, dickhead."

"Fuck you, asshole, your mom would've," Logan retorted. *Ah, pure poetry.* Faith rolled her eyes. "Besides," Logan continued. "At least the bitches still look for mine."

"No, bitch is lookin' for yours. Right, Joe?" Mikhail poked the older man in the ribs.

"All I know is I worked my ass off up here while my bitch sat at home," Joe complained, hooking his overalls. Faith rolled her eyes again. *Here it comes.* "Until I came home and found her fucking her ex." The man hadn't stopped bitching about that for four months.

"Not me," croaked Jesse, a middle-aged man that looked ancient from his years on the sea. They all eyed him as he broke into a smile that missed several teeth. "I just buy my bitches." This brought an uproarious guffaw from the collective, and Faith just grinned and shook her head.

"Shut up! Didn't y'all notice we got a lady here?" Cooper lifted his observation over the wind. All the men eyed Faith as if they just discovered her gender. She wanted to kill the deck boss. "Grab your mallets and get to work or we'll be out here all day! Logan on the bow with Jesse! Mikhail, Joe, on the stern. Pearson and I'll take the deck. Go!"

They all left, grumbling over their respective purgatories. Faith hefted her own mallet and chipped away at ice on the block. Oddly enough, she didn't mind the hard, repetitive labor that took anywhere from four to eight hours to complete. It allowed her contemplation time without a lot of talking, only required vigilance over the weather and sea's escapades, without the worry she'd slice her hand open on the bait table, or make a mistake with the flying pots.

Cooper tilted his head and leaned on his mallet, watching the men leave, then up at the stack of pots that blocked the eye line to the wheelhouse. The posture registered in the corner of her eye. *Don't do it... Don't do it.* He wrapped his arms around her waist and rested his chin on her shoulder... *Fuck, he did it.*

"Get off me."

"Capt'n thinks we'll be in port in about two days," he murmured. "Then it's you, me and a bed."

Faith gritted her teeth, and an exasperated sigh. "Take your fucking hands off me, Coop." Her voice was deceptively calm. When he continued to hold her, she stepped forward, turned, and positioned the mallet between them.

He grinned what he must have thought was an ingratiating smile yet merely came across as a sleazy leer to Faith. "Come on."

"Come on, what? We went over this shit two weeks ago, just stop!"

"Oh, Christ, Faith, are we doing that again?"

"We never stopped! We had sex one night, five weeks ago, in port, when we were both shit-faced. It doesn't mean you can put your hands on me, and I've made it clear the whole thing was a huge mistake." She rolled her eyes at his stupefied expression, and turned back to her work, throttling the ice on the rail with brutal determination.

"Fuckin' bitch," he muttered under his breath. "Sure weren't so frigid when I was fucking you, now were you?"

"Fucking tiny little dick, it wasn't even worth it," she muttered under her own breath at the same time. "Goddamn asshole."

As she pounded her mad off, Faith's mind engaged once more. She needed to get off this boat and move on. It didn't happen often, but she'd broken one of her cardinal rules. No sex with a co-worker, but that night she missed her family, they'd just come off a shitty run, and she'd gotten plastered. Something which also didn't happen often.

She understood when a group of people spent months out at sea in cramped, volatile and often life-threatening conditions, they learned about each other quicker and more in depth than those in *civilian* life. Proficient at fading into the background, and observing everything around her, Faith wanted to learn how to get acknowledgment for her work ethic, not her ass. To her way of thinking, you earned respect. A nice ass just came from work, and a lot of genetics. Appreciated but not rewarded and certainly not respected. So, with twenty-eight total years of experience, she built and tested five strict rules over her career, both for herself *and* the men she worked with.

One: While at sea, she would do what it took to camouflage or tamp down the rather more interesting parts of her anatomy and blend in with the men, as much as she could.

Two: She worked on a boat for only a short duration, perhaps two to four years, and left only after she'd proven herself or if the crew dynamic didn't work.

Three: She arrived on deck first at the start of a shift and left last at the end of each shift, with perhaps exception of the deck boss.

Four: Faith shared cooking and cleaning duties but made it clear to everyone involved she would not be in charge of the domestic duties. She spoke and behaved like the men, volunteered for duties everyone hated and took her turn in every chore, like everyone else. Her skill at those mundane tasks, and fortitude of keeping up with the rest of the men, granted her respect from even the saltiest of sea dogs.

Five: She didn't flirt, kiss and under no circumstances engaged in sex with anyone, for any reason, onboard a work boat, with no exceptions. She'd bent that rule two times, with men she worked with, and even though they both happened in hotel rooms, she regretted it.

When she left the environment of work and stepped onto land, she allowed herself the freedom of womanhood, albeit a reserved one. Most of the time she left the atmosphere of the crew she worked with to do so. However, sometimes... correction, two times... she got desperate. Cooper resulted from an alcohol-induced regret. Well, that, and engaging in celibacy for two years. So, she went against her better judgement and allowed the itch inadequately scratched, after drinking the better half of a fifth of whiskey. Cooper changed after that and treated her differently ever since. As if seeing her naked brought back the caveman in him. She needed to run... or leave... yes, leave again, and do something different.

Fifteen hours later the ice cleared, the last few strings of pots collected and sorted, and the deck secure, Faith remained outdoors, smoking a cigarette. The sun pulsated with streaks of orange, magenta and gold out of the earth's horizon like a child defying its parent just one second longer before going to sleep. Sunset, her absolute favorite time of day, where just one fleeting moment of warmth and beauty, reminded her of her father. The last dregs of amber slid into the earth and the tang of the sea pervaded deep into her nostrils. She blew the smoke out of her lungs from pursed lips in a long thin stream, then gave a nod of her head, and made her way to the wheelhouse to tender her resignation.

Two days later, after they arrived in St. Paul and offloaded seventy-nine thousand pounds of Alaskan King crab, Faith left the F/V *Rosemary Sue,* eighteen thousand, six-hundred thirty-seven dollars richer for sixteen and a half days' worth of work. She disembarked to the scowls and furious faces of the crew and headed for the phones to call the most beloved man in her world.

CHAPTER 13

For Mack, the past seventeen years provided a dichotomy between loss and gain. He missed Faith. The simple presence of her, but also the compatibility, fun, excitement, and peace she brought to his life. However, he also built relationships with both of his sons they never shared earlier in their lives. Now, their schedules ran opposite of their past, and he only saw Faith in snapshots of time.

Even more of a physical presence at fifty-three then in his youth, Mack resembled a powerful locomotive. His massive arms with thick rope-like muscles, were the canvas for seven separate tattoos, including an enormous King crab, the name and image of his boat, the *Je Suis Prest*, each of his children's names, a very busty Rosie looking over her shoulder with seductive eyes and a simple wooden cross covered in fire and ice roses and emblazoned with *Pearson* in the center. His hair, a wispy, grown out mullet, cut by his own hand whenever it obstructed his vision, now held streaks of silver in it. The deep gravel of his voice mellowed into excellent whiskey poured over rough sandpaper from hard living, and a thirty-eight-year, three-pack-a-day tobacco habit. Eyes of intense icy steel, from a face covered in a week's growth of scraggy, graying beard, observed everything.

The old skipper also mellowed with age. No longer the impulsive, explosive man of his younger days, he mastered self-control and observed more than he spoke. Out of necessity, he took in a situation and made life-affecting decisions with quick authority. Now, a respected captain, known for landing crab, Mack counted among the elite of his peers.

After the catch offloaded into large nets, he sat in his worn leather captain's chair, as they cruised back out to the fishing grounds. A whiskey in hand, he gazed down from the wheelhouse at both his sons sprawled out on the decks. They engaged in some kind of half-assed wrestling match, trying to push each other's faces into the slimy codfish.

At thirty-one, Mack's eldest son, Charlie, possessed the same build as his father in his youth. Tall and muscular, with the same cool gray eyes and thick, jet black hair that tickled the length of his collar. However, his golden coloring, thick, long, dark eyelashes, high cheekbones and full lips were gifts from his mother. Despite his parents' tumultuous example in early childhood, Charlie's temper stayed even and relaxed, unless riled by his younger brother, when it exploded with retribution.

Mack's gaze shifted to Brady, who held the honor of resident brawler in the Carter clan. Mack's youngest, more high-strung and quick-tempered than his father and brother, stood taller and lankier than both too. His deep-set eyes boasted the same thick, dark lashes as his brother's, yet beheld a golden-brown hue rather than gray.

The boys drove each other to competitiveness and desired to win favor with their captain and father at all costs. Everyone who met the Carter brothers liked them, even when the butt of their practical jokes and goofiness. Something that occurred a little too often to Mack's liking.

"Enough!" the captain bellowed over the intercom. "Jesus, you both look like a couple of girls, knock it off." When Brady threw one extra punch to Charlie's arm, their father rolled his eyes. "Goddamnit, I said enough, Brady!"

As the boys skulked off, Mack returned his thoughts to Faith. The boys and she formed a united trio of siblings growing up, and they missed her as much as he did. Each year, the visits seemed fewer and more far between. They once spent enormous chunks of their summer playing, wrestling, fishing, camping and four wheeling together. Now, they communicated via phone, text, and email, and it just wasn't the same.

Once they were back on the fishing grounds and approaching their last string, a voice crackled over the radio and into Mack's thoughts.

"Mayday! Mayday! Mayday! Commsta! Commsta! Commsta! This is fishing vessel, *Battling Gabe*." Heavy static replied. He tuned in and raised the volume, when finally, the Coast Guard responded.

"Station calling, this is the United States Coast Guard, Kodiak, Alaska, communications, over."

"Oh, okay... okay... This is the fishing vessel, *Batting Gabe*. We are taking on water, it's coming on quick! Our position is..."

"Shit." Mack scowled as the terrified greenhorn captain relayed his coordinates. Mack, two hours away, could do nothing but listen. He didn't know the man well and only met him three weeks prior at the Unisea Bar. His first impression, *this kid's as green as the algae in the harbor.* He recited the traditional words for safe recovery he learned from Nels during their first season fishing together. Mack wasn't a religious man, but like every other captain, he practiced spirituality with religious fervor. Too much death and destruction occurred not to.

As the drama unfolded, another mayday crackled over the line, but this time the distinct and well-measured voice was well known to him. The *Scaup's* captain, Andy Rasmussen, and his crew loved to hold competitions with Mack and his crew. Most of the time they bet on how many crabs they caught in a single day, but were also known to bet on just about anything. An evil wind blew over the Bering Sea tonight. One of their men fell overboard without a survival suit on and three to five minutes meant life or death, and the man fell in eight minutes prior.

"Position... 58.4 degrees... Wait, hold on." Andy's voice turned stressed and agitated, "We have him, Coast Guard, repeat, we have him, standby, over."

"Fishing vessel *Scaup*, this is Commsta, Kodiak. Roger, understand man overboard retrieved. Standing by, over." The radio continued to crackle for about ten seconds before Andy came back on.

"Yeah, Coast Guard, this is *Scaup*. Jake's doing CPR, and we're trying to warm him up, but I think he's gone, over." "Fuck..." Mack drew a hand through his hair. As the Coast Guard relayed instructions, Mack switched to the other tragedy. The boat capsized, and sank into its watery tomb, but the crew all made it out alive, in survival suits and were in a life raft waiting for rescue. Mack exhaled a deep breath, but knew it would devastate Andy, to lose of one of his crew.

Two hours and several tense calls to various boats in the area later, the skipper's phone rang again. He gave it an irritated glance and muttered to himself about how much time he'd already spent on the phone and radio that morning. Trying to maneuver next to a pot, he answered the phone on the fifth ring.

"Carter," he snapped.

"Hey, Pop." Faith's voice, like a salve on his frazzled nerves, brought a genuine grin to his face.

"Hey, baby, how you doing?"

"I'm unemployed but deliriously happy." Her grin seeped through the phone, and he shifted the receiver to cradle it in the crook of his neck and shook out a cigarette. Placing it between his lips, he pulled back on the throttle, as the boat eased alongside a buoy. "Everything okay? You sound a little fried?"

"One of the fleet just lost a man." As the men scrambled to bring the pot onboard, Mack lit his cigarette and bounced his leg up and down in the seat.

"Oh, shit... how?"

"Overboard, with no survival suit. I don't know all the details yet."

"Did you know him?"

"Probably, but I don't know which one it is yet."

"Christ, I'm sorry... Are you coming in soon?"

"I've got one more string and I think we'll have her done. If we grind, we'll be back Dutch to offload the day after tomorrow, then it's two weeks off before Opilio's, baby!"

"Perfect timing."

"What, you coming out?"

"Yeah, I'll take a flight out in a couple of days. So, no rush."

"That bad, huh?" His brows creased and eyes narrowed as he feathered the throttle, and kept his eyes starboard, alert for rogue waves as the men worked the rail. The exhaustion in her voice, evident, but something else bothered her too.

"No, not bad, have you heard of anything there?"

Mack brightened. "Sure, the *Je Suis Prest* always needs a hard, able-bodied young deckhand."

"Thanks for the young part, I ain't feeling that love but you know there's no way in hell I'm working on your boat, Mack."

"Come on, I'm sure you've made your point by now, don't you think?"

"Nope."

He groaned and scrubbed a hand over his face. No use arguing. The girl possessed equal parts of her parents, either of which gave new meaning to the word, hard-headed. "Whatever, yeah, I'll ask around."

"Thanks, darlin' pop of mine," she said, voice full of sugar.

"Yeah, yeah. See ya in a few. I'll tell the boys, they'll shit."

"Yawp, I love you."

"Love you too, kid."

They both rang off, and he sat back, scrubbing a hand down his face again. Something about her voice, her incessant stubbornness, or the fact she still called him, pop, from time to time focused Mack's attention on memories of her actual father. Or maybe it's the man that just drowned at sea? He hoped now, as always, that his best friend approved of his care and keeping of Faith.

****

They arrived in Dutch Harbor at five o'clock the next morning. The *Scaup*, Andy's boat, just finished with their offload and the *Je Suis Prest,* waited next in line. Mack trained both boys on docking, and allowed Charlie to take the boat in, as Mack scanned the harbor. A police car with its lights flashing, parked close to the docks.

"The ambulance must've already left," Mack noted.

"I wonder who it was." Andy shook the cop's hand and watched the officer drive away, before ambling up to Mildred's Cafe.

"We'll find out soon enough."

As Charlie turned the engine off, the stress of keeping everyone safe and filling the boat transformed into a memory. Just then, Brady walked into the wheelhouse from outside, automatically dipping his head in the doorframe to go over the offloading procedure and schedule for those keeping track of the numbers.

"If we get that asshole Todd again, you guys have to stay right on him, Brady, okay? He screwed us out of damn near five K last time because that dipshit greenhorn left to call his girlfriend."

"You got it," Brady said. "What time does Faith land?"

"Ah, six-thirty tonight, something like that. If we're all set, you and Charlie can come, if ya want."

"Ye-ah," Brady said and left to hand out orders.

Mack stood up in the quiet room, feeling like half his ass was still stuck in the seat. As he stretched both his arms toward the ceiling, and twisted his back to work out the kinks, his eyes fell on his boat's logo and remembered the first day he'd seen it.

"Damn girl," he muttered, then quirked a smile, excited to see her. He grabbed his old bomber jacket, and Camels off the instrument panel, then shouted his intentions to his younger son, before walking toward Mildred's for a decent cup of coffee, and a chat with his friend. As Mack walked up the hill to the small café, he gazed around the snow-covered hills and could just make out the old World War II bunkers half hidden in the mountainside. He breathed in through his nose deep, creating ice crystals inside, and smelled the fresh, pure bouquet of snow on the air. He opened the door and Mildred, *Christ, she must be over a hundred now,* sat on a stool at the register, folding napkins.

"Well," she said, looking him up and down. "Look what the cat dragged in."

"Well," Mack said back, matching her tone. "Look what the angels left for me."

She giggled and gave him a big hug. After spending a few moments to catch up, Mack ordered a cup of coffee, then turned to find Andy Rasmussen sitting in a booth alone, talking into a cell phone, pissed. As Mack approached, Andy finished the call.

"No, goddamnit," He ran a hand through his receding blond hairline, leaving the top to stand up in tufts. Something he seemed to do throughout the duration of the phone call. "Dude, I'm not waiting for you to ask your mother." He hung up and scrubbed a hand over his face, then noticed Mack.

"For the love of God!" he said, holding his head. When he lifted it again, said, "Hey, Mack." He reached for his large mug of black coffee and gestured at the open seat. "How did it go out there? I saw you come in earlier."

"We got it done," he replied. "How did you guys turn out?"

"We cleared three sixty, so not bad."

"I heard ya on the bitch box two days ago and tried to get a hold of you. You all right? What happened out there?"

"Fucking John," Andy said, exasperated, then took a sip from his coffee, and leaned back in his chair. "We went north like we talked about. It's early, and we get hit with some weather, right? John's been smoking shit all morning, and I had no idea he even brought it on my clean boat." Mack remembered John was the reason the Rasmussen's made their boat clean. "He's at the rail and trips over his own goddamn feet. One foot goes into the line and instead of cutting loose, he's so fucked-up, he tries to stomp his way out of it. Just greenhorn shit." Andy gestured with his hands for emphasis. "So, he loses his balance and in he goes. Our actual greenhorn loses line of sight, so Jake runs over. It takes time, but he sees him, throws the sling. He thought the stupid prick went under the boat. We couldn't find him for five minutes, when suddenly he comes up to the surface. He was dead before we got him onboard, but we went through the protocol." Andy locked hands around his head and stared at the table for a few moments. "Not even a flicker."

Mack noticed his friend's hand shake, so, reached into his pocket and withdrew two cigarettes, offering one to Andy. Mack nodded his head but gave an imperceptible shiver himself. He knew men that perished just that way. High on dope, and falling into oblivion, not even aware of their own demise. He kept nodding as Andy relayed the rest of the story of putting him on ice and bringing him into port.

"So, now I've got to be the prick that spends two seconds thinking about the fact one of my men just lost his life, while at the same time trying to find his replacement as fast as possible before the break and Opilio's." The captain let out a long exhale. He picked up his coffee and still shaking from the nerves and fury of it.

Mack sat quietly, thinking about what John must have gone through, the same way re-lived Nels' death. High or not, upon hitting the water, his body released air from his lungs, making it harder for him to breathe. The force of the blood pushing against the walls of arteries increased, trying desperately to protect his core. Mack closed his eyes a moment and remembered the rest of the chart in the safety class. The vital organs all syphoning blood and energy from the limbs, rendering them useless, until it lost its ability to generate heat through shivering. John's body, not coherent in the first place, more than likely died of a massive coronary after the first five minutes. *A fucked up way to buy it.*

"How many horns you got?" Mack asked, understanding his friend's need to talk logistics, rather than feelings.

Relieved, Andy all but spat out, "One, and I'm not having two. I got Jake, Booker, Tristan and Brandon, but I'm not having another damn greenhorn with no training going into that weather. Not after this." He picked up his mug again and drank deep. "So, I was trying to find..." He waved a hand in a helpless gesture. "... someone. You haven't heard of anyone looking?"

"No, man, we're just coming in too. I haven't even been to the bar yet and..." Mack stopped and looked at Andy.

With twenty-six years behind the captain's wheel, Andy remained in good shape. A proud Norwegian with an old soul, his clear, blue intelligent eyes observed Mack with expectation. Faith's surrogate father's mind raced with possibilities.

Andy inherited the *Scaup* along with his brother, Jake, when their father died eight years earlier. However, the older man taught Andy to take over the operation when he turned twenty-two, and the man ran a tight, safe ship. Mack drank beers with all the men who worked onboard too, and maybe, except for Booker, respected each one. However, as far as superstitious captains went, Andy, like his father, ranked among the highest. Coming off the bad karma he invariably thought he now possessed, Mack needed to tread carefully. Andy also knew of Faith and that she fished and belonged to Mack. The *Je Suis Prest* skipper recalled a conversation with the man, who implied he'd never take a woman on, no matter what the circumstances. Despite all that information, the match seemed ideal for all involved, so Mack tried to work it out in his head quick.

"What?" Andy asked with hopeful anticipation. "Do you know someone?"

"Yeah, actually, I think I might." Mack sipped his coffee, and took a deep drag off his cigarette, playing for time. "I got a call the other day from a crabber, I know. Been in and around the business about twenty-five years."

"Really?" Andy's attention piqued.

"Yeah, practically grew up on a boat," Mack said, steering clear of gender, nor correcting Andy's assumption, Faith was male. "One of the best I've seen. Devoted to making money and hauling ass."

"Okay. Wow. Can you throw him anywhere?"

"Yawp, works and knows every job onboard, engineer, deck boss, deckhand, and no qualms about getting dirty." This last statement characterized Faith's ability to not complain, and the implication of her capability at any job, but didn't feel above prepping or hanging bait. Andy's eyes lit, like a hunter circling its prey, and smiled.

"Okay, now the tough question." Andy leaned back in the booth. "When can he get here?"

"It's funny you should ask, I just got a call the other night, that's why I didn't think of it right away. Plane gets in tonight. You around, or are you and Jake going straight home for the break?" Mack asked somewhat hopeful they already occupied a flight home, and unable to meet Faith in the flesh, until right before the season started. A man could dream.

Most seasoned veterans worth their salt already held positions with a particular boat, going into Opilio's. Rougher seas from winter storms with more ice and freezing spray to build up on a boat, Opilio season resulted in more danger for the fleet. Having one inexperienced deckhand or greenhorn might be okay, but a captain needed veterans to come aboard and acclimate in haste. If Andy just agreed, Mack might postpone the inevitable discovery of Faith's gender for just a while longer.

"No, as it happens, with John and the complete mess, we postponed until tomorrow. Kylie..."

"Kylie?"

"John's girlfriend will be here in an hour, and it's going to be rough, since she thought he was clean again. Wanna all meet up for a drink later at Unisea, after I'm done talking with her?" Resigned, Mack gave a reluctant nod, and Andy relaxed back

171

in his seat with a chuckle. "Great. Like I said, we fly back tomorrow. If we stayed any longer, the women in our lives would come uncorked on us for sure. Are you going to meet up with Nels' girl this year?"

Before Mack answered, Andy's cell phone rang. John's girlfriend arrived early and saved Mack from having to lie. "I gotta get back too and make sure my boys aren't playing video games instead of watching the scales."

"Sounds good. Hey..." Andy stuck out a hand, which Mack shook. "Thanks man, I appreciate this, you just saved my life." He went through the door, then held it open for Mack.

"Oh, no problem," Mack muttered and felt like a shit at the deception, yet still couldn't help a tiny smile from surfacing.

CHAPTER 14

As the two skippers parted ways to go to their respective ships, Andy stepped a little lighter and breathed a sigh of pure relief. He trusted Mack's judgment. His old friend sent many fishermen their way over the years, and most made huge contributions to their family's organization. Whoever the guy, his friend wouldn't recommend him unless he delivered.

After consoling John's distraught girlfriend, the *Scaup* captain just wanted to get someone hired and get back to his wife, Debbie, and their three girls before Christmas. The season, long and arduous, culminating in the death of one of their own, left his nerves raw and his waning. Elated he didn't have to spend the entire holiday break on the phone disrupting other families and getting divorced in the process, Andy smiled, and whistled an old Norwegian ballad his mother taught him, breath encircling his head.

The delicious heat of the wheelhouse nearly caused him to moan in ecstasy. His brother sat in his captain's chair, feet up on the instrument panel, and head laid back on the seat with his eyes closed, blowing smoke rings.

In polite company, their mother liked to call Jake, nine years junior to Andy, her inspiration, which sounded a lot better than a surprise pregnancy at thirty. Even though he stood, six-foot, four-inches tall, the younger Rasmussen tended to look more like a deckhand, strong and muscular but lean. Where his brother and captain carried a little more around his middle, and stretched up to only an above average five-eleven height. Jake craved physical activity. He ran the deck, fixed the machinery and hung out with people. Andy, a classic first-born son, worried the seas, and the men on the rail. Uptight to a fault about his responsibilities, he excelled on the bridge, and his men considered him more of a loner. Andy never experienced the relaxed, laid-back, and charismatic nature which came so easy to his brother.

"Having fun?" Andy asked. "Don't think you'll be taking that seat anytime soon."

Jake didn't open his eyes or hesitate, "Naw, I work for a living and you owe me fifty-five K, right?"

"You want that in tens and twenties?"

Jake chuckled, sat up in the chair and peered over at his brother with deep sapphire blue eyes. His light, golden-brown hair, thicker than the captain's, much to the latter's chagrin, needed a haircut. His weathered, handsome face sprouted a five-day beard, which only made him more attractive to every woman he met.

Andy could never hold it against him, though. He and his perfect bride just celebrated their twenty-fifth wedding anniversary, his hellish days of dating behind him. Plus, the men shared a strong, mutual love and respect for each other, that only brothers understood.

"So, that was fun." Jake noted about the season. "What the fuck happened?"

"Did you know he was back on that shit?"

"It's weird, I never even had an inkling this time. Booker said he'd acted funny on deck and confronted him but..."

"Why am I just hearing about this now? We talked about it all night, last night. Why the fuck didn't he say anything then?"

"I think he was a little freaked. Man barely said two words, but I can tell you it's why he wasn't standing next to John. He was coming over to tell me and when we turned around, Masterson was already in the water. Tristan ran over, but it was too late, he couldn't see him."

Andy took off his coat, hung it on a peg, then walked over to grab a weather report. He sat down in the chair next to his brother and let out a long breath.

"Well, what are we gonna do?"

"I think we've got a solid line on someone else."

"Now?" Jake jerked his head back with disbelieving eyes. "Tell me you didn't just entrust our season to some pimply, pre–med college puke, looking for adventure?"

"No. I called around and thought that's where we were headed, though. Mack has someone, a friend of his that's seasoned and coming in tonight, looking for work."

"If he's seasoned and worth a damn, why's he looking now?"

"I didn't ask, and he didn't say."

"Jesus, Andy, it could be anyone. You were so pumped about someone, you didn't ask, did you?"

"All right, how many guys has Mack sent us, five... six? And besides that one, which wasn't even Mack's fault, they've all worked out. Hell, he got us Tristan. This guy'll be here around ten and we're going to meet up over at Unisea. If either of us doesn't have a good feel for him, we won't take him, and we'll still have plenty of time to try and find someone else. So, top crawling up my ass." Andy scanned the deck and empty balers. "Are we all done down there?"

"Yeah, we're set," Jake answered. "Brandon, Tristan and Book are at the bar, waiting for me to drive them all to the airport in a couple hours." "Well, all right, let's go." Andy balled up the weather report and banked it into the trash can as Jake grabbed their coats. He handed one to his brother, and they each armed their way into them, before stepping out onto the icy decks, just as it started to snow again.

****

With matching bored expressions, each of the Carter men eyed the drones filing off the small plane. Men in monotone plaid shirts, heavy jeans and quilted down vests, all shuffling to pick up bags. Most wore boots and stocking caps and full-grown beards.

Out of the pack came a flurry of activity and a massive amount of long red curls trailing behind a radiant smile and a face glowing with excitement. Faith dropped her bag and launched herself into Brady's outstretched arms, wrapping her arms and legs around his neck and waist. Charlie sandwiched her between, and flung his arms around them both, sinking his face into her hair.

Mack hung back, a prideful smile scoring his face. Two long years passed since all his kids occupied the same space, even then just for a long weekend. In fact, five years passed since he'd spent any quality alone time with Faith at all, and hoped she wanted to stay for a while.

She drew back from Brady and kissed him squarely on the mouth, then did the same thing to Charlie before her eyes searched and connected with his. Her face lit up like the first day of spring on the water.

"Oh my God!" she yelled and ran for him, repeating the process. He held her a long time, not wanting to set her down, and breathed in her soap and lavender scent.

"You look great, darlin'," Mack said and kissed her forehead, throwing an arm around her shoulders as she threw hers around his waist. They walked down the corridor as the boys trailed behind.

"Holy shit, look at that shake," Charlie said loud and emphatic. "Now that's an ass!"

"I like her rack," Brady said, grinning as her shoulders tensed and hunched. "Holy shit."

"Shut up." She shot over her shoulder, then did a double take at her muscular brothers. "You two look like hammered shit, when's the last time you went to a gym?

"Yeah, kiss my ass," Brady said.

"Kiss mine," Faith said, giving it a wiggle. "It's righteous, didn't ya know?"

After stowing her gear in the truck, Mack drove them down Gilman Road toward town and the Unisea Inn to check in. They all decided to spend the brief holiday in Dutch Harbor, rather than travel back to Seattle.

"When does Rose fly in?" Faith asked.

"Tomorrow." Mack's truck devoured the slushy road, as the snow fell in thick flakes. "So, I think I got something for you."

"A job?"

"Yeah, they're in a bind, and you said you wanted a change of scene, right?" He side-eyed her, while the boys tried not to laugh in the back seat. He narrowed his eyes at them through the rear-view mirror, causing them to quiet, but Faith's antennae engaged at the exchange.

"Right," she said apprehensively, then shifted her whole body to face him. "You told them I was a girl, right, Mack?"

"Oh, I told them all about you darlin', and how long you've worked in the industry. How well respected you are and stuff."

"Mack," she said, as if speaking to an unstable two-year-old. She smelled a large rat driving the truck. "You told them, right? You know how skips get." The boys burst out laughing, as the gig was officially up. "You didn't tell him, did you?" She whipped the back of her hand hard against his shoulder.

"Ow."

"Jesus Mack, you did not do this to me."

"Do what? Help you find a job," he said, voice rising. Better angry than guilty. "No, thanks, Pop, for helping me out?"

"Thanks for helping me out?" she parroted.

"*You* did it before."

"One time to get me started. Christ, this guy's a case too, isn't he?" She jerked a thumb back toward the boys. "Judging by the two morons in the backseat, he is. Right, Mack? Off-the-wall, superstitious freak!" Frustrated, she sniped, "Now I'm supposed to go in there, right? With him all excited thinking he's got some kick-ass veteran *man*, and I show up with my tits and twat." Laughter exploded from her brothers as Mack winced. "He's going to shit his pants."

"Jesus Christ, Faith, do you have to be so fucking crude?"

"Ah, yeah, because I grew up with a bunch of slobbering Neanderthals with absolute potty mouths. Even sweet innocent girls, such as myself, get a little jaded. And you," she said, punching him hard in the arm again.

"Ow, damn it."

"You have just made my life ten times harder." She slammed back in her seat, arms crossed against her chest, sulking as she turned toward the window. However, he could almost swear he saw a teeny little smile.

****

By the time she checked in, unpacked and showered, then received Mack's message calling her downstairs, the clock read eleven thirty-seven. Her prospective boss and his brother just arrived in the bar after dropping off their deckhands at the airport.

She dressed in baggy jeans, a gray tee-shirt, gray oversized *Je Suis Prest* hoodie, boots and ball cap, before grabbing her room key and heading to the bar.

The hazy, smoke-filled room reeked of deep-fried foods, smoke and hops. Her brothers faced each other on opposite ends of the bar, both talking to ugly women, engrossed in their every word. Charlie faced toward her, she caught his eye, and smiled, before shaking her head. *You go, bro.* A cool, calculating smile answered her.

Mack sat with two men, both facing away from her. *You chicken shit, you sat them like that on purpose.* He said nothing as she walked around into their field of vision. Without a doubt, he tried to keep up the charade as long as he could. Both men raised their eyes and smiled at her approach. The older man, handsome in a quiet way, looked about fifty. Maybe even mid-fifties, with his weather-beaten face. A quiet, commanding presence of a man that takes everything in before deciding. The skipper, no doubt. The other man, maybe late thirties, early forties, could only be described as crazy good-looking. A man who resembled Brad Pitt and Rob Lowe rolled together, usually sat pretty high on the conceited-arrogant-asshole scale. She smiled back at the men, and only then did the skipper seem to realize he beheld a girl.

"Oh no, I think we're good here, thanks sweetheart," Andy said, mistaking her for the waitress and darted a questioning gaze back at the men. "Unless anyone needs another round?"

Faith drew in a deep, irritated breath, lifted her chin and peered down her nose at Jake, who gazed back with a hesitant twitch at the corner of his mouth. *Oh, yeah, he's getting it.* At least she'd give him marks for *some* intelligence.

Squaring her shoulders, she shifted her eyes back to Andy and stuck out a hand. "Actually, I'm Faith. Mack says you're looking for a seasoned deckhand to help you through the winter, that right?"

Confused, Andy stared first at her face, then her chest region, then at her outstretched hand. In complete bewilderment, he checked Mack's face, then his brother's.

Jake, long legs sprawled out in front of him, an elbow on the table, and hand supporting his chin, serpentined a slow, genuine smile across his face. He flicked his index finger up over his lips and used only his eyes to measure his brother's reaction. Since the skipper didn't appear to snap out of it any time soon, his younger brother outstretched his own hand, and shifted his gaze back up to Faith.

"That's right. I'm Jakob Rassmussen, deck boss. You can call me Jake. This is my brother, Andy, he's capt'n." *Rasmussen,* the name sounded familiar. They shook hands and Jake returned his observation to Andy, whose face started to turn colors. A gurgle of laughter escaped from the younger man, before covering it up with a cough. Mack never stopped peering into his drink.

"Oh, for chrissake!" Faith said, disgusted, and all three men jerked their attention to her, as if slapped. "My father," she gestured at Mack, "is an asshole. It's not his fault, he was just born that way. He didn't tell me about any of this," -she waved a hand at them and the table- "until I got here, a little over an hour ago."

She flicked an accusatory glare at Mack, who had the excellent sense to stay quiet. "Look, I don't have time for any of your good-ole-boy superstitious bullshit. I've lived on a crab boat since I was eight-years-old. I became a full share deckhand at sixteen, and I've worked as deck boss and as an engineer." Her glare now fell on Jake, who stared back in fascination. "I just left my last job because it was time for a change, not because I couldn't hack it. I work well on the hydraulics, stack, rail, bait, wherever the fuck you want to put me. I'm a fast learner and I don't expect to find your boat to be the space shuttle. Either you want me or not. I'll be on the pier tomorrow at seven a.m., so you have the night to decide. Right now, I'm tired and I want to go to bed."

She grabbed Jake's drink, the closest and fullest, with three fingers of some strange, yet horrific alcohol, she discovered. Nevertheless, she drained it in one large gulp, turned on her heel and left the bar. All three men stared in her wake, open-mouthed. Her stomach roiled by the time she got upstairs, and puked.

"What the hell was in that?" she asked out loud. *The idiot didn't even have the sense to drink whiskey.* She shuddered with disgust and lifted a hand to her mouth and the lingering taste of vomit and licorice, before sitting down next to the toilet, and flinging her arm across the closed lid. At least the first pissing match went to her. She reached up and grabbed her toothbrush off the counter, smiled for a few seconds, then put a hand back on her stomach as it roiled again, then lifted the lid for another digestive pyrotechnic experience.

When she woke at her customary four a.m. for a long run, coffee and a western-style omelet, she felt like herself again. She dressed and made her way to the *Scaup,* with most of the boats remaining in the harbor, waiting their turn to offload or clean up, before the brief break. Mack informed her before they met, her would-be employers always did a quick head-to-toe inspection before leaving for the airport. She rolled her shoulders back. *Here we go.*

****

The Rasmussen boat, a one hundred-thirty-seven-foot -foot fishing vessel, close in capacity for pots and crab storage to Mack's, rather contained a wheelhouse-forward, then house aft. Faith climbed onboard, just as Jake came out onto the deck above her. She sure hadn't softened up at all and stood glaring up at him. She rolled her shoulders, squaring herself up for yet another battle. He threw both hands up in surrender, and the tension broke. Chuckling despite herself, she shook her head as he walked down the steps toward her.

"I know, I know, I'm sorry," she said, not looking sorry in the slightest.

"Wow, lying to the boss right off. That's ball-sey." He grinned at her. "You knew exactly what you were doing last night. So, hat's off to you. How'd that absinthe taste?"

"Is that what it was? I thought it would be whiskey," she admitted. "Jury's out on if it was better going down or coming up." She raised her eyebrows, then scanned the deck. "And just to set the record straight, Mack really did not tell me anything about what he'd done until about an hour prior."

"Well, after you left, the two of them went four or five rounds." He smiled at the memory. "Hell, we knew Mack had some weird arrangement involving a daughter. We even knew you fished, but never saw you around. Where ya been hiding all these years?"

"It's not that strange. Mack became my father after my real dad died." She stated it so bluntly, he didn't question the validity of the statement. "When I turned twenty, I wanted to prove myself and go it on my own. Usually, I offload at Kodiak, the floating processors, or further down the chain. But I've also spent some time off the east coast. Fishing for swordfish with the Gloustermen."

"Gloustermen? They're hardcore." Surprised, his eyes took in her appearance, now that the full light of day beamed on her. Attractive... with all those freckles and exotic-looking eyes. The hair that peaked out of her stocking cap ignited to red flame as the sun struck it. She packed on a little more flesh, but as long as it didn't hinder her stamina or performance, he didn't see any issues with it, and daughter or no, Mack wouldn't have set his name to her if she wasn't exactly what he said. Technically, he never lied to Andy, a point made often the night before.

"So, what's the verdict here?" She slipped on a pair of Ray-Bans.

"Well, Andy and I talked about it for a while last night and we'd both *love* to have you join us on the *Scaup* this winter for Opilios." No way would he portray the actual content of their conversation.

"Uh-huh." Her vivid eyes scanned his from behind the sunglasses. "Now who's lying?"

He chuckled again and raised both hands. "Okay, well, I'd love it because we need the help. Andy's kind of on a trial run with you." He twisted one hand back and forth, while looping his other thumb in a belt loop. "He's always been kind of superstitious when it comes to fishing. Gets it from our dad."

"But you're not?"

"Not nearly as much as my brother. I did some checking, and you're pretty well respected. If the earth doesn't come and swallow us up whole, you can stay after the first turnaround. It's the best you're gonna get from Andy, and I'd take it before he changes his mind. Deal?"

"Sure." She looked around the deck again, then back at him. "Maybe you aren't such a conceited prick." "Sorry?"

"Just saying, maybe I was wrong, too." Speechless, he tried to think of a clever retort, when she said, "I understand you're running a system check this morning, want some help?"

"Ah, sure." A little surprised he hadn't thought of that, but what better way to appraise her knowledge and ability. She followed him below to the engine room, where he handed her some ear protection, and over the course of the next three hours she left no doubt in his mind about her abilities.

****

Debbie Rasmussen, Andy's wife, picked them up at SeaTac airport and caught them up on the going's on at home, as well as the Christmas holiday agenda.

"So, I asked your mom what she wanted to do this year, and she said dinner at her house. Is that okay?" Debbie asked in her soft, girlish voice, then eyed Jake with cornflower blue eyes in the rearview mirror.

A petite woman, with a cap of golden blonde hair, and what could only be described as a perky personality, Jake adored his sister-in-law. It took a special woman to succeed as a fisherman's wife. Withstanding the months of solitude, and knowing the danger her husband experienced, most women found themselves incapable of the sacrifice, and didn't last long in a relationship. The profession also brought havoc to the family unit. However, Debbie raised their three girls, Calie, Analisha and Megan, essentially alone most of the year, and did it well.

"Sounds great to me," Jake replied from the back seat, eagerly awaiting a hot shower and an ice-cold beer. "I'm easy." "Yeah, I've heard that about you." Debbie giggled and her eyes softened as Andy raised her hand up to his lips, to brush a kiss across her knuckles.

****

Christmas morning, Linda Rasmussen opened the door to Jake, the last to arrive for dinner.

"Hello, darling," she crooned as he leaned in to kiss her cheek. "We still have about twenty minutes until dinner. So, fix yourself a drink and come into the kitchen." Linda, also a petite woman, would never be described as perky. She contained an air of sophisticated class that surrounded her like perfume, and she governed her family the same way, even when her headstrong husband still drew breath.

Elliott, stoic and commanding, knew better than to return home and try to impose his will over her domain. Her hair transitioned into white, and her clear eyes that twinkled the color of a cadet's uniform missed nothing.

Jake strode over to the bar, shook Andy's hand and kissed Debbie on the cheek. Their girls ran to launch themselves into their uncle's arms, and he kissed each one, before fixing himself a drink. By the time they sat down for dinner, the clock clicked into the six o'clock hour, and they clasped hands, closing a circle, and intoned in unison:

"Bless us, O Lord, and these thy gifts which we are about to receive, from thy bounty, through Christ, our Lord. Amen. So may it ever be." Then they all squeezed hands and filled their plates. The discussion soon fell to the men's impending season and the circumstances that led up to their new deckhand.

"John..." Linda said. "What a waste of a life. So utterly senseless. Who did you find to replace him?"

"Oh," Debbie sang. "You aren't going to believe this, Mom." Linda smiled and turned her attention to her eldest son.

"Well, we were shorthanded, and I thought I was going to spend these two weeks calling people, trying to find someone that knew their ass from their elbow."

"Language, Andreas," Linda said serenely, pronouncing each syllable. "Only at the table is all that I ask."

"Sorry, Mom," Andy said. "So, I see Mack and..."

"Mack Carter?" Linda asked.

"Yeah, do you remember him?"

"Yes."

"So, he said he had a guy..."

"No." Jake smiled, slicing a piece of ham. "He said he *knew* someone."

"Fine," Andy said, exasperated. "He said he knew someone that would be awesome. That they'd lived and worked on a boat for like twenty years or something. So, of course, I'm thinking he's been in the business for decades, knows what it' about and all is great." He paused, the green bean casserole on his fork hovering next to his mouth, and looked at his mother. She waited for the punch line. "It turns out to be some girl he adopted or something. A girl! Dad would flip his lid if he knew that."

The table erupted into talk and riveted, Linda transported herself back to a conversation she'd had with her husband all those years ago. Home just two weeks, he set the phone in its cradle, as she walked into the room. His friend, Nels Pearson, died in the waters just off Sweden. He told her Nels had a little girl who'd already lost her mother and grandparents, and lived on the boat with him at only eight years of age.

She remembered how Elliott behaved back then. He believed the girl brought unwelcome karma to the boat and to Nels. She, of course, thought the idea preposterous, and just agonized for the child and remembered the look of utter hopelessness and loss in the girl's eyes at her father's funeral. She always admired Mack for taking up the reigns and caring for the orphan. And now, that little girl's all grown-up and part of her son's crew. What kind of woman must she be? No, her husband would have prevented her from setting a toe on his boat, but her sons didn't. Pride bubbled inside her.

"What does she look like, Uncle Jake?" Calie asked.

"Well, she's kinda good-looking, but chunky."

"Chunky" Analisha asked. "How can she work on the boat? Won't she get tired?"

"Good point," Andy retorted.

"Why does she want to work on that disgusting boat, anyway?" Megan said.

"Megan!" Analisha said. "Don't call Daddy's boat disgusting."

"Do you think she's pretty, Daddy?" Calie asked Andy.

"Yeah," asked Debbie. "Do you think she's pretty, Daddy?"

"Hell, no," Andy glared at his brother for even suggesting the topic. "She's dumpy and's got a lot of sass in her."

"Language, Andreas," Linda warned.

****

The holidays flew by for Faith and the Carters, too. They ate Christmas dinner in the Chart Room at the Grand Aleutian Hotel, then rang in the New Year aboard the *Je Suis Prest* on a small excursion along the northern part of the Aleutian Islands. Faith enjoyed the time she spent with family. Too much time passed, since they all hung out together and she missed it. In a day or two, the fishermen would return to their boats. In fact, she expected the *Scaup's* crew back in two days' time.

Mack drawn away on a call, and Rosie already in bed, Faith found herself alone with her brothers, drinking nightcaps, with things on her mind.

"So, how have things been going with Dad?" Faith asked.

"Good," Charlie answered. "Becoming a hermit but okay."

"What about you guys... seeing anyone?"

"No," Brady said. "The last one I went out with was nice, but not ready to settle down yet."

"I settle down with a new one every night," Charlie bragged.

"Stop it," Faith scolded.

"Come on, I'm just kidding. Everyone's so..." He waved his hand in the air and didn't finish his thought. "What about you?"

"What, seeing anyone?"

"Well that, and how are you feeling about the new set-up?"

"First, no, I'm not seeing anyone, nor do I have any interest in seeing anyone. Your gender are pigs."

"Thank you," Brady quipped, rubbing his nails on his shirt, then holding them up to admire them. "My pleasure. And two, I don't know what to think about those guys. What do you know about them?"

"Andy's a class act," Charlie said. "The rest of the guys are cool. I don't know their horn very well."

"Yeah, I don't either," Brady confirmed. "Had a couple beers with him, but that's it. Jake's cool, though."

"Can't he bench like three hundred?"

"Something like that. He does like to fuck a lot of women, so keep your hair in your hat." Brady snorted at his own joke.

Charlie laughed too, before adding, "Oh, and Booker... you are going to hate him."

"Oh man, he's a first-rate dickhead," Brady confirmed again. "One of those guys that doesn't get that he isn't tall, good-looking, or has a personality."

"Oh, one of those guys." She laughed.

Two days later, she woke early, and padded to the bathroom to relieve herself and brush her teeth, when the phone rang.

"Pearson," she said.

"Hey, want to go for a run?" Charlie asked.

"Yeah, you ready now."

"I'll be down in five."

"Okay, see ya in the lobby." She made it in four, alert and ready, wearing head-to-toe black spandex, and a down periwinkle-blue running vest. With most of the fisherman still gone, she dressed for comfort. The sun still shone, but an ominous black to the north bruised the sky's canvas, promising a new storm front shortly. Faith secured her wool beanie to keep her ears warm and hold back her long red braid. The duo fell into the easy five-mile pattern they'd shared their entire lives. Snow packed deep on the roads yet lay in tufts along hillside. The cold bare branches of the trees, spidered out black as winter closed its grasp on the small harbor and town.

"Man, it got cold overnight." Charlie puffed as he kept pace with her, his nose and cheeks red with the effort.

"Yeah, it's gonna make for an interesting season." She glanced at him when he wheezed. "Jesus, Charlie, how much you smoke these days? You sound like old Mr. Campbell, remember?"

"Shut up, it's cold, and I haven't been running a lot." After a few more yards, he asked, "Hey, you want to take the summer off this year?"

"Why?" She panted. "What are you guys up to now?"

"No." He laughed. "Nothing bad, Dad just said something about it the other night. It could be kinda cool to take a breather and just hang out together. We could go up to Ross Lake, catch some fish, hang out at the cabin. I don't know, it's been a while and Ma wants to see ya, too."

She smiled and picked up the pace to run up a hill. "Yeah, that would be a lot of fun. I'm in if you guys want to do that."

He grinned and increased his pace to move in front of her. Their competitive nature surged forward, and raced the last half mile to the hotel.

CHAPTER 15

Jake, Andy and Brandon, a fellow deckhand, flew in earlier than expected. The skipper dropped off the childhood friends and co-workers at the Unisea hotel to check the crew in for two days to get the boat ready for the arduous season. They stood at the desk talking as they waited for their keys. Brandon, a new father of two months, was telling Jake another fun story. The deck boss, his greatest weakness being children, got a kick out of watching the pride on his old friend's face.

"Did you at least bring pictures?" He grabbed their keys and turned around to head up to their rooms, as Brandon patted at his pockets.

Jake snickered and rolled his eyes around the room when his gaze fell on a leggy redhead, with an incredible ass encased in spandex, holding a purplish-blue vest, heading away from him toward the elevators.

"Come on." Jake pulled Brandon's shirt and walked down the corridor.

"Wait, I haven't got them out yet. Oh, here they are." He pulled them from a front zipper pocket. "Damn, Jake, what's the rush?" He glanced down the corridor where Jake's attention seemed captivated and noticed the tall redhead. "Oh."

Neither man saw her face, facing the opposite direction and too far ahead of them, with a guy no less, but as she turned and jumped onto the elevator, neither men had time to spare for her face and groaned.

"Oh, man... Nice rack," Brandon said, and Jake sent him a reproachful expression.

"You're married to an incredible hottie and have a perfect brand-new, kid. Don't you think it's time to spread some wealth, dude? Besides, if you ever talk like that again, I'm telling Amy and she'll kick your hairy ass."

Brandon chuckled. "As if you're so deprived."

"I am alone in this world." He slapped a hand to his chest. "And need an excellent woman, with a great ass, to take care of me and stroke my hair after a season."

"Yeah right, it's your hair you want stroked," Brandon retorted. "It's funny, I never remember you having a problem getting women, Jake. Remember the Knutson twins? I mean, how fucked up do you have to be to have sex with a guy with your twin sister? That's just weird, right?"

Jake gave a theatrical sigh. "Yeah, they weren't very wholesome. I feel kind of used and dirty." He frowned as the doors closed on the elevator.

"Ah, the tragedy of it all." Brandon laughed. "You want to sit around and wait for her to come down again?"

"No, I'll need to find another wholesome girl somewhere."

"Well, we *do* have a new deckhand," Brandon suggested. "Didn't you say she's a little granola-ly?"

"She's *not* my type, bro."

"Oh, she said, no?" Brandon waggled his eyebrows, and Jake raised his. "Since when did you have a type, anyway? And what is it, exactly?"

"Um, Mr. Rasmussen? Jake?" The desk clerk from California, with long caramel hair, huge blue eyes, and large grapefruit breasts, pouring out of a fuzzy V-neck sweater, bounced up to them. Flirting with the deck boss throughout check-in, she now held out a yellow post-it with one hand, while flipping her hair around with the other. Her high girlish voice rushed out in a babble. "Ah, that get-together I was telling you about with me and my girlfriends? Well, if you want, we could pick you up tonight." Her eyes darted to Brandon, then leaned in and laid a hand on his boss's arm.

Jake glanced over at Brandon too, who crossed himself behind her back and shook his head. He narrowed his eyes at his best friend and eyed the underage girl. "I'm so sorry sweetheart, I've gotta work tonight and..." He added, as she geared up for another attack, "I'm out of commission until after the season and you're eighteen, sorry."

"Well, maybe when you come in to offload, I can change your mind." She squeezed his bicep and stared into his eyes, unblinking, and tried a pouty grin, then turned and wiggled away. He exhaled a breath of relief, and chanced a glance at Brandon, who waggled his eyebrows at him again.

"Shut up... I'm telling Amy." He held out his hand for Brandon's picture and grinning leafed through them.

****

Faith and Charlie stepped off the elevator and headed for their separate rooms to shower. She scanned her card in the door, then walked in, kicked off her shoes and stripped down to bare skin. She turned on the shower, removed her watch and went to set it on her nightstand when the message light blinked on her phone and she bent to retrieve it.

"Hey Faith, its Andy. Jake, Brandon, and I just got in. It's about six thirty. When you get this come down to the boat, we'll go over stuff, get contracts signed and get some things started, okay. See you soon, bye."

She glanced down at the watch she just set down. He finished the message just as she walked in. She wanted to start on the right note, so rushed through her shower, dressed and arrived in the marina twenty minutes later.

Outside, the sun shone, but she clamped her down jacket around her a little more. Damp hair escaped around her ears a little, allowing the frigid wind in. She pulled her hat down a little more and breathed in through her nose. The pungent sea, decomposing fish and bait in dumpsters, came alive in her nostrils. Almost at the docks, someone called her name and she turned around to see Jake and another man walking toward her.

"Hey, Faith," Jake said, rubbing his gloved hands together, a little breathless from the cold. "This is my good friend and fellow deckhand, Brandon Meade."

Faith looked at the man, who sized her up in return. At forty, Brandon possessed average height

196

and a powerful body, albeit somewhat relaxed into a comfortable softness around the middle. A beard made his homely features comforting, and his dark eyes seemed to sparkle under his cap. Faith liked him immediately and shook his proffered hand. He raised his eyebrows, as if not expecting the reality of her presence at all.

The trio, along with Andy, moved through a thirteen-hour day filled with system checks in the engine room, hydraulics, electrical, water systems and instrumentation panel onboard. Every vital organ the boat needed for health, and to create a safe journey for the harder season fell under scrutiny.

At the day's conclusion, the senior deckhands went back to the inn to clean up, then head out to the airport to pick up the remaining deck hands, Booker and Tristan. Andy stayed to organize and clean out the wheelhouse, and left two hours later, exhausted. As he walked past the *Je Suis Prest* he glanced over to see Faith, head bent, working hard to help Charlie and Brady repair part of their own sorting table. He couldn't deny the woman's dedication or stamina.

****

The next morning continued from where the first left off, except for a much earlier start. Jake introduced Faith to the greenhorn, a Californian named, Tristan Bailey. A sweet twenty-year-old kid, strong and eager, Tristan's young, angular face, possessed the deep tan of one raised in a warm climate. His dishwater blond hair, streaked by the sun and surf, curled around his face, and his impressionable hazel eyes, displayed a readiness to get back on the water for part two of his first full season.

Oh, yeah, Faith grinned, *he's infected by the bug.* Excited about her new crew, Faith yearned to go fishing in a way she hadn't for a long time... then she met Booker.

Christopher Mariano, better known as Booker. Mack informed her the night before that at thirty-eight, the man didn't have much to show for his life, except a lot of DUIs, some misdemeanors for fighting and one felony conviction for drug possession. His small head and thick neck, covered with dark wiry curls, blended into and out of an uncontrolled beard which turned into a thicket of black chest hair. It left Faith wondering if he ever truly evolved from the caveman days. His eyes, so small and dark, appeared black, and pierced through her. Where she liked her other crew members, her visceral feeling for this man hovered around distrust and dislike.

Booker, a man who seemed to like bathing his body odor in cologne rather than water, leered up at her. Up because his stature measured several inches shorter than Faith's, to his obvious chagrin. He tried to see through her clothes, rather than look her in the eye for the entire length of their first meeting.

"Hey, Faith, you're sure a cute little thing, aren't ya?" he asked. Knowing it petty, she took great delight in stretching to her full six feet and ignored his question by sticking out her hand instead.

"Nice to meet you... Christopher, was it?" she asked.

"Yep, that's what the bitch named me." He guffawed at his own inappropriate joke, then frowned, drawing his bushy eyebrows together when Faith didn't see the immediate charm in it. He locked his gaze on her nondescript bosom and baggy clothes. "Personally, I like my middle name, Donato, it means, *given by God.*" He gave her an ingratiating smile.

She snorted. "You're kidding, right?" The rest of the men laughed at her response.

"No, I'm not kidding!" he said, mood shifting from lasciviousness to pure maliciousness. "Look it up." His face reddened as the men continued to laugh. "You're a little thick, ain't ya? I tried to be nice before, but you aren't any prize, as far as I can see. Maybe lose a few bricks, someone like me might take a second look, but as it stands now, I'm not even sure how your gonna keep up with us."

The other three men shifted, as if thinking the same thing, yet too well-mannered to voice it. They all waited to see Faith's reaction and to their surprise, she howled. In fact, she laughed so long and hard, knowing Booker tried in vain to figure out if she laughed at him, or what he said.

"Oh, God," she said, wiping tears from her eyes. "God, that was funny." Faith turned to him in all seriousness before she smirked. "And an enormous relief to me, thank you."

"What?"

"That I'm not looking for a repugnant, narcissistic little man with an IQ of fifty and clearly a very tiny prick." She bit her lip, causing her shallow dimples to appear. "It's such a colossal relief to me that pressure is off." The men roared out their glee. "Whew, wow." She smiled at him and, still chuckling, walked inside to get some scrub brushes.

****

Jake knew Booker still tried to work out what "repugnant" or "narcissistic" meant, and chuckled. *Damn it, I'm liking this girl more and more.* He walked past the sputtering Italian to help Faith.

They scrubbed and cleaned the boat from the inside out, then started the laborious and often tedious process of inspecting the mesh on the pots.

Tristan sat next to Jake, asking every question known to man about the pots. "What size is a normal-sized crab pot?"

"About ten foot by ten foot by thirty-inch."

"How does it work?" Embarrassed by his own question, he stammered, "I-I'm sorry, they just told me what to do last time and I never asked."

Jake sighed, he needed to find patience. After all, he'd once been a greenhorn too. Glancing over at the others, he noted Booker and Brandon engaged in a competition to see who could get through their inspections quickest, and Faith peered at her allotted pots in blissful quiet solitude. He sighed again.

"Okay. See this webbing covering the frame?" The kid nodded. "Obviously, this makes it so the crabs don't get out. The funnel-shaped hole in the side here," he pointed, and the boy nodded again. "The crab crawls in there, but the flap folds down so it can't get back out that way either. So, that's the reason we're inspecting and changing the mesh size, because the Opilio's are a lot smaller than King Crab and could just crawl out of their size hole. When we go back to King crab, we'll switch it out again to the bigger mesh. Right?"

"Yeah, they're so heavy," Tristan observed. "The pots, I mean. When I came on, they don't look like they should be so heavy."

"Well, the mesh doesn't weigh shit but an inch and a half of metal frame, plus the line and bait set up... eight hundred pounds tacks on quick. That's why you have to be so careful in weather. I've seen people lose fingers and break hips... all kinds of shit from getting crushed behind or between the pots."

"It's physical."

"Yeah."

"So, how is she gonna do it then?" Tristan nodded toward Faith.

Jake snorted. "Women *are* excellent for things other than the kitchen or the sack, Bailey."

"No, I know." The kid's face reddened. "It's just it's hard for me and I got at least fifty pounds on her."

Jake looked over at Faith again, cinching the opening together with a lashing, then back at Tristan. "She's been doing it a long time, so I guess we'll find out soon enough." Her eyes shifted to his, and she winked. *Goddamn, she heard the whole thing.* He shook his head and got back to work.

Using the hydraulics and their own bodies, they stacked and latched a hundred and ninety-five more pots to the deck. Booker stepped to the rail for a smoke break with Tristan and engaged his favorite pastime... complaining.

"We're only in port two days and they think the princess is some kind of fucking Jason Bourne. When we get out to sea and she can keep it up like that, then maybe I'll get impressed. Twenty bucks says the bitch will need to get airlifted for seasickness."

"I don't know." Tristan said. "I like her."

"That's because you want to fuck her." Tristan winced and drew his head back. "Believe me, she's got holes, so she might be good enough for that."

"No, I got Julie for that. I mean... for... you know, um, being with. And you've got Ashley, or did something happen again?"

"No man, she's in Seattle," he volleyed, like that explained everything.

Monogamy wasn't the man's strong suit. Jake shook his head nearby, as he stood shifting his weight against the cold, on his own smoke break. Mariano, had changed in the years since the deck boss knew him. Always a braggart and a little too self-important, Jake understood it came from Chris' old man and his views on fatherhood, women and relationships. He'd always given Booker a pass because of it and the pain the kid endured. However, the kid was now a man, and the man gathered lather to continue the diatribe. So, Jake flicked his cigarette into the water and told everyone to get back to work.

****

"Okay, Gumby dash, here we go. Ready... Set... go!" Andy held a stopwatch and eyed the numbers racing forward in a blur.

The *Scaup* equipped each member of the crew with a rolled-up orange neoprene survival suit, stuffed into a bag and had sixty seconds to get it on, for eligibility to fish. At the skipper's go, they yanked the suits out of the bag and unrolled them like a sleeping bag on the floor, stepped into them, then pulled them up like pants. Booker, Brandon and Tristan each shoved arms into the two sleeves and tried to stretch the neoprene up over their shoulders.

Faith and Jake each put one arm into a sleeve and pulled the hood up over their heads. As the others struggled with garments, zipping and hoods, the couple jammed their other arms into the free sleeves and zipped up their suits. Each life-saving device contained a lot of room with oversized hands and feet so that the bearer could get into it wearing bulky clothes and shoes.

"Thirty-five seconds," Andy announced.

Faith finished securing her neck, wrist and ankle straps first, with Jake only a second behind and the others finished right at the sixty-second mark.

"Time! Hey now, we have a new winner," Andy called. Jake gave Faith a frustrated look at coming in second, but the company moved onto inspecting the suits for holes, and patent tubes to inflate the flotation part. After they determined strobes, whistles and reflective mirrors worked, Andy commanded, "Okay, get in your raft."

The collective groaned at the part that required them to jump into the freezing cold water and heave themselves into a life raft. Though uncomfortable, everyone paid the requirement the respect it deserved each season. Unless a greenhorn, most men knew someone that used the routine they just performed in a real-life scenario. Along with the procedure, each boat contained an Emergency Position Indicating Radio Beacon (EPIRB), which activated when it hit with water and sent out a radio signal to the U.S. Coast Guard with its coordinates, saving some from a watery death. Last, the crew and its captain went over an abandon-ship procedure, explaining their place of muster and the system of protocol.

The Rasmussen family took their crew's safety seriously, especially in light of John's death. The brothers didn't know it, but the more stringent system they practiced was implemented by their father after the death of Faith's father. Many fishermen in the area did.

Andy just wanted to control what he could before fate overtook him. He never left the harbor on a Friday. He didn't allow suitcases on board, or leave without his father's medallion around his neck, a pack of Marlboro's in his pocket, or his coffee mug full with straight black coffee and one shot of Bailey's cream in it. No one spoke of good fortune without knocking on wood. Jake always stepped onto a boat with his right foot first. Booker never left the harbor sober because he believed it helped with seasickness. Brandon always called his family beforehand and smoked his favorite cigar as they motored out of the harbor. Though new, Tristan took to wearing his dad's old Noodle golfing hat.

Andy's extreme breech in conduct in having a woman onboard as a crew member did not go unnoticed among any of his peers. As for Faith, she didn't believe herself a superstitious person, but did start each season with her father's silent prayer of thanks and protection for herself, her crew, Mack and the boys.

****

In the wheelhouse, the elder Rasmussen brother poured over nautical charts and weather reports. Jake walked around the corner carrying two mugs of coffee and handed one to Andy, before scanning the charts himself.

"How's it going down there?" he asked, knowing Jake would understand what he really asked.

"Good. She's good. Works hard. Has a lot of stamina and holding her own plus some with Book."

"Well, we haven't seen her at sea yet," the captain reminded him.

"No, but I think it's gonna be okay. She's a lot stronger than I thought and has smaller hands to get into some of those latching's easier. That might come in handy rather than one man in and another one out doing it."

"Okay, fine. So, where are we now?"

"Groceries," Jake answered with a deep sigh. "Anything special you want this trip?"

"Does she cook?" Andy asked, ignoring his question.

"I don't know," Jake shot back. "But there's not a snowball's chance in hell I'm asking her."

Without another word, Andy got on the deck intercom. "Pearson, come up here, will you?" She nodded and entered the wheelhouse a few moments later. "Do you know how to cook?" he asked without preamble.

"Sure." She narrowed her eyes and embellished, "when it's my *turn* to cook."

Ignoring her irritation, he continued, "Jake does most of the cooking onboard, but he hates doing breakfast and sucks at it, besides. Isn't that right?" He glanced over at his brother, who cocked his head to one side and stuck up a middle finger.

"You've never starved on this boat, asshole," Jake retorted.

Faith smiled. "You guys are a lot like Brady and Charlie." They both whipped their glares at her. "I don't mind doing breakfast," she said, breaking up what would have been an impressive spat. "It's what I do best, and it's easy."

Andy gave his brother a superior and satisfactory grin. "See there. So, why don't both of you go in and do the groceries?" He grabbed the keys to the company truck and threw them in their general direction. Jake made a half-assed grab for them, but Faith stepped in front of him and caught them one-handed.

"Let's go," she said and started for the steps. Jake put his hands low on his hips with a bewildered look on his face and followed her. Andy overheard them as they made their way to the door.

"So are you driving?" Jake asked when he held his hands out for the keys and she rejected him.

"I've got the keys, don't I?" She retorted and dangled them in the air. Andy chuckled. *She can handle more than the Italian.*

CHAPTER 16

"So, what do you think so far?" Jake leaned his forearms on the handgrip of his shopping cart as they walked down the canned food aisle. "You're taking the heat from Book pretty well."

"What a fucker." Faith spat out the words as she tossed several cans of corn into her own cart. "Why is there one on every boat?" Jake chuckled. "Come on, seriously, why do you guys put up with him?"

"Well, as much as he complains... when we go out there, he gets the job done. He's a helluva fisherman." Jake grabbed canned green beans and started throwing them into his cart.

Faith nodded. "And is that the only reason? Don't get me wrong, it's a good reason but..."

"We went to school together since second grade. Same with Brandon. Booker's better once he relaxes and gets used to you. He just has a big bark."

"Like a Chihuahua?"

"Exactly," Jake laughed. "Exactly, like a Chihuahua. He's a lot better around his girlfriend too." They turned the corner to go down the next aisle, filling their carts with groceries, then unloaded them onto a pallet in the back before continuing.

"He does *not* have a girlfriend." Faith removed the last items from her cart, then started down another aisle.

"Sure does."

"That's disturbing on so many levels."

"Her name's Ashley. She's almost inverted, she's so small, but she loves him, and he seems to understand he got lucky with her." He paused. "Well, most of the time."

"But it was like rutting season in the bar last night."

"He's a guy without a conscience, gone for a long time at sea, without his woman." Jake shrugged and grabbed twelve boxes of Ding Dongs.

"And that makes it okay?" Watching him, she drew her brows together. "What are you, twelve?"

"What? The guys like them." He grabbed some Fruit Roll-Ups. "Here you go... fruit. Happy now?" He pointed and dropped several more boxes into the cart. Faith rolled her eyes at him, and he returned to their conversation. "When you're a woman up here, trying to make ends meet, you can name your price and if a guy's horny enough, he'll pay it. You understand that, living up here as much as you do, let alone the only woman aboard a crab boat."

"No, I don't. Because I'm not a ho, and I don't have relationships with men onboard the boats I work on."

"Oh yeah, is that like a, "don't date anyone at work," thing?" He flung up his fingers in air quotes.

"No, I've had relationships with guys I like from a boat before. I just don't have sex or anything *on* the boat."

He stopped the cart and looked at her. "So, you're saying it's okay for you to fuck off the boat, but not on?"

"Yeah, I guess... sometimes."

"Is this a new rule of yours since meeting Mariano?"

"No," she snickered. "I've had that rule since I was sixteen." She grabbed five boxes of cinnamon and walked a little further. He didn't follow her anymore, and she turned to look back at him. "What?"

"I thought you've been on a boat since you were eight?" he asked with suspicion.

"Yeah, so?"

"So, your telling me you're a thirty-seven-year-old virgin?" He grinned, discovering the joy in teasing her.

"God, no! Why would you say that?"

"Well, if you don't have sex on boats, and you live on boats, but have only had relationships," -he made quotation marks with his fingers- "With men you work with off boats... whatever the fuck that means... What you're saying is you're a prick tease, aren't you?"

She guffawed. "No. You *can* have sex in other places other than a crab boat, you know. Come on Jake, you need to expand your horizons and give your ladies some romance."

Now Jake guffawed. "Just so I'm straight. You do *like* to have sex? With men?"

"Jesus, how did we get on this topic?" She turned to face him and spoke slow. "Yes, I *love* sex. Sometimes it's with guys from the boat, sometimes it's with guys I meet back home, sometimes it's all by myself."

She turned and a broad smile crossed her face as she walked off and left him to ponder that golden nugget. He looked after her, a little shocked, then tried to give some back.

"But if you're doing it with yourself on the boat," he yelled down the aisle. "Isn't that the same as sex? Or is this one of those 'I didn't inhale or have sexual relations with that woman', kind of deals?" He hoped to shock or better yet embarrass her.

"Masturbating isn't the same as having regular sex," she yelled back even louder. "Sometimes I know better what to do with my own fucking body than a fumbling, irritating, incompetent man."

She rounded the corner, and disappeared from sight, and leaving customers to stare in her wake. He stood frozen in the aisle, mouth open and blushed crimson. An elderly, heavy-set woman, wearing a huge tiered skirt over her pants and a red bandana kerchiefed on her head, stooped to pick up a bag of dried peas from the bottom shelf. She straightened and eyed Jake.

"She's got something there, handsome." Smiling, she revealed several missing teeth, winked and walked toward the cash registers.

"Oh my God," he blurted out in a breath and raced to catch up with his fellow deckhand.

They spent thousands of dollars on the groceries to keep on top of the five thousand calories the crew intended to burn each day while fishing. Since the goal of nutrition aboard is quantity over quality, they chose many high fats, carbs and proteins to substitute for sleep. Jake also counted the juice, water and Gatorade, on the second pallet, calculating the three gallons consumed daily by each of the six souls onboard. After purchasing all the costly items and organizing their delivery for later in the day, they made a last stop at a supply store to buy a new dog clamp for one that broke in the galley. Without it, scalding dishes or pots of boiling water could fly off a stove top burner in rough seas.

Jake and Faith arrived back at the *Scaup* to a flurry of inspections from Alaska Fish and Game and others required before they could leave the harbor.

After hours, Faith walked from the *Scaup* to the next slip over and the *Je Suis Prest* to help Mack and the boys get ready for their trip. Jake and Andy walked up to the wheelhouse to make the last preparations to their itinerary. Enjoying a companionable beer, a flurry of activity next door caught their attention. Walking out onto the upper deck, they turned their attention to Mack's boat as Brady, Faith and Charlie wrestled on the deck. Mack leaned against the rail and smoked a cigarette, while holding his own drink, laughing. He raised the glass toward his neighbors. They returned the gesture and reached for their own cigarettes to light up.

Brady held Faith's arms down as his older brother sat backwards on her legs and held onto her feet with all his might. One boot and two pairs of socks lay in a crumpled heap as Charlie tickled her bare toes. She bucked, screaming obscenities and threats at them while she laughed. Finally, they let her go and her body sprang up like a spring. Brady grabbed her hat, causing the very loose bun under it to pull out from its bindings. Her wild copper hair tumbled out and caught in the setting sun. Something in Jake stirred, until she punched Brady dead in the face, then turned and booted Charlie's groin. All five men groaned and flinched in reflex, grabbing at that tender part of their anatomy.

Andy winced in imagined pain. "Aww, shit! I don't think we ever did that even in our worst fight." He paused, looked at his brother and jerked a thumb toward his new employee. "She's cool, man. I like her." Jake smiled too as he let go of his own balls.

"I'll tell you one thing, though," he said as they went back into the wheelhouse. "Don't ever debate her in the grocery store."

****

Faith watched her brothers roll around, clutching the injured parts of their anatomy and swearing at her. She strutted back to Mack, who chuckled as he pulled out another cigarette, lit it and handed it to her. Thanking him, she took it and had a small sip of his whiskey.

"So, you ready?" she asked on a deep sigh and turned her body to look out into the harbor, resting her forearms on the rail. He followed suit.

"Yeah, I think we're close. They'll be bringing the new bait tomorrow." Mack gestured towards the freezers.

"Were you able to get the bin boards fixed?" she asked, indicating the long boards in the tanks that segmented the crab, so they didn't crash into the side of the hull or each other. To do so could cause the crab to release a toxin creating a chain reaction killing them all. "Lucky you noticed that."

Mack blew out a stream of smoke. "Yeah, we got that taken care of too." Mack finished his cigarette and flicked it over the rail. "You guys ready too?"

"Let's see." She counted on her fingers. "*Fish and Game* gave us a green light. Groceries got delayed, so we'll need to get that loaded. Check out of the hotel. Then we have a last system check, and I guess they have someone come on to bless the boat, and I think we're there." Faith finished her cigarette and crushed it out on her heel before putting the butt in her pocket.

"So, are you all adapting to each other? Are they treating you okay?"

"Yeah, it's fine. It's always a little tough at first, because they don't think I know anything."

"How long does that last?" He asked, turning back around to face the deck and leaning back on the rail.

"Usually the first turnaround. I gotta prove myself just like everyone else. You were right about the guys, they're cool." Then added, "Well, maybe except for Mariano."

"Yeah, he's always been a horse's ass. Keep holding your own baby, you'll be okay." Mack caught his sons coming up behind Faith, so he distracted her. "Why don't you go help your brothers limp back to *Unisea* and buy them a drink?"

Her sadistic laugh turned into a squeal as both boys knelt, each grabbing a leg and yanked down her jeans and sweats, leaving half her ass exposed.

"You little shits." She turned and tried to fumble her pants up as both boys turned and ran like hell to get off the boat. Mack howled with laughter and followed them out, shaking his head.

****

Leaving port always left Faith's body vibrating with happiness, as much as the docks hummed with activity. She grabbed her gear from the hotel room and headed downstairs to check out when Jake came out of a room next to the elevators, pulling up his jeans and throwing on shoes.

As she approached, he turned, face flushed and said, "Hey."

"Hey," she said back. "Have a late night there, Jakob?"

"Yeah, just had to go over some figures," he said, winking at her.

She giggled at the spectacle he made. "Yeah, how many figures we talkin'... two... three?"

He just gave her a sexy grin back as she stepped in the elevator.

"Hey, hold it for me." Not able to catch his balance and get on in time, the doors shut on her amused face.

Some boats were heading out that day, others in the days to follow. Only after an *Alaska Fish and Game* inspection and the official signal for the crab season to start could a boat fish. Many captains traveled to their chosen fishing grounds to wait, so no time was wasted once the countdown sounded.

Faith checked out of the inn and stowed her gear in the wheelhouse. An empty bunk below Booker's, mournful of an occupant, taunted her, but she prayed it wasn't hers. She peeked into Brandon's bunk area, and saw Tristan's gear on the lower bunk, and feared the worse. Before she could ask, the groceries and supplies arrived, and they spent the next two hours organizing it all, before she resigned herself to her fate.

The layout for the sleeping arrangements interested Faith. Andy inhabited a good-sized cabin just off the wheelhouse, with its own tiny bathroom. Jake, as co-owner and deck boss, lived in a much larger room than his brother, without a bathroom but with a door. His room, located across from the large communal privy, also held medical supplies and the overflow of groceries.

Booker's bunkroom looked down the entire length of the hallway toward the bathroom at the other end, and Tristan and Brandon's bunkroom laid between the two. Resigned, she grabbed her stuff from the wheelhouse and walked down to her own private hell. If one thing could break her during the trip, never having a break from the dipshit could do it.

She peered inside. The nine by nine room contained an L shaped style bunk bed, at the foot of which rested a three-drawer, dresser system and shelf for books or other items a crabber might find handy at night. Corkboards attached to the walls, ceilings and underside of bunks, waited for pictures and letters from home. *That's a woman's touch.* Faith smiled, then frowned. Booker strewn his shit not only over his bunk but all over hers, too. She dropped her bags and put her hands on her hips, then swung around to locate her nemesis. Pissed, she took the first couple of steps and ran hard into Jake, expelling each other's breath.

"Whoa, what the..." Jake began, then noticed her face. "Hm, Booker?"

"Yeah, where's the little shit?"

"What happened?" Jake chuckled.

"He left his shit all over my bunk, thinking, what, I'm gonna to put it away?" She pointed toward the messy room. "So, I'm gonna go fuck him up."

"As much as I want to see that," Jake crowed, "I have to tell you, that shit isn't Book's, it's mine. I was just getting water and coming back to deal with it."

She turned back to face him, and the couple now stood close in the tiny hallway. He needed a shave and smelled of sweat from the work they'd completed, but also the earthy pine scent of the soap from the hotel she possessed on her own skin. His eyes scanned hers, then dropped to her mouth, and his own lips parted. He took two steps back, inhaled and cleared his throat.

Confused by what just happened, she asked, "What do you mean? Where am I sleeping then?"

"Ah, I thought you might like mine." He jerked a thumb down the hall.

Her eyes widened and then narrowed, drawing her eyebrows together, then opened her mouth to say something, before closing it again. More confused, she opened her mouth again and closed it again.

"You look like a guppy," he said and turned up the corner of his mouth in a half grin. "I don't believe I've ever seen you without a quick comeback." He waited, and when she didn't speak, he said, "Look, it's no big deal. I just thought you might want a room with a door. In the middle of a trip, I don't care where I sleep. Most of us get dressed out here, so I thought it might be a little awkward for you."

"I've seen men get dressed for work before. I usually get dressed in the engine room," she replied, touched he'd thought about her comfort. "What I mean is, I don't care where I sleep either. I don't need it, but it's nice of you... for the dressing thing, I mean... to..." *Oh my God, I sound like an idiot, shut up.*

"Well, I'm sure we'd all enjoy the show, but we're here to catch crab and make money, right? So, don't sweat it." He brushed past her to stow his gear.

"I..." She started, stopped to consider, and tried again. "I don't enjoy having special privileges on a boat. It sets the wrong tone. It's better I sleep out here and..."

"Faith." Jake stopped unpacking and turned to her, exasperated. "You're not getting special treatment. Half the time I sleep in the galley anyway, and all the other guys know it. No one enjoys bunking with Booker, that's why Tristan put his shit in Brandon's room last night. It'll be better all-around if you guys can be apart from each other from time to time. Okay?"

"Okay," she conceded. "Sorry, it's just I gotta be careful. Thank you."

"Don't mention it... seriously... don't."

She smiled again and moved toward his room. With all the supplies, Faith discovered her actual living space was the equivalent of the other sleeping areas, yet with this room, she could in fact close the door and that made all the difference.

With the last of the groceries, gear, inspections and safety drills complete, the captain gave the signal. The crew of the *Scaup* could take one final hour to make personal calls home, finish any business that couldn't wait for the weeks and months to come, or to stretch their legs on land before leaving on their arduous journey.

Faith walked over to Mack's boat. They still needed their last inspection before Mack would give his own hour warning. Faith also discovered the night before the *Je Suis Prest* traveled in the opposite direction from her boat. She found him in the wheelhouse, absorbed in his charts, with a pencil behind one ear, another in his right hand, and a cigarette in the left. His foot bounced on the stool rung, and a mug of coffee held down one corner of the chart. His reading glasses perched vicariously on his nose as he studied the papers in front of him.

She leaned against the doorjamb, watching him smoke and twitch. For the first time in Faith's life, she thought he looked old, tired and more than a little stressed.

"I have never seen a man more in need of a woman's care than you, Mack." His head popped up, and he set his cool gray eyes on her. "Don't you ever take care of yourself? You look like hammered shit."

"Yeah, I have one of those at home, remember? The only time she doesn't bitch is in the sack." He took a drag and smiled as the smoke floated out of his mouth and around his head.

"Oh, my God. You did *not* just say that, that's disgusting."

"Far from it," he said, and bent his head to study the chart again. "She's great in the sack."

"It's a soul crushing day when you discover *all* men are pigs."

She walked over to him and he lifted an arm to drape over her shoulders, but his eyes remained focused on the paper in front of him. Faith tightened her arms around his middle and looked down at the charts too.

"I haven't heard Rosie bitch since I was fourteen. And I'm serious Pop, you look stressed, and you're smoking a lot."

Mack looked down at her, arm still around her shoulders, took a drag and stubbed out his smoke in the full ashtray.

"Look, kid, I'm about to go out on a trip. I'm always stressed out before we go. So are you, and so is every other guy here," he said, gesturing toward the window and the water beyond it.

"I don't get stressed," she said and squeezed her arms tighter before taking the sludge he called coffee and dumping it down the sink. She crossed to the mini-fridge and grabbed two waters before returning to him, untwisting the top and setting it in his hand. "I get excited."

"I'm excited too, but you're lying if there isn't some fear." He paused. "I'm fine baby, I just want to have a good season and get everyone back safe, that's all, okay?" He looked down at his hand and noticed the bottle, peered around for his coffee and when he didn't see it, shrugged and took a swig of water.

"Okay, fine." He raised his arm again and drew her closer, then using the same hand, took her hat off and pulled her head down to kiss it before handing the hat back.

"So, you guys out of here?" he asked, as if realizing there must be the reason for her presence in his wheelhouse in the middle of the day. She stepped away from him and coiled up her hair again, before shifting her hat back into place.

"Yawp, Andy gave us an hour to wrap things up, I've got about forty minutes left," she said, checking her watch. "I need to go to the store quick, so thought I'd come say goodbye, first."

"Okay, well, give a shout out every once in a while, on the squawk box, if you can, and be safe." He reached his arms out once more, and she stepped into his embrace, resting her head against his chest, and the steady thump of his heart. After a full minute, Faith stepped back and smiled up at him.

"You too. I'm gonna go out and find the boys."

"Okay."

She walked away, then stopped, so just her head and hand were visible around the jamb. "Oh, and Mack?"

"Yeah, babe?" He answered, not looking up. When she didn't answer, he shifted his gaze to her.

"Call Rosie, okay?"

"Yeah, yeah." He waved an unconcerned hand at her and watched her cross the deck to disembark the boat.

When Faith darted a glance back up to the wheelhouse, a cell phone rested at his ear.

CHAPTER 17

As the men and Faith finished boarding the *Scaup*, they gathered in the galley. The powerful aroma of *Pine-Sol* and grease hung thick in the air. The captain introduced Reverend Alma Wyatt, a small, older woman, with short gray hair and a pair of horn-rimmed glasses that magnified her warm brown eyes. She stood before them in jeans, fur-lined boots and a warm jacket, wearing a sash with religious symbols of a fish, a cross and Roman numerals on it. Most boats Faith worked on performed some kind of prayer before going out to sea. A moment to surrender yourself to your faith in hope of protection and security for yourself and the people on the sea with you. Each crew member, including Faith, removed their hat, and lowered their heads as the Reverend intoned.

"We pray, O Lord, for all those as they go forth and brave the peril of the sea. Grant them Your strength and protection over the course of their journey. Give them Your presence, O Lord, in times of loneliness and special need. Bring Your love and peace and to their families in their sacrifice. Almighty God, we pray for the captain and this crew to ask that You guide their minds, hearts and hands. We pray that You bless this vessel and make it impervious to danger. Heavenly Father, we ask that You make the seas plentiful to give each devoted servant just reward for all their hard work. Eternal Lord, who created these tumultuous seas, please receive into Your almighty and most magnanimous protection these men and this woman. To the fleet in which they serve, that all may return to enjoy the bounty of the land. With thanks of Your blessings and benevolent protection to praise and glorify Your holy name. In this we pray, Amen."

"Amen," the small congregation intoned in unison. Andy raised his head and sought each person who worked for him, and gave them a nod, a promise to do everything within his power to keep them safe.

"Okay, let's go!" He clapped his hands, and the rest of the group followed suit. "Let's get out of here!"

Faith stepped onto the deck to remove and store fenders as the boat pulled away from the wharf. The Carter men perched out on deck, observed their departure. Mack, coffee in one hand and a cigarette in the other, leaned his forearms on the rail, as the boys stood next to him, each smoking their own cigarette and waved. She waved back at them, then continued to coil line. She'd never sailed away in another boat, with all of them watching before, and the sensation felt odd. Charlie and Brady both turned and dropped their pants, giving an impressive and hairy BA. Andy laid on the horn as everyone hooted and cheered with laughter.

As the trio faded from view, she chanted the prayer Nels taught her to ease her worry while he worked. She spoke it at the start of every season.

"Blessed be to sinners, waiting for loved ones on the sea. Help them in their calling to bring them back safe to me. I lay my head in safety and warmness of my bed. Take away my fear for them and feelings of such dread. For I know Thou art with them and in Your arm's, so true. That even if they perish, I'll see them one day soon."

They motored out of the harbor past the rusting hulls of ships, at one time, also full of hope for the upcoming sea son. As the harbor vanished into the mist, the crew scattered. Booker sat at one end of the galley table, to sort through some CDs, as Tristan challenged Brandon to a duel on a game box. Jake turned to the kitchen to start dinner. He and Faith talked in the grocery store about making something special the first night to reward everyone for their hard work of the past few days. After securing the door to the outside and stowing her all-weather gear, she pulled up her oversized jeans and rolled down the waist band, drawing her puffy sweatshirt over the top of it.

Rounding the corner, she entered the stifling hot room and pushed her sweaty hair off her face and under her hat. She pulled the sweatshirt from her body and exhaled through pursed lips.

"Hey, you ready for help?" Faith asked, as the deck boss flipped the steaks in their marinade, and sprinkle garlic butter on top of them.

"Sure." He scanned the produce. "Ah, how about scrub and poke some holes in the potatoes?"

"Are you baking them?"

"Yeah." She nodded and walked to the sink to wash her hands, then collected her supplies. *Fuck, it's hot.* Perspiration rolled down her neck and into her clavicle. She pursed her lips again and let out another stream of breath. Jake stood in jeans, tank undershirt and bare feet, as did the rest of the men, except for Booker who insisted on just wearing his boxers.

Jake lifted his head and rolled his shoulders as if loosening up. He turned to her with a question hovering in the air he didn't ask. His gaze darted up to her hat, then what could only be a bright red, perspiring face.

"It's warm in here, right?" She closed her eyes and nodded her head. He padded over to the thermostat. "Jesus, it's set to eighty. All right," he called out. "Who's fucking with the thermostat?" No one answered, but guilt radiated off Booker and she narrowed her eyes at him, as he pretended to remove an imaginary shirt. *God, the man's an asshole.* "Aren't you burning up?" Jake arrived back at her side, and he reached up and removed her hat, bun once more loosened from the day's activities, bobbed down to the base of her neck.

"No, I'm used to being warm." She snatched up the butter and tin foil, glaring at Mariano. "Do you want to start the potatoes first? I'll do them quick, then make a salad." She glanced at him for his answer, but he only blinked at her, as if trying to work out a puzzle. "Jake?"

He snapped out of it. "Ah, yeah... potatoes, first."

****

Jake studied Faith as she coated her small hands with butter, greased the potatoes, then wrapped them in the foil for baking. Something seemed off about the woman. The room so stifling he expected her to burst into flame, yet she refused to remove a stitch of clothing. Maybe self-conscious. She pulled up the sleeves of the sweatshirt to reveal slender but strong arms, and placed the potatoes on a baking sheet, before sliding them into the oven. Her long thin neck, with the ridiculous bun puffing behind it, looked out of place with the rest of her body. Something was off.

As if to test a theory, he moved toward the refrigerator, and in the cramped quarters placed his hands on her waist, in a pretense of moving behind her. She wasn't big at all. In fact, he'd bet just about anything she wore clothes several sizes too large for her. *Why would she do that?*

They ate their dinner and talked about the upcoming season and location of their fishing grounds. Each crew member revealed their journey into fishing, yet Faith spoke little of her own experience. After dinner, the cooks left the clean-up to the others, and Faith asked Jake if he wanted the first shower. However, he needed to spell his brother for a few hours, so refused and they said goodnight. To his utter delight, Andy told him he'd wake him for a shift change in a few hours, and by the time the younger brother showered and climbed into bed, he yearned for blissful oblivion.

"So, off we go again, bro." Booker climbed up onto his bunk, passing gas with each movement.

"There you go, a little gift from me to you." He giggled and sprang onto his bed.

Jake rolled his eyes, already missing the seclusion of his room. He glanced down the hall at the closed the door. No, she needed the privacy more, however small.

"How do you like the way I fucked with the princess?"

"Yeah, about that." Jake made his words distinct. "Knock it off."

"What? Why? She's a tight-assed bitch. Walking around here like she's all that. I gotta take her down a peg or two."

"No, you don't. I want this trip harmonious, and you aren't starting it off any other way. You read me?"

"Yeah, I guess..." He made his voice into a high falsetto. "The fat ass is sensitive and..."

"Book, did you hear me?"

"Yes, I heard you."

"Okay. I'm wasted, and I'm turning out the light, all right?"

"Yeah, tomorrow we hit it hard."

"You got it," he said and closed his eyes to delicious silence. She's insecure. The thought made him open his eyes again. Booker made comments about her weight all day. Girls did that when they're insecure... wear big clothes because they think it makes them look smaller. He thought of the wallflowers at the beach. They always wore half their wardrobe into the water, *didn't they*? He did not take Faith as someone insecure about their anything, but stranger things happened. With that small part of the puzzle solved, he closed his eyes again, and within minutes the sandman sang.

****

After dinner Faith went to her room, shut the door, and peeled off every scrap of fabric glued to her body. As she laid naked on her bed, she rested a hand on her stomach. If this went like that boat six or seven years ago, she'd need to rethink her layer plan. The coolness of the cabin seduced her body, and she sent up a prayer of thanks to Jake for insisting she take his room.

Jake, she conjured up his face, and ran a hand to her breast. She tensed when she realized she thought of him *that* way, so willed herself to ease the tension in her shoulders and face. The man had amazing abs, and that ass. She moved a hand down her abdomen, to the sweet spot between her legs.

"Hmm." Relaxing her body more, she used the fingers of her other hand to play across her nipple. The delicious pulls and tugs across her tummy taunted her, as she remembered his sexy smile coming out of the hotel room. She stopped her ministrations. *What the fuck are you doing?* He attracted attention all over town with the female population and even left a parting gift with one adoring fan, hence the hotel room.

Frustrated and horny, she took a cold shower and got back to her room before anyone else made it to their bunks. Warning herself she couldn't start anything with the deck boss because they were crew members now, she needed to put any attraction on the back burner, or the season promised a poor end.

At five thirty on opening day, Faith's internal clock went off, and she rose, dressed, and went into the dark galley to make coffee. Jake sat at the kitchen table, his hair standing on end, and wearing a bleary-eyed expression on his face. Grunting at her in acknowledgment, he nodded in the coffee's direction to show he beat her to making it.

"Morning," she said with a cheeriness she didn't feel, and poured herself a large mug of coffee. He grunted again. "I wanted to go out and get started on bait. How many sets-ups do you want?"

"I imagine." He stopped and gave an enormous yawn, then stood wearing sweats, the same undershirt tank, and bright white socks. "Andy's gonna do some prospecting... wait, I'll ask him." With an effort, he disappeared up the stairs to the wheelhouse and Faith followed, an extra cup of coffee in her hand.

"Why didn't you wake me up?" She overheard Jake ask.

"You needed it more than I do, right now. I'll tell you when to come in. Ah," he nodded at his new deckhand. "Thanks."

"Energizer Bunny here wants to know how many set-ups." He gave her another one of his grins, and she raised her brows, giving him a side smirk back in reply.

"Well, I'm gonna lay some prospect strings," Andy pointed to a map. "Maybe fifteen, twenty pots in each string, across here and here." He showed a section of water, then sniffed. "After, we're gonna go over to a couple other spots and do the same thing."

Faith knew the secret for good crabbing is to understand their movement. In the back of a moving crab community there are the small, slow and roughed-up crab. In the middle are the combination of good crab and old, but the section in front is where the desired schoolies dwell. The biggest, fastest and best crab available. When a captain is on that, he is on the crab. An Opilio, or Snow crab, is the largest fishery in the Bering Sea region, and can move five to eight miles per day, so prospecting to stay ahead of the crab and always collect the keepers is the primary goal.

When Faith volunteered to start the bait, she showed her colors as a good deckhand. Prepping bait, one of the worst, most tedious jobs onboard a crab boat, and one often left to greenhorns, trying to prove themselves. Faith sipped her coffee and nodded, then got dressed in her gear and got to work. She took the frozen herring and other fish products, and chopped them into sizeable pieces, before running them through a grinder carefully, as it didn't discriminate between fingers and fish. She placed the mixture into bait bag and hooked it onto a grid for the baiter to grab along with a fresh codfish sliced up the middle.

By ten thirty, the sky lightened, and she greeted it with yet another cup of coffee in hand, sighing at the moment of solitude, and taking in the sight. The sun rose over the horizon before almost immediately descending again, with the day spending eighteen hours in darkness.

"All right, let's go, let's go!" Booker yelled and clapped his hands over the wind. He and Tristan climbed the thirty-foot stack and unlatched the pots from one another. Jake walked over to the hydraulic controls and the huge crane groaned into motion. Grabbing one of the onerous pots off the top of the stack, it swirled in the wind as he brought it down to the deck. It towed over the floor and reached the pot launcher connected to the starboard rail.

Brandon and Faith grabbed it and secured it to the platform as Jake engaged hooks, called dogs, to keep the enormous pot in place. The man and woman unhooked the crab pot door from each side and removed the three hundred feet of coiled line from within, along with a green buoy, a red buoy and a torpedo buoy attached to the line. Faith ran to the bait area and unlatched a thirty-pound bait set-up, then laid on her back inside the pot, and hooked it in the center before climbing out again.

The duo closed and secured the door and waited for Andy to broadcast Fish and Game's countdown. When the buzzer sounded, Jake made the platform tilt up, and they all watched the pot slide into the water. Brandon grabbed the shot, or length of line attached to the pot and flung it out into the sea, as Faith seized the buoys and flung them out just seconds after.

"And so it begins!" Brandon yelled with obvious enthusiasm. He and Faith went to the rail and watched the pot disappear beneath the water's surface, then high-fived.

Eighteen hours later, Andy navigated the boat back to the beginning of the first string of pots. Jake spotted their buoys and threw a long line, at the end of which held a grappling hook, and snagged the short length of rope floating between two of the buoys. He pulled the line in a little before looping it into the power block, or mechanical winch that bore the weight of the pot.

The power block hauled the container by its bridle up the side of the boat, and using the hydraulics, Jake brought the crab pot up, where Brandon and Booker steered and set it into the launcher once more. The machine coiled the rope in a can, but with the pot full of crab, they re-baited and set it into the water again, rather than stacking it to move to a different location.

Pot after pot came up full, and they sorted the crabs into keepers and non-keepers depending on the legal size. The keepers traveled down a shoot into the large holding tanks filled with circulating seawater below the decks, and the non-keepers were flung back into the sea.

****

"You're doing great," Jake said, as he lit two cigarettes and handed one to Faith.

"Thanks, so are you." He grinned, caught in the misconception somehow she would fail.

"Sorry." He leaned against the rail as the boat slid through the water. "It must be hard being you." Her head snapped up with an expression that screamed, *you asshole*, and he snorted. "No, I mean, it must be hard doing what we do, knowing you're going to get a whole lot of shit for it, you know? I'm sure every time you switch a boat, you're essentially starting over with the looks and distrust and everything."

Her face relaxed, and she drew on her Marlboro in thought, then blew out the smoke in a long thin stream. "Yeah, I guess."

"Why do it? It's not a judgement," he rushed on. "I'm just curious. You're a bright, good-looking woman. Why do this?"

"Because I love it and it connects me with both my dad and Mack."

"And if you weren't doing this?" He gestured to the surroundings. "What would you be doing?"

"Honestly, I have no idea. I've never thought about... maybe captain."

"Do you have your license?"

"Not yet... you?"

"Yeah, my dad wanted both of us to get it, in case one of us got incapacitated."

She nodded, then considered him. "What about you? You could definitely be doing a hundred other things. Why do you do this?"

"Same reason, I guess... family." Jake turned and looked out to sea, Faith walked up beside him and followed suit. "But I'm not like Andy. Fishing's in my blood for sure and I would never give it up on every level but..."

When he didn't say anything else, she twisted her head to look at him. "But?"

"I'm not opposed to doing something else either."

"Like what?"

"I like building things and working outdoors."

"Building things? Like what?"

"Anything, furniture, sheds, remodeling... I'm working on a big gazebo at my house right now."

"Wow," she replied, impressed. "Seriously, that's cool." She gave an impish grin. "You'd have to give up skulking around *Unisea* hotel rooms."

"Hey you two," Brandon called. "Ready to get back to work? Andy said we're a mile out."

"Did you say skulking?" The couple each grinned at each other and took a final drag on their smokes before stubbing them out. "Skulking, hmm, I think I like that," Jake said and walked back to the block.

****

"Christ, I'm beat," Booker breathed and glanced across the battleground of their dinner. His eyes fell on Faith. Halfway through their season, and even *he* couldn't complain about her work ethic anymore. He'd relaxed the rather hard points of aggression toward her, but still didn't think her worthy of a compliment either.

"Did Andy say we're going right back out?" Tristan asked.

All the seasoned deckhands laughed. "Yeah, I'm sure we'll be right back out," Jake responded. "Come on T, you know my brother by now." Jake eyed his best friend, who fell asleep in his mashed potatoes and banged his hand as loud as he could on the table.

"Brandon!" The man jerked awake with most of his dinner stuck to his face, and the table erupted into laughter.

"I'm fried," he announced on a yawn, without apology. "I'm going to bed."

"Me too," Faith said, fisting her eyes and yawning. "When did he say when we'd be in?" She jerked her head towards the wheelhouse.

"I think we have..." Jake broke off as the man of the hour rounded the corner. Andy's receding blond hair stood up in tufts on top of his head and large dark circles bruised underneath his eyes.

"Hey, Andy, how long do we get to sleep?" Booker whined.

"You get a full eight minutes," Andy deadpanned, and laid his plate on the counter. "Nighty-night." And without another word, he went back up to the wheelhouse.

"Tristan, it's your turn for clean up tonight," Jake ordered. "The rest of you can go."

He rose and headed up to the wheelhouse. He asked Andy if he needed a break and received the answer he desperately wanted to hear -no- and headed for the facilities and his own bunk. As he passed by Tristan and Brandon's bunk, the father didn't bother to finish undressing and lay sprawled out on top of his covers. Jake smiled after he made eye contact with the greenhorn, who'd stripped down to his thermals and laid in bed reading.

As he approached his own bunk, Booker's snore resonated down the hallway, as the door to his old room remained firmly closed. *She must be out too.* He stripped to his underwear, pulled the cool sheets and blankets up to his chin and slipped into oblivion.

It didn't last, and he jerked awake from a wave, shifting the boat, but it quickly settled back into a rhythmic rocking and creaking. Closing his eyes again, he waited for sleep to come. When it didn't, he got restless, and reached for his cigarettes, placing one between his lips. A movement to his right shifted his focus, and he strained his eyes to see if something wasn't secure.

His eyes rounded with shock and his mouth dropped open as Faith moved toward the bathroom. Thinking the men unconscious with exhaustion, she'd forgone her usual costume of tee shirts and layers of sweats and wore only her thermals. The stretchy fabric clung to her body like a second skin, and her hard muscles under the thin clothes rippled as she tiptoed across the hall. The cool air in the cabin made the nipples of an incredible pair of breasts strain against the crew neck, and he noticed her stomach abs, flat and rigid, might be better than his own. She turned and her ass, so small and toned, had him wanting to take a bite out of it. Jesus.

Jake closed his hands into soft fists and without taking his eyes off her, raised one to scrub over his face and mouth, displacing the forgotten and unlit cigarette. Thigh muscles contracting with each step, she opened the door to the bathroom, and the light spilled out onto her beautiful face before she closed the door.

He shook his head as if clearing cobwebs and thought he must be dreaming. When the toilet flushed, he waited to see if he conjured up that body himself, but as she opened the door, and turned to switch off the light, and the image from the inn came into full focus. The tall redhead with the incredible ass is Faith.

The clothes made sense now, but also didn't. She covered up an incredible, well-disciplined body created by years and years of hard physical labor. Most women with that kind of physique exploited it, just to get a man's blood boiling, just like his was now. He'd never be able to look at her the same way again.

CHAPTER 18

They arrived in Dutch Harbor early the next morning. As the crew offloaded, Jake couldn't help but examine Faith in the light of day. Her movements and the way she interacted with the guys. She blended in and made herself invisible. When Booker made his observation calling her out as different, obvious signs of rage flamed across her face every time. However, the few times she lost it and gave him a backhanded retort, she withdrew further into herself after.

It shouldn't be that big of a deal. So, why did she make it into something it didn't need to be? Lunch concluded and Jake and Faith made another quick run into town for some fresh vegetables and toiletries.

"First turnaround, what's the verdict?"

Faith smiled as the scenery blurred past them. "Good, I like it." She glanced over at him, and he returned the smile. "How long have you been fishing, Jake?"

"It'll be... wow... twenty years this year."

"Did you fish with your dad before that?"

"Yeah, but I guess I don't consider that in the count because I did all the grunt work. What was it like to be surrounded by all of this at eight?"

"Good. All I wanted was to be with my dad and Mack. So, they could've made me pump out the head every day and I would've been happy."

"I just can't get over that. As a kid, that's all you want is to hang out with your dad, be loved by your mom, but... I wanted to hang out with my dad too, but I'm not sure I would've looked at it the same as you back then."

"Believe me, I would've loved to have a more traditional childhood with my parents, but you take what you can get, and now I couldn't imagine living any other way."

They pulled into the parking lot, and Jake moved the gear into park. "But don't you want that someday? That life you didn't have with your folks?"

A flicker of something like loneliness passed over her features, and in that moment, he wanted to kiss her, and take away that pain, but a wall went up behind her lovely eyes. "Sure, someday. Well, this is getting deep, let's get groceries, before I ovulate right here." The moment passed as soon as it started and chuckling, she got out of the truck. The encounter left Jake ill-tempered and frustrated. He understood what happened to him now, was the exact reason women shouldn't be onboard boats. They mess with your head, both of them, and he'd spent way too much time thinking about Faith Pearson.

****

Before the *Scaup* left again, Faith checked in with Mack. They too landed on crab and were maybe two days behind them to offload.

Back onboard, Faith noted the shift in Jake and thought she maybe stepped over the line with the personal conversation. Snappy and irritated, no one seemed safe from his wrath. The thought made her scowl, and as she turned to stow some line, she ran straight into him and a shower of curses.

"You know what, fuck off, Jake." She threw the line at his feet before fisting her hands on her hips. "What's your goddamn problem today?"

"Why can't you just stay out of my way?" he shot back.

"What did I do?" Concerned, because she didn't want to lose the gig, and her chance to live and work close by Mack and the boys.

"Just get the fucking port side fenders stowed, okay?" He threw up his hands and moved to the hydraulic machine. The rest of the crew on deck watching the show, turned and pretended to go back to work.

"Look, Jake, I don't..."

"Just do it!" he yelled, gesturing with his hands for emphasis. "Jesus!"

Faith glanced over at Booker, who slithered a grin across his face at the exchange. He nodded at Tristan, but the greenhorn shot a look of sympathy back to Faith. Unbelievable. Faith turned without another word and marched over to port side to retrieve the fenders.

Goddamn asshole, what the fuck is his problem? One minute they're talking and the next she didn't even recognize him, *the prick.* She glanced over at him, *with a great ass.* He stepped indoors, and she continued to stew. He didn't get to flatter her or bully her and wanted words with Mr. Rasmussen.

As she stepped inside, wet footprints made their way under the engine room door. Faith squared her shoulders, grabbed some ear protection and advanced for battle. She found him checking the hydraulic lines, and not wanting to scare him, waited for him to turn around. When he did, he didn't seem surprised to see her.

"What do you want Faith?"

"I want to know if I did something wrong?" She took a few steps toward him to shout over the noise. "Are you or Andy unhappy with my work?"

"No, it's fine..." He stepped toward her and shouted back. "We're good."

She stepped forward again. "Because, if it isn't, there's..."

"Look, I said, it's good." He waved his hand at her in dismissal, and rage exploded inside her.

"Oh, it's good now is it," she screamed, advancing on him, causing him to widen his eyes and back up a step. "Because you said so? Is this how it is with you? Cool one second, moody as shit the next. Well, fuck you Rasmussen!" She jabbed a finger at him. "And don't you ever wag your hand in my face again when I'm trying to talk to you, asshole."

She turned and walked toward the door. Jake caught her arm and spun her around, then crushed his mouth to hers and sucked in her bottom lip, before opening her mouth with his. Their tongues danced as his cock twitched and pushed into her body through their clothes. She changed the angle and took the kiss deeper. Someone moaned, maybe they both did. His arms wrapped around her body, and he sucked in her bottom lip again. He tasted like salt and sea. The rigid muscles of his back tensed, and she wanted nothing more than to fuck him on the floor, with the machinery churning around them.

What am I doing? I'm in the goddamn engine room! Faith jerked back and pushed him away from her, eyes glazed. Breathless, she pointed at him from across the small space and said, "That will *never* happen again." Before he could respond, she opened the door and walked out of the room.

That night at dinner, both brothers sizzled in bad moods. Andy, because frigid winds from the Arctic Ocean meant to collide with some warmer weather from the Pacific, wanting to make all their lives a living hell in short order. Jake, well, Faith knew all too well what bothered him. It bothered her too. As they listened to their skipper's report and instructions about the incoming storm, Faith yearned for the privacy of her room to think. She hadn't seen what happened between them coming at all. Not that she hadn't imagined it, but rather thought it indicative of her thoughts alone. *So, now what?*

The next few days, with everyone hypervigilant and on edge, tempers flared with increased regularity. Faith laid on her back in the middle of a pot hanging bait when Jake barked out orders for her to spend more time prepping bait than hanging it, she glared at him but walked over to prep more bait. Shortly after, he ordered her to stop prepping and start cleaning the area. So, on hands and knees, she cleaned out some bycatch that slid into a mucky heap under the prep station. A shadow fell over her and she peered back over her shoulder. Jake stood behind her with an unreadable expression. He opened his mouth to speak, but said nothing, just raised his hand in a *whatever* motion, and walked away. She stared after him but stopped reacting to his tantrums, understanding clearly they needed to talk.

****

Over the next week, Jake didn't know why the whole thing bothered him so much. He understood her stubbornness. Hell, he even understood the clothes. Hadn't he worked on enough boats, fishing for salmon during the summer, where more women stayed onboard to fish? Maybe not on his brother's boat, but others. Some of those girls used sex to their advantage to do less but get paid the same, or they liked the men fighting for their attention and used what they could to get a reaction. However, just as many girls stayed there for the work, and wanted fair treatment for fair work. During the summer and in warmer climates, they dressed for that kind of weather and fishing. They didn't hide their bodies and got reactions from the men, whether they like it or not. Most viewed it as a necessary evil to do something they loved. *But why?*

Jake knew how people saw him and tried not to let it go to his head. He'd never in his life needed to scour around for a beautiful, sexy woman. Not only did Faith look like a guy with all that shit on, but she acted like one too. He didn't like tomboys, *did he?*

Using the hydraulics, he shook off the eight hundred plus pot. They fished the area well and now just pulled up blanks, which further dampened everyone's mood. They needed to empty, stack and move all two-hundred-fifty pots to another location just to unload the whole damn thing again. A nuisance and a drain on their dwindling endurance. *Fucking Andy. Just once he needed to come down and shovel the shit.*

Tristan and Booker set the pot in the launcher, so they could remove the few keepers in it. However, Tristan missed securing the heavy pot on the lift with the dogs, and it slipped from its hold, just missing Faith and Brandon on the other side of it, sending it crashing onto the deck.

"Goddamnit, what are you doing?" Jake snarled. "You're gonna fucking kill someone. Stupid idiot. What the hell?"

"Sorry Jake, I thought it was on." Abashed, Tristan shrunk where he stood at the continued diatribe.

"For Christ's sake, Jake," Brandon snarled back in exasperation, "It's not like you've never missed a hook, is it?" He turned Tristan. "Look, you know securing the pot is as import ant as staying out of the line. Do either wrong and someone can die or get fucked-up. Got it, kid?"

Tristan nodded his head. "Sorry B." Sheepishly he peered at Faith. "Sorry, Faith."

"We're cool."

Saying nothing, Jake rolled his eyes back to the horizon and took a deep breath. He pulled out one of his cigarettes, cupped his hands against the wind and lit it in one fluid movement. Then, clenching it in his teeth, he stepped back to the hydraulic controls to pick up and stack the pot to the rear of the deck.

"It's so fucking cold out," Booker complained. He pulled his hand, bloodless from the frigid temperature, and held it up for everyone to see. The man complained the entire morning about his misery, the pitchy waves, the lack of sun, how much his body hurt, keeping the facts fresh in everyone's mind.

At his threshold, Jake told him to shut up and work on the opposite end of the deck.

"Gosh, what crawled up your ass today, Jake?" Booker replied without a hint of reproach. Jake, who'd been looking at Faith, turned to see his old friend grin at him. "I guess it's time to get back to town, unless you can get our on-deck boy toy to open up for you." He grinned and pretended to ride a horse, even slapping an imaginary ass. "Yee-haw!"

The final tenuous break in Jake's self-control snapped, and he lunged at Booker, curled back his fist and let fly. It connected with the deckhand's nose with a sickening crack. Booker's head flew back, and he lost his balance, stumbling back onto the deck, groaning. His hand rose to his nose, which streamed with blood.

"You sonofabitch, you broke my nose." Booker's eyes watered from the impact and pain. "What the hell's a matter with you, Jake?!" he screamed. "Jesus!"

"You just never know when to shut up, do you Book," Jake shot back, reaching down to pick up some rope that fell off the pot. "You never have."

"What the fuck did I say?" He tried to pinch his nose to stop the bleeding but stopped when it brought on a fresh wave of pain.

"Just shut up and do your fucking job!"

"Jake!" Andy's voice boomed over the two-way outside loudspeaker.

"What?" Jake shot back.

"Get your ass up here now!"

"Oh, for Christ's sake." Jake closed his lids over rolling eyes, threw down the rope and stomped across the deck to go inside. When he got to the bait area, he kept his gaze forward and slammed the door behind him. Faith, Brandon and Tristan, unaware of the verbal exchange that led to the physical one, looked after him perplexed.

"What do you want, Andy? I have work to do and so do you," Jake said without preamble as he came into the room.

"What in the hell is going on down there?" Andy asked. "I need you guys focused on the weather and the waves, not beating each other senseless on the deck."

"Nothing. Booker's being a fucking dickhead again."

"So you break his nose? When isn't Booker being a pain in the ass?" Andy queried. "Jake, you can't lose control on the deck like that, you're the fucking deck boss. What message does that send?"

"Like I give a shit," Jake muttered.

"I don't know... you used to." Andy pushed the engines forward and surveyed his brother's angry face. "Come on, what's crawled up your ass?"

"Didn't get any sleep."

"For an entire week?" Andy eyed the horizon, then glanced back at him. "Well, do you need everyone to cover your ass so you can get some now?" An updated weather report crackled over the radio, moving the poor weather up by two hours. After listening, he turned the radio down again and glared at Jake. "Damn it, you know better than this."

"Is that all," Jake asked.

"No, that's not all. I got weather moving in, asshole. I got a greenhorn that's scared shitless to do anything because he thinks he's gonna get fired. I got you down there raging on everyone and breaking one of our deckhand's nose. Pull your fucking head out of your ass so we can get some work done and get out of here." Andy steamed. "You aren't the only one that's wiped and wants to go home, Jake, but we gotta get some shit done here or we'll be standing with our dicks in the wind when this goddamn front moves in! Your mood is dangerous to everyone on board, so fix it! I'm moving to shelter behind Hall Island. Get everything ready down there."

Jake left the wheelhouse and started for the hydraulics without another word to anyone. After the last remaining pot came aboard, Tristan and Booker climbed the stacks and latched them together, as everyone else secured the deck and boat for the oncoming storm.

Andy, able to hide behind Hall Island, dropped anchor and they all waited for the storm to pass. With the skipper in the wheelhouse and the others asleep, Jake went to the galley for a drink. Upon his arrival, he discovered Faith doing the same. She flipped through the pages of her book, but looked up when Jake came in. He poured himself a drink and sat at the table with her.

"Hey," he said.

"Hey."

"Can't sleep?"

"Just having a night cap then I will." She sipped, then set it down, and admitted. "Not gonna lie, I love storms."

"You would." He laughed as silence fell over them. "Look, about the other day..."

"Yeah, about that?"

"I'm sorry." He swallowed the whiskey and let it burn down his throat. "Look, I don't know what the fuck happened. I guess we seemed to connect from the start, then had a lot of success, a little stress, and I don't know... it happened."

"A moment of weakness?"

"Yeah." Some of her hair escaped from the braid she wore, and her emerald eyes sparkled under the night lamp. *God, she's pretty.*

"It's just that, I kinda pride myself on doing excellent work." She pressed her lips together and raised her eyebrows at him. "You've moved through everyone on this boat and I don't know, it seems like you got pissed at me first, and then the other thing..." The dishwasher gurgled and changed cycles. "If this isn't working out, I can always find another job. It wouldn't be the first time, sure as hell won't be the last. I just don't know how to do my job without some clear boundaries, Jake."

He considered her concerned face and felt himself soften. *She's resigned herself to the fact she won't be working for them much longer.*

"I'm an idiot."

"Yes... you are, but it still doesn't do anyone any good if this overlying tension sticks. It's dangerous."

"You're right. Andy said the same thing." He glanced around the room. "So, we'll hide out here and wait out the storm, then get back to work for the next month until we're done. Deal?"

"Deal." They each drained their glasses and stood to put them in the sink. A wave caused the boat to shift, taking them by surprise, and he reached out to steady Faith at her waist.

She smiled up at him, and dropped her gaze to his mouth. He mirrored her reaction.

"Thanks." She stepped away from him and walked toward her room. "See you tomorrow."

"Yeah," he called and went to pour himself another drink.

****

As the weeks turned into a month, the fishing stayed consistent with averages in the mid-four hundred range. With pots soaking, the deck hands took a much-needed break before the last push of the season started. The crew, digested a huge, gratifying meal, and turned to storytelling.

"Amy thinks he'll be rolling over soon," Brandon said, entertaining everyone with his son's antics. "I guess he's smart for a five-month-old." Faith exchanged an indulgent look with Andy.

"All the doctors' say kids are smart to their parents, B. I mean, what else are they supposed to say? Hey, your kid's stupid and ain't doing nothing." Booker snorted. "Come on, you idiot."

Faith's face pinched. *Leave it to Booker to spoil the dream.*

"I think it's wonderful, Brandon," Faith said as if Booker said nothing. "And just wait until you get a hold of him. God help everyone."

Brandon's fallen face exploded with an appreciative smile at Faith, and Booker rolled his eyes.

"Well, I *know* Gabe will be smart. He has Amy there to teach him." Those first precious months of missed milestones with his newborn and wife haunted Brandon, and he settled for watching them all on video. "Everyone knows if your ole man's a fisherman, he's a non-present man. Your dad was a fisherman too, wasn't he, Faith?" Brandon asked, curious about her, and raised his eyebrows in question. "Didn't your mom have something to say about you being on the water so young?"

"My mom..." Faith paused in personal territory, and not a place she felt most comfortable in. However, like the older man, she decided on honesty. "My mom died in childbirth," she murmured.

"Oh shit. Faith, I'm sorry," Brandon flushed red.

251

"What happened to the baby?" Tristan asked, innocently.

"The baby?" Confused, Faith looked at the greenhorn for a moment, then realized what he meant. "Oh, no, it was me. She died giving birth to me." She tilted her beer bottle back for a swallow as the table went silent. "Guys, it's okay. It was a very long time ago, and I never knew her at all."

"I thought your dad was some hotshot fisherman, though. Ain't that right?" Booker retorted.

"Yeah... he was."

"So, he said, *fuck it,* I'll bring my brat onboard?"

"Hey Book," Andy said. "Lay off."

"What?"

"I went to live with my mother's parents until they died. First my grandfather, when I was eight, then my grandmother died a few months after him." Her voice sounded hollow, and tinny. "I found her in her bedroom. She committed suicide." Fenella and Angus's warm smiles and soft, inviting faces filled her vision. At this, all the men stopped eating and stared at her.

"Is that when you went to live with your dad?" Andy asked. "You said you've been living on a boat since you were eight."

"Well, I can tell you, my dad didn't think the boat was for an eight-year-old girl, that's for sure. He wanted me to go to this all-girls school, where you live in all year, but the nearest one was pretty far away." She took a deep breath. "I told him I wouldn't go and I think he knew I was serious, so he let me stay with him and Mack on the boat." She squirmed a little. A long time passed since she'd thought, let alone talked, about her early life.

"What about school?" Andy asked, shaking her from her thoughts.

"Oh, well, my dad was emphatic about school. He said he'd be damned if his only kid would be an idiot." They all laughed, and Faith went on. "We talked to everyone that could help us get set up with some homeschooling. It was hard to do back then because it wasn't very popular." Her gaze darted around the table and met Jake's gaze. "After weeks of cutting through a lot of red tape, we got permission for special circumstances. I worked," - she threw up her fingers in quotation marks- "during the day and did my schoolwork in the afternoon. I don't know, school was easy. I graduated when I was sixteen, then got my engineering degree."

The men all blinked at her, then at each other.

"Check out the big brain on Faith." Tristan chuckled, breaking the tension.

"What happened to your dad?" Booker asked, curiosity getting the better of him.

She stood and walked over to pour herself a whiskey. She sipped it, then turned around and leaned back on the counter. "When I was fourteen, we were going to our cabin out on Camano Island to go swimming and have a kick-ass Fourth of July party. I wanted to spend the summer there, you know, just being a kid. It had been a while. My dad said we could take the summer off, but then a friend of his from Sweden asked if he wanted to go fishing just off where he was born, and where his own father fished."

Faith took a deep breath and went on, almost oblivious to the men sitting in rapt attention. "He would have known the crew made it. I think there was time for him to know it." Her mind fuzzed in and out. "He must have been so scared." She wasn't sure if she said it or just thought it, then blinked and the intimate moment broke. She'd said way too much. Exposed and vulnerable, she needed to get out of that room. "Then he died and left me to Mack. Ah, you know what... I'm gonna just..."

****

She walked out of the room, leaving silence in her wake. Jake looked down at his plate on the table.

"Fuck," Booker elongating the vowel. "That's some hardcore shit, right there."

"Can you let me out B?" Jake asked. Brandon scooted off the bench seat and let his friend stand. The deck boss walked to the hallway, grabbed two coats and stepped outside.

She stood at the rail with her back to him, and her face in silhouette. The story, her bulky sweatshirts and bulging jeans, the same hat with wisps of hair breaking free around it in the crisp frigid wind, made him realize she didn't just insulate herself from men and the weather. The full force of his ridiculousness weighed in on him.

As Faith gazed out over the sea, the clear black sky put on a diffused, colorful light show as the strains of the northern lights ghosted their way across the sky. Jake approached her with her coat and she smiled as he held it open.

"Thanks." She said, as her teeth chattered. "Forgot about that."

"Yeah, well, light goes out, so does every shred of warmth." He held it open wider as she put her arms through the sleeves, then shook out two cigarettes, lit them both, and handed one to Faith. He thought for a moment before saying, "So, you know there're rumors all up and down the docks about you and your dad and Mack. Your dad is legendary, but no one had it right. I didn't know any of that, because most of the old-timers are gone now. I wish you'd said something before."

"Why?" She turned and rested her elbows behind her on the rail. "So you could make me feel better? That isn't my style, and neither is splattering my entire life story for everybody to hear. There must be something in the wind tonight." She flicked ash off her cigarette and watched it float away. "Mack and I talked about it once when he asked me if I wanted to stay on the boat with him, but that was it. We only talk about the good times, and that's the way I prefer it. I overstepped tonight."

He blew out a smoke ring. "You're such a fucking liar, Faith."

"No, I'm not. It happened over twenty years ago, and I learned to make my peace with it. None of that affects me now." She gave him a warning look. "I know it kinda sounds the opposite from what just happened in there, but I'm not a whiner. I'm just tired or something."

He didn't reply, just listened. The water lapped at the boat's hull, as the wind howled across the deck.

"I mean, yeah, it sucked, but I know that sometimes shitty things happen. My dad always told me that death is part of life, and some get more than their fair share of it." She studied her hands. "But he also said it's better to be with someone you love for a little time than not at all," she recited.

"And you get to know people I guess, let them in, hang out?" The northern lights danced with haunted abandonment. "Way I see it is you flip everyone off and hide." He gestured at her outfit. "No emotion."

"How the fuck would you know anything about me, Jake," she challenged. "Who are you now, Dr. Phil? You think you can psychoanalyze me and say I just need a good man to come and rescue me from my miserable life? I don't need you or any of that shit."

"You must not watch Dr. Phil much. He'd say something like, you don't need a man, you only need to, ya know," -he gestured- "empower yourself or some shit." He blushed at her astonished expression. "In the summer, my ma makes me watch it with her." She blinked at him, then guffawed.

"Well, whoever then, Oprah, or who's the guy that has people come on and beat the shit out of each other?"

"I have no idea."

Faith chuckled, then inhaled the last remnants of her cigarette, before crushing it on her boot heel. She blew the smoke heaven-ward and brushed the free strands of hair from her face. "The thing is, Jake, I appreciate you thinking you had to come out here and say something, but I'm fine. I just kinda surprised myself, going as far as I did with it tonight. I never do that, and I'm kind of embarrassed."

"Yeah, I understand that. No need to be, but I get it." He paused and leaned on the rail. "But I'd also like to think we've become friends too." He regarded her. "Is that wrong?" She half shrugged, half nodded.

Shifting gears, he asked, "Why don't you work on Mack's boat? I mean, I know you said you wanted to prove yourself, but you've done that in the last, what, fifteen-sixteen years."

"Seventeen."

"Why not get yourself a sweet little gig there and be with your family?"

Faith spent some time thinking about that before she answered and decided once again to go with honesty. "It isn't just about proving myself. And since you're the son of a fisherman, I bet you understand that fine. But when I lived with just Mack, I was fourteen. He had Brady and Charlie, and they were little. You know the story... he never saw them. Rosie and Mack fought about it all the time... fought about me. They didn't know it, but I heard them."

The wind picked up a little and blew more of her hair out of its bun and her hat. The sky darkened just a little more and the sodium deck lights came on.

"Mack and I became so close because I'd spent most of my life with him, and my dad was his best friend. So we had that bond. Charlie started talking about wanting to come work with him, Brady not long after that. They said nothing, but I knew the time was coming when I needed to leave, so they could have their dad back. I damn well wasn't getting in their way anymore, and now... I just need to depend on myself, is all. It's important to me to not have to depend on someone else."

Jake took a final drag off his cigarette and threw it into the water. He understood, with the losses she'd experienced, it might be normal to rely solely on yourself.

"Who do you hang out with Faith? You never talk about any friends. You have all those damn rules about men. When's the last time you went on a date?" He looked at her, squinted and then blurted, "I saw you one night a while back."

"What do you mean... you saw me?"

"A while ago, you got up to go to the bathroom and... you weren't wearing anything. I mean, um, just..." He gestured up and down his body to show clothes. "You know..." The words hung in the air. "Um..." He closed his mouth and jammed his hands into his pockets.

Her face flushed hot with embarrassment.

"Look, I appreciate... I mean, I think there's a compliment in there somewhere, right?" He nodded. "I don't do this, and I'm not trying to play games or whatever men think women do. I just..." She stopped, thought better of her words and said, "Look, my life makes little sense to people, but it makes sense to me. It's simple and neat, and I'm sure if you analyzed it, I've got all kinds of issues about when I was little. It's not that I don't like people or hate men or anything, it's just I haven't found too many I want to hang out with."

She turned and placed her forearms back on the rail and leaned on them. "I don't understand most women any more than most guys because I haven't been around many of them, except for like Rosie or something. And in my experience, most guys in this line of work aren't into friendship all that much. At least not with me. I've just found dressing like this and being one of the guys works." She stood up. "And that's from years of trial and error and experience, by the way."

"I didn't mean you don't belong here, Faith." Jake breathed. "It's just, you seem kind of alone." He took a step closer and removed her hat. The wind picked up her hair, carrying it across her face. "I think you're cool. You're different, and... kind of a puzzle, I'm not going to lie." He paused, searching for words. "Not to sound like a creeper, but I want to be friends. Someone you could trust... you know? Lame?"

"I do trust you." She almost placed a hand on his cheek, before rolling her eyes. "Oh my God, how stupid is this? We gotta get some sleep or we'll be toast tomorrow." She walked toward the door, stopped and turned back to him. The wind blew his hair back and his cheeks and nose were rosy from the cold, and he gave a hesitant smile.

"Thanks, Jake." She smiled back, then opened the door and Jake lit another cigarette.

****

Andy watched from the darkness of the wheelhouse. *Well, that's interesting.* Jake leaned back on the rail and blew smoke out in obvious thought. Andy couldn't lie, Faith surprised him with her ability on this trip. She was anything but bad luck. She did her job well and got along with the crew, Booker notwithstanding. Now, he remembered his brother's tirades, and wondered if she affected at least one member of his crew after all.

He needed Jake at top of his game, not worrying about having sex with some chick, no matter what happened in her past. Still, he wasn't unfazed. Jake never experienced a serious relationship in his life. His younger brother dated some of the most amazing women he'd ever seen. At one time, Andy's jealousy over that raged, but then he met Debbie, and Jake didn't know that kind of love. Any feelings of envy evaporated, and he merely wished the same for his brother. He glanced up at another very large swell coming, and thought, we'll give it a few more hours of soaking.

CHAPTER 19

Faith woke up to a change in the boat. *We're here.* Time to get off this boat and get away from everyone so she could think. They completed their season with tremendous success and now the summer waited for them. Mack wasn't due for another week. He needed to finish the season and make some quick repairs before making his way back to Seattle. So, she had two weeks to herself, just waiting for her. She got up and walked past Jake's room just after Booker farted in the top bunk and she wrinkled her nose in disgust. *God, he smelled like the ass of a dead rhino. Disgusting piece of shit.* She made her way to the coffeepot and discovered it already full of coffee, causing a small fist pump. She turned to get a pan when she noticed Jake sitting at the table with a coffee cup in hand, suspended in midair as if about to take a drink. With only the small light above the stove on and his eyes closed, a soft illumination caressed his features, softening them. She smiled to herself as she studied at him. *She still wanted to fuck him... badly.* Feeling someone in the room, he opened his eyes.

"Hey," he said and yawned. "You don't have to be up yet." He set his mug down and rubbed the palms of his hands together under the table, trying to create some heat. "Why don't you try and get a little more sleep?"

"The boat's crawling Jake, we gotta be getting close to the harbor," she said. "I couldn't get back to sleep now if I tried."

He glanced at the clock and realized he'd slept for a while. They had maybe two hours before docking, and mere moments before Andy's voice would boom down the intercom. The deck boss observed his coffee, as if it just appeared, and the corners of his mouth turned up in that damn sexy smile. Faith moved through the kitchen, beginning to find the ingredients to make a breakfast scramble.

"So, what do you got planned for when we get back?" he asked, shuffling into the kitchen to get more coffee. His sweats laid low on his hips, without a shirt and those sweet dents low in a man's back that she loved, tantalized her.

"I'm gonna take a long, scalding-hot bath, to get the inner core of my bones warm again, then sleep like the dead for at least twenty-four hours." She smiled as she cracked eggs. "Then maybe buy a car. I've never had a car of my own before."

"Never?" he asked, surprised. "Do you know how to drive?"

"Yes, of course I know how to drive."

"Sorry. What kind do you want?"

"A 1968 candy-apple red convertible Mustang."

"Wow?"

"Oh yeah. Black leather interior. I'm hoping to get over 220 horses." A dreamy expression crossed her features. "What about you?"

"I'm going for a long, scalding-hot *shower*. Sleep like the dead for, hmm, yeah, twenty-four hours sounds good, and then it sounds like I'm looking for a Mustang." He took a sip of his coffee and eyed her as she stopped whisking the eggs and drew her eyebrows together.

"You want to help me look for a car?" she asked just to make sure she understood, then poured the egg mixture into a pan and placed it in the oven and set the timer.

"Sure." he replied. "I don't know if you know it, but I've got a house just a couple blocks away from Mack's new house."

"Yeah." She poured herself a second cup of coffee, then joined him at the table. "I think Mack said something like that when we saw them that time." She waved her coffee mug, indicating the one overnight *Je Suis Prest* and *Scaup* shared during a turnaround a few weeks earlier.

"I can't wait to get off this damn boat."

"What are you going to do with *your* summer?"

"I've got a million outdoor projects to do. Finish my gazebo, build a shed, fix my roof." He eyed her. "Maybe we could hang out."

She smiled into her coffee, then met his eyes. "Yeah, that would be great."

Just then Booker came into the room clad only in boxers, with a full-on morning erection and hands down his pants. Scratching the protruding member, he yawned before he gave a loud and emphatic fart and grinned.

"Seriously?" Faith pursed her lips together, wrinkled her nose, and rolled her eyes before she closed them, as Jake snorted with laughter.

After breakfast, the crew members, wide awake with coffee mugs in hand, stepped out onto the deck. As the harbor came into focus, each threw fenders and gathered lines for docking, content knowing that another successful and safe season now laid behind them.

When Andy handed her a check for forty-seven thousand dollars after the offload, she folded it and tucked it into her jeans pocket. The crew took a vote and went home rather than stay the night in Dutch, so after dinner and drinks at the Unisea bar, they left and started the trek of the long journey home.

From the Gulf of Alaska, past Canada and into the Straits of Juan de Fuca, they entered Admiralty Inlet and sailed into the waters of the Puget Sound and Shilshole Bay, before finally coming to rest in Fisherman's Terminal, one week later. As the journey progressed, the men grew more excited to see their families, and the infectious glee caused Faith a little homesickness, as well. Rosie surprised her men and flew up to take the boat home with them, and for a moment, Faith wondered if she shouldn't have stayed. However, two weeks of absolute quiet also sounded blissful.

As the wharf came into view, a small congregation of people stood on the pier waving and calling to their loved ones. Once docked, Booker almost boyish, climbed over the rail first and down the ladder to grab a small petite woman with long golden blonde hair. Faith smiled at the scene until he strangled the poor woman with his tongue.

Brandon climbed down next as his wife and son sunk themselves into his arms. He held the adorable baby up to the sun, with tears collecting in the corners of his eyes. Amy, a tall, solid woman with shoulder-length brown curly hair and rimless glasses, watched her husband with silent tears running down her face as the three became a unit again.

"He's so big, baby. He's gotten so big," Brandon said over and over.

Tristan climbed down third, with just enough time to throw the line at Faith when his girlfriend, Julie, took a running leap and straddled him around his waist, hands plunging deep into his thick hair. She almost knocked him over as she kissed him, and Faith chortled at the spectacle.

Andy lowered himself down the ladder with Jake just behind him. The stoic and stalwart skipper greeted a darling, well put-together fifty-something woman with loving enthusiasm. She cupped his face in her hands, before bringing her lips to his, her chocolate-brown bob swinging around their faces.

"Oh, babe," Andy exclaimed. "Look at your hair, it's dark."

"Too much?"

"No, I love it. You are so beautiful. Hey girls!"

Behind them a young model-like girl with long honey-colored hair in her twenties leapt at Jake, much like Julie did with Tristan, and Faith's entire face fell. The woman planted a loud, smacking kiss on his lips. He smiled at the girl with love in his eyes and squeezed her hand before turning to his sister-in-law to give her a hug. Two other girls, identical to the first, came running down the pier and sprang into his arms in the same manner, calling him Uncle Jake. Relief flooded through her as she studied the reunions on the dock.

****

Jake turned, thinking Faith stood behind him, but when he turned and lifted his eyes to the deck, she threw a buoy far aft, so sprinted up the ladder to retrieve her.

"Come on," he grabbed her hand. "Come meet everyone."

After Jake brought Faith over to the group and made the introductions, Andy announced the bulk of the unloading and clean-up could wait until the following day. They all negotiated one o'clock and Brandon, Booker and Tristan left immediately, eager for time with their loved ones. After several trips to and from the boat, and assurances from Jake that he'd lock up, Andy and his family left too. Analisha, Andy's eldest daughter, had driven Jake's truck to the marina for him before leaving with her family.

"Ah, quiet at last," Jake said a little, raising his hands to the heavens, and Faith smiled. "Can I give you a lift home, since we're almost going to the same place?" he asked, as she jumped down from the boat, her battered canvas duffle bags in hand.

"Really?" she asked. "That would be fantastic, I was just gonna catch a cab." The car noise from the Ballard Bridge sounded foreign to Jake's ears, and

266

the hum of the city made the exchange seem awkward with no buffer of people or fishing between them.

"Yeah, no problem. Come on."

They drove across the bridge and into the Sunset Hills district. He drove past his house, which overlooked Shilshole Bay and the Puget Sound, but pointed it out to her, before rounding the corner toward the Carter house. She hadn't seen their new house yet and commented it was much bigger than she'd imagined. Climbing down out of Jake's truck, before he got out himself, she turned back to him.

"Thanks for the ride. It was a great season."

"It was. So," he said, before she could sprint away. "Sleep tonight and clean up tomorrow? Sorry your entire day of sleeping got taken away."

"It's okay." She laughed. "I'm glad we waited. Everyone needs to be with their families tonight. At least I'll get the hot bath and a solid ten before we have to be back there."

"How about I pick you up at nine-thirty? Mack can't have anything to eat in the house. You want to grab a bite before going in?"

"Sure. Thanks. I'll see you at nine-thirty." Closing the door, she stooped and lifted her two-heavy bags before walking up the narrow path. Jake waited for the light to come on inside and tried not to think about her dumping everything, stripping off her clothes and laying naked in a tub somewhere.

"Goddamn, that woman's gonna be the death of me," he muttered and drove to his own waiting shower and bed.

****

Faith dropped her bags in the foyer and viewed the Carter's house. Rosie made it shine. The spacious rooms and cheerful colors, all inviting and well put together. She walked by a buffet containing pictures of Charlie, Brady, Mack, Rosie and herself, yet also perched there were several of Rosie with friends Faith didn't know. She peered at one, her surrogate mother's head thrown back in a belly laugh. Beautiful, yet eyes still lonely. What had her life been like? Wanting to escape her tiny little town? Getting pregnant? Married? Not only married to Mack, but her and Nels too. She never knew where she stood with Rosie, but somehow the woman had always been there when she needed her most. She made a mental note to do something special for her that summer.

Faith went to the refrigerator and as suspected, Mrs. Carter stocked it well. However, she didn't want to admit that fact to Jake because she wanted to spend time with him. Time off the boat. A six pack of Budweiser beckoned, and she opened a bottle and sipped.

"Ahh," she said to the quiet emptiness. "God, that's good." She walked to the adjoining living room where a large flat screen television, well-stocked bar and oversized couches and recliners made of worn leather, also whispered their encouragement to her to lie down.

She drank from her beer, moving past the living room and other spaces to the bedrooms upstairs. The master bedroom appeared warm and inviting, but it wasn't until she opened a room at the end of the hall that her mouth fell open.

In colors of sunshine yellow and summer sky blue, the room welcomed her. A huge king-sized bed with starfish on the pillows amassed most of the room. The nightstand and headboard contained real bleached white shells, starfish and sand dollars. Her mother's rocker sat waiting in the corner, with a soft angora blanket folded over its backrest.

She gasped when she turned and a large group of photos collected on one wall. Each member of the Carter family beamed out of their own photo, all surrounding a picture of herself and her father. Rosie made this *her* room. Unable to control the stinging in her eyes, she turned around in it. Above the door coiled in rope spelled out the word, welcome.

Two other doors, one containing a closet with a handful of women's clothes inside and the other, a small bathroom with, to her utter delight, a bathtub in it. Next to the tub, several round balls stacked high in a dish, and she brought one to her nose. Lavender and vanilla. Figuring it must be something for the bath, she threw it in and watched it fizz, spiral and dissolve into a fragrant foam. The water merely warm, she rotated the taps to a hotter temperature, and steam soon wafted up toward the ceiling, and followed her as she returned to the bedroom to peel off her clothes. Noticing a long dresser, also her mother's, with a mirror attached to its base. She opened the drawers to discover Rosie set to work there too. Underwear the kind with no butt, two lacy bras, socks, shorts and tank tops all waited cheerfully for her to wash off the sea, the job and the rules of that life so she could begin the new ones. Smiling, she reached for her cell phone to call Mack's wife.

****

The crew worked on the *Scaup* through the next day and into the early evening, but when they finished this time and Jake drove her home, the entire summer and early fall laid out before them. Making a date to look at some cars in the next few days, after completing all the tasks requiring their immediate attention, like bills, laundry and sleep, the couple parted ways.

By the time Friday came, Jake wanted to see her again very much. The days, still clinging to cooler weather and rain, had the sun peeking out in intervals. Before he could get out of his truck, Faith came out the house, turned to lock the door, then ran over to it. She wore well-worn Levi's, a green cotton sweater the color of her eyes and an old, battered leather bomber jacket, with no makeup and her long glorious red curls pulled through a baseball cap. It surprised him to see her like that, and he smiled as she opened the door and slid on a pair of aviator sunglasses.

"Hi," she said, a little breathless, jumping in and filling the cab with a fresh soap and lavender aroma.

"Hey." He grinned back, as she hooked her seatbelt.

"We match," she giggled, and his eyes shifted down at his outfit. Jeans, boots and a steel gray sweater, with a darker leather jacket over it, though sans the baseball cap. Instead, his brown wavy hair curled on the collar and around his ears. He did shave but needed a haircut.

"So, you sure you want to do this?" she asked. "You can still get out now."

"Not a chance, Red. Where are we going first?"

They spent the day looking at four different cars and were happy to see the best was saved for last. She paid in cash and since she bought the car in West Seattle, they met at a bar and lounge called the West 5, for beers and dinner.

"Oh wow, this place is so cool," Faith noted, looking at the red and cream interior, with a glowing neon crown and old Rainier sign illuminated at the far end of the bar. The stools at the counter, cushioned and tacked, matched the rest of the old retro-chic charm.

"Yeah, it *is* cool. It's been around for years now, the guy that owns it put a lot of time and energy into keeping it laid back and kitschy like this."

"Did you say kitschy... perfect word."

"Yeah, I try to come here in the first couple weeks after I get back. Hey, Dave, how you doing man?" He shook hands with the proprietor. "Dave Montoure, Faith Pearson. Faith this is Dave, the owner of West Five, and a good friend." After they exchanged some pleasantries, the couple sat in an old-time booth, ordered and found themselves alone again. "So, what's going on for you this next week?"

"Oh," she said, exhaling, and leaned back in the booth. "Well, for the next few days not much. I called Rosie, they'll be in by the end of the week and she wants to do some stuff next weekend."

"What kind of stuff?"

Faith squirmed a little and a flush spread across her freckles. "Oh God." She hesitated, then blurted, "She thinks I need to look more like a girl. I came home and found some clothes she bought for me but she's taking me to some spa thing in B.C. to get some different summer clothes or something."

"Summer clothes? What... like a swimsuit?"

"I guess." She flashed him a look of pain and slight panic. "I don't know. I haven't taken a break for a very long time, so I just have a couple pairs of jeans, tee shirts and work stuff." She peered down at her clothes. "Rosie bought this."

"It's nice. What else could you need?"

"Right?" she exclaimed. "Yes, that's exactly what I said."

"Why don't you just go back to your house and get that stuff." He paused. "Where *do* you live?"

"With Mack."

"Oh, where's your stuff then?"

"I don't have stuff," she said and took a sip of her beer.

"What about your furniture?"

"I don't have any, except for a few pieces of my mother's and they're in my new room now."

"Oh," he said, interested. "So you never bought a house or an apartment or anything?"

"My dad's cabin is still out on Camano Island, and there's a couple of beds and some stuff out there. We all share it but I haven't been out there for several years, now."

"Don't have furniture. Just bought your first car. You're kind of a nomad." She laughed at how ridiculous it sounded.

"Yeah."

"That's a real trip." He thought for a minute, and asked, "What do you do with all your money?"

"Oh, that. I just put it in the bank and take it out when I need it."

"You don't invest it?"

"Yeah, I do. Most of it in fact, but not in like a house or anything, just the market. Whatever the agent guy says to do."

A little shell-shocked, he tried to do the math. Working and earning a salary since she the age of fourteen -granted at the beginning it isn't much- but he'd bet she made a little less than he did now, and minus his owners share. Times that by twenty-some odd years and that would make it in excess of...

"Four million dollars." She smiled as the realization dawned across his face. "It's always so fun to watch people's reactions when they figure it out. It's a lot, I know. I built it off work, a trust fund from my grandparents, and the annual share Mack insists on giving me. Well, that and some great investing. The thing about it is, I don't care. I don't need much to live on. Money doesn't mean that much to me, and I'd give every cent I have to get my dad back, every single dime."

CHAPTER 20

Faith had to admit facials, massages, deep conditioners and haircuts with Rosie was nothing to turn your nose up at. The shopping, she could do without but Faith came back with a new wardrobe, feeling fantastic, albeit several hundred dollars poorer.

The Carter family reunited, unpacked and rested, before they barbequed, fished, went to the batting cages, and Pike Place market, often taking Jake with them. However, Jake was ready for something a little more private with Faith.

"Pearson," she stated, accepting his call.

"Hey Pearson, this is Rasmussen."

She chuckled. "What are you doing, Rasmussen, bothering me on my summer break?"

"I'm getting my boat ready, hoping you'll come out on it with me tomorrow."

"Oh yeah! What time?"

"Maybe nine-thirty? It's supposed to get hot, so bring sunscreen, we're going swimming. I'm guessing you and Rosie found a swimsuit by now?"

"Yes." She laughed. "I'm not sure about it but Rosie liked it."

"So wear it, and I'll see ya in the morning."

"Okay, sounds good."

Jake arrived at nine-thirty sharp. A balmy ninety-seven degrees out, with blue skies and a perfect warm wind, he couldn't wait to start the day.

Walking up the path to the Carter home, he felt like a teenager picking up his date for the prom. Though he lived close by and respected Mack, he didn't know the man all that well. The skippers did more together, and he suspected Mack would be like a dragon-at-the-gate kind of dad. He could see the large man in the kitchen, leaning on the counter with a lit cigarette in one hand and a mug of coffee in the other. He laughed at something Faith said. She stood behind the kitchen island, her hair in a messy knot at the base of her neck with sunglasses perched on her forehead. She wore a UW hoodie with cut-off sleeves, as well-defined, tan arms, gesticulated, emphasizing whatever she said. Charlie and Brady sat on barstools on either side of her at the island, both mirroring their father with their own cigarettes, coffee and smiles. Rosie walked to Mack and wrapped her arms around his body, leaning her head into his chest. Raising an arm, he laid it around her shoulders. Every one of them animated, and plain to see, very much a family. Faith appeared young, relaxed and happy. He stepped onto the porch, took a deep breath, and rang the bell as he blew it out.

Charlie answered the door wearing board shorts, an unbuttoned Hawaiian shirt and shades hanging off the back side of his head. "Oh hey, Jake." They shook hands, and he gestured for him to enter. "How you doing, bro?"

"Good, how about you?" Jake smiled, stepped aside, then followed the kids back to everyone else. "Good to be home, right?"

"Fuck yeah! That last run was a bitch, yo."

"You guys ever figure out the engine?"

"Yeah, I don't know. You might wanna leave that one alone with my dad."

"Thanks for the heads up." He considered Charlie's appearance. "You guys going to the beach?"

"Naw, man, Faith said we could come out with you guys." He pivoted to conceal his evil grin and walked into the kitchen. "Come on in, we're all back here."

Jake's face fell. *Fuck!* There went his perfect day with Faith on the water. He came around the corner with a smile plastered on his face, trying not to show his disappointment. The kitchen smelled like cigarettes, coffee, bacon and fresh bread. Faith, Rosie and Mack looked up as Brady turned around on his barstool.

"Hey, Jake," Mack said in a relaxed, raspy voice and extended a hand, which Jake shook. "Where you guys going today?"

"Ah, San Juan's, not sure where yet." He turned to Charlie and Brady. "You guys got a favorite spot you want to go to?" The kitchen quieted and Rosie realized her son's prank.

"They're teasing you, Jake." She snapped a towel at Charlie's butt, but he danced away from it.

Giggling, Faith turned to bus the table and entered Jake's full view, causing his mouth to drop open. She wore high Levi's cut-off shorts with bits of frayed threads hanging down onto her tan, hard-toned thighs. When she leaned over to put the dishes in the sink, the denim strained against her incredible ass.

****

Brady launched into a loud embellished story about a particular string of pots as Mack watched Jake gape at Faith, struggling for control, and not without sympathy.

His surrogate daughter, a beautiful woman, seemed clueless or disinterested in the effect she had on men. In his mind, it was one of her best traits. Chalking up men's catcalls to men living on a boat for a long time without the benefit of female companionship. In her mind, they referred to any woman, not necessarily her specifically. She didn't play the coy, deceptive games that many other girls played, because no one ever taught them to her. Even if they did, she would think the deception unfair and ridiculous. Before she turned to see Jake's face, Mack thought he'd give the man a moment to compose himself.

"Hey, Faith," Mack said as he gestured Jake outside. "Why don't you grab the rest of your stuff and meet us out front when you're ready, I'm going to show Jake that new engine."

"Okay, just be a few. Let's take my car?"

"Sure." The two men walked outside, and after Mack opened the garage door, Jake leaned across the engine to inspect it. "Wow, this is clean, Mack. Who did you get it from?"

"Norman Rudolphson. Nice, huh? He gave me a fair price."

"How much did he…" Jake began when Mack's deep register interrupted him, not willing to beat around the bush.

"Look Jake, I've always liked you, man. I know she's not mine by blood, but she's my daughter just the same." He pulled out a cigarette and offered one to Jake, who took it and held it against Mack's proffered lighter. The older man took a deep drag and blew out the smoke. "You've got yourself quite a reputation there, man, and it follows you. My girl's not gonna be another knot in your cherry stem chain. You got me, chief? It's safe for you to assume that I'm not bullshitting you, in any way."

Jake considered Mack's colored-filled face. "So, we're shooting straight here?"

"Yawp."

"Well then, I don't know what's going on with Faith and me. It's been going on for some time now, though. There's… something and I just don't know what it is, yet." He glanced back at the engine. "Yeah, I've been around the block more than her, but a lot less than you, I expect." He turned and saw Mack's mouth twitch. "I'm not looking to have sex and dump her, if that's what you think. I just… like her… and we became friends this season." He looked confused. "And… I don't know what it is," he finished.

Mack glanced back at the engine again too and took a drink from his coffee mug. He remembered Jake lost his own father just a few years back and took it hard. Andy and his brother were close, but because Faith intertwined with their livelihoods. Andy might find it harder to talk to his junior about her, and Jake *did* appear out of his element. However, Mack, also a man, understood what the guy wanted from his daughter, no matter what he professed.

"Okay, understand this, then." Mack looked him in the eye. "She's a grown woman that makes her own decisions. I'm not, nor would I ever want to be, in the position to tell her anything about her sex life. She's important to me, Jake, and she's important to her brothers, and Rosie. She's also been through too much in this life. So, if she *is* just a piece of ass, walk away now and find someone else to scratch the itch. If not, well, then you have my blessing."

The back door slammed, and they both saw her stride across the lawn toward them. Mack saw Jake's eye scan the length of her and grin. Just before she got to within earshot Mack leaned in and growled, "But remember this boy, you hurt her, well then, me and the boys are going to fuck you up... in pieces." He slapped Jake on the back, his voice and mood lightening. "Hey darlin', have a great time, okay?" Jake turned and watched her kiss him on the cheek.

"We will. See ya." She smiled and turned to him. "Okay, you ready?"

"Ah... yeah." He smiled and darted a look back at Mack, who winked at him. The trio walked around the house to the front yard, where they saw Charlie and Brady in the back of his truck sitting in a canoe.

****

"Sorry about the morons," Faith said, still trying to stifle a chuckle as they drove to the marina, with the top down on her Mustang. "They think they're hysterical."

Jake glanced at the road, then at Faith. "Oh yeah, they're a riot." Relieved when Mack told the boys to stop being jackasses, and to put the canoe away, he snorted at the remembered expressions on their faces.

"When's the last time you took your boat out?" Faith asked, and his grin broadened.

"Last summer." He tilted his head down and peered outside. "And it turned out to be a great day."

"Yeah." Faith grinned, peering out at it too. "Today marks the longest time I've had off in five years. Bad, huh?"

"Why so long?"

"Well, at first I just wanted to throw myself into work." She thought some more before shaking her head and laughing. "Then to be honest, I don't know. I just love being out there."

"Yeah, me too. Pathetic, aren't we? Well, today we'll make up for it."

"Deal. Oh, look!" Faith pointed across him out the window at Lake Union. A hundred sailboats glided along the water with majestic reverence. "They're so cool."

"Do you like sailboats?" Jake asked, interested. Sailboat people were a different breed.

"Yes... well, I guess I can appreciate them," she said. "I mean, I think they look beautiful, but I don't think I'd ever own one."

"Ok, I've decided you can come aboard *Krigerens Hjerte*."

"What the hell's a Kri... Kriger... heart?"

"Cre-ga-rens Yat-te. The Warrior's Heart," he explained. "It's the name of my boat."

"Christ, between your family and Mack, there is enough sentimental national pride and testosterone to last generations." Faith rolled her eyes. "That's a Norwegian thing, right?"

"Yes, of course it's Norwegian," he said. "What else would I name a boat?"

"Oh, I don't know, um, *Morning Star* or *Jenny* like on *Forrest Gump*." He stared at her with such unabashed disgust it made her laugh until she vibrated. "Okay, okay, Norwegian pride. Fine."

"You're such a Swede," he accused, miffed.

They drove for a few minutes in silence before Jake asked, "What about Mack?"

"What?"

"You said between my family and Mack... I've never known Mack to be, um, well, sentimental, all that much."

"He's very sentimental about things he feels strong about," -she paused- "That didn't quite make sense, but you're right, it's only a couple things."

"Like what?" Jake asked, curious now about the salty skipper that could reduce him to a crimson stain.

"Well, like my dad and mom."

"Oh yeah?"

"Yeah. So, my dad married my mom, who was a full-bred Scot. She was a lot younger than him, like around ten years, but they hooked up. I guess, according to Mack, my dad fell hard and even though he felt the same way about Sweden that you do about Norway, he learned some Gaelic from my mom's parents." She smiled. "He wanted her to kind of stay alive for me."

They left the freeway and turned into the marina where he kept his boat moored, parked, then he turned off the ignition and shifted his body to look at her.

"Dad and Mack were saving to buy their own crab boat and my dad wanted to name it for my mother. You know, for Scotland. At first, he thought, Middleton, my mother's last name. Their family motto was *Fortis in Arduis,* which means strong in adversity. But my grandfather hated my dad and Mack, and the feeling was very mutual. So, Dad decided he didn't want to name his boat after him. After my dad died and Mack finally got the boat, he named it *Je Suis Prest,* which was one of my dad's favorite expressions." She smiled and gazed out over the water, before saying, "It means, I am ready."

Jake observed her for a long moment, thinking, then said, "Shit, that's a great metaphor. And that's Gaelic?"

"It is a great metaphor, isn't it?" She seemed pleased he understood. "No, it's Latin. Well, it's old French, derived from Latin. I'm not sure why I told you about the Gaelic. It's just something cool about my parents."

"Wow, all this time and I never knew what that meant. He was right to do that," Jake said, thinking of Mack's boat. "It's what I would've done too."

They got out and walked down the pier. Faith stood dumbfounded when she stared up at the sleek sixty-foot cruiser complete with fly bridge and sundecks. Jake disappeared below deck and came back carrying a cooler of beer and water up to the bridge, and she still stood on the finger-dock.

"What are you doing?" he asked, eyebrows raised.

"This is huge," she exclaimed. "You could like, live on this."

"I did for a long time but decided it was becoming just a little too much time on the water." He grinned at her and reached for her hand. "So, welcome aboard."

The teak decking and outdoor shower used for rinsing off after swimming gleamed, inviting their use. Thick carpet covered the floor in the galley which boasted rich colors in various hues of taupe. Everything was comfortable, classic and oversized, with three staterooms, two heads and clean engine room. When he showed her the master berth, she looked in wonder at the king-size mattress, thick and plush.

"I know it looks impressive now but believe me, it came ridden hard and put away wet."

"A charter?"

"Yeah, a brewery. They took people out and partied *hard* on it. I got it for next to nothing, gutted it and lived aboard while I spent five years turning it into this."

They embarked and were soon planning over the clear, crisp water for Roche Harbor on San Juan Island. As the day progressed, the weather got warmer and by the time they reached the harbor, the air floated thick and stifling hot. They motored in, sitting up in the exposed fly bridge. Jake removed his tee shirt, uncapped a bottle of water and drank.

Faith watched the people on shore and turned to point out a small blond girl of about three, who dumped a bucket of water on the head of her older brother. She laughed and turned to see Jake drain the last contents of his bottle. A small rivulet of water ran down his chest and torso, tinted golden tan, just to the top of his low-slung cornflower blue board shorts and a jolt of pure lust exploded inside her. She dropped her own water bottle on the deck. His eyes caught the movement and gave her a questioning look as he recapped his bottle and threw it into the trash.

"Whoops," he said, laughing. "You okay?"

Without waiting for an answer, he turned back toward the wheel as she rolled her eyes at herself and her idiocy. He scanned the area for a place to anchor, eyes shaded by his Oakley aviators. The muscles in his biceps and forearms contracted as he moved and shifted the gears, and his broad shoulders, chest and abdomen laid smooth, as a perfect V of muscle dove into his shorts and narrow hips.

Unlike Faith, men didn't hide their bodies on the work boats. Though they didn't walk around naked... Well, except for that one boat when they all played a prank on her and walked around three days in their off time completely naked. Many walked around in thermals, boxers, sweats or jeans. Some with shirts, some without. Jake wore jeans or sweats with a tee shirt most of the time. As he faced away from her now, her eyes dropped to his ass. He filled out his shorts and at that moment her hands itched to round over him, run fingers down his chest and... She dropped her water bottle again.

"Damn it!"

"Faith?"

"What." She snapped her neocortex back to attention. *What in the hell's the matter with her?*

"Hey, where do you go?"

"Off island," she retorted and then finished with, "Do you want to stay here?"

"Off island?" he asked, creasing his brows together.

"No, I mean, here. Do you want to stay here at Roche? It's pretty crowded." He turned around to face her, one hand still on the wheel.

"We can tender in."

"No, let's go someplace where we can go swimming."

"Okay," he perched his sunglasses on his forehead and peered at his chart plotter.

Faith stood. "I'll make lunch."

"Sounds good," he said, studying the screen. "Want to go over to Sucia?"

"Yeah, I like the hikes over there."

As Jake motored over to the small island and anchored in a private cove, while Faith prepared the club sandwiches. She dressed a deck table, before setting the plates down along with some potato salad from the cooler, and two beers. They sat eating on the warm covered patio a million miles from Alaska's frigid waters.

****

After lunch, Jake suggested they go for a swim. As he went to find towels, Faith walked on deck, unbuttoned her shorts and shook them off, wearing tiny peach colored bikini bottoms. He groaned as he walked out and saw her, then held his breath as she stretched to remove her heavy sweatshirt. Her bikini top, though brief, fashioned into a halter that contained high full breasts within the fabric. Her waist, long and thin, created a perfect eight pack, and her glorious hair threaded down from a ponytail in a perfect waterfall. She removed the band and the loose curls rained fire down her back. She fingered the waves back into the ponytail, securing the strands that escaped.

His penis, with a mind of its own, twitched. Worried his attraction revealed itself in an all too apparent way, he moved toward the rail and slammed his leg into a bench.

"Fuck!" he shouted as his shin throbbed and pulsated. "Goddamnit!" Faith turned around and watched him sit down on the bench hard, holding his shin, an enormous bruise already mottling across it.

"Oh God, what did you do?" She walked over to him and knelt. "Let me see it."

Fuck, she's too close. "No!" he said, then gentled. "Really, it's fine, let's go."

"Let me see it, you stupid baby." She pulled his hand away and inspected the knot growing under the skin. "You klutz," she laughed. "You're as bad as I am today."

Her hair fell off her shoulder and tickled the top of his thighs. Her breasts were inches from his fingers. He stood up, colliding with her body, knocking her hard on her butt.

"Ow, are you giving me a matching one for my ass?" she retorted.

His body quickly betraying him, he decided any more words or hesitations would only bring him further embarrassment. So, he took two strides, reached the rail and jumped into the cool water below. She sat for a full three seconds by herself before her own competitive nature piqued and she jumped in after him.

They swam for over an hour, racing, dunking and splashing until chilled and more than a little tired. Swimming to the boat, Jake reached up, lowered the step ladder, and moved to the side to help her onboard.

He hopped on deck after her, as she squeezed water from her thick hair. She grabbed two towels and threw one at him, hitting him in the face, then dried herself off with the other. The afternoon's easy, carefree mood evaporated into awkward shyness again, as her nipples strained against the fabric and cold, and suddenly he didn't want to play the game anymore.

CHAPTER 21

He crossed the distance between them, standing four inches away from her, then reached up and removed the band from her hair. Her heart thumped in her chest, as she breathed in suntan lotion, and sea, and man. Placing her hands on his chest, it rose and fell faster.

"I like your hair down," he breathed, running a hand down the length of it.

"Okay." Her eyes darted from his eyes to his lips, as her fingers slid down his chest and sides, causing gooseflesh to rise.

He rose a hand up and skimmed it across her clavicle, and with no memory of doing so, her hand moved to the front of his shorts and cupped him. His eyes first widened, then narrowed in warning.

"If this starts, don't tell me to stop." Her hand caressed him. "I fucking mean it, Faith." She looked back up at him and nodded. "I'm not going to tell you to stop, Jake."

His hands dove into the thick, tangled mass of her hair and he covered her mouth with his. He groaned like a wounded animal, and his tongue met hers in a private dance, as his hands moved down her shoulders and back, then molded around her bottom, and drew in her heat.

"Jake." She panted when they broke the kiss, but he already moved to her neck.

Her nipples stiffened into pebbles, pressing hard against his chest, breaking loose months of sexual tension. Desperate for her taste, he tugged the bikini top down and feasted on her breasts, sucking in deep, and rolling his tongue over the tip. The stubble of his light beard, rough against her skin, aroused her even more. Wanting his flesh on hers, she moved her hands to the sides of his shorts and yanked down hard until they pooled at his feet. He jerked and groaned in pain.

"Shut up, you like it," she said, then added, "Sorry, did I hurt you?" A noise only described as pleasure crooned out of him in answer. She held him full and rigid in her hand, massaging and milking him.

"Faith." He panted and released the hand he placed on her breast to plunge down her swimsuit, bringing one hand to the front. Finding her ready, he thrust two large, rough fingers deep inside her.

"God!" she yipped and couldn't quite catch her breath.

Fingers still inside, he lifted his eyes to hers and watched her struggle, then lowered them to her parted lips and only then did he release her womb. Jake brought both hands up to cup her face, fusing his mouth to hers. In a moment of clarity, they both realized they stood out in the open, on the back of his deck in plain view of anyone that bothered to turn into their hidey hole.

He lifted her legs, and she clamped them around his waist as he took her down the steps to the master berth, bumping her head on the door jamb.

"Ow." She laughed and rubbed the offended area.

"Shut up, you like it." He carried her into the cabin, and kicked closed the door, then leaned her against it. By mutual agreement, they slowed down. He helped her remove her top and kissed her slow and deep. When their lips parted, he turned her and backed her up to the bed, until it forced her to sit. She blinked up at him, and as he stood in front of her, erect and desperately needy, she lifted him to her mouth, but before taking him in, he groaned and pushed her back onto the bed.

"No..." he said. "I wouldn't last ten seconds."

"I'm not too far behind you," she admitted. "Believe me."

Pressing her thighs down, he used his middle finger to enter her again, and scrape along her nub, moving his other hand to play across her abdomen, never taking his eyes from hers. She ground against him, her breasts moved to the rhythm of their bodies, making them bounce.

"I want to feel you inside me." At her word, he stood and sheathed himself into the slow embrace of her body.

"Christ, you're tight."

Thrusting himself deeper into her folds, caused her back to arch, and her breasts to lift, nipples teasing his chest. The deep delicious pull grew more urgent, as he slid his fullness in and out, stretching her, and knowing soon she'd find release.

"Jesus, Faith!" he pleaded, pain and pleasure battling within him. "Please..."

"Mmm..." She placed a hand on each side of his ass and brought him into her as deep as he could go. He pulled out until almost outside of her before thrusting in once, then a second time. Intense sensations of pleasure exploded within her, and their bodies locked in frozen unison, as he filled her.

After several moments, he seemed to turn from a solid to liquid state. "I'm not sure I can move. Am I getting heavy?"

"A little," she admitted and stroked the contours of his back, "but I'm not sure I want you to go yet." He pumped into her twice more, laughed and rolled off her and onto the bed.

"Honey, after that, not a chance in hell."

They were quiet, feeling the boat rock beneath them, water lapping against its hull, as the afternoon gave up and evening descended.

After a while he asked, "Do have any idea how hard it's been being around you and not be able to touch you?"

"I do now," she retorted, and they both chuckled. The window in the ceiling above them doubled as a door onto the deck of the bow. Three stars dotted the black canvas of the heavens. She laid her head on his chest, red hair fanning out and one hand resting on his forearm, as she stared up through the glass. "Bad?"

He continued to stroke her arm. "Completely blue-balled. You should know, I had some very dirty dreams about you." He paused and shook his head. "I was such a dick to everyone." They laid in silence for a while before Jake spoke again. "The last few weeks, seeing you... I don't know... this is kinda new for me."

She listened and with the declaration her eyes opened and widened just a little more. It took a long time for her to get comfortable with someone too. She'd loved five men in her life, but never been in love before. The way she'd describe her feelings for Jake... pure confusion, and she didn't know if she should trust it. Friendship, yes, and now lovers and intense intimacy but...

"What are you thinking about?" He pushed her hair over her shoulder, stroked her cheek, then locked his hands behind his head.

"When we were on the boat and you got so mad," she started, looking over to meet his eyes. "I thought I'd have to look for another job, and it bugged me because I didn't know why you were so angry. I thought I was gonna lose the gig and working close to Mack."

"I'm sorry about that, baby, more than you know."

"But... I also knew I wouldn't see you again, and knew I'd miss that... miss you." She blushed and when he said nothing continued, "I guess I care about you too, more than I want to admit and it scares me, Jake."

"Scares me too."

"You getting angry is the reason having a relationship can be bad."

He sighed in relief, smiled and rolled to his side, propping his head in his hand and ran the other hand down the smooth silk of her back.

"Maybe we can figure it out though, you think?"

"I don't know... maybe."

****

They woke as they fell asleep, face to face with mouths open as if paused in conversation. The blankets cocooned around them, keeping out the morning cold. The sound of gulls calling out for food sounded somewhere in the distance. Though not at all conscious, Jake's numb arm trapped under her head demanded attention.

It took a full minute to disentangle himself and focus on the woman next to him. Jake couldn't believe he'd just spent a memorable night with Faith, so beautiful in sleep. He ran his hand over her cheek. The sun streamed in from the skylight, setting her silky hair aflame, as it fanned out in stark contrast to the white sheets. Feeling alive in a way that only great sex and the promise of a new relationship could provide, he leaned over to kiss her forehead. She didn't move except to close her mouth.

"Now that's what I call a fantastic date," she murmured and smiled. "The best part's no headache." She sighed. "I'm so fucking easy." She opened her eyes and shifted her gaze to meet his. "Last night happened, right?"

Saying nothing, he reached up and peeled back the downy blanket. His eyes moving with his progress as his hand slid down over her back and the curve of her bottom to her thigh and back up again, just because he could.

"You are perfect," he said without a hint of derision.

"You're biased." She smiled and rolled onto her back. "You just got laid after being out at sea for months. You'd think a troll was perfect."

"I don't think so." His eyes clouded. "Let me prove it."

****

They arrived back at Mack's early that evening and walked to the front door hand in hand. Jake brought her fingers to his lips and brushed a kiss over her knuckles. "Are you sure you don't want to come back to my place?" he asked, hopeful. "You still haven't seen it and I could open a bottle of wine and throw some steaks on the grill, or something." She cocked an eyebrow at him.

"Or something?" she asked. He grinned like a kid, trying to get a last piece of candy, and brought his arms around her waist.

"Well, yeah, anything would do," he said, raising his eyebrows at her.

"You're insatiable." She laughed, but said more seriously, "I want to Jake, but Mack and the boys are back, and they made me promise we'd be a family this summer. Plus, I've never dated around him, so I'm not sure how he'll like it."

"Would it change anything?"

"No, but I *do* respect him and I need to get a feel for where he's at. I need to keep balance. What are you doing tomorrow?"

"I'm fixing a trellis, then maybe yard work." He kissed the side of her neck, then collarbone, adding, "Unless you tell me you want to do something more interesting."

"Maybe I'll come over and help you."

"What, and do yard work?" he asked, raising his head to look at her, then drew his brows together as if she'd gone crazy.

"Yeah, I'm not an idiot, I can pull a weed."

"No, I know, it's just... it's not much fun."

She lifted his face and kissed him, opening his mouth to let her tongue mingle with his, losing herself in the sensations. They separated, and she leaned her forehead against his.

"Are you *sure* you don't want to come home with me?" He hummed into her ear.

"I'm positive I *do* want to come home with you, but we gotta settle for tomorrow night," she whispered back, a little breathless, and he growled low in his throat. Resigned, he nodded his assent, drew in a deep breath and kissed her forehead. Turning, he walked back to his truck, and as he reached for the door, he glanced back at her on the porch. She had her hands in the back pockets of her shorts and watched him with mussed wild hair, and the slow, sexy smile of a woman recently bedded well. *Christ, Mack's gonna be pissed.*

****

Mack walked back into the living room from pissing. *Sportscenter,* three fingers of *Crown Royal* whiskey and a quiet house, his idea of heaven. He stopped short at the exchange on the front porch and clenched his jaw. It's one thing knowing something happened, but another thing seeing it. Sitting down in his chair, he picked up the remote and switched through all the channels, taking several large gulps from the glass, unsure of his role. *Upset? Fury? Beat the shit out of him? All the above? Christ, she's thirty-seven years old.* At least with boys you could throw condoms at them and say stay safe, but his girl going out to get some, well... He took another deep gulp of the warm amber liquid and clenched his jaw, as the door opened and quietly shut it.

"Hey babe. Have fun?" She jumped and turned toward him, cheeks rosy and guilty like a teenager. He clenched his jaw yet again.

"Oh... yeah," she said. "Um, what are you drinking?"

"Crown, want a belt?"

"Sure." She walked to the bar and poured herself three fingers, sipped, and sighed.

"Where did you guys go?" Mack asked.

"North side of Sucia." Brightening she said, "Holy shit, have ya seen his boat? Do you know what he named it?"

"Yeah, some Norwegian Kris Kringle shit or something." She laughed at his tone.

"Krigerens Hjerte."

"Oh yeah, that's right. So, you like him?" Mack asked, wasting no time. Never a traditional father with a lot of bullshit rules, Faith always loved that about Mack, and their exchange of information, without judgement.

"Yeah, I like him. This last trip was hard."

"Hard weather, hard gig, or hard following the rules?" At first, Faith's rules seemed unnecessary and overkill to Mack, but as the years rolled by, he appreciated their position and rigidity in her life more.

"Well, the weather was usual, the gig was okay and there's only one asshole on board."

"Christopher Mariano?"

"The little shit." Her face contorted into disgust. "The rules were kind of hard, but I didn't realize that was it. It's just... I like him, Pop."

"Jake's a good man, Faith. His entire family are quality people. You could do a lot worse."

"But..." she prompted.

He paused on the phrasing of his response. *Fuck it.* "Well, it ain't no secret, he's had his share of women, darlin'. It's not that he treats anyone bad, but he doesn't stick around and commit to any one person either, Faith."

"Oh God, Mack, and you think I do? For Christ's sake, I've never been with a guy longer than four months."

Mack considered his glass, raised it to his lips and drained the contents. "That doesn't make it a good thing, darlin'," he commented and rose to pour himself another shot.

"Come on." She followed him, drained her glass and held it out for a refill too. "Please don't tell me you want to see me settled in a pleasant house somewhere with babies all around. Because if you do that Mack, you're gonna fucking piss me off!"

He raised his head and took a long, hard look at her. Her long, massive ropes of silky red hair were every which way from the night and day's activities. The look of a woman who just experienced a gratifying, sexually charged night, and he should know what one looked like. Her vivid green eyes bore into him, face flushed with a wicked temper.

"Slow down, Faith," he cooed and raised his hands, before placing them on the counter. "Of course that's what I want for you. It's what I want for the boys too, and your dad would've wanted it just as much as I do." When she opened her mouth, he raised a hand. "But I fully acknowledge I'm an asshole for saying it. All's I'm saying is it seems different. You're a little different with Jake and I just don't want you to get hurt because you got laid for the first time in God knows how long."

Her expression softened. "Okay, I'm sorry." He poured their drinks and handed her a glass. She laughed. "It has been a long time, you know."

"I don't want to hear or know about it," Mack said, raising his hand, and moved back to his recliner, whiskey and remote. "Just keep on leaving me in the dark, baby, or I'll wring his fucking neck." She went to him and draped arms around his neck, kissing him on top of the head.

"You know I love you, right?" Not waiting for an answer, she ran off to her room to shower and change. Mack finished his drink, never once looking up for the score.

CHAPTER 22

Humid and dry, the evening blew a warm breeze through Sunset Hills and down to the water. The Carter family spent a wonderful day waterskiing, wake boarding, and swimming at Lake Goodwin. Faith planned to go over to Jake's for dinner that night. She walked the short distance in faded Levi's, brown leather flips flops and a thin, earthy green silk wrap blouse with a deep V neckline. One tug brought on all kinds of possibilities.

"Wow. You look perfect." he said and raised a hand to her face to draw her in for a kiss. He went for jeans too, and a comfortable white shirt, left unbuttoned, with a towel around his shoulders. His feet bare and his hair mussed and damp.

"Am I early," she asked, wrapping arms around his waist.

"No, I'm late." He placed hands on both sides of her head and drew her in for a deeper kiss. She rested her hands on his ass and burrowed into his neck to smell his aftershave. "Mmm, you smell good."

A hungry look passed over his features, and she pushed him away. "Later." She kicked off her sandals and walked into the house. "Oh my God, Jake."

His house, a 1920s Tudor style home, overlooked the Sound and the Olympic mountains. Jake spent every dime he'd made buying and restoring it and his boat to their graceful splendor. The rooms, open and spacious with finished bamboo floors, done in tones of warm yellows, diffused creams, and rich variant shades of taupe, all possessed breathtaking views.

A large game room, set up with a full bar, pool table, foosball, and large flat screen TV occupied most of the basement. His bedroom and living room, done in various tones of creamy whites and browns, with filmy white curtains framing large, open windows, welcomed anyone that entered them. The kitchen, spacious and well appointed, contained a door to an enormous wraparound deck where he set up their dinner table. All the spaces indicated a feeling of lived in, not cluttered.

"This house is amazing," she said, turning a circle. "I didn't know you could do stuff like this. Sorry," She broke off, embarrassed. "I didn't mean... I just thought you were just a guy who liked toys." He grinned at her flustered face and handed her a glass of merlot.

"It's okay, I just wanted something nice for when I came home. And before you go on thinking I have home decor super powers, my mother helped me out a lot with the decorating stuff."

As if on cue, a beep from a car horn sounded in his driveway. Andy, Debbie and a petite, well-dressed older woman stepped out of a newer SUV.

"Are you fucking kidding me," Jake snarled.

Confused, Faith observed the car and upon seeing her skipper realized Jake's carefully planned and seductive evening now circled the drain. Disappointed too, she plastered a smile on her face and tried to think of an excuse for her presence that Andy wouldn't call bullshit on.

However, families always fascinated her, and she was eager to see how the stalwart, cool and commanding Andy did when confronted by his mother and wife. Maybe she'd luck out and he'd become just as uncomfortable as she believed herself was soon to be.

****

Andy watched the scene unfold from the car. Not surprised to pull into his brother's driveway and see him entertaining a beautiful, curvy redhead, he flattened upon discovering the woman was his frosty, hardcore deckhand.

Debbie glanced at her husband, then did a double take at his open mouth.

"Andy, you're making a fool of yourself, close your mouth." Then she noticed the woman on Jake's front landing, which caused her mouth to drop open too. "Where did *she* come from?"

"Who?" The matriarch asked, whipping her head around and focusing her eagle eyes on Faith. "Well, who's this?"

"That," Andy replied, closing the door. "Is my new deckhand." He pocketed his keys, muttering, "Well, fuck me," under his breath.

"No, we met her that day, didn't we?" Deb whispered. "I thought you said she was dumpy?" She ran her gaze down the woman, then over at her shocked husband. "You kept that one under wraps."

"Well, if you remember, she sure as hell didn't look like that on the boat," he retorted through gritted teeth.

"Andreas, language," his mother chided, the called, "Jakob, sweetheart."

"Mom," her son said, approaching the trio, buttoning his shirt. He leaned in to brush cheeks with each woman, then shook hands with his brother.

"Jakob." Linda Rasmussen beamed at her youngest offspring. "So, I told Andreas and Debra, if the mountain won't come to Muhammad, then Muhammad must come and sit on the mountain."

She raised a hand to her son's cheek as everyone chuckled. Linda glanced over at Faith and said, "Wow, looks like you've got some good taste, at least, dear." Linda gestured to his guest before they came within earshot. "She looks like she's got some fire in her belly. Just look at that hair, and those eyes." Faith approached them and extended a hand. "Hello, dear," Linda said, extending her own hand, and the two shook. "I'm Linda, Jakob's mother. Have we interrupted something?"

Faith thought the older woman looked familiar but couldn't place her. "No, not at all." She smiled back. "We were just gonna have some dinner on the deck."

"Well, Andreas brought some steaks along, so maybe we could crash your little party." She patted Faith's hand.

"Sorry," Andy said to his brother as he tried to hide a smile and ran his eyes up and down Faith and the brevity of her top that with the wind, left nothing to the imagination. Jake scowled at him, and Andy said on a laugh, "Look, I tried to warn you, man, but you wouldn't pick up the damn phone." He nodded his head at the redhead. "Did you know this whole time she looked like that?" He pulled out a pack of cigarettes and lit two, handing one to Jake.

"About halfway through." Jake said, took it and inhaled a long deep drag, then blew it out quick.

"Hi," Debbie said, and surprised Faith when she pulled her into a hug. "We waved to each other on the pier but didn't really have any time to talk. I'm Debbie, Andy's wife."

"Right. Hi, I'm Faith Pearson." She pulled away, out of the older woman's grasp. "Okay... good... well." She gestured toward the house. "I guess, come on in." She glanced back at Jake and raised her eyebrows.

"We'll finish our cigarettes and be right in," Andy said for him. Jake glared back at his brother. He didn't know how she'd handle this... their quiet yet interfering mother. Andy raised his eyebrows in an, *I don't give a shit* look back and sucked on his own cigarette.

"Look, don't get pissed at me. You should've gone to see her, dude," Andy blamed, hands raised. "I already had my turn with all this shit, why do you think I got married?" Several feet ahead of them, Debbie and Faith walked in front of them and toward the house. "Holy shit, look at that ass."

"Stop looking at her ass, Andy!" Jake scolded but smiled. "I can't believe you didn't tell me about this sooner."

"She doesn't want all the bullshit, so she tries hard to keep it quiet and just do her work." He studied Andy's reaction. "Come on, you gotta admire the fact she's thinking of the boat drama."

"So, what? This" -he gestured at Faith- "has been going on since the boat?" Irritated, Andy tried to see all ramifications this recent development would have on production and harmony on the *Scaup*. "I thought she didn't do that."

"No. We've only... we just, um." Jake didn't have a clue what to say. "We only started hanging out after we got home. Mack lives just around the corner... you know that. We've only been seeing each other for a couple of days." Jake walked to the can sitting outside his house for smokers to stub out their cigarettes, ending the conversation.

Andy eyed him and decided not to press it but knew his brother had done more than just eye the redhead, and needed to think about that carefully. Jake turned to see if his skipper followed.

"Well then." Andy extended an arm toward the front door. "Let the games begin."

****

"So." Jake's mother leaned back on the couch with her glass of wine. "How long have you and Jakob been seeing each other then?"

"Ah." Faith struggled. "Well, we're not –ah– I work for Andy and Jake on the boat."

"Remember, Linda, we had that long talk at Christmas, about how they hired Faith, and what Elliott would have thought."

Faith endeared herself to Debbie's mother-in-law despite her late husband, without even knowing it. "Oh, yes." Linda met Faith's gaze, like the revelation dropped new light on the whole thing. Her eyes ran down Faith's top. "He would have hated it, my dear," she said, causing Faith to take a huge gulp of wine. "One hundred percent would have gone through the roof. So, well done, my darling, well done." She raised her glass to Faith, who took another hefty swallow. "These boys are just like their father, especially this one," she said, jerking a thumb at Andy. "And for you to have pulled that off, well, you'd have to have some kind of spark about you, wouldn't you?" Faith locked eyes with Jake in a silent plea for help.

"She's done well, Mom," he said, running interference, then eyed Andy for reinforcement, who gave it with a simple nod, causing Jake to shoot dagger stares at him. "She's one of the best we've had on the boat. Made Opilio's a lot easier after John died."

"Oh, yes, John," Jake's mother said, clucking her tongue. "That ninny." Her eyes shifted back to Faith. Time to see what she's made of. "I've always told my boys I wanted lots of grandchildren. Andreas and Debra have sure held up their end. Three of the most delightful angels you ever seen." Her eyes darted from Andy to Jake, who shot her a warning look of her own, then back to Faith. "But Jakob here, well, he has to stop chasing girls and start catching them so he can settle down, get married and give me some more. Do you like children, dear?"

"I-I don't... um... know any," Faith stammered and slugged back another huge gulp of wine, draining her glass. "Excuse me, I'll just..." She trailed off and sprinted for the kitchen.

Debbie sat, legs crossed, fingers around the stem of her own wine glass. Her eyes dropped, apparently pained at how uncomfortable everyone seemed, except for Linda and Andy.

"I think I'll go help her find another bottle," she said, and made her way for the kitchen too. Andy leaned back in the chair, enjoying the show.

"Mother!" Jake hissed. "Knock it off." He finished through gritted teeth.

"What?" his mother said, brushing her hand over her coiffed silver hair, then straighten the pearls at her throat before taking another sip of her wine. "What did I say? She's exquisite Jakob, and you would have beautiful babies together. There, I said it, and that's my two cents."

Andy took a sip of his beer and swallowed as he laughed, causing a coughing fit. Jake snarled at him with disgust.

"Choke on it, asshole," he spat.

****

Debbie walked into the kitchen but didn't see Faith. A flicker of movement shifted her attention outside to the back deck where Jake strewn several hurricane lanterns. The table illuminated two place settings. Faith sat at the table, smoking a cigarette.

Her heart plummeted. They didn't expect to have their romantic evening ambushed this way. Next to Faith laid a glass, with three fingers full and a bottle of whiskey. Debbie stepped outside, and Faith's back stiffened, then relaxed when she discovered Andy's wife.

"Don't mind Linda," the mother said, as she approached the table and grabbed the other tumbler. She poured a healthy amount and raised her glass. *"Sláinte,"* she said to the younger woman.

"Sláinte." Faith raised her glass and drained it. "Don't worry about it. I just get irritated easily."

"Mrs. Rasmussen can do that to you."

"So, what, she doesn't like me?"

"Oh no, she likes you a lot," Debbie said as she sipped her whiskey. "She's just trying to see what you're made of. If you're right for her boy. She did the same thing to me, but I didn't figure it out until much later. Those first couple years with Andy were rough when she was around, trying to toughen me up." Debbie paused and said with all sincerity, "She is one of the most amazing women I've ever known, though, and would give everything she had to any member of her family, if they needed it. May I?" Debbie gestured toward the cigarettes. At Faith's nod, she lit one and inhaled. "I've quit these things, but every once in a while."

"Yeah, I don't smoke as much on land as I do on the water." Faith admitted. "It's a filthy habit." She poured out two more glasses, handed one to Debbie, then leaned back into her chair, and propped her feet on another. Debbie followed her example, and both women remained quiet for a time.

"She had a hard life raising those boys, Faith. She was essentially a single parent. Elliott was a good man, but he could be fierce." She took a drag, flicked off ash and blew out the smoke. "Things went his way, and she had to learn to stand up to him or lose herself. It didn't help that their father could do no wrong in those boys' eyes."

"Yeah, dads *do* have that inside tract," Faith agreed. "I wonder why that it?"

"Because a mother's love is unconditional." Debbie sipped and sighed. "When Andy I first started dating, I didn't understand what she was about, but over the years she's helped to make me understand it all and be strong when Andy's out at sea. You're out there with them, so you don't know what it feels like to be back here at home, worrying if you'll get the call. It can be lonely and not just a little hard."

"Believe me," Faith said, "I know what that feels like." Faith scanned the darkness and released the smoke from her lungs. "Especially getting the call."

"Well, you know Elliott died a little over eight years ago. Lung cancer ate him to the bone. He was strong, like the boys, but by the end, she could pick him up off the bed. It hit them all pretty hard. I think she just wants to make sure they're loved and cared for. She actually really admires empowered women like you."

Faith looked up as if she'd just discovered something important and stubbed out her cigarette.

"Sure has a blunt way of putting things," Faith mumbled and drained her glass. "Okay, thanks."

"Ready to go back into battle?" Debbie asked, stubbing out her own cigarette, excited to see what Faith would do.

"Yawp." Faith squared her shoulders and went back into battle.

****

However, the rest of the evening moved on without incident, and Faith understood what Debbie meant about her mother-in-law and a small flame of respect flickered to life. After dinner and more drinks, the trio of interlopers rose to leave. Faith said goodbye to Andy and readied herself for Debbie's hug, then walked over to help Linda, standing a little out of the way, into her light sweater.

"You're good for him, Faith." The lady nodded toward the open door her sons, and daughter-in-law just vacated, then faced the redhead. "You aren't like one of those drippy girls he used to be so fond of." Linda buttoned each pearl button of her sweater.

"I remember you from my father's memorial."

"Yes, I know all about your family, Faith. Elliott knew your daddy. Not well, but he respected him. I remember the day he came home and told me about his death, and about you. How you lived with Mr. Carter. I'm not sure if the boys ever knew about it, but you have always stayed in my mind. When Andreas came home and told me he'd hired you on, I remembered. Now, I see you with my Jake and, well, he needs someone to challenge him. I think you might have the backbone to do it, don't you?" She smiled when Faith said nothing. "Thank you for not trying to deny that there's something between you. Any fool can see it. Just don't push him too hard, will you dear?"

"I suppose I'll push him as hard as he needs. That isn't always nice and comfortable." Faith scrutinized Linda's eyes. "I know when I get pushed too hard. I push back... harder." Linda smiled and placed a hand on Faith's cheek.

"Yes, you're very good for him." She turned and hummed as she walked to the car, but before she reached her son, she turned again and said, "I imagine he'll be good for you too. Maybe knock down a few of those walls you have so firmly in place. Good night dear." She punched at imaginary blocks, turned and waved.

Faith walked back into the kitchen and poured herself another glass of whiskey as Jake finished his goodbyes. She opened the back door and stepped out onto the deck, sipping from the glass as the warm wind blew her hair back.

He moved behind her, arms moving to encircle her small waist. She closed her eyes and leaned back into him. "I'm sorry about that, I..."

He trailed off as she reached up and ran her fingers through his hair, still looking out at the beautiful glow of the stars and house lights reflecting on the water. He bent his head into the curve of her neck, breathing her in, as the silk of her blouse billowed against her body, and noticed the small tie at her hip, holding it all together. He reached over and did what he wanted to do all night and gave it a gentle pull.

The top billowed open, exposing the round curves of her breasts. He left one arm wrapped around her waist, as his other hand stroked and played with her.

"Make love to me, Jake," she whispered. "Please." Without saying another word, he turned her to him, then picked her up and carried her to his room.

CHAPTER 23

"You're going to be cleaning and grilling all the fish I catch, like a little bitch," Faith lifted her chin at Mack in challenge.

"Keep it up big mouth. I smell a wager coming on." Mack set the tackle box and rods in the dinghy as Faith chuckled.

"That's okay old man, I'll take your money from you anytime you want."

On the Skagit River in the North Cascades National Park and north of Ross Dam, stood Ross Lake. Though they contained power, the twelve cabins and three bunkhouses built on floating logs couldn't be accessed by roads. In fact, the family needed to take two boats just to get there. They brought in their own food and drinks and needed to pack it all out when they finished their long weekend as well. Serene and perfect for any outdoorsman, most people forgot life continued to buzz miles away when they stayed on Ross Lake.

"You don't know dick about fishing," Brady spat out of the side of his mouth, then glanced at his brother, who texted a new girlfriend on his cell phone.

"Oh?" Charlie retorted, not taking his eyes off his phone. "And who's been fishing more with Dad, huh, genius? You're an idiot." He glanced over at his brother's line. "And you're using the wrong bait."

"Shut up." Mack glared at them. "You're grown-ass men. Charlie, put the phone down, you know there isn't any service up here."

"Yeah, shut up," Brady snarled at his brother.

"Fuck you..."

"Both of you shut up," Rosie bellowed from onshore, where she was reading a book. "Jesus, you'd think you were both two years old."

"Welcome to my world, babe." Mack called and she grinned. A tug came on Mack's line, and he waited to see if he had a fish on. Receiving an answering tug, he yanked and reeled hard. A six-inch trout flopped around wildly on the bottom of the boat. He grinned at Faith. "Now... who's gonna be cleaning whose fish tonight?"

"The day isn't over, ole man." As if on cue, a tug came on her own line and she dropped a seven-inch trout next to Mack's, saying, "Mine's bigger than yours."

His congested laugh echoed off the September hills, which were beginning to change colors. *God, he missed her.* Talking on the phone, emails and brief stays here and there over the years weren't the greatest substitute.

"Rose, you want to try," Mack called.

"Hmm, let me think... No," she retorted. "I'll eat them."

"So, you need to take Rosie somewhere nice for your anniversary. Thirty's a big one," Faith said, lowering her voice. "When's the last time you swept her off her feet?" Faith glanced over at her surrogate mother, deep in her romance novel again.

"I dragged her by her hair and threw her over my shoulder last night."

"Seriously?"

"Seriously, none of your business." Mack reeled in a little and took a sip of his beer.

"Come on, maybe go to Hawaii or Mexico. I'm thinking you should put some time in there."

"Why are you all butterflies and rainbows?" Mack grinned. He shaved, which always looked strange, more youthful, but nothing could hide that raspy, gritty voice.

"Yawp, that's me," Faith said. "That damn glass is always half full." The boys, having no luck, motored beside them.

"What about you and Jake?" Mack asked her.

"What about him?"

"Well, before too long we'll be going back out there."

"And you two guys have been like rabbits. So, how's that gonna work?" Charlie asked, grinning.

Faith reeled in her line and placed her rod down. She opened the cooler and grabbed a beer, then surveyed to see if anyone needed another. She popped tops, and handed them out.

"Yeah," she said, leaning back into the boat and taking a long swallow. "I'm not sure what to do about that."

"Hey." Charlie turned to face her. "I'm just kidding, you don't have to do anything about it, just have fun."

"Yeah, when summer's over, it will sort itself out. Jake's a cool guy," Brady said.

She looked over at Mack, who considered the water, and sipped from his beer. "Things don't always got to be going somewhere, Faith. Just let things come and see what happens," he counseled.

"Is that what Dad did?"

"Every day of his life, baby." Mack looked away, reeled in his line, laid the pole down and said. "You know he wanted you to have sisters and brothers, besides these two yahoos."

Charlie and Brady pretended to look offended, and they all drank companionably before Mack continued. "You'd be, I don't know, a doctor right now. When Murron first died, he was so afraid *he'd* mess it up too bad. As much as I hated your grandfather, he and Fenella were bringing you up right. Nels thought so, too. When they died, he just prayed you could come out happy, but didn't know how to get you there, Faith. Now you gotta do it yourself. That goes for all of you. You're all old enough to figure this shit out for yourselves and decide what you want."

"Is that what you did, Dad?" Charlie asked in all seriousness.

"Hell no, I've made so many damn mistakes they're writing a how to book on them. In the early day's I got it all wrong, especially with you two morons, and your mother." He gestured towards the boys. "I'm not the best for expert advice, but you," - He gestured at her with his smoke- "You ain't no pussy Faith, you're a powerful woman who never gotta be a kid. If you want to be happy, you're gonna have to let all this shit go some time and just be happy."

****

The next two weeks passed in a blur. Faith and Jake spent most days together, working at his house, finishing the gazebo and doing yard work, having barbeques with their families, and spending nights making love together. Yet every day, as the season drew nearer, Faith got more anxious. There was nothing definitive she could put her finger on, just pressure over a decision she thought she needed to make.

Jake felt it too and wanted to do something special for her. So, he enlisted Debbie and Rosie's as co-conspirators. Both women, eager to help, couldn't wait to take the putty into their hands.

Phase one: Faith didn't own a single dress. She never wore makeup in her life, and styling her hair comprised of ponytails, braids and buns. Debbie, ever the fashion plate, took her shopping to give her a brief "girl" lesson at Nordstrom's and began collecting dresses for the special evening until she tasked both her arms and Faith's with piles of them.

"I'm gonna need to try all this crap on?" Faith complained. "How long's this going to take?"

Debbie rolled her eyes. "Faith, this is important. We don't know which one is the perfect one until it's on. Don't you want to watch his eyes roll out of his head?"

"Oh, and I suppose a dress will do that? Won't standing there naked, you know, later, do the same thing?"

Debbie blew out an exasperated breath. "Sometimes wearing the right dress gets them all excited for what comes later. They have to suffer all night, right? Wanting to take it all off you." She focused on Faith's blank face. "It'll make sex even better. We'll be at this all day, honey, so just wrap your mind around it right now. We've got a lot to do before six." Resigned, Faith grabbed the dresses and went into the fitting room.

"Don't forget to come out and show me what they look like," Debbie demanded, taking out a nail file. "I mean it, or I'll sit in there with you."

"I have to come out there and show you every time?" Faith whined, then mumbled under her breath, "I'm a goddamn grown woman!"

"Glad to hear it," the older woman sang over her shoulder. Two hours and several cat fights later, the new friends chose the perfect dress. Relieved and knackered, Faith sat down on the bench next to Debbie who immediately popped up and announced like a cruise director, "Okay, on to lingerie."

"What? Why do I need that for?" Faith almost pleaded. Debbie ignored the question and walked into the intimate section of the department store. Faith followed behind her like a scolded puppy and looked up at a mannequin in a provocative pose wearing a thong. "Okay, but I'm not wearing that thread up my butt. Do you understand me, Deb? I won't do it."

Her warden gave her an evil smile and peered over at the part of the anatomy in question.

"Honey, you will with an ass like that. Do you understand? Sometimes we must bear our perfections and accept that looking hot is sometimes uncomfortable. Welcome to womanhood," she pronounced, and more quarreling and swearing ensued. Faith agreed on the thong and a demi bra but drew the line at garters and stockings.

"Not one chance in hell!" she yelled, and Debbie, knowing which hills to die on, considered Faith's long tanned legs. "They'll look better without them, anyway."

The trickiest part of the day came with shoes. The crabber never wore a pair of high-heeled shoes before, let alone stilettos. Debbie didn't want her to look like an idiot that evening so agreed to a lower-heeled sling back. They still took some getting used to, but they worked.

Phase two: Rosie, a stylist and esthetician, understood how to make hair and makeup work, and took on Faith's beautiful, thick hair, and face color for the night. At this point the "putty" stopped arguing and just drank whiskey, eyeing Mack's wife in the mirror.

"Thank you," she mumbled. "I'm sure I was the biggest pain in your ass today, but I appreciate everything. I'm not sure about any of this and I'm positive I'll screw it up, but thank you anyway, for all of it."

Rosie stopped curling her hair and glanced back at Faith's reflection. "Do you know I hated you?"

"Oh... well... okay."

She picked up a small section of hair and wrapped it around the wand before releasing the curl. "I did. Not because of you really, but because of your mom."

That piqued Faith's attention. "My mom? How…"

"Mack loved her. He loved her since high school. We used to scream and fight all the time, and he told me so during one of them." She collected another section of hair and once more curled the hair down around the wand. "Said I was no Murron. I was already pregnant then. I had stopped taking my pills." She released the curl and looked at Faith in the mirror. "Because I wanted Mack. I loved him."

"Oh, Rosie."

"I thought if I could take care of Murron's kid, then have one of my own he'd love me as much as he did her." Tears sprang up in her eyes. "But of course, he didn't. It also never helped that we couldn't work out our problems because he was always going back out to sea." Faith just watched her in the mirror, eyes stinging. "I felt like she took my husband and you wanted to take their father away from my boys."

"Rosie, I…" Roslyn lifted a hand.

"Of course, you wouldn't mean to. Which made it all the more infuriating. When I came to you that day… right after Fenella killed herself and I saw how broken you were. I realized you were just a little girl trying to survive. You weren't trying to take Mack away, any more than your mother could help Mack from falling in love with her, but I couldn't compete with a perfect memory."

The curling iron rolled down another shaft of hair. "But I didn't take you in because even if it wasn't your fault, he'd have given all the attention to you, for Nels' sake. In Mack's mind, Nels saved him. He would have come home and spent all his time with you, not his boys." She released the curl. "So, I said no to raising you, because then when Mack came home, he'd already spent most of his time with you and could give something to the boys. I'm not proud of it." Faith stared down at her lap. "When you were twenty and left, I knew what you were doing. You were giving the boys and Mack each other, sacrificing your own happiness for them."

"That wasn't the only reason, Rose."

"I know, but by then I already loved you in your own right. You're hard not to love, and by doing that, in some weird way you became my daughter too. In doing that Mack and I finally made peace. I know he loved her, but he loves me too, and it is enough."

Tears slid down Faith's cheeks and Rosie stooped in front of her and wiped them away.

"I love you, Faith."

"I love you too, Mom."

****

Jake arrived at five to six, and Mack ushered him in, poured each of them a drink and they sat down to wait. It relieved him both the boys left on their own dates, as the night promised awkwardness to spare. He glanced over at Jake in his black suit, creamy yellow shirt, haircut and

320

tanned, clean-shaven face. *I'm glad it's not me, the poor bastard.*

"So where are you going?" Mack asked, trying hard to make small talk.

"Palisades," Jake responded. "You know, Elliott Bay?"

"Oh yeah, I hear it's, you know, good." *Kill me now!* Jake shifted, uncomfortable too, and glanced up as the bedroom door opened, and Rosie walked out. Each man grateful just by the simple presence of her.

"She's just finishing up." Rosie considered Jake. "You look handsome, Jake."

"Thanks." Unable to stand it, he walked over to the door and knocked. "Ya ready?"

Faith stood in the mirror gazing at herself. Rosie created a smoky look, making Faith's eyes seductive and alluring. Her lips, tinted the same red as her hair, looked like sex itself. She wore a silk crepe inky black dress that molded to every curve of her body. The thin jeweled spaghetti straps plunged into a deep cowl, exposing the swell of her breasts. It nipped into her waist, pleating crisscross to just above her knees. Her hair up in a messy up-do, played over her freckled shoulders.

"You look... fantastic, Faith," he said, and flushed an even deeper crimson. Walking over to her, he leaned in to kiss her and held out her arms.

"I better because I'm never doing all that again." He chuckled. She took in his appearance and replied, "You clean up pretty good too, Rasmussen. Are you ready?"

"I am." He held out his arm, but she grabbed his hand. "Ready to face the firing squad."

She stepped out into the living room and her eyes shifted from Rosie to Mack. He brought his hand to his mouth, vee'd his thumb and forefinger down the sides of his jaw, and they met in the center of his chin. His shining eyes met hers and he expelled his breath. "Christ, you look like your mom, Faith."

Her eyes darted to Rosie, but the older woman winked and nodded.

****

"She looked beautiful, didn't she?" Rosie said in a soft, light voice over his shoulder. With a nod, he took another gulp of whiskey, then turned and set the glass down on the coffee table. He pulled Rosie into his arms and did something he'd never done before... danced with her.

"Yeah, she did." He brushed her hair away from her face and kissed her as they swayed in a circle. "You wanna go do something tonight?"

"Hmm." Delighted Rosie set her index finger in front her lips as if considering the ceiling. "What should it be? Dinner... Movie... Candlelight?"

As he listened, he shook his head and grinned. "No, something you *want* to do."

She laughed and her gold bracelets clinked together. "Oh, well then... it's gotta be you." She giggled as his face knotted in concentration.

"Thank you for what you did for Faith."

"Mack, you're an idiot." She twirled away from him. "I did that for you."

"Do you remember when we first met?" He asked, turning her around and unzipping her dress. She turned and began to unbutton his shirt. He pulled it over his head and threw it on the floor.

"Do *you* remember when we first met? You were pretty drunk." She asked, stripping off her dress and standing in her slip.

"*Me?*" Mack spun them in a slow circle. "You were laying on top of me but kind of moved to your back, and you had an *Elbow Room* coin stuck to your cheek."

"Oh my God." She giggled and unbuckled his pants. He let them fall to the floor and stepped out of them. "I must have looked ridiculous."

"No. You were beautiful. You didn't have a stitch of makeup on. Your hair," he brushed it from her face, then kissed her. "Was all over the place and you had a coin stuck to your face. I know this is going to sound weird, but that was the second I think I knew you were for me."

"What?"

"Imperfect. I've said a lot of fucked up shit to you over the years, honey, and we aren't no angels, but we go together, right?"

"Imperfect angels?"

"Yeah, imperfect angels." He smiled and continued to dance her back to their bedroom. "Wanna tarnish your halo?"

"Absolutely." She grinned and reached back to slam their door shut.

****

By the dawn of the next morning Jake and Faith laid curled up in front of the fireplace, naked. The fire, warm the night before, caused them to shirk the fluffy comforter half off them in the middle of the night. However, now chilled, Faith bent to reach for it and stopped to consider her lover. He laid on his back, hands folded across his abdomen, his chest rising and falling with each content exhalation.

She grinned just as content, then frowned. In two days, she needed to start the shift from this world to her existence at sea. The thought jolted through her and she looked at him again. How would he handle what she needed to do once they were back onboard? An innocent smile danced across his face, and her heart melted. *She loved him.* She knew she loved him, but what in hell could she do with that in her world?

Her stomach dropped, and she stood trying hard not to wake him. Faith scanned the pretty room... the pretty man... this pretty little life. Her dress laid carefully on a chair. *When did she start setting things nicely on a chair?* Heart thumping, she walked to the bathroom, washed her face, and brushed her teeth with a toothbrush in a drawer he cleared out for her. She peered at the object as if it sprouted wings, then opened the drawer all the way. She placed deodorant, a razor, and a hair tie in it. Not able to face how quick and easy she let her guard down and centered him in her life, she turned to the shower and twisted the knobs to scalding hot.

Stepping in, she allowed the stream to wet her hair, then turned her face into the spray. A tiny burst of cool air whooshed into the large tiled space, as Jake brought his hands around her waist, leaning his chin on her shoulder, and hugging her back to him.

"You should have woke me up," he said, sexy and sleepy, then reach for the shampoo. He massaged it into her hair, and she closed her eyes, allowing him to care for her. "What do you want for breakfast?" He turned her and guided her into the stream to rinse out the suds.

"I've never gone out like we did last night," she admitted, ignoring his question. "It was great, Jake, thank you for all of it."

"Ditto," he said, watching the shampoo slide down her décolletage and onto her breasts. He cupped them and ran his thumbs over her nipples, abandoning the cleaning ritual altogether. She breathed out, and he leaned forward to kiss her, running his hands down and over her bottom.

She let her fingers glide over his chest, as he backed her to the wall, and lifted her into the air. Faith wrapped her legs around his torso, tilted her head and kissed first his upper than lower lip before he opened his mouth to hers.

Holding her, as she leaned back against the wall, he impaled her on himself, pinning her harder to the wall, and moving slowly in and out. Their eyes watched each other as pleasure and emotion suffused through their bodies. Her breaths came in quick, short bursts as the water camouflaged her tears, and she climaxed the instant after he did, pressing his forehead to hers, then he said the words she couldn't say.

"Christ, Faith, I don't want to leave."

****

She walked home after breakfast, and as her cell phone rang, she glanced at the caller ID. Debbie's face smiled back. No doubt calling to ask her about the date. Unable to think, Faith screened it and opened the front door. Mack and Rosie's clothes laid strewn about and she smiled. His snore evident, she proceeded to her room and changed into black spandex shorts, a sports bra, and her favorite gray *Je Suis Prest* tee-shirt. Lacing up her shoes, she tucked in the laces, and hid her cell phone securely in her sports bra, before walking outside and starting to jog.

She ran from the Sunset Hills to the Greenwood District, and finally Fisherman's Terminal. At first, she tried to empty her thoughts, then she tried to face her dilemma head on. When she couldn't do either, she just got pissed. By the time she arrived at the marina, she had a full head of steam, and stood between the *Scaup* and the *Je Suis Prest*, who moored side by side, but didn't know which to check on first.

"I can't even figure *that* out," she muttered out loud.

"Stop trying," Andy said, painting the ship's name on some new buoys. He popped his head over the rail and saw her standing there, perplexed. "That's what works for me." He stretched his back and tilted his face to the Autumn sun. "What are you doing here? I thought you'd be out having fun on your last two days."

"I'm running," she said, stating the obvious. He nodded and bent his head back to his work, smiling.

"From what?" he murmured.

"What?"

"Well, are you getting anywhere?" he asked with a laugh. When she said nothing, he asked, "You all packed and ready to go?"

"I will be. Do you need some help up there?"

"Nope, after this I'm not doing one more damn thing on her for two days. Everything else will keep until Dutch. You coming to the barbeque?"

"Yeah, tomorrow, right?"

"Alki Beach, two o'clock. Tell that brother of mine to let you get some sleep, you'll need it." She nodded even though he wasn't looking and walked away. "And Faith." She stopped and turned around, a look of total bewilderment on her face. Andy stood up and wiped his forehead with the back of his hand. "Relax, things have a way of working out, whether you like it or not."

CHAPTER 24

Booker held Ashley's hand and strutted into the picnic area, goosing Linda Rasmussen. The old woman jumped a foot then hit him upside the head hard. Andy's youngest daughter, Calie, built sandcastles with Brandon and Amy's eleven-month-old son, Gabe, in the sand, while everyone else played volleyball.

Faith almost forgot about Booker and seeing him now made her stomach drop at the thought of the long months to come.

"Hey, hey, peeps," Booker yelled. "How you all doing? Ready for another season?" Not wanting a response, he announced, "I got news."

"Hey Book, have a good summer?" Tristan asked, spinning the volleyball in his hands.

"Oh, yeah, I got my old lady knocked up twice." He held up two fingers, turned and patted her butt.

"Chris," Ashley said, pretending to hit him, then noticing everyone's confused faces clarified, "Well, he's kind of right, I'm two months pregnant and we're having twins." Her faced flushed a cheerful pink.

"Yep, and getting married, right after Opilio's, baby." He clapped Andy on the shoulder as the captain extended a hand.

"Congratulations Book, guess you're growing up before our very eyes."

Faith, for the life of her, couldn't figure out what a beautiful, intelligent woman like Ashley saw in Mariano, but she gazed at him with undeniable love in her eyes, and Faith couldn't begrudge the girl her happiness.

Booker scanned his audience and Faith knew when his eyes fell on her. He made no comment but a few hours later, cornered her as she came out of the bathroom.

"So, I guess you lost the freshmen fifteen, huh?"

"Yep, guess so," she returned. "Sounds like you had a real productive summer there, Booker."

"Yeah, well, it works for now, doesn't it?" He sneered at her. "Kinda like you and Jake. Not up to par, so you figured you could pave an easier path by blowing the boss. Fuck, I wish I had tits."

"You don't need tits Booker, you're a big enough dick." She threw a shoulder into him as she walked.

"Yeah?" he called after her. "We'll see about that."

****

After the game and dinner, the evening ended early. Everyone wanted to spend the remaining time left with their families and loved ones. In that moment, Faith didn't quite know where to be. She wouldn't see Rosie, Mack and the boys much over the next eight or nine months, but she wouldn't be with Jake during that time either. Not in the way they'd grown accustom to. Deciding to split it, she spent the rest of her evening with Mack, Rosie and her brothers, eating barbeque and playing games, leaving at midnight to go over to Jake's.

That night the couple laid awake most of the night talking, kissing and making love. At around three o'clock, her body curved into his, both facing toward the open windows, and fell asleep. Jake woke to the warm sunshine peeking over the mountains, and her lavender scent blowing over him. Her emerald green eyes opened to his, and they smiled at each other. They made love, showered together and ate breakfast, before closing up his house. Jake's mother and Debbie took turns checking in on it whenever he left for Alaska, and Analisha would drive his truck back from the marina for him, after they left.

Faith wanted to see Rosie and pick up her gear before leaving, so they drove the short distance to the Carter house and loaded it into the back of Jake's truck. Faith hugged Rosie goodbye, each woman feeling the closeness that developed over the summer revelations. They exchanged quiet words until Mack came out and offered a hand to Jake.

"We'll see you up there," Mack said as they shook.

"You're right behind us, right?"

"Yeah, just tying up a few loose ends." Mack shifted from one foot to the other and Jake suspected he wanted to say something else but didn't. Rather he turned to Faith and said, "Felt like old times again."

"Yeah, it did," she said and hugged him. "Maybe do it again next summer?"

He released her and looked into her eyes, "I'd really like that darlin'."

She grinned and the couple walked back to Jake's truck. She looked at her car and called out to Rosie. "Give her a spin every once in a while, Rose."

"Oh, you know I will."

They grinned at each other, as Faith climbed in the truck and waved out the back window until they crested the hill.

By taciturn agreement the couple said very little to each other on the ride to the marina, but the tension swirled and gathered forming a dark tumultuous cloud. When the truck slipped into a parking stall, Faith moved to open the door, but Jake reached out a suppressing hand to stop her.

"Okay, so what happens now?" Already frustrated, he took a deep breath and exhaled. "I know we should have talked about this a lot earlier, but what... I can't touch you or anything, right?"

"Right." She stated it so plain and without apathy, it pissed him off.

"So you've done this before, right? You just turn off? I mean, what do you do if... you know... you..." He trailed off. *Damn it.*

"You mean, what do I do if I want to have sex with someone I'm working with?" she asked.

"Yeah, I mean... No, I don't just mean that... I..."

"Jake." Faith took her hand off the door but was careful not to touch him. "Get into the job. As soon as I step foot on that boat, I'm changing into my gear and becoming a deckhand." She already did, he noted.

"Yeah, well, maybe it's just that easy for you, but this isn't a casual fuck for me, Faith." "It wasn't for me either," she retorted, face flushing red. "But it's time to get back to work."

"And you think the guys are going to give a shit, if..."

"Yes, they will. None of them want reminding of what they're missing back home. I don't need people thinking this," –she gestured between them– "is a way for me to get out of working hard."

As the girl from the summer vanished before his eyes, Jake glared out the window. *Christ, is this what she was like during the season?* He couldn't remember.

"Great, and I'm supposed to do what?"

"For the next few weeks do what I do."

"Okay, what do you do?"

"Learn to practice a lot of self-love." He just stared at her with deep blue troubled eyes.

"Yeah, thanks for putting that image into my mind. I appreciate it, Faith."

Her laugh sounded cruel, and he hoped it only some kind of protective mechanism that carried her from his reasonable argument. She sighed.

"Okay, when we're in port, and we have time... there you go," she said matter-of-fact.

"There you go, what? When we're in port, and have time, we'll run up behind *Millie's* and fuck next to the dumpster, or have an actual conversation about us?" He ran a frustrated hand through his hair. "*No one* is going to care if we're together. They all know it anyway, and they don't care."

"I'm sorry, but they will... I will. You're part owner of this boat. I can't have people not trusting me or treating me different because I fuck the boss. It leaves too many questions and accusations about my position on deck and as a crew member. It's not good, and it's not safe. I just can't go there, Jake. Not now." His gaze darted toward her.

"Why not now?" he asked with suspicion.

"I'm not getting into this." She launched herself against the door.

"Wait..." He got out too and ran around the truck. "Don't go pissed off."

He grabbed her hand and cupped her cheek, pulling her close, then leaned his forehead against hers. He bent down to kiss her, and when they separated, she smiled at him, squeezed his hand, and bent to pick up her gear again. She walked ahead as he pulled his own gear out of the bed of the truck and followed slowly behind.

He approached the *Scaup* just as Andy laughed and kissed his wife goodbye with open candor. He scowled and noticed Tristan and Booker saying goodbye to their women, too. *Christ, it's easier if she stayed home.* Blanching at his thought, he swore at himself, knowing it illustrated her exact point.

Faith picked up her gear after hugging Debbie and the girls' goodbye, then climbed on board and his belly clenched. Making his own way toward the boat, he said his goodbyes, and turned toward Andy.

"We need to get going."

"What do you think we're doing?"

"Let's get underway," Jake snapped. "Now."

"I'll get onboard when I'm goddamn good and ready," Andy spat back. "If you're in such a big fucking hurry, why don't you go prep the boat." Jake stomped over to the passageway.

"It looks like it's going to be a rough cruise this time, sailor." Debbie said, watching Jake step through the opening. She added, "Let them work it out, Andy. It's going to be hard on them." She wrapped arms around his neck and kissed away the irritated crease between his brows. "I love you... I'll miss you... Be safe and come home to me."

"I love you too, and I will," Andy said, his face lightening. "But if he thinks this trip's going to start off like this, I'll pull his head out of his ass for him." With one arm around his wife, he reached the other arm out to his daughters, who all squeezed in. "I love you, girls. Take care of each other."

Jake walked several steps, then turned when Megan shouted goodbyes to them all. Faith waved and passed him without saying a word, and he looked down at the deck, before moving back to the rail.

"Bye, baby," he said to his niece, and met his sister-in-law's gaze. "Deb, I'm sorry, take all the time you need."

"It's okay," she said. "It's going to go fast, Jake. Just wait and see."

****

The week-long trip to Dutch Harbor transitioned smoothly. Once there, the *Scaup* started the checklist of outfitting, prepping and inspections, like every season before it. With several days of work and Jake not ready to let go of the closeness he and Faith had over the summer, they shared breakfast and coffee at the café together alone before going back to work on the wharf.

"Fern and Brock said they're waiting for us to come by with the grocery order," Faith said, pocketing her cell phone, as Jake came back to the table from using the restroom. He scooted into the old vintage booth and sipped his coffee. "I said it shouldn't be too much longer tomorrow, right? They said they had a couple of boats coming in for their supplies today. So, if we're coming in today, come early."

"Yeah, we'll make that work, and just plan it for tomorrow. There's still a lot to do." Jake laid his arm on top of the booth and stretched out his long legs on the bench seat. "I also want to flush the hydraulics, they're always a little sticky at first." She hunched over a grocery list, scribbling down items. She had made one consolation for Jake. He wanted her to work in comfort, stating the job was hard enough without adding extra elements of discomfort. She relented and though still wore the same types of items, they just fit better and stayed out of her way.

She glanced up to see him smile at her, and she smiled back and leaned across the table to...

"Well, fuck me." They both looked up to see Booker grinning down, as if finding the golden lottery ticket. Faith scowled at the way his voice curled over the words, and leaned back into her seat. "Isn't this cozy? Sorry to bust up what was sure to be a damn fine show."

Jake sighed, rolled his eyes and said, "I'm gonna go pay and then we can get out of here."

She nodded and took a final sip of her coffee, before turning to rise out of the booth when Booker lifted a foot to rest between her legs on the seat. He laid an elbow on his own knee and leaned in, bringing his furry face a whisper from her mouth. He hadn't brushed his teeth yet, and his breath snaked through the air, stale and spoiled. He smiled and fixated on her upper lip until he broke away to look at her.

"Look, bitch. I'm done with you. You show up at the beach, in your tiny shorts, ass hanging out and tight little top, flipping your hair all around to get *everyone* going. Now you're closing everything up tight again to push him off the edge, right? I know your game. So, let me just say this, be very careful and watch your back." His eyes locked on her lips again. "Stop fucking with my livelihood and we'll... Argh!"

Faith shot her hand out, grabbed his balls, clenched and twisted with all the strength she could muster. Booker changed colors and sounded like a high-pitched rusty gate blowing in a stiff wind. He dropped to one knee and fell on his side, holding the offended area, as Jake turned and moved toward them. So, she leaned over and spoke in a very low growl.

"You want to play with threats? I'll give you a threat, you disgusting pig. Fuck with me again, and I swear to God, I'll use the fillet knife to cut off that miserable little toothpick in your rancid pants and hang it with the cod on the next pot. Do you honestly think I lived with Mack and the boys and never learned how to defend myself?" Jake reached them and when the smaller man didn't answer, Faith twister harder. He squeaked. "Do not speak to me again, unless it pertains to work, not for any reason. Do we understand each other now, Christopher?" He nodded, and she released him.

"What the hell was that?" Jake asked, chasing after her. He left Booker on the ground to recuperate and compose himself. "What was that, Faith? What happened? Goddamnit." He grabbed her arm and spun her around to face him. "What?"

"That," she screamed, pointing at the café door, "is the fucking reason I do what I do! Because of little shitheads like that. He may be your friend Jake, but I will not put up with his bullshit anymore." He reached out for her again, but she held up her arms. "Stop... don't."

"Okay," he said, holding up his own arms. "Just, can you at least tell me what he said?"

"No," she replied and walked back to the boat.

****

Andy gave the one-hour warning, two days later, and Faith climbed aboard the *Je Suis Prest* to say goodbye. Word got around the dock that Faith dropped Booker to his knees, but neither one spoke of it. Mack didn't ask because it wasn't their way, and knew Booker probably deserved it. They sipped whiskey's and smoked in relative silence. When it came time for her to go, she just rose and walked over to him, wrapping arms around his middle. After a few moments, he pushed her back.

For thirty-eight years of age, she sure looked like a broken little girl.

"You know, I was nineteen-years-old when I met you. Just a little punk ass kid. Me and you, we grew up together, didn't we?" She nodded and smiled sadly. "I'm happy I didn't fuck it up too bad, but damn it, Faith... what in the hell are you waiting for?"

She didn't answer his question. He didn't expect her to. She just told him how much she loved the summer and being together again. As the *Scaup* left the harbor and the dark purple and gray wake crested into silver, Faith waved to the group on the dock, then moved to finish stowing the fenders. A horrible sense of foreboding dropped like lead in Mack's gut.

CHAPTER 25

The first week of the season seemed hardest for Jake. However, he realized if he let go of the physical aspect of their relationship, he could spend quality time learning about Faith, in a way he hadn't over the summer. How she thought about things. What she liked and wanted from her life. Though not ideal, he did as she said, and eased sexual frustration in the dark by himself.

Even Booker changed. His words not so plentiful, his swagger not so pronounced. He and Faith ignored each other. Jake suspected she finally proved herself to him that day in the café, and the steady tension that charged the deck the year prior turned to mist.

In early November, the King crab season was coming to a close, the weather reports across BHF radio called for gale force winds of thirty-five knots or over forty miles per hour and seas of over thirty feet tall, making rogue waves much more likely.

Faith staggered with coffee for Andy and secured the covered mug in his cup holder, before dumping his overflowing ashtray.

"Thanks." He squirmed in his seat. "Hey, take this a second, I gotta piss like a racehorse, and she's a bitch out there."

"Sure," she said, and sat down in his vacated seat, maneuvering the throttle to full reverse as the boat came down the next wave, then punched it full forward until the wave hit them, trying to keep the boat straight.

"Bit blustery, wouldn't ya say?" He came out of the bathroom, zipping up his pants.

"A bit." She chuckled. "Are we setting soon?"

"Yep, almost there." They switched places again. "Thanks, I really needed to do that."

"You bet." She held onto the extra seat in the wheelhouse as he plowed down another large swell. "I'm going back out. Do you want anything to eat before I go?"

"Naw, tell everyone we'll set the last six and go hide for a while until this thing blows over." He maneuvered the boat, and sent her an appreciative grin. "We'll eat then."

"You got it," she replied, and left the wheelhouse to go back outside.

Andy peered at the ominous dark sky approaching and gave orders to the crew via the intercom. He thought about how many heated debates ensued over who possessed the worse job on the fishing vessel, the mental exercise of the wheelhouse or the physical strain of the deck. He may stay warm and dry, but Andy considered the seas and believed he won the contest on this night.

Trying to navigate the strings of pots became a full-time challenge for him, as he tried to keep the weather on the port side so the crew could do their job on the starboard. However, in doing so he spent much of his time in the ditch or valley between the waves. A very dangerous and rough place to occupy in good conditions, let alone a storm.

By the time they got to the last pot, the weather worsened to hurricane conditions. The winds howled and fast approaching the promised seventy-seven knots, or eighty-eight miles per hour, and the seas rose from thirty-three to forty-two feet. Andy wanted to set the last pot and hurry to get the crew inside to safety, before they were blown off their feet. The pots could soak while the *Scaup* and her crew sought refuge, but Andy was nervous he waited way too long.

Faith yell something to the crew, and Booker moved off the rail and went to clean the bait table under the roof of the upper deck. Tristan stowed crab bins, also under the deck, while Faith and Brandon set the last pot onto the launcher, as Jake worked the controls, and the dogs clenched onto the metal rungs.

****

After Brandon secured the pot door with Faith, he walked over to help Tristan stow the rest of the crab bins. Jake pushed the release lever and sent the huge container over the rail, then ran over to help Faith throw the line and buoys. He couldn't remember if he'd shut down his equipment in his haste to get off the deck, so turned and walked back to look. Noticing a movement off the starboard side, his gaze shifted and his blood ran ice cold. An forty-eight-foot rogue wave with teeth barreled down on them, hungry, just as the boat started to maneuver out of the ditch. Time slowed as he turned to find Faith, who walked toward him but did not yet see the wave.

"Faith!" he screamed. "Rogue!" With no time to do anything else, he wrapped one arm around the hand-hold of the block, and reached out his other hand for hers. *God, oh God, no!*

Andy's voice bellowed from the speakers. "Rogue! Rogue! Hang on! Hang on!"

The wave hit at just the right position on the rail, pitching the deck and boat sideways. Icy water flooded over the side as Faith reached her hand out to Jake's. The force of the wave blew over her and swept her off her feet at the same moment she clutched onto Jake's wrist and he grabbed hers, creating a tenuous link. The water hurtled Faith towards the opposite rail and Jake's eyes tried to focus on the unfathomable depths of the sea below them with only one rail between them and the abyss. It took him a fraction of a second to register the angle of the deck and calculate what it meant. Faith turned her head, trying to limit the amount of water she consumed. In doing so, she took in even more liquid and her grasp weakened.

"No, goddamnit, Faith," Jake screamed. "Don't let go! Hold on to me!" Jake's grasp loosened from hers, and from the rung of the hand-hold. He pleaded with God to help him, and let go of the block, just as the ship rolled over and slammed down with tremendous force. Looking like a rag doll, Faith's head slammed into the deck boards with a sickening crack, splitting her head open and rendering her unconscious.

The slap of the vessel righting itself sped life up once more, while gallons of water rushed over the sides and back out into the murky depths. The couple water-planed across the surface as the remaining water slithered back into the sea. Jake leaned down and peered into cold, flat eyes staring back at him. He screamed her name over the wind with no response... not even a flicker of life. He reached his hands under her, and with Brandon's help, carried her limp body inside to the boat's galley floor.

****

Andy watched the drama unfold in helplessness from the bridge, as the wave came out of nowhere. When the men brought Faith in, he stumbled and slid down the last three steps. He ordered and shoved Booker to take the wheel and find shelter, as another wave moved the massive hull sideways. Anything not secured to the floor or wall flew around the room, and the human inhabitants, took hold of whatever they could find for balance.

When the vessel righted itself, Brandon lifted Faith so Jake could remove her sweatshirt and tee-shirt underneath, leaving her in her bra. He laid her back down as Andy leaned over her mouth to listen for breath sounds and feel for a pulse. *Was that something?* The room shifted and pitched. She didn't have breath and her lively emerald green eyes were now dark and stared without seeing.

"Oh, Christ man, I don't think she's breathing, Jake." Andy's voice cracked. "She's not even shaking, man."

"Faith..." The voice sounded like a song. *"Mo nighean..."*

"Mama." She tried to focus, on diaphanous being. "Mama? I can't see you."

Jake, the picture of concentration, ordered his brother to begin CPR as he lifted her chin, pinched her nose and breathed air back into her lungs.

"We are here, *mo nighean.* Right here." A whisper fluttered across her chest.

Tristan threw up into the sink, and sat down hard on the galley bench, shaking from fear and the scene unfolding before him.

"It will be okay, *mo brèagha ros.*" Nels's whispered.

"Daddy?" Faith grew excited, and she tried to reach out and find him but her arms remained still. "Daddy?"

Brandon sprinted into the sleeping berths, stumbling on the blankets and sleeping bags he brought back with him. He fell into a door jamb with a hard slam to his shoulder, and white-hot pain shot down his arm.

"You must wake now, Faith."

"But I wanna stay with you," Faith whined.

"No!" snapped her father. "Then everything that's happened will be for nothing. All the things I've wanted for you are right in front of you. You... must... live. Now open your fuckin' eyes, girl," Nels ordered.

Jake screamed at Brandon to bring the portable defibrillator and set up to use it when Andy flung out a hand to stop him.

"Wait, wait, wait." He re-positioned his fingers on her carotid. "Okay, okay, wait now, I feel... Okay... I got it, I got it, it's fast."

"Faith!" Jake screamed in her ear. "Open your goddamn eyes!" After a few more moments, she squeezed her eyes shut as she tried to breathe. Finding her pathway blocked, she struggled and choked. Jake and Andy rolled her to her side, where she violently vomited out the Bering Sea from her stomach and lungs. She took the first glorious breaths of fresh air and life, choked and vomited again. The reek of her sickness filled the cabin.

The center of her vision diffused into color as she came out of the oily blackness, and by the time she finished being ill, her mind started to re-engage. There's danger... something... danger. And then her mind filled with him.

"Jake..." She croaked out his name, her own voice raw and raspy but panicked. Her system revolted, and she gagged and threw up again. Andy held her head steady and kept her on her side.

"I'm right here, baby," Jake said, trying to keep himself from going over the edge.

The information didn't get through and she said his name again on a plea, desperate for the knowledge if he lived or died. She opened her eyes, but everything blurred in one palette of color, and she dry-heaved several more times.

He drew his arms below her underarms and around her back to lift her body to his. One hand fisted in her tangled hair as he wept.

"I'm right here, baby. Faith, I'm okay... you're okay... I'm right here. Don't you fucking go anywhere. You hear me?"

Andy rocked, sat back on his heels and laid one hand on his knee and the other one up to his mouth, shaking. He closed his eyes for a moment, then opened them to focus on Jake and the woman. His brother convulsed with cold and spent adrenaline. Faith shivered from the freezing water clinging to their clothes, hair and bodies.

"Shivering," Andy noted out loud. "Okay, that's a real good sign. Jake, take her into my cabin," he barked, then turned to his greenhorn. "Tristan, help Brandon get all these blankets and bring them to my bunk." He did a double take on Brandon. "Are you okay?"

"Dislocated shoulder, I'll keep for a minute."

"Okay, sit down and don't move." He turned his attention back to Jake, who still clung onto Faith. "Jake!" he bellowed, and his brother's head jerked up. Andy enunciated each word, "Take her into my cabin. Both of you have got to get out of the rest of those wet clothes and get some blankets on to warm up, now!"

By this point, Jake shook so hard he couldn't pick up the limp, lethargic woman. On an oath, Andy picked her up himself and carried her into his stateroom. He laid her on the bed as Tristan approached with his burden. The skipper grabbed the blankets and threw one at Jake, who stumbled in behind him. He secured one blanket around Faith, before turning to yank off his brother's wet sweatshirt, tee shirt and thermal top.

However, before unzipping his pants, Jake swatted his hand away. "Okay. I got it. I got it."

"Okay, get her out of hers too, then both of you get wrapped up in the blankets." Andy shoved Tristan ahead of him, ordering, "Get some cold compresses for Brandon's shoulder and get some cider going for them. I gotta go upstairs and find out where we're at real quick. I'll be back in two seconds."

"Okay."

Jake unzipped his pants and allowed his jeans and underwear to fall to the floor. He stood naked and as Faith shook hard enough to make both their teeth rattle, challenged him in removing the rest of her clothes. Closing her eyes, she started to drift off, just to have him shout at her again. Grabbing four of the blankets, he wrapped her in one and laid her back onto the bed, then picked up a second one and cocooned himself in it before he laid down beside her. He shook the last two blankets over the top of them, and spooned around her for added heat, relying on Andy to come back soon with something warm to put inside their bodies, now that the outside inched toward homeostasis.

A scream sounded from the galley of Brandon getting his shoulder put back into location.

For now, he just wanted to hold her, feel her heartbeat and watch her breathe. He rubbed the woman's arms fast, then brought his own around her, and buried his head in her hair, as tears rolled down his cheeks.

****

347

With the heat of his body and the blankets, Faith recovered, slowly. *Did a freight train run smack into her?* That's the only logical reason for her head and body to throb as it did. She blinked open her eyes, and the light hit them, causing a blinding shock of pain and a wave of nausea to flood through her. Conscious of Jake's powerful arms around her, she lifted a grateful hand up and laid it over his arm.

"Jake." Her voice sounded foreign, more like Mack's than her own and somewhat disconnected from her re-engaging brain. She reached another hand up to press against her left eye, then ran it up her forehead, pushing hard to force out the pain. She ran it through her hair, toward the back of her head, when he reached up and stopped her.

"You've split your head open back here, baby, don't touch it until we can get some stitches in. How are you feeling?"

"Like hammered shit," she said matter-of-fact, and closed her eyes again. "Can you turn the light out, my head hurts."

"No wonder, you used it as a basketball up there. Let me look first though," he said and shimmied around her to look at her pupils. They were uneven, but only a little. He scrutinized the open wound, spreading the matted hair out gingerly, as the blood trail appeared lighter than before. *She'd definitely need stitches.* He checked her grip, which seemed weak, but before he switched off the nightlight said, "I'll turn this off, Faith, but I'm sure you have a concussion and you have to stay awake for a while."

"Is everyone okay?"

"Yeah, everyone's fine."

"What happened? Was it a wave?"

"Yeah, a big one. We'll talk about it more later okay, just lay here. Does anything else hurt?"

"My head." She twisted a little, and added as an afterthought, "I think my ribs a little too."

"I think you have a concussion," he said again, and his forehead creased with worry and he pulled blankets back to check her ribs. No bruising or blackness, to indicate internal bleeding, caused him to breathe easier. "Andy should radio the Coast Guard."

"Don't even think about it, Jake. I'm fine. I just need a little sleep."

"Not if you have a concussion," he argued. He stood and threw on a pair of Andy's sweats when a knock sounded at the door. "You can forget it, for a while anyway. Here's something for you to eat. And you're gonna need to get started on antibiotics, half the sea went into your body."

"I don't want to eat," she whined. "I'll puke again."

"Well, you're gonna try," he chided over his shoulder. "I sure as hell ain't telling Mack that you're dead because we didn't get you warmed up right." He opened the door to Andy, who came in and set a tray with warm soup, crackers, Gatorade and a giant container of Tylenol on the slight excuse for a dresser.

"Hey, how you guys doing? Man, you'll do anything to get out of a little work," Andy said, trying to joke as he scanned his injured crew member. She didn't look good, so he leaned over and whispered to Jake, "She's bleeding somewhere, there's a lot on the carpet out there. I'm gonna call Commsta?"

"No! Goddamnit!" She raised her hand off her head and into the air in an emphatic gesture. "Just shut up and give me a minute, okay?" Faith struggled to sit up and held her head with both hands. One brushed over the wound, and greasy waves of pain and nausea pocked her consciousness, causing her to whimper and pale. When she pulled her hand down again, her palm felt sticky. "My head's just bleeding a little. Head wounds do that, you know."

"Man, how can you even see in here?" Andy said and flipped on the light.

"Awck! Jesus Christ!" Faith howled in agony and Jake reached up and turned the light back out. "Are you assholes trying to kill me? Both of you get the fuck out of here," she said with gritted teeth and rocked as she dry heaved again at the smell of the soup.

"You can't fall asleep, Faith. I should stay," Jake argued. "Get the fuck out!" she screamed, and holding her head threw a book at their retreating backs.

"Man, she's like a pit viper," Andy said, a little miffed, and climbed the stairs toward the wheelhouse. Jake just grinned, thrilled at her responsiveness, and followed his brother up the stairs to give her a few minutes to cool off. Loitering in the wheelhouse, the other three deck hands looked up as the men walked in. At first, no one noticed the small split in the greenhorn's forehead where he slammed into a corner.

"Dude," Andy said, getting a closer look. "You're gonna need stitches, too." He peered into the young man's clear eyes, and checked for equal and reactive pupils. The captain breathed out a sigh of relief when he held up a finger and Tristan tracked it with no problems. "All right, let's take care of that in a minute, okay? I've got a big job to do on Faith too, and neither of you want me doing it when I'm shaking, right?"

"No, it can wait." Tristan confirmed.

Brandon, his arm in a sling, walked over to a cabinet and pulled out a bottle of Andy's good whiskey. He pulled five Styrofoam cups out of a plastic sleeve and poured out four fingers in each cup.

"How's she doing?" Booker asked, as he accepted a cup from Brandon. Jake peered out into the darkness and the outline of the land-mass. Booker maneuvered them to shelter, and he slapped him on the back, in encouragement.

"Good job, Chris." The newbie skipper gave a nod of thanks. "She's doing good, she's yelling at us, so that has to be a good sign, right, when a woman's yelling at you? Thanks for taking the wheel, man."

"No problem. That was some crazy-ass shit." When no one replied, he continued, "It was a good thing that was the last pot or we would've all been out on the deck. Jesus, that was so close."

"All I know is I looked over and saw nothing but a wall of water, man. And then we like flipped or something." Tristan gesticulated wildly, adrenaline still pumping through his veins and his youthful body didn't seem to have the sense as the rest of them. He, too, took his cup of whiskey, sipped and made a face.

"I saw you two disappear, man, and I thought you were fucking dead," Booker said. "What do you think Andy, were we at ninety degrees?"

"Man, it sure felt like it." Andy ran a hand through his hair, standing it on end, and took his seat in the captain's chair, as Brandon handed him his cup. "Thanks, dude."

Brandon handed a cup to Jake and kept one for himself.

"What I don't understand is how you held onto her for so long," Brandon queried in awe. "I mean, that was some freaky shit of nature, man. That force should have ripped her straight out of your hands long before we righted."

"Well, at one point she drank half the Bering Sea and passed out," he whispered, commanding all four men's attention. "She became dead weight, man, and I was losing my grip on the block. If the boat hadn't righted when it did, it'd be a different story now." Jake shuddered at the memory and they all drained their whiskey.

Nodding their heads in agreement, each crabber looked at their own spot on the floor. However, Andy didn't take his eyes off his brother. He let go of the block, because he would not let Faith go over the rail alone, and when Jake caught his brother's eyes, he realized Andy knew the truth. They spoke a thousand words between them in that moment. Andy broke eye contact first and swiveled his seat to observe the darkness.

Jake aped the gesture. On the water fishing for as long as he could remember, the life, excitement, fortitude and the absolute sense of accomplishment, all ran through the deck boss's veins. Close calls, accidents, men overboard, men caught in the line, broken bones, even a man's death, but Jake never felt the level of fear from the water before, then he did that day.

"You guys go on downstairs," Andy said. "Tristan, get cleaned up, and I'll be down in five minutes, to get you fixed up. Brandon, could you look in on Faith?"

"Yeah."

The men rounded the corner, talking about what transpired and what they were going to eat before bed. Jake poured them out another glass of whiskey and handed Andy his cup. He could almost see the words forming in his mind. The superstition toward women on board so ingrained in him and now look what happened.

"It wasn't her fault," he said, answering Andy's unspoken accusation.

His brother spun around in his chair, and Jake saw something he'd not seen on his face before... fear.

"You let go, asshole," Andy spat out, stood and jabbed him in the chest with his finger. "Let go because of her." He pointed down toward his cabin. "How's that not her fault? If a man had been on board..."

"If a man had been on board, we would've all been dead," Jake interrupted, voice raised. "Faith told the guys to go get things cleaned up quick, because she made them cinnamon rolls. If a man had been there, I wouldn't have been able to fucking hold on to him before we righted and maybe that man might have been Brandon, or Tristan, or even Booker, not some phantom stranger you've cooked up in your head. Jesus Christ, Andy."

The skipper lowered his head and glowered at some of the instruments. The boat rocked under the shelter of the calm cove. He leaned forward on the panel and held his head in his hands, then ran them through his hair.

"You would've gone," he said and looked up at him, daring Jake to contradict him.

"Yeah, I would've." Jake didn't take his eyes off his brother's. "And if that had been Deb, what would you have done? I'm not gonna apologize for making that decision, Andy. I love her." He rose from his chair as if electrocuted and laughed as he realized what he'd said. "Oh Christ, I love her..." he tried again. "I love Faith. Jesus, I guess it only took a fifty-foot wave to realize it."

He leaned against the wall and folded his arms across his bare chest, then asked in all seriousness, "What do I do now?"

"Well," Andy chuckled. "Congratulations, life as you know it is over. You get to act like a schmuck, like the rest of us." He scowled out the window, then sighed and said, "You go tell her, you idiot. And she feels the same way. Then you get married and have fun making babies. But first, you go downstairs and make sure the girl in question isn't in a damn coma." Jake grinned at him like a kid.

"Thanks, brother." He turned and made his way for the stairs, but just before he vanished down them, said, "You know I'm okay? Right, Andy? Everyone's gonna be just fine."

****

As the storm passed, the captain spent the next couple of hours tending to the sick. Andy placed four surgical staples in Tristan's forehead, gave Brandon another cold compress, then carefully shaved a small patch of Faith's hair, and punched in nine staples to piece her skin together again.

Andy called Commsta and asked if Faith required immediate attention. Talking through an extensive checklist, they all agreed to bedrest, with the understanding she receive immediate medical attention if her symptoms changed and once they docked. Shortly after that conversation, they received a phone call from an enraged Mack, who heard the distress call, and only after Faith talked him down from reigning death upon the entire *Scaup* crew and their families, did he agree to meet her back in port.

At Faith's insistence, they continue, Brandon captained the vessel, as Jake, Booker, Andy, and Tristan all hauled in the full soaked pots, before motoring back to harbor.

Jake woke with a start from a fitful sleep, filled with terrifying images of not holding onto to Faith. He panicked more when he realized she wasn't next to him in the bed and reached over to click on the light. The clock read four a.m. and he reached for some clothes to go find her.

As he approached the empty galley, he smelled the appetizing aroma of brewed coffee, as a cacophony of snores and other bodily melodies resulted from the men. At the foot of the stairs to the wheelhouse he listened for any sign of conversation between Faith and Andy, but only the hum of the machinery and electronics whispered back to him. Her jacket and all-weather gear didn't hang in the usual spot, and Jake knew she'd gone outside. Confident his brother watched over her, Jake grabbed the largest mug he could find and poured the dark caffeinated lifeblood into it. The rich aroma snaked its way into his nostrils and he smiled.

Dressing in his own all-weather gear, Jake lifted the handle, and pushed open the creaky water-tight door. She stood near a single column of stacked pots at the aft end of the boat. Faith's forearms rested on the rail, her hair secure in the hat, so it wouldn't whip around in the wind. She smoked a cigarette, deep in thought, and stared out to sea.

He came up behind her, not giving a damn about her rules, and decided, on the spot they needed new ones... compatible ones. Jake wrapped his arms around her waist, and she tensed, straightened, then relaxed and leaned back into him, laying a hand on top of his, she reached the other to stroke the stubble on his cheek. *Maybe the new rules wouldn't be such a hard sell, after all.* The colors of the sky changed as the sun rose and magentas, purples, reds and yellows bounced off the clouds and sky, creating a breath-taking display. He brought his cold cheek down to hers and rested his chin on her shoulder.

"This has always been me and my dad's time." She continued to stroke his cheek. "Whenever I could, at sunrise or sunset, I'd try to get out here."

"Do you want me to leave you alone? have your time?"

She turned to face him, two large, deep bruises already forming in the sockets of her eyes. "For a long time I thought there was, like a curse or something on all of us, and I would wind up like my parents and grandparents. I thought that was it, the other night. I even saw them, but... I didn't die here, Jake. Maybe it sounds stupid, but it feels like all the nasty shit broke and it's all now."

"Maybe it is." He stooped to look into her eyes, once again normal and equal. "I love you, Faith."

She scanned his eyes, then reached both hands to his face to bring him closer, as he put a hand on either side of the railing, to box her in.

"I love you too, Jake," she said. "So much it hurts sometimes... not touching you, when I want to."

"Well, I'm right here." He grinned. "What do you wanna touch?"

She couldn't help the giggle that escaped her but rolled her eyes and tried to adopt a harsh tone. "You're ruining my tender movie moment here."

"Oh, is that what this is?" He chuckled. "Am I mistaken, or are we having a movie moment on a crab boat?"

"Yeah, it feels so weird. Maybe you and I can figure out a compromise, but you need to understand I can't just forget everything either, or change because *you* say so. This way of life has been working for me for a very long time now. And I believe, with everything I am, that it's good for the crew... morale... everything."

"I understand what you're saying, but you've also gotta trust that I've been friends with these guys since we were in elementary school. As long as we aren't throwing it in their faces, they'll be okay with it, Faith. And I'm not an idiot, I know we need to keep a harmonious deck." He brushed back some strands of escaped hair that whipped across her face. "It hurts not to touch you, too. I really thought I lost you, baby."

He leaned down and kissed her, light at first, then deepened it, moving her head to the side and stroking the side of her neck. He ran his tongue along the smooth underside of her top lip and she tightened her embrace. They broke apart and waited.

"See, the earth didn't swallow us up. A wave almost did, but not the earth." He chuckled.

"Do you want to get married?" she asked, surprising them both.

"W-what?" He took a step back, so shocked it made her chuckle. A flood of emotion filled him as he gained his feet again. "Aren't I supposed to ask you that?"

"I've been so fucking afraid to get close to anyone because I felt like I was a plague, killing everyone important," she said, ignoring the question. A seagull swooped down to sit in the water. "Mack told me what he wanted most for me was happiness and a normal life." She met his eyes. "I'm terrified, Jake, but I do want this. I don't know if I can give up this life and be the woman that stays home with the kids…"

"Do you honestly think I would ask that of you?"

"No, I honestly can't wrap my head around anything like that right now. I don't know how it will work or what it will look like, but I trust this. I want you… want us."

"Man, so, when you change the rules you really change them." He tucked more flyaway hair back. "Do you have a ring?"

"No, I've only just asked. Besides, everyone knows that if you leave a proposal up to a guy, you'd be waiting until hell freezes over."

"Well, can I do it right and ask Mack first and stuff?"

"Oh, do that." She giggled. "He'd get such a kick out of it." Jake wasn't too sure about that. "But for now it's just you and me."

"It's always gonna be you and me. I want you to be my wife, more than I've ever wanted anything in my life." He touched his lips to her forehead and then to each cheek before kissing her on the mouth.

"Jesus, get that crap off my deck! You guys are making me sick." Andy's voice boomed over the loudspeaker, and the couple sprang apart, glaring up at Andy, who choked on his coffee from laughing so hard.

EPILOGUE

Faith: Well, honey, your granny just passed on and that makes three huge losses in your young life. In going through Fenella and Angus's things, I realized I didn't have my own affairs in order, and if life's taught me anything, it's to get things organized, so no one else needs to do it. So, I made a will, and put this letter in with it, asking Mack to give it to you on this very special day.

If you're reading this, and I'm not with you, well then something very wrong must have happened. I can't tell you how gutted I am for that, sweetheart. You've been through so much and to think I may have caused you more pain, well, that eats me up inside. Close your eyes darlin', and know I'm not too far away.

When I first met your mother, she lit my soul on fire. Does your young man do that for you? Something tells me he does. If he doesn't, run like hell. In fact, go get Mack and read the rest of this letter in his truck! Your ma, she took me as I was and somehow didn't see a broken old man but someone who still had a lot to offer. Murron and I didn't have much time on this earth together, but it's so much more than you got with her. I loved that woman something fierce, and she loved you ten times more.

For a short time, I resented the fact I couldn't have you both, or with one here, I couldn't have the other. Whenever I felt that way, I remembered what your grandmother would always say about how hard your mom fought for you. I keep going back to the day we found out she was pregnant. She glowed, Faith. She was the most beautiful woman I ever saw and you are the spitting image of her, honey. I think about how different things would've been for you, if she had lived. I imagine my life would've been a lot lonelier, you not out there with me, but your life might have turned out very different.

I know Mack's there and you're his, as much as you ever were mine. I always knew he'd be the perfect daddy for you, if I couldn't be. You two were the best thing that could've happened to each other and you both blessed my life so much.

You're our legacy, Faith, and you came from a lot of love. Today, on the day you're getting married, I hope you know that same love I knew so many years ago. It makes me so damn happy you got me bawling like a baby right now. Don't waste a single moment on sadness for us not being there. We are beaming right where we are! Be well my daughter, mo brèagha ros.

Your devoted father, Nels Pearson
****

Faith folded the letter and held it close to her chest. With an hour before she walked down the aisle, she walked over to the window for some better light and read it again.

Mack sat back in his chair, wearing a suit with his tie looped around his neck and shirt not all the way buttoned up. He held a glass with his classic three fingers of whiskey in it, studying her. The sun shone through the window, igniting her hair to flame. Rosie swept it up at the sides, with a waterfall of flowers and fiery curls extending down to the middle of her back. Her dress, a simple sheath made of creamy silk, possessed a thin silk cummerbund of the Middleton tartan at her narrow waist. She wore little makeup, just accents here and there, as the light on her created the illusion of glowing from within. Her head bent over the paper and didn't have a trace of sadness on her beautiful, serene face.

A pain filled his chest as he sat there. A woman grown and about to marry Jake in a small ceremony in his backyard. Correction: their backyard, now.

Mack stood as she walked over to him and buttoned up the last few buttons of his shirt. They both eyed the tie with dubiousness about how to tie it and Faith tossed it onto the chair he vacated, then reached up and undid the top two buttons of his shirt, so he could remain comfortable.

"Do you know how hard it was for me to keep that from you some days?"

"Yes. I do," she murmured. He drained his glass and stood up to straighten his suit jacket. "Who would have thought you could look this good?" She giggled, raised onto her toes and kissed his clean-shaven cheek.

"And here you thought it was my witty intellect and sparkling personality." He grinned back at her. "So, are you ready to do this then darlin', or do I need to go get my truck?"

She took a deep breath and exhaled as she glanced back at the paper on her bed.

"Je suis prest." She smiled and Mack escorted her out to make her promises.

****

Faith stood by another window with the light streaming across her face and hair. She twisted her solid gold necklace with Mack's king crab charm around her fingers. It seemed like a million years ago she'd taken those vows with Jake, instead of a mere six.

Mack groaned, trying to readjust himself, and Faith glanced back at him. He tried to sit up, slipped and banged his elbow hard against the rail, wincing. Faith placed his hand back, knowing he wanted to do most of the work himself.

"Leave off, goddamnit!" he growled at her.

Faith stepped back, heart breaking inside, as her powerful man tried once again to maneuver himself in the hospital bed. He stopped when the exertion triggered a massive coughing spasm. Faith grabbed the towel nearby and held it to Mack's mouth as he continued the wracking wet heaves. She pulled it away, and a large gruesome blood stain covered the cloth. Faith's hands shook as she set it down and gave Mack a cool glass of water, but he refused.

They diagnosed the sixty-one-year-old skipper with metastatic small cell lung carcinoma five months prior, and his diagnosis didn't give him much time left. The once huge and intimidating frame, was now emaciated and fragile. Because the cells compressed the nerve attached to his vocal cords, his strong, gravelly voice became hoarse. Faith wanted to insist he drink something when the oncologist walked in with a smile.

"Okay," the small, wiry man said, as he reached into his pocket and clicked open a pen. "Well, Mr. Carter, let's see," He flipped through several pages in his patient's chart before looking up and squinting at him though his rimless spectacles. "So, how are we doing today?"

"We," Mack said, mustering every ounce of strength he had to sit up, "ain't doing nothing except having" -he glared at the doctor with derision- "what'll probably be a massive waste of my time." He coughed again, and breathless, said, "Does anyone like that bullshit you try to reassure us with?"

"Mack," Faith whispered and held out the cloth again. He pushed her hands away.

"Well, let me tell ya, Doc. I" -he gestured to himself- "am fucking dying and you," -he gestured back to the doctor- "are still an asshole in a damn bow tie." The doctor raised his hand up to his neck.

"A-ah, be that as it may." The doctor cleared his throat.

"All right," Mack said with a cheerful tone and a condescending smirk.

"Er, we've just gotten your scans back." The doctor moved to a light machine and pointed to some splotches and small nodules. "It's what we thought. If you look here, here and here" -he pointed to part of the splotchy area- "we want to do a biopsy to be sure but..."

"I ain't doing a fucking biopsy." Weary, he leaned back in the bed.

"Mr. Carter, I feel I should be clearer. We believe it's metastasized to your liver. Remember now, that means we feel it has spread..."

"Can ya do me a favor, Doc?" Mack said, resigned. "Two... can you do me two favors?"

"I believe we can prep you and..."

"No," Mack said, breathing fast and deep now. "First, I want you to stop saying we, like we are in this together... We ain't." Mack glanced over at Faith. Tears shimmered in her eyes. He tried to make a fist but winced in pain and placed a hand on his upper abdomen. He tried to gather his courage to take another lung full of air. "Now, here's the most important thing, Doc, are you ready?"

"I..." The doctor glanced at Faith, then leaned toward Mack but still kept somewhat of a safe distance. "Er, yes, Mr. Carter."

"I want." Mack's voice cracked with emotion. He stopped, closed his eyes, breathed hard through his nose, and said, "I want you to go call my sons and my wife." His upper lip twitched in pain. "Call them and tell them to come home, it'll take a few days." Mack eased back down onto his bed and closed his eyes as if to sleep. "So do that now, okay Doc?"

Concerned at this change of neurological function, the doctor turned on his heel and left.

"They went to get some dinner, Mack, remember?"

"I know, but it'll keep him busy and thinking."

"Mack, please..."

"No," Mack whispered, eyes still closed. "We talked about this. I did this shit to myself. I didn't need any goddamn help living and I sure as hell don't need any help dying."

She lay down next to him, careful of the vast array of cords, wires and tubes. He rested his chin on top of her head and looked past her to Jake. He stood in the door holding hands with their five-year-old daughter, Murron Rose. Her bright red hair curled in every direction, reminding him of Faith as a little girl. On Jake's shoulders, supported by his father, sat their three-and-a-half-year-old son, Carter Pearson, who scanned the area, trying to decide if he should be happy about his circumstances or not. Murron recognized her grandfather and ran to his bedside, giggling.

"Papa!" she said. She lifted her arms and hopped from one foot to the other, wanting someone to pick her up.

"All right, baby." Faith lifted her onto Mack's bed and sat her on her bottom before she reached out to take Carter from Jake and bring him closer. "Be careful, Murron, Papa has some owies."

Jake came over to the bed and reached a hand out to shake Mack's. "So, did you catch the game?"

"Naw man, they had me doing all kinds of shit around here. I heard they won, though. What happened?"

Jake took Carter back but within Mack's reaching distance and launched into the play-by-play. Faith gave Murron a coloring book and some crayons from her bag, then stood back and watched the scene unfold. Jake gesticulated over a play. Mack held Carter's chubby hand, and Murron laid the coloring book on her lap and asked Mack to pick a color. When he gave her the green color *Crayon,* she flipped to the back cover and drew a crab. A thousand memories flooded into Faith, and the anchor to all those memories laid in the bed before her, dying and leaving her alone again.

After Jake and her kids left, Faith got up and made a big production of cleaning up his room. "Faith... come here, baby." She turned to him, eyes overflowing with tears. "Are you gonna make me watch you die, Mack? Because I just don't think I can do it."

Mack thought for a long time, listening to the irregular beat of his heart on the monitor. Her hand shook in his.

"I just don't want you to fear it anymore, honey. Your mom and dad got dealt some shitty cards and so did you and so did I." He lifted her chin to look at him. "Now your mom, well, I knew her and she wouldn't have done it any other way, having you here instead of her. Your dad died doing the thing he loved. Your grandpa's needing some ice cubes and a fan about now, but..."

"Mack." Faith gently hit him.

367

"Ow." Mack smiled. "Your grandpa died the way nature intended. I'm dying because I chose a path that led me here. You have a choice to make, Faith. You can die like your grandma, sad, senseless, leaving people that need you behind, or you can stop all of this right now and take everything you learned and everyone you love and give it to those two babies and your husband."

"And what, live happily ever after?" she all but spat.

"No baby," he said, almost dreamily. "There's no happily ever after, there's just after." He looked so tired. "You know... real life."

"Okay, Mack," she said wearily, watching him smile and close his eyes. "I will."

Mack never regained consciousness again. Rosie and the boys arrived as Mack's body started to betray him. Charlie snuck in five airplane whiskeys, handing one to his mother, brother, and sister, and keeping one for himself.

"I thought Dad would have the last one but..."

Something close to a gurgled sob came out of their father's throat, and Rosie stood up from the hospital chair and moved to comfort him. Faith took the bottle from Charlie and went to the small eating table to grab a paper cup, with an absorbent sponge resting inside. She poured out the water and refilled it with some whiskey, then placed the swab in the whiskey to soak. She handed the shots out, including her own, and they drank a toast to Mack. Rosie used the swab to wet her husband's lips.

Ten minutes later Mack tried to sit upright, pleading, "I can't! No... wait... I'll try. It's not a calm sea though, we got weather coming in. Watch starboard, Charlie... Brady, watch for rogues."

The boys both glanced up at Faith, uncertain what to say. She clutched Rosie's hand and leaned over by Mack's ear to say, "It's okay, Daddy, you can take us in now. We've topped off the tanks. We made it, and we're all safe." Her voice hitched and broke. "It's okay to rest now, Daddy. It's okay to go to sleep."

Faith held Mack's hand, and visions popped up in sync with Mack's heartbeat. *Beep.* Drawing Mack a picture of a green crab... *Beep.* Her grandfather's pipe as she snuggled on his lap... *Beep.* On her dad's shoulders as he walked on the pier... *Beep.* Her grandmother's hands tying ribbons in her hair... *Beep.* Her first time on the boat, and Mack teaching her how to fish... *Beep.* Rosie rocking her to sleep... *Beep.* The Fourth of July with the boys... *Beep.* Schoolwork in the galley... *Beep.* Prepping bait... *Beep.* Sitting on Mack's lap after her father died... *Beep.* Her daughter... *Beep.* Her son... *Beep.* Her Jake... *Beep.* Her family... *Beep.* She wasn't alone after all... *Beeeeeeeeeeeeeeeep.* And through her tears, she smiled.

THE END

ACKNOWLEDGEMENTS

First and foremost, my father-in-law, Charles Anthony Heckman Jr. When I first wrote *the Catch*, I was taking care of you. Though you are very little like Mack in the unimportant ways like looks, language and occupation, you were the driving force behind some of the most important scenes between him and Faith. I have missed you every day since you were taken from us.

To my husband, Jeff. It's hard to believe it's been so long since we started this journey together, and every day you humble me in the way you support my passion and love me. We have endured many storms and rogue waves together. You are truly a remarkable man with so much love to give. Thank you!

To my darling daughter Paisley, thank you so much for being the first to read and critique all my books. Your constructive criticism and support, mean so much to me. You are so loved. The main character, Faith, was named for you as the courage you read in her, is the courage I've always seen in you. It's been my biggest joy watching you become a butterfly.

To my son, Charlie, who makes me smile and believe in myself, every day of my life. The mischievousness of the Charlie and Brady characters is the wonderful adventure I received from you. Your extreme love and joy in simple things keeps me grounded. I love the light and joy you bring into my life.

To my assistant Andrea Florescu. Thank you for being so patient with me as I went crazy trying to get, *Releasing the Catch,* out in time! Having you come on board and get my business sorted out has been an absolute God-send! Your enthusiasm and excitement, renew my spirit each day.

Thank you to N.N. Light for your editing services, and for making my manuscript even better.

Thank you to *Celtic Butterfly Publishing* for publishing my book and understanding my vision in re-writing it.

To all my family the Heckman's, Rudy's, Gregory's, Coyle's and Garcea's, thank you for all of your support of me over the years but especially since I started tapping on a keyboard, and writing down my stories. Each and every one of you bring me so much light, and joy, it would take far too long to write them all down. However, this is my attempt to hopefully let you know, how much of a blessing I consider you all. Love you!

DEE'S CORNUCOPIA
EXCERPT

"**M**y God, it's hotter than a billy-goat's ass in a pepper patch out there," Dee announced as she entered the office furnished with the rich fragrance of leather, old wood, coffee and tobacco smoke.

Her boss, Bert Norton, sat hunched at his desk, puffing on his ancient pipe. His gaze snapped to hers, and he gave the merest hint of a smile before frowning at her crass expression. The two fellows, also occupying the room, stood a little straighter at her appearance, but gave each other surreptitious glares. They wore identical uniforms of scarred leather boots, dusty work trousers and damp cotton shirts, right down to the sweat-stained field-hand hats squeezed together in their enormous fists.

"Ah, sorry?" Dee phrased it almost like a question and raised her eyebrows at all the testosterone in the small space.

"Deidre, please, take a seat." Bert gestured to one of the broad wing-back chairs occupying the area in front of his desk.

The two imposing men shifted their weight from foot to foot in apparent agitation and she concluded it would be even more uncomfortable sitting in a chair, shorter and more insignificant than she already felt. Possessing a vagina created enough of a disadvantage chasm already.

"Thanks, Mr. Norton, I'll stand. No sense in giving anyone the upper hand," she quipped and slapped her hands on her hips, shifting her own weight from side to side. The corner of her boss's lips twitched, but he sighed and they both looked over at the two workers.

One of the men, Beaker Sparks, of medium height, and strong, muscular build, grunted as she studied him, and frowned. The only remarkable thing about the field-hand? The size of the white-head marring his chin. His icy, steel gaze peered down a nose too long and broad for his pocked face in a way that left her feeling exposed and undressed.

He'd tried to step out with Dee since her arrival at the Sugar Grove Plantation two years prior. However, with each rejection he became more ardent and acquisitive, until the girl reached her boiling point and punched him dead in the face when he got too handsy one day.

Taken unaware by the retaliation, Beaker stumbled in front of the mixed lunch assembly and fell, appearing as if the petite creature knocked him on his ass. Afterward, the man took to impugning her character, even hinting she'd given him a gratifying blow job during a lunch break in the outhouse. Dee gave Sparks a look that suggested he wasn't worth the lump of cow shit she walked in daily, and it caused the muscles in his jaw to clench and his nostrils to flare like an Adirondack moose ready to charge.

Her eyes darted to the other man, and the only thing she'd learned about him was his name, Arthur. A delicious dream boat, Arthur, stood taller than Sparks by several inches, and Dee by more than a foot. His wide muscular shoulders and massive chest tapered down into a trim waist. Brilliant clear blue eyes with a detonation of gold and green encircling the pupils searched the young woman's face, captivating her attention. He'd worked at the company a little over two weeks and labored in the fields two zones over with the harvesting equipment. The few girls that worked on the plantation or in its office, all had eyes for the mysterious new employee and Dee now understood why.

"Walker," Norton began without preamble. "These two men have been brawling over you, and it's disrupting my lunch hour."

"Really?" Dee sighed with exaggerated innocence and tilted her head to the side to consider both of thcm again. "Hmm." She exhaled hard through pursed lips. "Okay, well, I'm probably too young for both of 'em, but seeing as Sparks there is a genuine asshole, I think I'll take the tall drink of water here." Arthur's eyes widened and his eyebrows lifted.

"Ah, no, ma'am," Arthur drawled out Alabama. "I was tellin' Mr. Norton here, that the man was speaking wicked regardin' your appearance." He jerked his chin in Sparks direction, and venom shot out of those magnificent eyes. "There's no excuse for such language about a young lady."

Bert Norton and Beaker scanned the length of the young lady in question, and she followed their gaze. The wet heat left her bright orange work shirt clinging to her rather well-endowed bosom. Purple plaid trousers, also damp with sweat, clung to her thighs. She supposed she'd have to get used to this kind of attention now that she'd at last received her period and became a woman at the venerable age of sixteen.

"That right? Well, what's he been saying then?"

"Ah... well..." Arthur's neck and face flamed crimson, whether in anger or embarrassment, Dee couldn't decide. "Mr. Sparks here suggested that you've... ah... had relations in a public settin', and in the privy." He hesitated, and she lifted her eyebrows for him to continue. "Um, with several others watchin' y'all?"

Dee turned to glare at her nemesis, then at her boss. "Well, I can't fault his imagination, now can I? I wonder what Mama would have to say about that, Mr. Norton." Dee cocked her head to the side again, as if thinking, then answered her own question. "Oh yeah, she'd say, Dee, sweetheart, next time that weasel Sparks opens his mouth, don't bother punching him in the face, kick him the balls instead."

"No, your mama would wash out your filthy mouth with soap and tell you to stop leading guys on," Sparks spat in his high-pitched nasal register, and turned toward their boss. Arthur's fists clenched in reflex. "You gonna believe this horse shit, sir?"

"Naw," Dee retorted. She stepped forward and stared the jackass straight in the eye with all the supremacy her small stature could muster. "It's 1957, Beak. Mama would say break a foot off in the fool's fucking ass."

With that, she drew back her booted foot and kicked him with exactitude in the center of his scrotum. All three men groaned in immediate solidarity, and Arthur's powerful arm wrapped around her tiny waist, lifting her from the floor in restraint. She kicked out again, clipping her nemesis's chin, and popped his pimple. Beaker Sparks wheezed, clutching the most offended area, and gave an uncontrolled fart as he writhed around on the industrial carpet. Arthur set Dee back on her feet and stood between her and the fallen man. She returned her attention to Norton.

"Okay, so I guess we're done here then... right?" Without waiting for his stunned response, she spun around and punched out the door, calling, "That's real good too because it's time to get back to work."

The whistle announced the conclusion of the lunch hour, two seconds after she raised a finger to point at it.

Watch for Dee's Cornucopia in 2021

ABOUT THE AUTHOR

Jeny Heckman is the award-winning author of the paranormal-romance series, Heaven & Earth. When she isn't writing, you will find her boating with her husband, enjoying game night with her kids, cocktails with her friends, getting frustrated with photography or dreaming and plotting her next adventure. Jeny lives in the Pacific Northwest.

FOLLOW JENY

For the latest information on Jeny's book releases, contests, giveaways and news:

Newsletter: Monthly Giveaways!
http://eepurl.com/dDTPI

Website:
https://jenyheckman.com/

Facebook:
https://www.facebook.com/heckman.jeny

Twitter:
https://twitter.com/jenyheckman

Instagram:
https://www.instagram.com/jenyheckman

GoodReads:
https://bit.ly/3fd8RJA

BookBub:
https://www.bookbub.com/profile/jeny-heckman

Amazon Author Central:
https://amzn.to/3hfq6fh